M000096508

Living Life Riverside

Our Nightmarish Pursuit
of
the American Dream

by Richard W. Paradise

Copyright © 2017 Richard W. Paradise All Rights Reserved.
Editing by Dawn Petersen. Cover design by Kelly Spornitz

No part of this book may be reproduced in any written, electronic,
recording, or photocopying form without written permission of
the author.

Books may be purchased in quantity and/or special sales
by contacting the publisher at:

Eden Press
5416 West 97th Circle
Overland Park, KS 66207
edenpresskc@gmail.com

Printed in the USA

ISBN 978-0-692-86947-5

This is a fictional story based upon actual events. Other than the author
and his immediate family, all characters, businesses, corporate entities, etc.,
are fictional, and any resemblance to actual persons, businesses, corporate
entities, etc., is entirely coincidental.

Contents

CHAPTER ONE
The New Pioneers

*"Far better it is to dare mighty things, to win glorious triumphs,
even though checkered by failure, than to take rank with those poor
spirits who neither enjoy much nor suffer much, because they live
in the gray twilight that knows not victory nor defeat."*

— Theodore Roosevelt, *Strenuous Life,* **1900**

What force or forces could be strong enough to pull an intelligent, rational, moderately successful couple, married twenty-seven years, away from the safety of their
lifelong home, family, and friends while jeopardizing the financial security that they
had worked their entire careers to accumulate? How on earth could two well-educated,
professional, conservative individuals, who through careful utilization of these aforementioned attributes had reached the pinnacles of their chosen professions, willingly
and without duress or provocation, make a major, life-altering decision that was so
foolish on the surface to all others — all others from any point on the spectrum, higher
or lower, regardless of intelligence, education, or societal or economic standing?

In December of 2007, my wife and I made the conscious decision to leave
well-paying careers in which we were firmly established and risk everything we had
acquired on — now with 20/20 hindsight — what was the riskiest crapshoot of an
investment and profession that one could possibly imagine. I'm certain there are sta-
tistics somewhere that would prove this assertion correct.

On December 26th, 2007, with our decorated Christmas tree still standing and
never-to-be-consumed leftover prime rib from the Christmas Eve feast sitting in our
refrigerator, we loaded a 9' X 12' U-Haul trailer with our television, a sofa, chairs,

tables, lamps, bedspreads, pictures, throw pillows, and an indescribable collection of knickknacks and decorative froufrou and drove across the frozen Great Plains of Kansas, climbed up the eastern slope of the magnificent Rocky Mountains, and, late in the day on December 27th, pulled into the tiny town of Hot Sulphur Springs, Colorado, population 521, in the county of Grand. Then with criminal disregard to the fact that between us we had not one second of hotel, bar, and restaurant work experience, we signed papers that made us the new owners and proprietors of The Historic Riverside Hotel, Bar & Restaurant.

* * *

In 1980, my wife, Julie, and I married, both out of college for a year, and set up our lives in Johnson County, Kansas. Julie was a high school special education teacher, and I worked for a small manufacturing company that produced adhesives and sealants for the automotive and construction industries. We both worked our way up in our respective careers.

Julie eventually gained her master's degree in Transition, a specialty that involved transitioning special needs children from the loving, protective arms of the school district into the not-so-loving arms of society and the real world. She had more than twenty-five years with the district and had amassed about all that you could amass with regards to seniority and stature in the district and amongst her peers, not to mention the most rewarding aspect of the love and respect of a generation of special needs children and their families in the Shawnee Mission, Kansas, school district. You couldn't go many places in Johnson County — grocery stores, shopping malls, movie theaters — where Julie wasn't lovingly accosted by an ex-student or thankful parent. This commitment to excellence in her chosen profession was rewarded by a national Teacher of the Year award in 2006. She had truly reached the pinnacle of her chosen profession, not to mention being but a few years away from a fully funded retirement as an employee of the state of Kansas.

With the help of a few deep-pocketed investors, I had been able to build a small manufacturing business from scratch, a business that provided the commercial roofing industry with specialized asphaltic adhesives and coatings. Chances are that somewhere along the way you've been in a building in which the fruits of my labor were responsible for keeping the rain off of your head. It wasn't glamorous, sexy, or obscenely lucrative, but combined with Julie's teaching salary it allowed us the opportunity to own a nice home where we raised two children, and send them to private high schools and the state university; take a few trips to exotic places; drink reasonably good wine; and enjoy all of the comforts and technological trappings of upper-middle-class suburban living. We were even able to chunk a decently modest nest egg aside — not enough to hang it up at fifty-five, but a good base to build upon with our final ten years of paid employment.

We'd played life by the established rules and, relatively speaking, had come out as winners. So what comes next — just quietly and ingloriously ride things out on this even plane until my children and grandchildren stand coffin-side, tearful and grieving, all the while acknowledging and accepting of the natural ebb and flow of my own life?

Actually, that was the initial plan, as I'd seen it work out well for my father, and his father, and his father before him.

However, in late 2006, life threw me a bit of a curveball. The business that I started and built, the business that I was ultimately destined to buy from the investors and own outright, grew to the point that it was now unattainable, priced beyond my ability to self-finance and purchase. I quietly and dejectedly walked away from the quest to own the business that I had helped build, the business that I was destined to own. Alas, destiny is most often not in the hands or under the control of the destined, and the business which was in all actuality never to be mine, was sold to the highest bidder.

Without a doubt, one of the most unpleasant things about putting the company up for sale — beyond the obvious issue of me having to work for the devil I didn't know — was facing the reality that we would more than likely be purchased by a large corporation. I'd spent my entire working career calling on large corporations, and I knew enough about them to know that I wanted no part of them. It irked me that I was going to spend the latter part of my career doing what I had been successful at avoiding to this point.

After the back and forth of the ultimate purchase, the deal was signed and I was welcomed as a new member to the team. I felt that they sincerely wanted my experience, my advice, and my continued service. But this behemoth that bought us was a Berkshire-Hathaway-type conglomerate, involved in everything from restaurants to rocket fuel, and there was no question that they would ultimately be putting their brand on my backside.

Everything went pretty well in the short term, as teams of accountants, health and safety people, and engineers descended upon our facility, all telling us how things would pretty much remain the same as they'd always been, plus or minus a few little things here and there. One big change that I personally had a tough time adjusting to was that I was no longer captain of the ship. I'd literally started the business in my basement, and grew it and cherished it as I did my own children; now someone else was raising and disciplining my children while I stood back helplessly watching. Combine this with a truckload of new responsibilities for me, job tasks that I'd heretofore intentionally and successfully avoided like the plague — in a word: meetings.

In my first job out of college I worked in a small business that had one weekly meeting that seemed to be held for the sole purpose of calling people out — grinding axes, picking bones, and making your enemies look foolish in a public forum. I hated those meetings and swore that if I were ever fortunate enough to be the one wielding the gavel, those sort of "meetings" — not much different and certainly no more productive than a town square pillory — would not be a part of my corporate repertoire.

The meetings I was attending with my new employers weren't the "calling-out" sort of things I'd dealt with previously — they were much worse. I flew to Jackson, MS for a meeting that taught me the forty-three necessary steps of sending out a sample to a customer. For the previous twenty-five years of my career I'd been able to accomplish that with four steps: put the sample in a box, tape the box shut, address it, and call UPS for a pickup. This sort of thing went on and on, and nothing was ever accomplished; we just had meetings to report, argue, and discuss why nothing was being accomplished. To me and my let's-just-grab-hold-and-do-it existence in the business and manufacturing world of the prior twenty-five years, my new world was my vision of a complete hell. Don't get me wrong — they were all intelligent, good-hearted people with the very best of intentions. But we all know with what the path to hell is paved.

Towards the end of what I at the time didn't know would be the end of my tenure, I was summoned to the headquarters in Mississippi to have a meeting about how we would now go about doing something that we'd been doing simply and successfully for the past twenty years at our plant. Twenty people were assembled — engineers, accountants, health and environmental specialists, lab personnel, and upper management — to discuss something as elementary to me and my previous charges as how to open a door and walk into a room. All of the assembled brain power made cases as to how much it would cost, how unsafe it would be, what a logistical nightmare it would be, etc. In short, I heard thirty-five reasons as to why we now couldn't do something that we'd been successfully doing — albeit apparently inefficiently, unsafely, and ill-ogistically — for the last forever and a day. At the conclusion of the meeting, another meeting was planned to discuss in greater detail why we couldn't do this thing we'd been doing, and high fives and fist bump explosions from all assembled were in abundant evidence. Let the record show that I participated in but one fist bump explosion, half-heartedly.

To the casual observer, the half-hearted fist explosion that was reluctantly performed by me would not later be described as "forceful"; it certainly was not compelling, nor was it monumental. But this seemingly innocent act, played out at the finale of that Mississippi meeting between myself and the rest of the assembled employees that accomplished nothing beyond scheduling another meeting, shook the very core of my existence and set into motion a series of events that radically shifted the angle at which my wife and I were to repose for the rest of our days.

Seven hours after that fist bump, I was in my office at home, dialing the phone, waiting as it rang for what I was hoping would be a way out of my slow death by meetings.

"Riverside Hotel; can I help you?"

"Yeah, Abner ... uh ... my name is Richard Paradise. I don't know if you remember me. We stayed at your place four or five times over Christmas a few years back."

"Do I remember you? How could I forget someone named Paradise? Is your wife also named Paradise, and are you not in Paradise every night?" Abner laughed in false hilarity.

I was tempted to hang up at this point; I'd forgotten just how repulsive this man was, this proprietor of The Riverside Hotel. But the seismic force of the seemingly innocent fist bump explosion pushed me onward, much as someone who knows the downside of stepping into a large mound of feces but continues ahead anyway, feet first.

"Abner, I was wondering if by chance you'd considered selling The Riverside."

CHAPTER TWO

The Seeds are Planted

In the summer of 1993 we made our initial visit to The Riverside Hotel. It was the first stop in an extended trip for which the ultimate destination was a five-day visit to Julie's family reunion in Anaconda, Montana — a lot of driving in a 1992 Chevy Astro van with my 8-year-old daughter and my 5-year-old son, before they'd started installing DVD players in cars. Having lived through the trip, I can now say that was a good thing, as the kids were forced to drink in the scenery, as were Julie and I and any other of our generation fortunate enough to take a driving vacation. Remember, this form of recreation was pretty much new to the post–World War II civilized world, after the relatively recent advent of the affordable car, the interstate highway system, and the job where you got time off. How sad that we've quickly degenerated to the point where our offspring are entertained not by nature's beauty and familial interaction but only by HD, 3-D, I-Pads and Smart Phones.

The summer of 1993 was also famous for the Great Flood of 1993, where the heartland of our country — from the mouth of the Mississippi River in Minnesota through Iowa to the heart of the Mississippi Delta, and the mighty Missouri River back through the upper reaches of the Dakota's — was devastated by a five-hundred-year flood, not seen again until eighteen years later. The flood threatened my business, which was a few short miles from the point where the Kansas River (a.k.a., the Kaw) hooks up with the Missouri River. Three miles downstream from our manufacturing plant, trailer parks and a few businesses that had been there since the 1940s were literally wiped from the map by the overflow of the Kaw. The land today remains a barren, treeless plain of silt.

We headed west from Kansas City towards Denver and the Rocky Mountains on I-70. To many this stretch of road is the punch line to: What is the most narcoleptic section of interstate highway in the U.S.? Having now made this trek I can't remember how many times — forty, probably closer to fifty — I can tell you that stretches of this ride are singularly spectacular, tenfold more scenic than the I-70 that stretches through the equally Kansas-flat cornfields of Missouri, Illinois, and Indiana. Driving west out of Topeka to Salina, you will experience a nice stretch of the Flint Hills. If you hit them early in the morning or during a purple fall dusk, you will experience a vision like no other; mountains are quietly envious of this spectacle. The latter, western part of Kansas into the eastern stretches of Colorado gives you the gentle rumblings of the Chalk Hills, truncated by the jagged cuts and arroyos that exist with a vibrant purpose in the rainy spring, only to turn to inconsequential ditches in the summer and fall. It is a barren land, hard and spent, but its starkness whets your appetite for the beautiful yet brutal peaks and spires that lie ahead.

The summer of 1993 was the third time I'd made this trip, and the first time in my adult life. The first trip was in 1959 as a three-year-old in the back of a brand new 1959 Chevy station wagon (my memories of this trip are vague), the second in 1973 as a 17-year-old protesting the fact that he had to go on a family vacation (my memories of this trip are also vague). Now, as the father of a family, I was essentially heading into lands unknown and was exhilarated about the prospect of such.

Our lunch stop off of I-70 was Wilson Lake Reservoir, about two hundred miles west of Kansas City, halfway between Salina and Hays, Kansas. I'd picked the place out on a map because it was right off the interstate and had some decent looking picnic areas where our kids could run off some steam. Unbeknownst to me, two weeks before our visit an F4 tornado had savaged through the area. A short distance off the interstate, driving towards the picnic areas, the devastation we saw from the storm was otherworldly: the shell of an old gas station with its spidery, twisted canopy turned on its side and the pumps still standing; a large stand of once-majestic cottonwood trees transformed into a spot for a massive fall bonfire; picnic tables and fire grills a jumble of iron and wood nested ten yards off the shore in the lake, forty yards from their original point of purpose. Add to the aura the fact that there was no evidence at this "park" of any other human; we had the place so to ourselves that it felt as if we'd stepped into the twilight zone. Who would have expected such a surreal setting for the two-month-prior planned consumption of our simple travelers' picnic lunch?

Perhaps this was a deeper portent of things to come, not only on this trip but for our ultimate western journey.

Two nights were spent in Denver, me doing some business while Julie and the offspring hit the zoo and the Children's Museum. My doing business was central to our being in Denver, and totally central to our ultimate involvement with The Riverside Hotel. My boss lived and operated several other businesses in Denver. In one of those businesses I found a kindred spirit, Roscoe, who became one of my closest friends. We were both at similar points in our lives, with working wives and young children, toiling away for the same boss in related industries. And tied into the package was our mutual love of baseball, fishing, literature, and fine food and booze.

When I'd mentioned to Roscoe that we were driving west on vacation for a family reunion, a stop in Denver followed by a night at The Historic Riverside Hotel — a getaway staple for my Colorado buddy since his youth — was etched into the trip. One of the things I love most about Roscoe is his tendency to embrace his knowledge of prose and literature, and infuse it into every fragment of conversation. He can make a trip down the driveway to pick up the morning paper into an event: "The morning sun sparked the glistening snow into a field of blinding diamonds as I made my way towards the bundled journal, treading carefully ... cautious not to disturb the surrounding glitter as I bent to gather the previous day's news." Roscoe's propensity to elucidate on the most ordinary of tasks and events (certainly not a fault, as it is borne from the most genuine joie de vivre that I've ever encountered) made a trip to the Colorado mountains and an eventual visit to The Riverside seem as if we were in fact heading to Shangri-La.

The drive to The Riverside seemed endless, up and over Berthoud Pass, through one small town after another, before we took a right turn onto the main street of Hot Sulphur Springs, Colorado, heading slowly west towards Mt. Bross, the Colorado River, and The Riverside Hotel. The white clapboard façade bared itself to the south and the rest of the town as if it were one of the world's last outposts. It was truly as if all roads in Grand County led to this end, this juncture of farm, burg and field, river and mountain. I stood before the place awestruck; I knew that I was in the presence of time, history, and past generations. Good Lord, but the place had a feel!

As I walked up to and into The Riverside for the first time, bags in tow and eager for the experience, and, more importantly, eager for a cocktail after the long drive, I was greeted by the visage of this fantastically musty, cluttered old place — half-dead climbing vines clinging to the walls, window ledges, and door jambs; a homey living area dominated by a massive limestone fireplace; and a mounted trophy seven-point elk rack lording over the room. It was as if the old-timey feel of the outside had pulsed its veins straight through the interior. I'm certain that if you'd have walked into the place in 1930 not much would be different, save for the raging 19-inch television in the corner. The old man who sat in the chair, his eyes glued to that television, feebly greeted us as we entered.

Meet Mr. Abner Renta, the proprietor of The Riverside Hotel.

At that time Mr. Renta would have been my vision for the Gollum character in Tolkien's works: bloodshot, bulging bug eyes; sallow skin; and rotting teeth under a wild, unmanageable tangle of wispy, wiry hair. His lilting, high-pitched welcome and his hysterical falsetto of a following laugh most certainly would have chilled Gollum's icy blood. I clutched onto my bags, forgot about having cocktails, and looked nervously for the exit.

On the spot I began to question the accuracy of my friend Roscoe's tendency to creatively describe his past and present, thinking that possibly some serious drugs had played into his utopian worldview way more than I'd imagined.

After a slow rise and a dramatic flourish of the arm, Mr. Renta all but exploded, "Welcome to The Riverside! Go upstairs and pick any room you like!"

"Abner! Good to see you! It's Roscoe Cowerd. Remember me?"

"Of course I do. Is the rest of your family with you? Have you brought your dogs? I don't want the dogs down here."

"No, Abner, no dogs; just our friends from Kansas City and their kids."

"Wonderful! How nice. Nice to meet you. Will you be having dinner with us tonight?"

"We wouldn't miss it," interjected Roscoe before I had the chance to say, "Hell no!"

"What's for dinner tonight, Abner? We're all starved!"

"We've got ham and vegetable soup, pork chops, trout, and strip steak … all served with Spanish rice."

"That sounds great, Abner. Sounds like what was on the menu the last few times we were here."

"Well, yeah, I guess that's true; we got it down pretty good. Dinner is at six o'clock. Don't be late! And make sure you put the bath mat on the back of the chair after you shower!"

And so went my brief introduction to Abner Renta. Not in a billion years at that time would I ever have imagined that fourteen years later that I would be standing in this very room giving this grimy little man a check comprised of the better part of our lives savings in return for the honor of sitting in this lobby greeting strangers and telling them where they would be sleeping, what they would be eating for dinner, and at what time they would be eating it.

Who amongst us can at any time imagine and say for certain what will ultimately be?

Not one of us; if we could, we would be King eternally.

Yet we can all accurately make pronouncements as to what absolutely will not be.

It's funny how the unknown can so often soundly trump the absolute.

* * *

After a brief attempt at trout fishing in the Colorado River, a cleanup, and a few quick cocktails, we found ourselves in The River Room Restaurant, the early 1970s addendum to the western edge of the original 1903 structure that overlooked the stretch of river upon which I'd just unsuccessfully attempted to angle.

Our group of nine — four adults and five children — was seated at a large table, hungry and eager to order. More accurately, the kids were ready to order, as the adults with the cocktails were less eager to do anything substantive beyond enjoying the moment. The adult mood was sublime, brought on more by the place than the booze, as this warm room and its immediate proximity to the mountain, the river, and the setting sun had a wonderful effect on the road weary travelers.

WHAM!

Abner's easel chalkboard, which contained the evening's food offerings, slammed down next to our table for the threefold purpose of 1) abruptly and rudely getting our attention, 2) temporarily shutting up the kids, and 3) letting the adults know that their brief stay in La-La Land was now over. Welcome to Abnerville!

"I'm pretty busy, so I don't have a lot of time." (The restaurant was empty.) "Our soup tonight is Ham & Veg...A...Ta...Ble." (He said the word "vegetable" not only as if it had four syllables, but also as if it were four separate words.) "We have fried pork chops, fried trout, or New York strip steak, all served with Spanish rice."

"Is the trout fresh from the river?" I asked.

"It's from a river. What do you know about fresh trout, or rivers ... and why would you care where it's from?"

"Could we ask about — "

"MAKE YOUR CHOICES! I'm VERY BUSY! I'll leave you the board, but I'll be back in a minute ... **FOR YOUR ORDER!"**

'Wow, did I miss something?' I wondered. 'We're in this guy's place of business, ready to spend money, and he seems pissed that we're here. How could this be?'

From grades one through eight I had the honor of being educated by nuns — real nuns from the '50s and '60s, not these new-age nuns that are all about peace, love, and wearing civilian clothes. My nuns were first and foremost about knuckle-busting, skull-rapping discipline whilst they were uncomfortably suffering in restrictive costumes that obviously brought them to the point of wanting to torture the rest of the world as a way of getting things on an even keel.

Abner Renta's customer service style made me feel as if one of those All-Pro 1950s nuns were standing at the edge of the table not-so-gently tugging at the tender part of my upper ear, asking — no, demanding — "You don't want the trout ... *Whap!* ... You want the fried pork chop, and if you think you don't want the fried pork chop ... *Whap!* ... put your knuckles on the table and I'll make you wish ... *Whap!* ... *Whap!* ... *Whap!* ... you'd have ordered and enjoyed the fried pork chop."

Seven minutes later, Mr. Renta reappeared with an order pad in hand, noticeably very testy. Had Abner been dressed like a nun, I wouldn't have been surprised, nor would I have found it out of character.

"Alright, who's ready to order?"

I decided to jump right in to the fray.

"I'll have the New York strip steak, medium rare."

Abner's response: "I'll bring it cooked, but there's no guess as to how it will be cooked. You won't get sick if you eat it. That's about all I'll guarantee. *BWA HA HA HA!*"

"Ok, who's next?" I asked.

My wife, Julie, stepped up to the plate and ordered. "How about the trout? How's the trout?"

"We're out of trout. But we've got a few pork chops left, and a few steaks, cooked to the chef's liking ... *BWA HA HA HA!*"

"But your chalkboard has trout, and — "

"WE'RE OUT OF TROUT! DID YOU NOT HEAR ME? WE'VE GOT STEAKS AND A FEW PORK CHOPS!"

Sheepishly, Julie ordered the pork chop, and we ordered pork chops for the kids, as the thirty-dollar, eight-ounce, frozen steaks were but a bit beyond our budget.

The food was decent (being both famished as well as a little inebriated might have helped to soften the requirements of my particular palate), but the previously sublime atmosphere was darkened by the SS-like discipline that was exhibited by the owner.

Possibly at this point the first seeds to growing the ultimate weeds of our eventual demise were planted: 'Wow. This place is awesome. If we owned this place, we wouldn't be mean and offensive to our customers. We'd try to accommodate their desires rather than verbally beating them up for expressing their desires. Gotta think that attitude would ultimately be better for business. If only we owned this place ... '

CHAPTER THREE
A Little History

The building that now stands at 509 Grand Avenue, Hot Sulphur Springs, Colorado, whose construction date is officially noted as 1903, is comprised of four sections — one original structure and three later additions — that have been morphed into the seamless white façade of its current iteration. The original section of the building was a livery stable, constructed sometime in the1860s after the official founding of the town of Hot Sulphur Springs, which is on record as occurring in 1860. William Byers, who was the founder, publisher, and editor of the *Rocky Mountain News*, a Denver-based newspaper that ceased publication in 2008, the summer we moved to Colorado, journeyed to Hot Sulphur and was enamored by the idea of turning the town and the healing waters of the natural sulphurous hot spring pool into a tourist Mecca, much on the order of New York's Saratoga Springs, which Byers had visited some years earlier. Byers bought the springs from the Ute Indians, whose people had been frequenting the area for the previous thousand years as they considered the springs to be sacred grounds, for a reported sum of one hundred dollars.

While Byers' vision never fully bore fruit on the level of Saratoga Springs, or other Colorado natural hot springs such as Glenwood Springs or Pagosa Springs, the little town of Hot Sulphur continued to grow, mostly due to it being the governmental seat for the county of Grand. And this in and of itself is a pretty good story.

Grand Lake, some twenty-five miles northeast of Hot Sulphur Springs as the crow flies, was founded in 1881 to support the influx of miners who descended on the area with the 1875 discovery of gold, lead, silver, and copper in the surrounding mountains of the Never Summer and Indian Peak ranges of the Rocky Mountains. Those majestic peaks that now draw sightseers from all over the world were initially magnets for prospectors and independent men of commerce, the draw of the ore strong enough to pull the hardiest of men into this mostly uninhabitable and most certainly inhospitable stretch of real estate. It would follow that anyone who would give up the comforts of late nineteenth-century city life for the brutal conditions inherent in this 9000-feet elevated, isolated icebox would be greedy to a fault and tough beyond reason. This lethal combination of character traits, traits inherent in most who would be the fashioners of our Western frontier, would make for a violent, bloody start to the birth of Grand County.

Colorado was admitted to the Union as a state in 1876, and shortly thereafter county boundaries were drawn and county seats were established. The county of Grand was established with the tiny hamlet of Hot Sulphur Springs — centrally located in the hub of Middle Park and the county — being selected as the county seat. As the city of Grand Lake grew quickly with the influx of miners and merchants, some industrious Grand Lake politicians arranged for a vote of the people to move the county seat from Hot Sulphur to Grand Lake. The first election, widely in favor of the more populous Grand Lake, was thrown out as many of the votes were declared invalid, being cast by residents who had not lived in the county the requisite six months before being able to legally vote. Grand Lake barely prevailed in the second election, but prevail it did, and in November of 1882, the county seat was moved to Grand Lake. It's certain that many contentious exchanges, unrecorded in the history books, went back and forth between the political powers of the two towns before the fateful day of July 4th, 1883, when the lone county councilman from Hot Sulphur (one of four Grand County councilmen, the other three from Grand Lake), accompanied by the sheriff and deputy of Grand County and three other masked residents of Hot Sulphur, rode to Grand Lake with serious mischief on their minds and loaded guns on their hips.

As the July 4th county council meeting adjourned, with the Hot Sulphur councilman noticeably absent, the three Grand Lake council members exited the county courthouse and were summarily gunned down in the broad daylight as they strode out onto the warm main street. One was able to fire back at the masked assailants, but at the end of the day, all three Grand Lake council members were dead, along with the county clerk. The Hot Sulphur councilman was the unfortunate member of the marauding party who took the bullet from the Grand Lake bunch, dying several days later from an infection. The sheriff from Hot Sulphur, who was called to investigate the killing in which he, masked, had participated, committed suicide two weeks after the shooting. His deputy, also one of the masked murderers from Hot Sulphur, fled the county after the shootings and was later found dead on the Colorado-Utah border, identified only by the size of his feet, said to be unusually and notably large.

A few years after this murderous brouhaha, another vote to establish the county seat was called by the new replacement county commissioners (all of whom were residents of Hot Sulphur Springs), and in a resounding landslide, Hot Sulphur was selected and the county seat was moved back to where it has resided, unchallenged, since that violent Fourth of July in 1883.

* * *

As well as being the midpoint of the county, Hot Sulphur Springs was also roughly the halfway point between Chicago and San Francisco for the railroad, and in early 1900 the railroad made the town its major midway stopover for resting the crew and refueling the trains with coal and water. Hot Sulphur was simply referred to as "Coal Town" by the railroad workers and most others who knew of its existence.

The influx of railroad workers and hot springs visitors spurred the need for food and lodging, and in 1903, The Riverside Hotel & Café was officially opened for business by Mr. Charlie Free. Charles F. Free was born in Zurich, Switzerland, in 1873, and shortly after he immigrated to Canada with his parents. In 1890, at the tender age of seventeen years, he left the family in Canada and headed south, finding his way to Denver and then the mountains beyond, working primarily as a cowhand on one of the many ranches that inhabited the lush summer grazing valleys of Middle Park. He then found work for a short while at the grocery store in Hot Sulphur Springs before signing on as a teamster, freighting goods, supplies, and the occasional passenger down the Blue River Valley, thru Georgetown, on to Denver, and back. That simply had to be grueling work, as driving that route back and forth today in good weather on paved roads in a fancy car can wear one to a nub.

In 1900 Charlie Free gave up the teamstering© business, found a bride in Hot Sulphur, and settled down for a few years, working on a ranch outside of town. One assumes he worked hard but made little, wondering how he had the wherewithal to buy the old livery stable and build the aforementioned attachment that became The

Riverside in 1903. There's possibly more to this story, but only one's speculation will provide the supposed details. Charlie owned the hotel for ten years before selling it and striking out again as a rancher, which he did until he finally hung up his spurs in 1926, at the age of 53. Apparently Charlie found the frigid outdoors, the stubborn livestock, and the aroma of hay and horse manure easier to deal with than cranky hotel guests, picky diners, and drunken bar customers. There were many times during my tenure as owner and proprietor of The Riverside when I could understand Charlie's desire to be outdoors on the back of a horse instead of straddling a dishwasher or corralling a bloated, clogged toilet bowl.

In one of life's continuing string of "fact is stranger than fiction"-isms, Charlie's last known employment was that of a founder and the first president of the Middle Park Bank, located in nearby Granby, later to become Acme Savings & Loan. Thus, Charlie Free, builder of the building we bought, founded the bank where we received our loan to buy his Riverside; ergo, Charlie founded the bank that foreclosed upon us and eventually took back his Riverside.

After living a long and successful life in Grand County, Charles Free died in 1955 — the year before both my wife and I were born — and is buried next to his wife in the cemetery on the hill east of town, lying in eternal peaceful repose as he watches over the town of Hot Sulphur Springs, the magnificent Colorado River, and his iconic Riverside Hotel.

* * *

The new two-story structure that Charlie Free built in 1903 was roughly twenty-five feet in depth and seventy-five feet in length, and contained a narrow dining room with a kitchen in the back, paralleled by a narrow lobby, or gathering room, separated by a staircase that led upstairs to the owners' living area, which included a bedroom adjoining a sitting room, and five small guestrooms. There were no bathrooms at the time of construction due to the fact that there was no running water or indoor plumbing. As was common of the times, there were chamber pots in the bedrooms and a privy out back, certainly unheated — doubtful that Byers' *Rocky Mountain News* was read during the course of doing one's business. Because the hotel was located near the Grand River, as the river was known in 1903, the name being changed to the Colorado River in 1923, an abundance of clean, fresh water for cooking, washing, and drinking was no more than a short walk away. Maps indicate that the river's course has changed since the construction of the building; today the western edge of the building is but ten short yards from the riverbank, whereas back in 1903 the distance was more like the length of a football field.

The new structure shared a common wall with the livery stable; however, there was no interior congress between the buildings. As travel by horse and buggy was still the principle mode of transportation, the need for a livery stable was germane, yet, one of the earliest known pictures of the structure shows a pre-Model T jalopy of unknown make in front of the hotel, the hitching post with a horse and buggy attached still evident.

In 1913, Charlie Free exited the hospitality business at the expense of a gentleman named Omar Qualls, who hailed from Hot Springs, Arkansas. Mr. Qualls' wife was, as they said in those days, "in a sickly way," requiring continual access to healing waters, waters that were native to her Hot Springs, AR, and, as Mr. and Mrs. Qualls' luck would have it, also native to their newfound summer getaway in Hot Sulphur Springs. (There is but a little irony here, as I felt that I might possibly die, or at best become deathly ill, if I slipped myself into the sulphurous brew of those waters.)

Mr. Qualls and family would venture some one thousand miles in the spring of the year, traveling from one hot spring in Arkansas to another in Colorado. They would open and operate a five-room hotel and a small café from May through September, then close the place up for the winter and head back to the warmer climes of Arkansas' Blue Ridge Mountains. That business model worked well for Mr. Qualls for the next twenty years, a business model that I possibly should have adopted, as the off-season slump was critical to our ultimate downfall.

Sometime in the 1920s the original structure of the livery stable was transformed into additional housing for both hotel guests and staff, and running water and indoor bathroom facilities were added. The remodeled upstairs consisted of seven guest rooms and one bathroom — a toilet with a tub. The guest rooms were also equipped with sinks with running water (these impossible-to-buy-parts-for accoutrements were still in existence when we took over the hotel in 2007). The downstairs consisted of eight rooms: two used for storage, two for staff, two overflow guest rooms, and two "utility" rooms, used during the next few years as a barber shop and then as a doctor's office from 1935–1945. These rooms would ultimately serve as Abner's office and living quarters, and finally, after being gutted to the dirt and rebuilt, our living quarters. Also, as the two structures were adjoined so were their dissimilar rooflines — the livery stable had a turreted façade that denoted it as a stable as a steeple denotes a church or a dome a capitol — being replaced with a straight common ridge across the front of the structure.

In the 1930s an additional shotgun arm running the north-south length of the hotel was constructed, in parallel consort with the 1903 two-story structure. The purpose of this addition was not only to add four additional upstairs guest rooms but also to double the width of the restaurant on the first floor.

The fourth and final addition, the single-story River Room restaurant, was built onto the western side, or river side, of the hotel in 1970. Ironically, this newest section was the only part of the building that had foundation and structure problems. The slope of the room towards the river, from the rapidly sinking foundation, was so bad that a marble placed on most of the tables in the restaurant would have begun running westward and downward once freed from the fingers. None of the windows in the room — and the walls were all but windows so that dining patrons might enjoy the view — could have closed flush on a bet, the building was now so out of square. Apparently they just don't build things like they used to.

In 1968 construction began on the Eisenhower Tunnel, located approximately fifty miles south of Hot Sulphur Springs on I-70, just up the mountain from Dillon, Colorado, to the west and Georgetown, Colorado, to the east. The tunnel construction was expected to bring an influx of workers into the area, and they would need places to eat and sleep, and, of utmost importance, places to drink, party, and spend away their hard-earned cash on the weekends. The owner of the Riverside at that time, like many other purveyors of food, booze, and lodging in Grand County, was quick to cash in on the tunnel labor, thus the final addition to the building in 1970. The tunnel construction was expected to last three years but ran into numerous delays, including the discovery of a fault line and the deaths of six of the workers, and wasn't fully completed until eleven years later in 1979. Shortly after the tunnel was completed and the workers were depleted, The Riverside shut its doors until its 1986 resurrection at the hands of Mr. Abner Renta.

The records on all of this constructing, plumbing, and general building cobbling no longer exist, if in fact building permits or any sort of official documentation detailing construction were required. (All of this building possibly occurred before it dawned on the public trust that it had the legal wherewithal to filch its citizens for any act of or attempt at commerce from which they might profit.) The dates of additions and changes to the structure are but educated guesses based upon pictures that hung in our lobby that showed the progression of the building's architecture, starting with what we believed to be the first 1903 picture, which shows the six-window, two-story, clapboard structure with a large "HOTEL" and "CAFÉ" painted on the front, adjoined with the turreted building that housed the livery stable. The second picture was from approximately 1910, with the livery façade still evident but the two buildings made to look as one with the use of a faux brick and tar-paper façade. The next picture was taken in the 1920s, and the turreted rooflines of the livery stable are now absent, making it look for the first time in its twenty-year existence like one building. Finally, the fourth picture, taken in the 1930s, shows the hotel with the addition of the west wing, the fifteen-foot widening that ran the length of the hotel, adding four rooms upstairs and doubling the downstairs dining room and kitchen.

One of the things I loved about these pictures was the fun in dating them by the type of transportation that was parked in front of the hotel. In the 1903 picture there were horses and a hitching post; in 1910, horse-drawn carriages along with a few 1910 Model T Fords. The 1920s-era picture showed no signs of hitching posts, with equine power being replaced by a fancy sedan of unknown make and model. In the last picture, taken in the 1930s, a regal awning spans the front of the hotel, offering afternoon shade to a sporty 1932 Ford Coupe. These pictures were all taken in the summer, as traversing Berthoud Pass in a 1932 Ford Coupe during the winter would have been impossible, much as it can still be today, even in a four-wheel drive Chevy Suburban.

It was often while viewing these pictures that our guests would have their feeling of awakening to the history that engulfed them as they stood in the lobby of The Riverside. You could figuratively see the light go on in their heads; their eyes would widen and a smile would break the plane of their faces as many would finally get it with an, "Oh, wow! I'm standing here right now in this place that looked like that a hundred years ago." To many it served as a pleasant little lagniappe in addition to the food and room for which they were about to pay. It is a feeling we don't often get elsewhere in our daily lives in the cities and suburbs of America, and it was certainly one of the feelings that brought us and our dreams to live in Grand County in that magnificent building.

CHAPTER FOUR

Back to Mr. Renta

We would visit The Riverside eight times in total before our seriously fatal pursuit of purchasing the place, which would be comprised of the initial summer visit and one other, and six straight visits between Christmas and New Year's. Our Colorado-Riverside holiday ritual involved blowing out of Kansas City on Christmas afternoon, driving to Hays, Kansas, spending the night, and then heading straight the next morning to 7800 feet of Hot Sulphur Springs altitude and 139 pounds of Abner Renta attitude. There we would meet family and more often than not friends from Kansas City who we'd drag to this little jewel in the mountains, as The Riverside was an ideal place over the holidays to spend quiet, quality time with family and friends.

One irony of our Riverside pre-purchase winter visits to Hot Sulphur and the mountains was that never, *ever,* did we experience the brutal weather and driving conditions that are commonplace in that neck of the woods. We ignorant flatlanders would head up I-70 out of Denver every December 26th, the sky blue and the frost glistening, and marvel at the beauty of the snow-laden pines and icy peaks on clear roads all the way to our destination. Not once, coming or going, were we treated to the normalcy of a winter blizzard — the kind during which we bit our lips to bleeding and wore out our right arms sign-of-the-crossing whilst driving over Berthoud Pass — that is, not until we bought the place and there was no going back, and then, of course, we experienced them with Ex-Lax regularity. No question that timing is everything, as had we experienced the blinding terror of a normal blizzard trek over Berthoud Pass, our desire to spew our retirement dollars into a black hole in Middle Park would have been quickly and immediately squelched.

From that first visit in the summer of 1993 to the final visit in the winter of 2000 when we left The Riverside saying, "Never in hell will we come back here," Abner steadily transmogrified from a lovable old character's character to an utterly untenable asshole's asshole. I contend that many longtime customers continued to visit Abner and The Riverside in his later years only to savor the experience of seeing this miserable, ill-humored, insulting old fool in his not-to-be-topped-ass-holiness glory, much as you watch a NASCAR event for hope of seeing a wreck, or a hockey game a brawl.

Here are some examples of the snappy repartee that ultimately inspired us to find places other than The Riverside to spend our hard-earned vacation dollars when visiting Colorado.

To friends of ours who visited during one winter trip with their five-year-old: "Your son is very ill-behaved. I'm assuming that he's mentally retarded?"

To an overweight female guest in the restaurant, loudly enough for all to hear: "If you don't see anything on the menu that suits you, the Dairy Dine is down the street. Their hamburgers are *very good,* but they're *very fattening*. However, I don't suppose that would deter you from eating one."

To an innocent walking in off the street: "In what sort of a sty were you raised where you find it acceptable to enter this room without wiping your feet?" (The prospective customer proffered his middle finger in response and quickly left the premises without describing to Abner the sort of sty in which he was raised.)

Aloud to no one in particular as a female guest, clad in insulated ski pants, walked through the lobby: "The nice thing about insulated ski pants is that people aren't sure if they're looking at your fat ass or insulated ski pants — but then I suppose that all of our asses look fat in ski pants! *BWA HA HA HA!*"

These are a few of the zingers that I remember; there were a plentitude more that I thankfully succeeded in forgetting.

One of Abner's trademarks was his dramatic falsetto, creepy Tiny Tim freak show of a laugh, which was way beyond verbal description. Whenever you heard it, you'd cock your head in aural wonderment. Those of us who visited The Riverside and knew Abner would attempt to mimic the laugh — it was like Elvis', "Thank you ... thank you very much." Once you heard it you had to try and ape it yourself.

As the visits to The Riverside mounted up, the laughs lessened and the slyly caustic comments turned to brutal personal assaults. I don't remember a seminal event on that last visit that made us stomp our foot and say we were never coming back. Rather, it was just a general feeling of ill will that Abner consistently exuded towards us, his paying customers. We knew he needed our money, but we also knew that the last thing on earth he wanted was our company.

I never complained to Abner, never said anything like, "Dammit, we've come here for six straight years now, brought you a ton of business, spent a ton of money, but you've turned into a real asshole and we're NEVER COMING BACK!" I never did because I knew that he couldn't care less. At best, berating him and telling him the truth would have gotten me nothing more than one of his *"BWA HA HA HAs."*

Six years passed in which only one of those years we returned to the mountains for our post-Christmas family visit — and not to The Riverside — as the rest of our Christmases were spent in Kansas City, blissfully enjoying our home and family, replete with our own private toilets. Not one of us missed our Christmases past at The Riverside.

Then one day in late February of 2007, as a result of the previously described job-related series of events, I was pushed into making one of the most reckless phone inquiries of all time — asking Abner Renta if he would consider selling The Riverside.

The rotted-teeth grin that Abner displayed upon hearing that question beamed across seven hundred miles of telephone wire, a smile so profound that possibly the corners of his mouth deftly sliced into each of his earlobes.

* * *

So who was this Gollum-esque miscreant, Abner Renta, who found his way to a ramshackle old hotel in a desolate outpost in the frozen, unpopulated heart of Colorado, in the county of Grand, and turned it into a welcoming, charming, homey little hostelry for what seemed to be the ultimate purpose of taking easy money from innocent, unsuspecting people?

Raised in the barrio of East Los Angeles, Abner moved to Colorado to study at the University of Colorado in Boulder. Social Work was his degree (very odd … a degree you would normally pursue if you wanted to be in the business of helping the less fortunate), and he plied it for a while working for the Colorado Department of Labor & Unemployment, assisting the unemployed. Possibly the notion of working with and trying to fleece people that had nothing to fleece moved him into the hospitality industry, where logic would follow that if you were staying at a nice hotel, you had to have some money to spend/lose/fleece. It was there that Abner found his home.

Abner worked at a hotel in downtown Denver for the better part of ten years, honing his multiple Riverside-worthy skills of hotel and restaurant management: biting sarcasm, short sheeting, cost cutting, bill padding, making good eye contact while bald-faced lying, code skirting, pouring rotgut booze in empty top shelf bottles, dead-beating vendors, and tax evasion, to name but a few.

Abner pounded out of Denver in the mid-1980s with a suitcase full of cash and an illegal that he picked up at the Denver Greyhound depot, bound for the mountains in search of a place where he could practice his newly acquired art of hospitality on the paying public — far from the eyes of scrutiny. He stumbled upon a sleepy little burg in Grand County, one block north of Highway 40, and found a building nestled against the banks of the majestic Colorado River, a football field's length away from the base of Mt. Bross (a languid, lazy excuse for a mountain, but imposing nonetheless as it lorded over the town and valley like a fat uncle to whom both money and fealty are owed) and a stone's throw away from a natural hot springs pool that had been frequented by the Ute Indians and other nonnative denizens as far back as the first century — possibly further.

What Abner found was a magnificent but neglected historic structure: a white clapboard, many-windowed building that jutted its façade in broad defiance of the southern exposure that pounded it with three hundred days per year of a 7800-foot elevation dose of UV rays. The three-quarter-inch thick pine slats that comprised the cladding of The Riverside had seen and needed a century's worth of primer and paint to survive this environment. Shortly after Abner purchased The Riverside, the illegal-in-tow did a little scraping, then added a heavy coat of 1980s cheap white latex — that did for the place until we purchased it in 2007, desperately in need of a new coat of paint.

The Riverside had been unoccupied for the better part of seven years when Abner purchased it in 1986. The roof was shot, and water damage had all but obliterated the wooden infrastructure. Water — the stuff that we are all mostly comprised of, live for, die for, fight for, and order with or without gas at fancy restaurants — when left to its own devices, is brutal on buildings and building materials in general, and roofs in particular. This naturally destructive proclivity is magnified in a roller coaster-extreme climate like Hot Sulphur Springs. The building faces south to accept the warming rays of the sun for natural heat, while the roof slopes back away to the north so that the accumulated then melting snow drips and drains to the back of the building. That northern-exposure snow, seeing no sun from October thru May, builds up on that roof all winter — three to four feet is common. The weight of that snow constantly squats on the roof, forcing and flexing the substrate with cooling and warming, all the while opening cracks and crevices that the melting snow seeks out. Unabated, this force, this unyielding flex and flow, and then the ensuing melting snow and dripping water, can buckle the structure of a building and obliterate its walls and floors in a few short years.

When Abner found The Riverside, it was on the perilous end of being decimated by the innocent but destructive forces of cold, hot, sun, snow, ice, and water. I'm betting that Abner got a pretty good deal on the place.

One of the first things that Abner did, or rather had his indentured illegal do, was put a new roof on The Riverside. The existing roof was a flat, layered, hot asphalt and felt construction, known in the trade as a "built-up roof" — the technology dates back to the late 1800s and is still a solid option for a flat roof today, much unchanged in both materials and application techniques. As opposed to tearing off the old and applying new — standard protocol for a roof of this age and deteriorated condition — Abner went right over the old roof with interlocking metal roofing panels, roughly three feet wide and twenty feet in length. When I say "went over," I mean that the help screwed this roof down to the old substrate with thousands of 3/8" x 1.5" screws — that would also equate to thousands of holes being put in the roof, leading to thousands of additional opportunities for future leaks. Not the best roofing practice, but quick, cheap, and not demanding of a high level of skill for its application.

When the metal roofing panels were delivered to Abner, laid in bundles on the roof by a crane, Abner went up and cut the bundles open for the purpose of counting the panels. By God, he'd paid for 120 panels and, understandably, he was going to count and make certain that they shipped him the 120 panels that he paid for. All panels present and accounted for, Abner and the help turned in early for what would the following day be the grueling task of roofing. Abner didn't account for the possibility of an evening windstorm, which did occur, lifting all 120 panels (not simultaneously) and depositing them throughout the town of Hot Sulphur Springs. It is a miracle that no one was dismembered or beheaded, as these panels are sharp-edged sheet metal, capable of cutting someone in half given a lethal combination of proper angle and sufficient force, both of which would be available as these things flew through the air like big rectangular Frisbees. It would not have been a good first impression on the town of the new hotel proprietor had one of the residents, due to Abner's ignorance regarding the forces of wind when plied upon unattached sheets of razor-thin metal, been sliced in half whilst taking their evening stroll.

After spending the better part of the next two days collecting the panels and toting them back up on the roof, without the aid of a crane, the help began attaching what in most cases were bent, misshapen, and often out of square panels, square being important for the purpose of adjoining panel to panel in a tight, waterproof fit. This little whoopsie would be the cause of continual leaks and the resultant water damage from Abner's first day of new building and roof ownership until the day he handed the keys over to me, and then beyond.

* * *

About twenty miles north-northeast of Hot Sulphur Springs lies the village of Grand Lake, home to Colorado's deepest and largest natural lake and the headwaters of the Colorado River as well as being the western entrance to Rocky Mountain National Park. In the county of Grand, with all of the spectacular vistas, fishing, hunting, and recreational opportunities, Grand Lake can lay claim to being the first established vacation spot in the Colorado Rockies, dating back to the late 1800s. The setting of this cerulean jewel surrounded by sloping pine forests and the ensuing spires of the Indian Peaks is rivaled by few places in terms of its natural beauty. Sadly, at the bottom of this visually bountiful natural bowl lies the actual town of Grand Lake, replete with a faux-rustic Old West street of bars, restaurants, art galleries, souvenir shops, a bowling alley, and some less-than-quaint motels and lodging establishments. Oh well; we all gotta make a buck.

The historic Grand Lake Lodge, which opened in 1920, some seventeen years after the opening of The Riverside, was the crown jewel of Grand Lake. It was a magnificent lodge, with both elegant guest quarters and rustic cabins, and was the standard bearer for food, beverage, and lodging on the western slope of the Continental Divide. It would remain as such until a fire burned the better part of the place to the ground in the summer of 1973. The owners took a painstaking eight years to rebuild, careful to extract historic furnishings and memorabilia from the charred rubble, before finally reopening in the summer of 1981.

Why is this little north-northeast travelogue germane to the story of Abner Renta and The Riverside?

Approximately fifty yards north of the resurrected Grand Lake Lodge, just at the edge of the magnificent pine forests that surround this iconic structure, sat a pile of pre-1940s kitchen equipment that barely survived the fire, and only because the fire didn't get hot enough to melt the two-ton cast-iron gas stove, oven, and attached griddle that had been the heart and soul of the Grand Lake Lodge kitchen for the past thirty years. They'd been talking about replacing that big, old, outdated locomotive of a stove ten years prior to the fire. It was now dead and forever out of that kitchen, figuratively if not literally buried at the edge of the woods — for the kitchen crew, a silver lining in the dark cloud that was the destructive blaze of 1973. Truth be known, they'd hoped that it would sit there forever and become a permanent part of the flora and fauna, as the effort required of hauling it off would have been monumental.

Enter Abner Renta, a Middle-Park Gollum on his eternal quest for a magic ring's worth of cheap furnishings and equipment for his newly acquired mountain hostelry.

Abner bought the stove for twenty-five dollars, and had his bus-depot servant and probably fifteen others help load it onto a U-Haul trailer and install it in the newly remodeled kitchen at The Riverside in 1986, prior to the grand reopening. No big deal that not all of the burners worked, the flat top was half melted, it was rife with rust, or that the scald and char from the 1973 fire was welded to the exterior of this gargantuan hotbox. What was key was that it was cheap and it worked ... barely, but working versus not working at all, in a very black and white sort of way.

30

To a yellow paisley linoleum sheet floor, probably installed in The Riverside kitchen sometime in the 1930s, Abner and his servant adhered speckled beige as-bestos linoleum tiles. The perimeter of the kitchen was then outfitted with built-in plywood and pine shelves, cabinets, pantries, drawers, and worktables, all painted with a heavy coat of high-gloss white paint. It was here that utensils and dry goods were stored, and food was ultimately prepared. These cabinets and shelving were very well constructed by Abner's illegal, so well-constructed that they would end up being a screaming bitch to remove twenty-two years later in our effort to get the kitchen up to code. (Take a peek in any commercial kitchen — you won't see anything constructed of wood, as wood tends to have a soft spot for harboring bacteria.)

The dining room tables and chairs as well as all of the furnishings in the guest rooms were a hodgepodge assortment of yard sale, estate sale, and thrift shop items, an eclectic mix but functional and inexpensive. Bedding, sheets, and towels were also collected at various sales or secondhand stores — no boring, bleached white sheets for The Riverside beds. For a fact, if the linen wasn't loud enough to keep you awake at night, you wouldn't be sleeping on it in Abner's place. Many guests found the wacky sheets and funky furnishings charming, as it gave the place a "homey" feel; we got rid of them the first week we owned the hotel, with prejudice.

The dishware, glasses, and cutlery were also vintage garage sale — nothing was a set, no two pieces alike. It could be all but dizzying to look down at the swirls, stripes, and floral patterns on the plates before stabbing your fork at some of Abner's finest fare. Also, for certain an advantage to using loud, colorful stone-ware was its ability to hide the adhered flecks of yesterday's food that might have been missed by the no-dishwasher sink-dunking method of tableware hygiene that Abner chose to employ, as the Grand Lake Lodge apparently did not have a rusted, charred, barely working dishwasher for sale.

The final accoutrement to The Riverside was no bargain-basement, thrift-shop, fire-damaged piece of junk; rather, it was arguably one of the most spectacular pieces of furnishing in all of Grand County: the magnificent, historical Brunswick bar. Manufactured in 1895 in Dubuque, Iowa, and brought to The Riverside from its original home in Leadville, Colorado, in 1920, the bar was a burnished oak and cherry wood masterpiece of ornately carved borders and corniced columns that beckoned thirsty travelers to gaze in awed admiration, often forgetting that an icy beer sat sweating before them, waiting patiently to be consumed. When Abner arrived at The Riverside, the bar was stored out back of the hotel in one of the storage sheds amid a pile of clutter that had accumulated over the past eighty-some years. Enlisting the help of a few locals with the promise of a round of free drinks after the bar's assemblage, Abner had the booze-fueled locals lift, haul, and reassemble the bar in what had previously been a small storeroom off of the kitchen. After the twenty-year hiatus — the previous owner, for God only knows what reason, had taken the bar out of the building — the glorious Brunswick bar was back in business at The Riverside.

And so began Abner's tenure as proprietor of the newly refurbished Historic Riverside Hotel, Bar & Restaurant. He'd had the roof replaced, the walls wallpapered, the rooms furnished, the bar stocked, and the kitchen cooking in time for the start of the summer tourist season of 1986.

Twenty-one years later, he was pulling out every stop imaginable to convince a naive couple from Kansas with just enough money to get their asses in serious trouble that Hot Sulphur Springs was a garden spot that would rival Mecca, and that in spite of the seemingly high asking price, The Riverside was an idyllic yet affordable dream come true that we could make happen with the stroke of a pen.

CHAPTER FIVE

The Bait is Taken;
The Hook is Set

So back to my umpteenth-meeting-from-hell-induced phone call to the Riverside, when I was attempting to examine the possibilities of fleeing the corporate world for the safer, saner haven of Hot Sulphur Springs.

After our initial phone reintroduction when Abner said he remembered me and made the mildly obscene but totally in-character remark regarding my unusual last name, I got right down to my reason for once again subjecting myself to this sniveling little con man.

"Well, my wife and I have always loved your place, and I've just sold my business here in Kansas City and we're at a point in our lives where we're looking for a lifestyle change, and we've always thought about owning The Riverside. Any chance you're looking to get out of the business and sell the place?"

Unbeknownst to me, the smile was now back broadly, so profoundly that Abner could barely operate his tongue to get words through his lips. The high-elevation afternoon sun was reflecting off of his fully exposed rotted dentia, the reflection from his ragged incisors in the front window of The Riverside all but blinding Abner to the point where he couldn't concentrate. But he summoned the necessary wherewithal to answer in something like a hissing purr, coyly, "Yes … yes … I might be interested in discussing a sale of the property. But it would have to be to the right people … people that would care for the place, people that would love the place, as I have."

'Oh my,' I thought, 'beyond the financial, he has additional qualifications for who he'll sell to. Could we be so honored, could we ultimately be selected, and would we be deemed worthy enough to ably carry his water at The Riverside going forward?'

33

I didn't want to be cast out from consideration before a proper vetting so early in the game, a vetting that might show me and mine not worthy to bear the distinguished mantle of Proprietor of The Historic Riverside Hotel, but I had to come right out and get a price, as I had a maximum number in mind that I was willing to offer. I feared that the number was maybe half of what he was asking. There was no sense going any further if the place was immediately out of our price range.

"So, Abner, I know there is a lot of water to cover between here and there, but so I don't further waste either of our time, do you have a number in mind that you'd sell the place for?"

Abner said immediately and emphatically — no doubt his arm was outstretched and his index finger pointed skyward in oratorical emphasis — *"I won't take a penny less than $800,000!"*

Now the drunken-pumpkin grin appeared upon my face. I'd imagined the place to be worth two million, maybe as much as three million, and my drop-dead point with what I thought we could offer was one and a half million. Here was a 13,000-square-foot structure on one and a half acres of Colorado River-front property — bona fide Gold Medal trout water that people traveled from all over the world to angle. I'd read that people spent as much as $3 million for 2500 feet of undeveloped riverfront property on the Colorado not but a mile or two upriver from Hot Sulphur.

"Well, that seems to be a price range that we can work in. Let me talk with my wife and get back with you."

I didn't know then, but know now, that Abner quickly lost the smile at this point and went heavy into a "gotta sell this white elephant at all costs as I haven't had a serious prospect with the money to make this happen on the hook for the past nineteen years" survival mode. "I recall you had a family and you seemed to love this place. Not everyone could take this on, but I remember that you and your wife and kids seemed like you'd be the type of people that would be perfect for this place. Wasn't one of your children retarded?"

"No, uh, that was one of our friends' children you're thinking about, and *he wasn't retarded!*"

"Sorry. Sorry. I've had so many thousands of guests the past few years, it's a wonder I can remember as many particulars as I can, given my advanced age and my poor health … (cough … cough). I really would like to sell this place to you, as I'm really starting to wear down."

"Well, Abner, let me talk with my wife, and I'm going to put a list of questions together and I'll call you in a few days."

And now, here was not only the first red flag of hundreds that I would fail or refuse to see, but, in retrospect, here was the biggest, football-field-sized red flag of all times regarding our magnum f-up in the pursuit and eventual purchase of The Historic Riverside Hotel, Bar & Restaurant.

Before I could hang up, Abner opened up to me, a virtual stranger, over the phone on our first phone call. "I've got a couple of other parties interested in the property … I think you should know that." (*'Damn!'* I thought.) Abner continued, "Unfortunately, I've got myself into a little issue on my property taxes, and I could use $10,000 to get up to speed with the county. If you could send me the money, we could put it towards a down payment, or, at the least, I'd pay you back at a generous interest rate when I sell the place to someone else if you're not interested in purchasing the property. And if you were to send me the money pretty quickly, it would certainly put you in a favorable position when I'm deciding on who to sell the place to."

At this point in the discussion, any normal human being would have not only turned away from this deal, they would have snapped their necks turning away and running as fast as their fat little shanks would carry them, all the while laughing with glee, screaming to and thanking the Good Lord above for not having gotten into a deal that would've involved sending big money on the come to a shifty, broke, tax-evading hotelier.

Reality and simple common sense would normally kick in, and you'd reply to this outlandish request with a: *"What? Do you think I'm out of my mind? I'm going to just up and send you $10,000? Are you insane?"* You would then hang up the phone, probably chuckle to yourself, and get on with your life.

I probably don't have to tell you that the $10,000 check was in the mail, heading west to Abner Renta, but a few short days later.

* * *

Abner was broke. Flat busted, in the hole, impoverished, financially depleted, in the red, destitute, insolvent — you get the picture.

However, of paramount importance to this story was the fact that I didn't get the picture, or worse and more to the truth, I knew but refused to get the picture. We found that Abner had a bit of a gambling problem, he being a frequent enough patron of the casinos in Blackhawk and Cripple Creek that he received Christmas hams from them. This revelation had me thinking, 'He's not broke because it is impossible to make a living in Hot Sulphur. He's actually probably doing real well and blowing all the cash in the slots!'

Abner hadn't paid his property taxes for three years. I learned, after not paying my property taxes the second year we owned The Riverside, that this wasn't the end of the world. Kind-hearted individuals would step up and pay your taxes, and when you could finally pony up with the money, you would pay your taxes to the county, plus a penalty and interest, which the kind-hearted knights in shining armor would reap. CDs were earning 2 percent and the stock market was anywhere from losing 100 percent to breaking even if you were lucky, while buying up late property taxes and cashing in on the interest when finally paid netted the investor 10 percent interest — risk free.

Here was the ugly part, and the reason why Abner pleaded with a total stranger over the phone for a loan of $10,000. You had three years to get right with the county, at which point the kind-hearted soul who saved your ass with the county by paying your taxes at the worst case would gain 10 percent interest, but at best-case scenario they would have first lien against your property when the Grand County Treasurer sold it on the courthouse steps, three years to the date of your delinquency.

Simply put, let's say I owed the county $6000 in property taxes on February 10th, 2004, for the 2003 tax year. I didn't pay the money, but some nice guy did, and the county is cool, as they get their six grand and don't even bother sending me a nasty notice. I pay $7000 one year later, for the 2003 tax, of which the nice guy gets $6600, and the county gets the $400 penalty. But if I can't pay the $7000 the following year, the compound interest grows into the next year and the next, until I hit three years past due.

Let's say I pay nothing for three years, as was Abner's case, then on February 10th, 2007, on the courthouse steps in the county of Grand, Colorado, my property is auctioned off to the highest bidder. The nice guy that plopped down that initial $6000 investment three years ago gets the first grab at his six grand and 10 percent compounded interest over three years. That's almost $2000 on a $6000 risk-free investment. In these and any times, buying up property taxes is a good investment. Instead of buying a dilapidated, haunted shithole of a hotel, possibly I should have looked at that as a means to making a buck in Grand County ... but alas!

Abner was two weeks away from that three-year delinquent courthouse steps auction. He was about to lose the thing that he'd put twenty years of blood, sweat, tears, and all of his monetary wherewithal into. His financial life was flashing before his eyes, and the ending was a cataclysmic event from which there was no recovery. At best for him we're talking homeless shelters, if they would have Abner and his cantankerousness.

The first $10,000 got Abner out of immediate trouble with the county and the really unpalatable "sale on the courthouse steps" thing, which was bearing down on Abner at a pace that made Father Time look like a lazy good-for-nothing slacker. The next $10,000 that we sent went towards the next year of unpaid taxes and "a little credit card debt that I've compiled," a nervous little laugh accenting this profession from Abner. After submitting this second financial resurrection we were now in for $20,000 and were a little more serious about buying the place. We figured, worst case, we'd get it back with interest if we didn't buy The Riverside and one of the multitudes of interested parties that Abner had on the hook did buy the place.

A visit to my banker in Kansas City to discuss my wild notion of buying The Riverside wrought the following discussion. This was a banker that had financed my business for years, through times both lean and hardy. We'd become pretty good friends, as friendly as a banker can become with a borrower.

"We've found this place in Colorado that we're considering buying. It's a historic hotel in a beautiful little town. It's something we've always considered doing, and now with the sale of the business, I think we've got the wherewithal to make it happen. I've got cash-flow projections and pro formas for the next five years that I'd like you to look at. Any chance UM Bank would be willing to consider this?"

"Without even looking at your numbers, I'd be pretty certain that it's not a loan we'd consider. Let's be honest. You don't have any experience in this type of business, and it's in a remote spot that we wouldn't be interested in investing in," said my friend, the banker, really looking out for me at this point, yet I failed to pay heed.

"But you've got locations in Denver! You're trying to establish interests in Colorado."

"Right, but they're pretty selective investments in Colorado. Here's the deal. We're hesitant to loan money to established Kansas City restaurateurs with locations around the corner from our banks, let alone your venture, someone new to the business trying to make a go of it in the middle of nowhere."

So my financially savvy friend, whose financial opinion I'd sought and trusted as gospel for the past twenty years had just sat me down, looked me in the eye, and told me in a fashion that a five-year-old would have understood that this was a bad deal and to make it but a funny point of cocktail-party conversation in my future.

"So, how serious are you about this deal?" my friend, the banker, inquired.

Sheepishly, "I've loaned him $20,000 to pay his delinquent property taxes, of which he's guaranteed that he'll pay me back when he sells the hotel."

His serious demeanor changed to a scolding. "Please tell me that you are kidding me? You loaned him money to pay his property taxes so the place wouldn't be seized and sold? Do you realize you could have gone out there and bought that place from the county for nickels, maybe pennies, on the dollar?"

I knew damn good and well that I could have done that. I knew that I could have told old Abner that I too had not a pot to piss in and he was at the mercy of the state. I could have shown up two weeks after denying Abner his $10,000 and probably bought the place for one-fifth of what we ultimately paid for it. I knew this, I thought about it, and St. Richard decided against it as a course of action — a course that would hopefully define me and my future, a course that would give me good karma going forward, knowing that I allowed a human who'd given his heart and soul to this place to walk away from that place with his head held high and some money in his pocket. I didn't want to take ownership of The Riverside under any other scenario.

OK, so my saintly actions weren't reciprocated by the seller. After the deal, on paper, I am not Saint Richard, I'm Schmuck Richard. But to this day I look into the mirror with aplomb, hoping that someone of a higher pose, someone beyond a banker, will note the good thing that we did and hopefully forgive us our many other earthly transgressions.

CHAPTER SIX

A Slight Case of Buyer's Remorse

As you head west on I-70, when you reach the 371-mile marker at the town of Genoa, Colorado, you get your first full view of Pike's Peak, one of fifty-three 14,000-plus-foot mountains in the state. Although that majestic crest is yet still some one hundred miles southwest as the crow flies, when the sky is clear, the smog is absent, and the light is right, it is a view that ignites, rejuvenates, and energizes the weary westbound traveler. I can only imagine the emotion that first view of the snow-capped peak inspired in Zebulon Pike and his crew, the sky then devoid of any twenty-first-century visual encumbrances, and they not having had the luxury of traversing the prior five hundred miles of flatness at eighty miles per hour in an iPod-playing Chevy Suburban.

To Zebulon Pike and to countless others, those mountains, those commanding peaks, were a welcoming sight, but to me they were an imposing sentinel, a massive opponent that I would inevitably have to dual. Yet I knew before the battle that there was no chance for victory — the only hope was for my meager survival on the heartless terms of this enormous oppressor, this never-ending wave of one granite Goliath after another.

The city of Denver sits in a slight depression, a bowl, after the steady but gentle rise of the land that starts at Hays, Kansas, elevation 2000 feet, and ends 3240 feet later at the eastern edge of Denver. It then dips a bit, just a bit due to the valley created by the Platte River, and then ascends at a rapid rate into the foothills of the Rockies. Natives to Denver likely have a very different view of the mountains than do I. They view them as old friends, always there to have a little fun with on the weekends. To me, they were my challenge, a big Brutus that always had to be dealt with, a little like having to walk home past the house with the mean dog, having no safe alternative route. I grew to hate those mountains.

My first ten to twelve encounters with the mountains were relatively friendly, i.e., there were no issues with the weather. We'd been to Hot Sulphur Springs on seven occasions and once to Glenwood Springs between Christmas and New Year's, and not once did we encounter winter weather on the trip; not once! So I was totally dumb to the reality of a Rocky Mountain blizzard experienced behind the wheel of a car on I-70. As luck would naturally have it, I got my first taste of snow and ice on that initial trek to Hot Sulphur as the soon-to-be-owners of the Riverside whilst pulling a loaded 9' x 12' U-Haul trailer.

If you've never pulled a loaded trailer, you've missed a chance to savor the taste of one of life's real shit sandwiches. As your car groans and strains with the slightest acceleration, you are certain that at any moment your transmission will hemorrhage and vomit itself into the middle of the road. No matter how fast you're traveling, there is a pervasive feeling that the trailer is milliseconds away from swaying itself to the left, then right, then left, eventually breaking free from the tow ball and somersaulting into the other lane of oncoming traffic. And all the while you're driving, the thought of this thing attached to the back of your car is more than you can bear, as every sudden noise or unusual movement causes your sphincter to pucker up near the bottom of your throat. To the novice, it is an experience that rivals very few for its propensity to thoroughly and most absolutely suck.

That first haul, December 26th, pulling out of Kansas City at 3:00 p.m., we encountered snow when we hit Topeka at around 4:30, some sixty miles west of Kansas City. It was a very light snow but enough to scare the bejeezus out of me — and it was getting dark. I felt as if I were working miracles maintaining a speed of 55 mph and not losing complete control of the car or my bowels. The snow really started to pick up around Salina and it was now totally dark, the swirling flakes in the headlight beams making visibility extremely difficult. It was also at this time that Julie complained that she was freezing, huddled in the heated passenger seat wrapped in a blanket, her teeth chattering like a pair of dime-store castanets. With the heater blasting it was probably eighty degrees in the car; I was so hot I'd stripped down to my Garanimals. 'Great!' I thought, 'she has a raging fever.' We made it to the halfway point, Hays, Kansas, at 9:00 p.m., Julie sick as a dog and me as physically and mentally exhausted as I could ever remember being. I was in dire need of both a martini and a diaper change, confused as to which need to first satisfy.

The next morning dawned clear and crisp, the prior evening's snow universally glazed and frozen to the surface of I-70 from Hays to the immediate outskirts of Denver. I think I remember saying something like, "Oh, yippee!"

Even in bright sun with unlimited visibility, the drive was harrowing. The combination of the car and attached trailer gliding over the glazed surface felt a little like roller skating on an ice rink — there wasn't one second, regardless of our speed, when I didn't feel like we were going to lose control. Seven long hours later we arrived in Denver. At this point most of the roads were clear and free of ice, with the only issues being spray from the roads and the constant need for keeping the windows clean, and hoping I had enough windshield juice to finish the trip as I had no intention of stopping and maneuvering highway ramps and Denver side streets with the trailer.

Through Denver and the traffic, I started the climb up into the foothills, which all who have made this trek know strains your car's drive train as you climb upwards at 5–7 percent grades. Pulling that loaded trailer up those hills had my Suburban's engine and transmission screaming at me. Onward and upward I went, but not very quickly.

I'd been debating with myself for the previous eight hours about my ultimate route over the Continental Divide. Would it be Berthoud Pass, a python of a roadway that climbed to 11,000 feet before snaking back down into Winter Park and on another thirty-five miles to Hot Sulphur? Or would I go the longer route over Loveland Pass on I-70, a slow, steady, steep straight up, followed by a log flume ride straight down through the Eisenhower Tunnel to Dillon and the Blue River Valley, then north on the flat but crooked, narrow, and windswept Highway 9? For whatever reason, I opted to take the straighter, longer route on I-70 over Loveland Pass and up Highway 9, which would ultimately have me entering Hot Sulphur from the west, our new home that would welcome us after this bitch of a traverse like a massive mousetrap would welcome a hungry mouse on an innocent quest for a simple bit of cheese.

No sooner did I pass the Highway 40 turnoff for Berthoud Pass and head for Loveland Pass than it began to snow hard. I suppose you'd describe the weather conditions as "blizzard-like." It was a very wet, heavy snow, the kind that accumulates faster on your windshield than your wipers can manage. I wanted to pull over and cry, but we were so close to our destination. This was for certain a classic example of "always darkest before the dawn." The Coloradans who shared the road with me flew by as if nothing were out of the ordinary, seeing a look of terror on my face and probably saying, "Poor bastard … not only is he from Kansas, he's pulling a damned U-Haul." If they only knew our ultimate destination and eventual purpose, they'd know that pulling a U-Haul over Loveland Pass in a blizzard would be one of the easiest parts of our two-year journey.

* * *

On December 27th, 2007, at approximately 5:00 p.m. MST, in front of family both immediate and in-law, a banker, a title company representative, a realtor, and Abner Renta, my wife and I signed papers that made us joint owners of The Historic Riverside Hotel, Bar & Restaurant.

Abner had signed his papers earlier in the day, and the money, $690,000, was already in his bank account. Nearly half of that money would immediately transfer to an individual who had loaned Abner $300,000 as an "investment" — an investment that not only earned the investor no dividends, but Abner had never even paid him a penny of the principal, as was their initial agreement and a condition of the loan. While this sucker made none of the promised gains, at least he got out whole.

We had arrived at the hotel at 4:30 p.m., having pulled that 9' x 12' U-Haul trailer, loaded with a sofa, chairs, our big-screen TV, and scads of other knickknacks, pictures, decorative items, and on and on, the first load of what would ultimately be three additional loaded 9' x 12' U-Haul trailers and two 25' Penske trucks comprised of all that we had acquired in twenty-seven years of wedded bliss.

The deal was for Abner to have all of his personal belongings out of the hotel at the hour of closing. The deal also included Abner leaving all of the furniture and fixtures germane to the operation of the hotel in place, as they were included in the price of the hotel. As you don't have to imagine, the opposite had occurred. Anything of worth, including most of the nice antique pieces in the lobby and the guest rooms, was noticeably absent, absconded by Abner and held in whereabouts unknown.

Still present in the hotel, particularly in Abner's living quarters, was his personal junk, trash, garbage … the effluvium of twenty years of packrat living … the very refuse of life that a person such as me or anyone would assume that they were paying hard money not to have to deal with. That refuse, he left for us.

Step back and imagine me for a second, going into this major life-altering venture, having driven through a blizzard, hauling a trailer with a sick wife and reluctant business partner, and walking into our new home, the previous owner sitting in one of the stained chairs that he was gracious enough to leave behind, sipping on champagne and chomping on celebratory shrimp that the realtor had provided, throwing the shrimp shells on the floor next to the worthless garbage that he hadn't moved from the hotel (not next to the antiques that I'd thought we purchased), and as I'm smoldering to the point of spontaneous combustion, he says to me, "I've got my personal effects in the back room, where I'll still live for a while, if that's OK with you? I've got nowhere else to go ... *sniff.*"

I took a Grand Canyon-esque deep breath and walked back into the living quarters. In one of the back rooms, actually the nicest back room — one that Abner and his kept illegal hadn't fouled — were Abner's clothes, personal effects, and, believe this or not, his slippers sitting neatly near the side of the bed, his robe laid neatly on the bed, and his toothbrush and a tube of toothpaste at the sink (this was a huge shock, taking into account the condition of his rotting incisors).

Abner sold us the building, cashed his $690,000 check, took and sold all of the good stuff out of the hotel, left the garbage and the trash, and still planned on living in the hotel rent free, with us, in the nicest room in the house.

If balls were cash, Abner would have the financial wherewithal to scare Bill Gates and Warren Buffet out of a game of Texas Hold-Em.

* * *

The deal was done and now there was no going back. Never in the history of people exchanging money for things, things large like hotels, things small like Little Debbie Nutty Bars, and things in-between like a full pallet of Little Debbie Nutty Bars, has there been a more immediate and intensely rueful case of buyer's remorse than with our purchase of The Historic Riverside Hotel, Bar & Restaurant from Mr. Abner Renta.

The ink on the deal hadn't even thought about beginning to dry before we began discovering a treasure trove of caveat emptors, so many of so many varying degrees that if I didn't already know the translation of caveat emptor, I would have thought for certain it was Latin for "Beware Abner Renta."

Walking upstairs shortly after signing the deal, I discovered (all of this new since the quasi mechanical inspection of the previous August — my last visit before the sale) a broken windowpane in the "John Lennon" room, kind-of fixed in the most half-assed, duct-tape sort of fashion, with subzero air rushing in; two rooms with nonfunctional heaters; one room with a sink so stopped up that a stick of dynamite wouldn't free its flow; the previously mentioned missing antique dressers, chairs, and other pieces that gave the place but a little charm; and, the coup de grâce, a ten-gallon aluminum stockpot sitting in a back hallway, half full of water that had leaked from a massive gash in the roof, next to a wall so warped and misshapen by the leaking water that it bowed a good foot out of square at its center point.

I know for a fact that this was the exact hour that my body decided for me that, in spite of my previous good health and clean living, I would need consistent doses of blood pressure medicine to remain in good health from this point forward, even as I rotted away in prison after having bludgeoned Abner to death with enthusiastic joy and a total lack of remorse.

Downstairs I went to the kitchen, my blood simmering at a steady temperature of 211°F. But it wasn't long before my temperature rose that significant extra degree. All of the commercial-sized pots, pans, serving trays, and dishes were gone; left in their stead were a few small ten-inch frying pans, beat to absolute shit and in such an awful state that you would be embarrassed to offer them in a garage sale, nor would a picker bother pulling them out of a trash can. And then there was the commercial ice maker — silent, room temperature, and totally barren of ice. This discovery made the cork officially pop.

I stormed out of the kitchen to the lobby, where Abner still sat in comfortable repose, still eating shrimp, still throwing the shrimp shells on the floor.

"Abner, where in the hell is all of the kitchen equipment ... the pots, the pans? And what's up with the ice maker? It's not working!"

"Oh," he said, quietly and coolly, not looking at me but casually examining his fingernails as if he'd just finished having a manicure, "you noticed that, did you?"

It was at this precise point that a demon that had previously been unknown to exist in me, locked deep into the recesses of my innermost person, exploded out of my soul, through my mouth, and into the lobby of The Riverside, making the famous chest-monster scene in Alien seem tedious.

I unleashed every sort of obscenity and invective that I could summon. The air in the room was searing and oppressive from my heated tirade as a continual stream of spittle flew from my rabid mouth, creating a fine mist that suspended in the atmosphere. This display was witnessed by my wife, my in-laws, the realtor, and, worst of all … my children, their eyes wide as pie pans as they had never heard me say anything harsher than the occasional "damn," and only once a "shit."

In response to this epic, Vesuvian explosion, Abner sat calmly, regarding me in a fashion as wan and detached from reality as if he were watching a PBS special on fog. No doubt this wasn't the first time that someone had dressed him down in such a manner. And really, what did he care? He had $690,000 nestled in his bank account, albeit for only a short while, and I held the keys to a 104-year-old haunted, wooden, broken-down turd, permanently parked in the middle of a frozen, out-of-the-way hellhole.

His lack of a reaction only made me hotter, and it was at this point that my two brother-in-laws stepped in, both knowing that I was seconds away from diving at this lying, thieving, pencil-necked bastard and strangling him until his bloodshot, bulging eyes popped from his sockets and rolled across the room, me laughing maniacally, gleeful as his face turned the color of Grape Fanta. They picked him up out of the chair, each grabbing an upper arm, and dragged him kicking and screaming across the floor of the lobby, through the front door of The Riverside, and threw him into the street.

Who would have imagined that this scene, this forceful ejection of Abner Renta from the pig in a poke that he had sold us, witnessed but one short hour after our purchase, would be my most joyful memory of Colorado, Hot Sulphur Springs, and our tenure as owners of The Historic Riverside Hotel, Bar & Restaurant?

* * *

It's easy to be philosophical and wax poetic about the laws of physics after you've been run over by a truck and survived. I can look back now and see with clarity the red flags that prior were obfuscated by my desire to live what I thought at the time was my dream job in my dream locale. The truth of the matter is that the night we signed the papers to purchase the hotel, I had such an immediate, almost suffocating feeling of dread and remorse that I literally became physically ill. My first night sleeping in the hotel and the new life that we'd just mortgaged our souls to obtain, I awoke at three or four in the morning with a high fever, bone-rattling chills, and a paralyzing bout of nausea. Maybe I had caught the bug that had tormented Julie the previous day, or perhaps it was nothing more than a nasty dose of altitude sickness for this unsuspecting flatlander? I think not; rather, it was a severe physical reaction to the notion that I'd just done something classically irresponsible and fatally stupid.

For a fact, the body's natural defenses to illness can quickly break down when exposed to severe stress, becoming impotent against the onslaught of a phantom virus seeking harbor in a fertile port that lacks the will or resistance to send it packing. If stress were luck, I had a boatload of it that night, enough so that there wasn't a lottery that was safe from me the night of December 27th had I a free dollar left to play, and, to wit, that transient virus found solid purchase within my stress-ridden body.

I made it through that miserable night, but midway through the next morning I walked out of the hotel into a frigid day, a bright sun in an emerald sky, headed west down Grand Street, staggered across the bridge over the Colorado River, and walked through waist-deep snow on to the isolated western riverbank until I was out of sight and sound of the hotel and any human who might be wandering by, and I vomited from the very depths of my person — profoundly, loudly, and violently.

As I trudged back to the hotel through the waist-deep snow and bitter cold that I realized was not just a winter vacation accoutrement but was now a part of my day-to-day existence, the gut-wrenching nausea was gone, but the feeling of dread persisted. As forcefully as I had expunged the bug that had so quickly invaded me and rendered me a staggering, vomiting slug, I knew that the real source of my heartburn was yet smoldering within me, both physically and mentally. Once back at the hotel, I went to the sink in our room and splashed cold water on my face, and then had a hard look at the man in the mirror and a subsequent discussion with same, and found that we were both in agreement: 'Buddy, you screwed up bad — HUGE, BIG TIME.' And similar to the fashion in which I had shortly before violently vomited, I now began to weep.

This was within twenty-four hours of our ownership of The Historic Riverside Hotel. Talk about your classic case of buyer's remorse.

CHAPTER SEVEN

Remodeling History

While we had ambitious plans regarding the improvement of this 104-year-old structure — redoing and adding modern bathrooms; installing a gas furnace for the main common areas; replacing the original single-pane windows with double-paned, screened, energy-efficient windows; upgrading the riverside deck; and putting on a new roof, to name but a few — remodeling the living quarters was a *must,* something that had to be done before we'd even consider occupying the place.

During Abner's ownership of the hotel, the living quarters were separated from the hotel lobby by two doors — always closed and somewhat foreboding. It was a bit of a mystery as to what was actually behind the doors, as Abner himself was ... uh ... a bit of a mystery.

During our tire-kicking phase of deciding whether or not to buy the hotel, we made four visits over the course of the spring and summer of 2007. We never saw the owner's quarters, the place where we might ultimately live the next who knew how many years of our lives, until the fourth and final visit. The truth was that Julie and I were both afraid of what lay beyond those doors, afraid it would be so despicable — much as the living quarters' chief inhabitant was despicable — that it would immediately squelch our desire to make this radical lifestyle change in this idyllic setting on the banks of the Colorado River. While we wanted a change, we didn't necessarily want to leave our house in Kansas City, a wonderful house that we built and raised our family in.

At the end of that fourth and final visit before the ultimate purchase/mistake, our cars packed and good-byes being said, Abner finally asked if we'd like to see the owner's quarters. With just the slightest bit of trepidation (I'm being sarcastic here) we headed through the foreboding doors, back into the unknown and heretofore unseen world of Abner Renta and his kept, illegal alien servant-slave. We were accompanied by friends from Kansas who went with us on this trip to see if we'd totally lost our minds, as they couldn't help but correctly assume.

In we went, me in front with the others lagging behind. I didn't spend much time in the place, and didn't talk about or discuss with the others what we were seeing. I had no questions for Abner, who sort of stood back very quietly, with the kind of sheepish look that people display after they've passed a silent-but-deadly fart and are waiting to see if anyone notices. I said good-bye to Mr. Renta and quickly left the building, waiting in front of the hotel for the rest of my party. In truth, a lingering fart would have been the most pleasant thing about his living quarters.

When Julie and our friends came out of The Riverside, the first words I heard were from our friend Ginny, who said, "Oh, Julie! That was horrible! I could just cry for you!" Not exactly what you'd refer to as a ringing endorsement of our possible future place of abode.

When we got in the car to leave, Julie started peppering me with question after question: did you see this, did you notice that, could you believe what was in that one room, etc. The truth of the matter was I didn't see or notice much of anything, as I walked through that place much like you'd walk through a busy hospital emergency room trauma ward — with your eyes straight ahead, not looking to either side for fear of what horrific sight to which you might be a witness.

There was a simple answer to this hell on earth, this fetid collection of cobbled-together rooms, shelves, nooks, and crannies that was the Riverside's living quarters: Don't view it as it is; view it as what it can be. That philosophy, adopted before I ever set foot in the place, was what allowed me to walk through and not be affected by the horrors contained in this subhuman dwelling. Pure and simple, the place had to be gutted down to the studs. Any vestiges of the previous owner had to be banished, banned, bazookaed, bulldozed, burned and buried — then fumigated.

We knew that very shortly after our purchase of The Riverside, a contractor would have to be hired to strip the living quarters to the bare earth below, down to the floor of the crawl space. This would be the first time in 140 years that the earthen floor would see daylight. Gone forever would be the four small rooms that had been Abner's home for the past twenty-some years. Gone forever would be the small, dimly lit, grimy bathroom consisting of a small toilet and a very large

(large enough for two!) claw-foot bathtub, dingy and gray from years of use and abuse. Gone forever would be the largest assortment of books, magazines, records, reel-to-reel tapes, cassettes, eight-tracks, laser discs, and VHS tapes west of the Mississippi and not in an actual library, piled on crude shelving to the ceiling of every room and stacked in every square inch of free space. Gone forever would be the endless miles of wires, extension cords, and speaker wire, all taped together and stapled along walls, trim, and molding — a collection of electrical conveyance that would cause the local fire inspector and building code administrator to flee the building in terror for their safety upon their first view of this rattrap that looked like it had been wired by a five-year-old who'd been trying to cut safety corners.

Our real estate agent was consulted and we were given the names of three "reliable" building contractors — reliable at least by Grand County standards, which we were to discover were without question the lowest reliability standards for hired labor anywhere in the universe. After interviews, proposals, and quotes were evaluated, the building contracting firm of Jack Legg Construction was hired to renovate the Riverside's living quarters. While they came with a few good recommendations, truth had it Jack Legg Construction consisted of two bartending ski bums from Chicago who, during a normal Grand County night of drunken debauchery (probably a Tuesday), set a friend's deck on fire, burning it to the ground, and then, in a fit of soberness possibly fueled by a tinge of remorse, rebuilt the deck in short order. Rumor had it that the deck rebuild was true, level, and square. They then deemed themselves building contractors and rode the tails of the Grand County building boom of the early 2000s, when $500,000 log homes were popping up throughout the Fraser River valley like mushrooms.

One full month behind the promised delivery date and 25 percent over budget, we moved into our new living quarters. The first room was a small office that contained my desk, our computer, filing cabinets, and the copy and fax machine. The original wood-slat floor was left intact, the thought being that during one of the slow, frozen, winter months I would make time to restore the floor to its original luster, sanding off the quarter-inch-thick coat of garish brown paint that Abner's illegal had slathered upon it. Next was our bedroom, which had a door between our room and the office that was costly but nonfunctional as the size of our bedroom was barely large enough to contain our king-size bed; walking through that office door into our bedroom would have me walking straight into Julie's slumbering head. We had a very nice bathroom with a large tiled shower that did not include a shower door in the price of the remodel, even though we were 25 percent over budget. Next was a nice, large-enough, walk-in closet, used as much for hiding good booze from our chefs as it was for hanging clothes. And lastly, a small family room with a sofa, a comfy chair, and a TV. Over the course of the next eighteen months I would sit in this room and relax, watch a little TV, take a little nap ... maybe twice.

So right out of the gate we put our architectural touch on that iconic structure, knowing that for us to have a shot at being happy in Hot Sulphur Springs we'd need a decent place to live. To the opinion of all but maybe Abner and a sewer rat, the dwelling as we bought it was not a decent place to live. Often I would sit in the office and think about those that had occupied this place before me — at one time there sat a barber chair; at another, an examination room for the local doctor. The thought of sleeping in a bed that rested on floor joists that were set in place in 1860 — by whom I can't imagine — often made me shudder, made me feel somewhat of a kinship with those foolhardy pioneers who braved the elements to construct a new life for themselves in this remote outpost, this outpost that now included plush carpet, crown molding, electric heat, HD-TV, and a couple of equally foolhardy pioneers.

* * *

The Historic Riverside Hotel, Bar & Restaurant is a 13,000-square-foot structure constructed primarily of wood with a hand-laid stone and mortar foundation, situated on the eastern bank of the Colorado River, some twenty-five miles from its headwaters. One of my biggest attractions in taking this blind leap from our comfort zone was the opportunity to be stewards and caretakers of not only this historical building but, most importantly, of the innumerable yet unrecorded stories and memories ensconced within the walls of this old place: the 104 previous Christmases celebrated, the weddings and wedding nights of hundreds of hopeful brides and grooms, the births of how many Grand County babies, and the jubilant hoots and hollers of countless New Year's Eve revelers and Fourth of July celebrants. How many prayed, toasted, and dined at Thanksgiving feasts; how many birthday cake candles were extinguished by the wind from how many beaming faces? How many all but tangible memories of how many lives and how many deaths in the course of The Riverside's 104-year history lingered in the halls and the walls of this sixteen-room structure that we ended up purchasing?

Very early in our ownership, this aspect of being a steward of memories as well as a caretaker of a historic structure became evident to us in a blissfully unexpected event that, to put it mildly, awed and humbled us with the responsibility that we had undertaken.

It was June 29th, 2008, and we had lived full-time at The Riverside for only three days. It was late in the afternoon, and the hotel was almost booked full. We were making last-minute preparations for the evening dinner crowd when I noticed two young men trying to get a very large, full-body wheelchair into our west hotel/ restaurant entrance. As the hotel was built many years before the Americans with Disabilities Act, it unfortunately wasn't up to code regarding accessibility. I went to see what could be done to help them get the wheelchair into the building. At this point I took the time to notice the inhabitant of the chair.

He was an elderly gentleman, probably in his early eighties, and he looked very much like my father looked shortly before my father died: pale, gaunt, and sallow-eyed. The man also appeared to be paralyzed from the neck down — no sign of movement from his torso or limbs. He was unable to communicate verbally, barely nodding yes or no to queries from the young men, who turned out to be his grandsons. But he seemed fully cognizant of his surroundings and of what his grandsons were saying. I immediately gained respect for these young men, as they were the epitome of love, tenderness, and human kindness in the way they cared for their grandfather — and care it took, as getting the chair from one cranny in the old hotel through the next would have tried the patience of most. Behind the boys followed their grandmother, who told me that today was she and her husband's wedding anniversary, that they had spent their wedding night in 1952, fifty-six years ago to the day, at The Riverside, and that her husband "didn't have too much time left, and we wanted to see the place one more time."

When I grasped what was happening here — jarring me from my immediate mental preoccupation with people checking in, the details of a big-dollar restaurant night ahead, and guests barking at the bar for high-profit rum and Cokes — it shook me. On the day of their fifty-sixth wedding anniversary, most probably the last that they would celebrate, this couple and their grandsons had driven to our out-of-the-way town from Denver, some ninety miles to the southeast over Berthoud Pass, to visit our hotel ... simply for the memory of it. I was immediately humbled to the point of embarrassment, now all but reverential of these people and their quest.

The wife took me upstairs — the husband stayed downstairs as ascending the narrow stairways was impossible, even with the help of the resolute grandsons — and showed me the room, "Elizabeth," where they spent their first night as newly-weds. (The rooms were all given female names versus numbers by Abner — with the notable exception of the "Lennon" room — lending to his lurid assertions that The Riverside operated as a brothel at some stage in its past; I believe this to be nothing more than a lurid assertion, knowing Abner as I did.)

The wife paused and bowed at the door for a minute, as if in prayer, and then slowly walked in the room and looked around. It was a very small room, the width of it barely able to contain the full-sized bed that resided within, one of Abner's beds that we had yet to replace, comprised of an old, thin mattress on exposed springs, very possibly the bed upon which they had spent their wedding night. She stood quietly for only a few minutes, then without speaking a word she left the room, passing slowly by me without acknowledging me, and went back down the stairs to be with her husband. She gently took his hand and told him that she'd found the room, and it was much as she'd remembered. There was the faintest at-tempt at a smile from the old lion. As he closed his eyes, he looked totally satisfied and complete.

I was dumbfounded, speechless, and choked up to the point of not being able to communicate with this family or any others in the lobby. When Julie came to me and asked what was wrong, I couldn't form words, as my throat was constricted from the emotional scene that I had just witnessed. In fact, to this day I have a difficult time retelling this story to people without tears welling in my eyes and my throat constricting, as I have burned in my memory the eager face of the man who was trying to relive in that instant one of his life's great memories.

I saw my father die, at peace, surrounded by his family in his bed at home. At the end he had a look of contentment with what he had done and resignation with the next, final step in his life journey. This man — this 1952 visitor to our hotel who chose The Riverside to begin his post–World War II journey into manhood and fatherhood — after hearing his wife of fifty-six years whisper into his ear, smiled and looked content, much like my father looked before his passing. I never knew for certain, but I would bet that sweet closure wasn't far behind this gentleman's last visit to The Riverside.

I knew that we had bought a hotel and restaurant, but it was at this point that I finally realized that we had bought much more than just a business; we were the stewards of this magnificent building and the memories and stories of thousands of unknown people. What an awesome responsibility it was to be caretaker to such a glorious old girl as The Riverside.

CHAPTER EIGHT
Living with Strangers

The first weekend that we owned The Riverside there was one humdinger of a blizzard, even by Grand County standards. Julie and Rachel (our French-degreed college grad daughter who was going to run the hotel until we could move out the following summer), who had been out shopping that afternoon, got caught in the storm while driving back from the outlet mall in Silverthorne. I was at the hotel by myself, and I started getting calls from soon-to-be-stranded travelers looking for accommodations. I knew we were going to be busy, so I decided to take a quick shower and get cleaned up for the impending throngs. I was using the shower in "Laura," the only guest room with a private bath, and just as I began to wash my hair — all lathered up with my eyes closed — the water went off. It didn't slow down and turn to a trickle, as if it were a water pressure issue; *it flat went off,* as sudden and final as a downward light switch. 'Oh crap!' I thought. I figured there must've been a massive break in the water main and envisioned a geyser spouting twenty feet into the air in the middle of the street in front of the hotel. What else on earth could make the water just stop — *snap!* — like that? These thoughts rushed through my mind in a matter of seconds, at which point — eyes still closed, hair still soapy — I reached down to the knobs *and turned both water knobs back on!* They both had been shut into the full off position, instantly and at the same time. Upon discovering this I said something other than 'Oh crap' and felt an icy chill go down my spine, the kind of icy chill you feel when you realize you've just encountered your first ghost.

I had my hair rinsed and was out of that shower faster than the winner of a Hot Sulphur beer-chugging contest. I then quickly dried off, threw on my robe, took the wet towel and bath mat, and headed back to my room to get dressed. After getting dressed I went back into the bathroom, fiddled around a little bit with the knobs (they seemed as normal as any water knobs I'd ever fiddled with), and tidied up the bathroom to get it ready for the evening's guests. (I recount this now as though nothing unusual had happened and I was cool as a cucumber; quite to the contrary — I was still shaken and shaking.)

All was in order except for a new dry bath mat. A short walk to the linen closet and a short walk back with a new bath mat, and there, over the back of the previously empty chair back, was a new, dry, nicely folded bath mat. I experienced another one of those spine chills, and then tried to calm myself and gather my thoughts. I know I took the bath mat off of the chair; I put it on the floor; I took my haunted shower, got out, dried off, put my robe on, PICKED UP THE WET BATH MAT, and exited the bathroom. After getting dressed I then went back into the bathroom and fiddled with the knobs, cleaned the sink and mirror, looked over the bathroom, and thought to myself, 'You need a new bath mat.' After a brief absence to the linen closet to get that bath mat, lo and behold, upon my return there on the chair was a new bath mat. I know I didn't put it there, and no one else was in the hotel — at least no other human comprised of flesh and bone.

So we'd been in the hotel but a few days and already the spirits were making their presence felt. Some Internet reading I did on the subject of the paranormal mentioned that "activity" can be ramped up when a new resident takes a place over. At least the ghost seemed to have a sense of humor, as well as a good sense of comic timing, as it chose to turn the shower off when I was in my most defenseless state — bare naked, soapy hair, and eyes tightly shut. And it was also nice to know we had a ghost who was willing to help with the housework and cleaning; this would come in handy when we had ten rooms to turn in a short period of time. It really would've been nice if we had a rich ghost, one that might have left hundred dollar bills scattered about. But I now know it was doubtful, nay, impossible, that a previous owner/resident of The Riverside would have any money left to throw around.

* * *

I swear to God, these were the first words out of our first restaurant customer's mouth: "My mother is gluten-intolerant. I don't know what's on the menu tonight, but I hope you'll be able to accommodate her diet."

Thinking gluten was maybe a type of fish, or perhaps a type of tofu, I promptly replied, "Nope, we're not serving gluten tonight. We've got prime rib, tilapia, an Asian pork dish, and a chicken dish!"

"And do none of those contain gluten?" he asked me in a somewhat challenging tone, appearing more than a little irritated.

This stopped me for a second before I finally asked him, "So … just what is gluten?"

He looked at me as if I had a dried turd balanced across the bridge of my nose. And so it began for me in the restaurant business in Colorado.

* * *

During the two hours prior to this seminal exchange, I had survived my first encounter with The Riverside ghost in the shower and guest bathroom; Julie and Rachel had arrived safely back at the hotel from their Colorado blizzard experience; I'd checked in all of our guests (thirty-six people in thirteen full-size beds and two twin beds) and turned down requests from countless more snowbound travelers. Those that weren't lucky enough to have snagged up a local hotel room spent the night on cots or blankets in the Kremmling High School gymnasium.

Thirty minutes after my crash course in "Dammit, I'm gluten intolerant; I'm mad as hell; and I'm not going to take it anymore!" I'm in the kitchen and the restaurant is packed. The only place I can be of any use is washing dishes. I'd long since been banished from the salad prep table.

"Hot pan!" yelled Thomas, my nephew with commercial restaurant experience who'd signed on as our chef, as he tossed a small sauté pan on the table that stood nearest to the three-compartment sink, the pan now fighting for space with the rest of the dirty plates, cutlery, water glasses, sauce pots, and pans that I was struggling to wash, rinse, dry, and put back into service. The first compartment of the three-compartment sink had hot soapy water in which the dirty dishes were washed; the middle sink contained warm water where the dishes were dipped for the purpose of getting rid of any soap residue; and the final compartment contained cold water with bleach, a final attempt at sanitation before setting them on a rack to air dry. That first sink had to be changed out quite a bit, as the residue of dirty plates and sauté pans floated on the hot, soapy surface like so much unappetizing flotsam and jetsam.

The bigger factor in my falling behind with the dishes was my morphing from restaurant owner/dishwasher into a fascinated observer of the stadium event that is high-pressure commercial food preparation. Never having been in a restaurant kitchen during the heat of battle, I'd never witnessed anything like the requisite speed, deftness of hand, and all-but acrobatic symmetry that these two chefs exhibited. Thomas had six pans going at once, all the time, without so much as a hiccup — sautéing vegetables in one large pan while the other five had either pork, fish, or chicken sizzling away in a pat or two of melted butter and a dash or two of olive oil. Thomas also had this thing going on where he would twirl in the air and click the metal tongs — "clack-clack, clack-clack, clack-clack" — together every time after turning the food in the pan or plating the entrée. He was really good at it, and at that early point in our adventure it hadn't yet gotten to be annoying. (I'm betting that there is now a common Spanish phrase in the commercial kitchens of California where Thomas now earns his living that goes something like: "Clack those one more time and I'll shove them up your *culo!*")

Gabe, our other chef and another relative, was nonstop banging out soup and salads, and doing the majority of the plating. He had also taken on the leadership role, as Thomas seemed to be at his best reacting to directions as opposed to giving them. This was amazing for me to watch as it unfolded; all of this was going on with a quiet confidence that would have made you think they'd been doing this together every day for the past twenty years. Possibly they were just stoned.

As the evening concluded — we shut the kitchen down at 8:00 p.m. as we were absolutely out of every scrap of food — I stood in awe of what Thomas and Gabe had pulled off. Not only were sixty-eight diners (including one gluten-intolerant septuagenarian) fed in an organized, timely manner, but they were fed food of exceptional taste and quality. There were lauds and bravos aplenty from all who had dined with us. I'm certain that if there were any food or service glitches they were minor, as most who dined with us realized they could be eating microwave mac & cheese in the Kremmling High School gym, and compared with that The Riverside had to seem like Le Cirque.

The only hitch to the evening came at the end, when some of our guests — a Russian couple with two small children; she spoke broken English and the others not a word — came to the restaurant at 8:00 with a brown paper lunch sack. I sat them and told them we had very limited offerings — I think all that was left was some pork and some rice. The woman then pulled from the sack two plastic bags, one containing a yet to-be-determined raw meat, the other some chopped raw vegetables, some sort of gourd thing, and asked if we could cook this for her family. I was a little dumbstruck, but what the hell; "Why not," I told her. When I brought the bags back to the kitchen and told Thomas and Gabe what was going on, they protested as loudly as if I'd asked them to cook while straight.

"Tell them, *No Way!* That is totally against the health code," said Gabe while standing amidst a room full of equipment whose mere existence within a hundred yards of a kitchen violated most every known rule in the Colorado health code. Some of the equipment would make them rethink the rules as to what is and isn't allowable in junkyards.

A little deflated, I went back to the Serbian nationals and told them our state law didn't allow for this sort of thing and they'd have to buy food from us if they intended to eat in this restaurant. I had to explain this slowly and loudly so the woman could understand me, and as she explained the situation to her husband in their native tongue, he unleashed at me what I'm certain must have been some Serbian invectives and were not intended to wish me well. But eat they did, and they paid in cash.

I was abuzz at the success of our first night, both from a culinary and financial position. All were equally excited as we cleaned the kitchen, washed and dried the dishes, reset the dining room, and generally decompressed from the rush of the rush. We were to repeat this performance the next two nights, including another 180-mile round-trip to Denver the next day to buy more stuff. Thomas and Gabe would continue to wow our guests every weekend for the next three months, bringing high-end, inventive cuisine to Grand County that was heretofore unavailable. I can't recall any of Abner's old customers who visited us those first three months saying anything like, "I sure miss Jamie's fried pork chops and Spanish rice," or "Grey Goose? No, I prefer the cheap Popov vodka that Abner used to serve."

By golly, unlike Abner, we may have gone belly up, but we did it with style!

CHAPTER NINE

Meeting Damien

We'd been living full time at The Riverside for a little more than a month, and our days and nights were filled with an endless stream — sometimes a deluge but most others a trickle — of hotel and restaurant guests from all corners of the globe. Many were one-night vacationers who tripped upon us late in the afternoon looking for a meal and a room. They were the kinds that were suited to the vagaries of The Riverside and the town of Hot Sulphur — no agenda, free-spirited, and up for whatever they would stumble upon. For the most part, immense joy and satisfaction were evident in their find of our little jewel with its warm atmosphere, quaint lodgings, and better-than-imagined restaurant.

While this pattern made me happy and helped pay the bills through our first season, there was a very noticeable bruise on my otherwise pristine piece of fruit; not one of our customers were local. Not one Mr., Mrs., or Ms. Grand who lived around the corner or down the street bellied up to the bar or had a family meal at The River Room. I'd expected, and heavily counted upon, the townsfolk of Hot Sulphur to more than occasionally saunter in and have a steak and a glass of wine. Two months into the venture, the lack of local support was profound.

And then, on a Sunday night in late July, early in the evening, in walked a local. He was alone. I had previously noticed him picking up mail at the post office across the street from the hotel, his large, white Suburban gliding ominously down the streets of Hot Sulphur like a predatory shark in a town of small fish, then slowly pulling to a stop in front of the post office. He would then step out and stride into the building like a baron amongst the lowly serfs. His business-like demeanor and appearance of purposefulness told me he was a man of means, a force to be reckoned with. He was possibly the mayor of Hot Sulphur, or perhaps the Grand County District Attorney — if not one or the other, certainly someone of a higher stead. Regardless of whom he was or what he did, he was a local, and he was walking into our restaurant on a slow Sunday evening. This was the crowd I was after; this was the crowd that would get us through the slow winter season ahead; this was the crowd upon which I'd based my business plan for success … this crowd of one.

I stumbled all over myself trying to make a good first impression, welcoming our local diner with probably a little too much gusto. Possibly he found me overly convivial, my greeting contrived.

"Welcome to The Riverside," I boomed, with a flourish of the arm. "Will you be dining with us this evening?"

Looking timid, he quietly responded, "Uh … yes." Possibly I had made our guest nervous. I decided to play it cool, tone it down a notch.

"Do you have a reservation?" I asked, as we stood in the doorway of The River Room, it empty and as devoid of guests as the "Free Prostate Exam" booth at the Annual Conference of the Society of Proctologists with Oversized Digits.

"Uh … no, no reservation. I didn't think I'd need one." He was very soft spoken, belying my initial impression of him having a booming basso profundo to accompany his size and swagger.

In a cheerful and reassuring tone, I offered, "Well you're in luck, as our best river-view table happens to be available" (along with our worst river-view table and every other table in the restaurant, which I'm certain we both thought but didn't say).

He ordered a Cosmopolitan, which was always a good beginning for me as I figured that anyone who started off with a seven-dollar cocktail was probably good for a second cocktail, and a steak, and wine with dinner, turning at minimum a quick fifty bucks into the Riverside coffers, which would at least come close to paying for the chef that evening.

Speaking of cocktails, prior to our purchase of The Riverside, I had an immense amount of experience when it came to drinking cocktails but hadn't for one solitary second ever worked in a bar where I would have gained experience actually making cocktails. In spite of this reality, I had the audacity when composing our first menu to feature three cocktails and name them "The Perfect Martini," "The Perfect Margarita," and "The Perfect Cosmopolitan." To that point, not only had I never made a Cosmopolitan, but I'd never even tasted one to know perfect from putrid. Not the story with a margarita, as I'd had a few of those and knew what I liked. And as far as the perfect gin martini went, I'd also had a few thousand of them ... probably one or two that morning before breakfast.

Our local guest savored the Cosmopolitan and ordered another as I detailed the evening specials, one of which on Sundays was always prime rib, which he ordered medium rare.

So I'd pegged our local visitor wrong, that business of him being a bold, cocksure mountain man of a mover and shaker. Quite to the contrary, he was timid and very reserved, extremely polite and quiet to the point of being shy. I decided to introduce myself, something I was always hesitant to do in the restaurant as most people who came in for dinner couldn't care less who I was so long as the service was good and the food better.

"I don't mean to be intrusive, but my name is Richard. I'm the new owner of the hotel. I've noticed that you're a local and, honestly, I haven't had very many locals dine with us. Thanks for coming in."

"I'm Damien Farmer, and I'm the owner of the Farmer-Scamwell Mortuary here in town," he said as he calmly extended his hand in greeting.

'Oh my!' I thought while I unconsciously let out a little gasp. 'He's the town mortician.' He was the guy who would ultimately deal with me should I live long enough to die and be buried in this town, which at that particular moment in time was my long-term plan.

Instantly I bought into him having the demeanor of a mortician, and certainly the well-groomed, somber look of a mortician as well; you can usually pick them out of a crowd of thousands. We chatted about our pasts, he coming to Grand County two years ago from Nebraska for the sole purpose of buying the funeral home and practicing his mortuarial art. There was no other funeral parlor in all of Grand County, so he figured he had a captive audience. Unfortunately, he figured as badly as I did. While he was the only game in town, the population in Grand County was so small that the game didn't have enough participants to sustain a decent livelihood let alone retire the note on the purchase of the funeral business or a restaurant. But alas …

* * *

Damien Farmer quickly became a regular diner with us at The Riverside, coming in at least twice a week for dinner and two to three times a week for lunch. He ordered steaks, cocktails, wine, and desserts, always running up a solid tab and tipping well to boot, often alone but other times with guests — always his treat, his tab, and his tip. Of major importance was the fact that the guests he was bringing in were other locals, and they were locals of stature, at least stature relative to Hot Sulphur Springs: a town council member, the food and entertainment writer for the *Sky-Hi Daily News*, and, ultimately, a bit of a coup, the unofficial Grand County gadabout, Daniel Handsy, who was socially connected to all of the high-end muck-ety-mucks from Denver who had weekend getaway homes in Grand Lake.

Damien prepped us prior to the evening that he was bringing Mr. Handsy to dine in that he cautioned us to be at the top of our game, as this gentleman's thumbs-up could make us or his thumbs-down break us.

It was another Sunday evening, and the restaurant was fairly busy. Damien arrived an hour later than he'd promised with Mr. Handsy, who was the spitting image in look, voice, and manner of 'Liberace,' almost to a level of creepy. No doubt he'd worked at it, and rather successfully. He walked into the hotel lobby, stopped abruptly, sniffed a few times, and looked around cautiously as if he possibly expected turds to start dropping on him from the ceiling. By his look and demeanor, I half expected him to ask me for some rubber gloves and a Hazmat suit before he dined with us. "Strike One" from Mr. Handsy on the atmosphere.

Due to their tardiness and our busyness, we were unable to seat Damien and Mr. Handsy at the already occupied choice corner table overlooking the river, which was where we typically seated Damien and his guests. This news was followed by a look of 'What else could go wrong?' along with a dramatic sigh from Mr. Handsy, so we were possibly already at "Strike Two!" before he even sat for dinner. When he did sit, I began telling them the evening's specials, in the midst of which Mr. Handsy picked up the salad fork from the place setting and began polishing it with his linen napkin.

"Water spots," he said dryly, a smile smugly breaking the plane of his pale visage.

He may as well have said, "Steeee-rike three; you're outta here!"

When I explained that one of our feature dishes at The Riverside was our garlic salad, which was served with every entrée, Mr. Handsy shuddered a bit and said, "Oh, Damien, I'll not be joining you for the salad course. You know I don't eat garlic. Only peasants eat garlic."

"Not a problem, Mr. Handsy," I said. "How about our soup, made from scratch here in our kitchen, tonight a tomato basil bisque, which has a cream base and a small amount of bacon in it that really makes it special."

"Oh really!" Not asked by Mr. Handsy but stated. "From my perspective, bacon would make it common, not special. I think I'll pass on the soup as well. I'll just have the rarest piece of prime rib you can bring me ... blood red wouldn't be too rare for me. And why don't you just start from scratch and bring me some clean silverware."

At this point I was the one who began looking for turds to drop from the ceiling, so I could hopefully catch one and artfully plate it next to his blood-red prime rib, disgusting and offending him to the point that he would hurriedly haul his Liberace ass out of our restaurant and back to Grand Lake — his ultimate thumbs-down appraisal of our place be damned.

Damien looked down, embarrassed for me but more so mortified at his guest's abhorrent disregard for rudimentary social skills, the irony coming in a flood as this epic display of a lack of decorum had been exhibited by one of Grand County's most elite socialites, the supposed local paragon of fine manners and good taste.

We never had the honor of gracing Mr. Handsy's table with spotted silverware again. Nor did we have the opportunity to host any of the other high-minded Grand Lake residents whom subscribed to the bible of Daniel Handsy. If a spot on a fork, or a salad dressing that catered to peasants, was the ultimate cause of our demise, I am at peace with that, especially faced with the alternative of what being successful in satisfying the whims of that upper crust would have ultimately sucked from my soul.

* * *

Before we knew it, Damien went from being our best customer to our best friend, showing up at The Riverside on an all but daily basis, and not just for meals. In fact, he seldom ate in the restaurant as a customer, now more often showing up in the morning for coffee, the middle of the day for lunch, and before dinner to help Julie set the dining room or even do dishes in the kitchen. (Remember that I previously mentioned the fact that the death business in Grand County was always slow due to the limited number of living inhabitants.)

This was nice that we'd made a friend but a little disconcerting that we lost such a good customer, as it was touchy for me to charge friends money for shared meals and drinks — my issue, and one that I'd wished from the start I had been able to overcome. Subsequent discussions I had with people in the business advised me that without equivocation you can never, ever give anything free to anybody. Cross that line once and there is no going back, so the obvious move was to never cross the line, not with family or friends.

Damien's lack of involvement in his business afforded him the opportunity to help with ours — gratis in exchange for the food and booze we were no longer charging him for — by serving as the maître d' at the restaurant; he would even wait tables when the need arose. He enjoyed taking care of people, be they alive or dead, and his well-coiffed, well-educated, gentle demeanor was a nice accoutrement to the white-table-cloth elegant ambience of The River Room.

One Saturday afternoon Damien showed up at the hotel with a large pan of bread pudding, saying that it was his specialty and he baked it for the dessert service that evening. This was nice on more than a few levels in that it freed the kitchen staff up from making desserts that day and allowed them to better prep the main courses; it brought something new to the dessert menu; and it was essentially free money in that Damien paid for it and made it labor-free. That sixteen-serving dish of free bread pudding netted us about eighty dollars that evening, and I was at the point where every dollar earned was essential.

This dessert thing went on for a while, as it seemed to give Damien something to focus on during the days when he had no funeral business, and perhaps it made him feel as if he were putting some skin in the game. I know that he enjoyed the accolades that came with diners going on and on about his desserts. And he was pretty good at making desserts — nothing that was visually stunning, but good, serviceable recipes that people would buy and enjoy.

So in a few short months Damien had transitioned himself from a local customer who quietly wandered in to our restaurant, dropping big bucks and solid tips during each visit, to a nonpaying friend who ate and drank the same amount as he did when he was a customer, and now had a place to hang and friendly people to hang with in exchange for the occasional hand with the dishes and a weekend pan of bread pudding or a baking dish full of berry cobbler. The reality of the situation, at that time, escaped me, and all seemed right with Damien, The Riverside, and the world.

CHAPTER TEN

The Three Portals to Hell

Each of the three sections of The Historic Riverside Hotel & Restaurant built before 1935 have their own separate foundation, constructed of native stone of irregular size and shape and tightly cemented together. The structure is as stout today as it was when it was built more than a hundred years ago. Each foundation also contains a crawl space, all differing in size and depth, with the first construction under the stable literally being a "crawl" space as the distance from bare dirt to the floor above is but three feet in height. The crawl space of the middle structure, which housed the hotel lobby, café, and five upstairs guest rooms and the owners' living quarters, is deep enough in the front end of the building to allow a person to stand almost upright, and narrows in depth as you move towards the back of the hotel. The third section of the building, the 1930s addition, has a real-life, honest-to-God basement, with poured concrete floors and enough head space to walk upright, assuming you're me and not Shaquille O'Neil.

In August of 2007, before purchasing the hotel, I visited The Riverside to meet with Tim, the man who was hired to perform the mechanical inspection. After learning that the roof needed to be replaced, the kitchen didn't meet all of the state health code requirements, and a host of other things that would have sent an intelligent person back to Kansas with a pocket full of cash searching for a new dream, Tim suggested we go down into the crawl spaces.

"Crawl spaces? Why do we have to go down in the crawl spaces? I really don't need to see the crawl spaces," I whined.

Tim had shown me the exposed foundations while we toured the outside of the building, demonstrating — I think he pounded his closed fist against them — how sturdily and solidly the foundations were constructed, and that was good enough for me. I didn't need to see them from the inside of a dark, mysterious, possibly big-hairy-spider-containing crawl space.

Tim said, "I've got to show you where all of the mechanical stuff is — the water main, the grease trap, the sewage main, the boiler … "

It was at this point that I really should have allowed myself to be beaten to death by an army of do-it-yourselfers bearing red flags. Grease traps, boilers, and sewage lines in a subterranean spider farm — and I was interested in owning this place?

The first space we toured, Portal Number Three — an outside entrance from the rear of the hotel — was the newest of the three, the one where you could stand upright. I entered cautiously and it was no big deal, as it was well lit, spiderless, and looked as if someone had actually attempted to turn it into a living space by apportioning off rooms and paneling the walls and ceilings with dog-eared cedar 1 X 4 fence slats. This space was important as it contained the two relatively new two-hundred-gallon hot water boilers. Abner had them installed when he purchased the hotel, replacing the coal-fired boiler that sat dormant in one of the little rooms, a permanent, immovable monument to yesteryear. I didn't think to notice at the time that in the event the boilers needed to be dealt with in the winter — that time of year in Hot Sulphur when it's extremely cold, there are thirty feet of snow piled in the back of the hotel, and the need for hot water in your shower is especially necessary — that there was no way you could access this basement to fix those boilers without blasting caps and a front-end loading tractor, as there was no entrance to the crawl space from the hotel above.

The back of the space contained an unpaneled storage area that was filled with old bed frames, mattresses, desks, chairs, doors … quite an assortment of old junk and furnishings not fit for the current hotel. If you had seen what was actually in the Abner-owned hotel at that time, you could only imagine what lay fallow in this space below.

On to Portal Number Two, this located under the original main building. There were two entrances to this space, which actually had a dividing wall making two separate sections of the crawl space under the one structure. I helped the inspector lift a 3' x 5', seemingly two-hundred-pound trapdoor, which guarded the entrance to the second section of Portal Number Two, from the floor in the back of the kitchen. It was very dark, and the cold air and dank, moldy smell attacked us as we peered into the space below.

"Looks good to me!" I said.

"No," Tim replied, "I've got to show you where the main kitchen drain runs into the grease trap. You're going to have to clean that grease trap fairly regularly to keep your lines from clogging."

This is sort of like when the professor says to the students in medical school, "You're going to have to put this rubber glove on and stick your finger in … ," and the prospective internist quickly switches over to radiology. But no, more fool me, as I forged ahead, bought the hotel, and, on more occasions than I would like to recall, stuck my finger up that grease trap.

On to the next crawl space for the first section of Portal Number Two, which was accessed through a trapdoor on hinges located in the main lobby floor, just outside of the public men's and women's restrooms. This crawl space was approximately five feet in height at its entry point and sloped down a little towards the front of the building, enough so that you could all but stand upright. Standing upright would come in handy if it were ever necessary to unclog the main sewer line with a high-pressure sewer line jetter, which of course was ultimately necessary.

This space also contained the main water shutoffs, which a person would have to quickly access and shut off in the event an old pipe burst, or a toilet got jammed up and overflowed. And, of course, both of those events ultimately occurred, more than once.

Finally, on we went to the crawl space for Portal Number One, this one under the original stable; this one the very shallow, literal crawl space.

Tim told me, as he struggled to lift the trapdoor, "There really isn't much under here except for water pipes and electrical conduit. No mains; no valves, breakers, or shutoffs. Not sure there's really anything to show you."

"Great," I smiled, "I'll defer to your higher knowledge of crawl spaces and pass on this one."

I never did go into this creepiest of crawl spaces, but it wasn't long before someone did.

* * *

It was Labor Day weekend, 2008, and the hotel was full for the entire three days. A full hotel meant nonstop busy: up at 6:00 a.m. making endless pots of coffee; chatting with and checking out people; starting laundry, cleaning rooms, and changing sheets; more laundry; helping with lunch-prep dishes; more laundry; lunch service waiting tables and swiping credit cards; doing lunch dishes; cleaning the dining room and setting up for dinner service; more laundry; chatting with and checking in guests; helping with dinner prep; more laundry; grabbing a bite to eat on the fly, a quick shower; doing dinner prep dishes, dinner service, bartending; closing down the kitchen; bartending until 12:00 a.m.; closing down, locking up, and then finally to bed, hopefully before 2:00 a.m. It would start all over again in four hours. And this was our dream job? *What in the hell were we thinking?*

It was Sunday evening of Labor Day weekend, maybe 10:30ish, when Julie came back from our living quarters into a fairly busy bar to announce, in a slight panic, that there was a snake in our bedroom. As I was busy manning the bar, I was unable to manhandle the snake, as would have been my normal duty. Fortunately our good friend and neighbor Tony the Sober Plumber was quick to step in and went back into our living quarters to slay the monster. After playing a little bit with Julie, telling her that it was a poisonous copperhead, he dispatched the eight-inch long, pencil-thin snake.

There's one nice thing about the Hot Sulphur Springs 7800-feet altitude and the long winters — virtually no snakes or big, hairy, tropical spiders. The only snakes to be found at that elevation are small, nonpoisonous black snakes, and the nine month winters never give them the opportunity to grow much beyond twelve inches in length. But let's be honest here — a snake is a snake, and you damn sure don't want them crawling around in your bedroom. Not even a tough guy like me likes that sort of thing.

Julie calmed down a bit as I tried to assure her that this was an anomalous occurrence and I doubted very much she'd see another snake in the living quarters. With the busy day we'd had, doors open and closing all day with people coming in and out, the slinky little reptile had probably slithered his way in to get out of the blistering, high-altitude, afternoon sun and found a nice, cool, quiet place to lie on our closet floor. So back Julie went to bed, and back I went to tend bar.

It wasn't five minutes before Julie was at the door of our living quarters looking anxiously into the noisy, crowded bar for the specific purpose of getting my attention. While I'd actually never before seen Julie's "RICHARD!!! There's another snake in the bedroom!" expression, I was pretty sure that I was seeing it now. And in fact, there was another small snake in the bedroom, and another, then another. They were crawling through small gaps between the floor and the trim that our crack remodelers had left open and unsealed. What was strange was: Why, all of a sudden at 10:30 on this Sunday night, were the snakes coming through all at once, right before our eyes? They even began crawling through another gap in the floor in the back bathroom. Was it a simple game of follow the leader — one snake made it through and then yelled back down into the crawl space, "Follow me, boys; I've found a woman up here to scare the dickens out of!"

Most of the snakes were really small, not much bigger than your average fishing worm. But they had that big snake head that a worm doesn't have, and they glided along the tile floor in that snaky manner that makes those of us wussies that are afraid of snakes even more afraid of them. No question, this was not a good situation, and there was only one thing that could put a temporary halt to this situation: duct tape. I grabbed the roll that I keep on my bedpost for nighttime emergencies and began taping the gaps in the floor trim molding, temporarily holding the little devils at bay. With the living quarters secured for the evening, Julie finally settled down enough to go to bed. I think she slept in the car.

The next day brought an end to the busy holiday weekend and a trip to the hardware store for a tube of clear silicone caulk to seal the gaps in the floor. I wasn't sure what I'd see when I removed the duct tape; i.e., would the little buggers start flying through the cracks in a Guadalcanal sort of onslaught? Fortunately that wasn't the case, as there was no evidence of snakes when the tape was removed, and I quickly went to the task of caulking the gaps, hoping it would dry quickly enough to offer the resistance necessary to forestall another p.m. snake blitz.

Caulk one up for polymer science and the fine folks at Dow Chemical, as the silicone cured and the reptilian assault was abated. That was good enough for me but not for my business partner.

"Do you seriously expect me to live in a house that's built over the set from an Indiana Jones movie?"

"Well, of course not, dear, but who's gonna … I mean, how would I … there ain't no way I'm going down into that crawl space after a nest of snakes. In fact, I wouldn't go into that crawl space after a treasure chest full of gold coins, and we could damn sure use some gold coins!"

The Internet was perused for methods of getting snakes out of your crawl space. I read numerous links with a myriad of suggestions — from the ASPCA green, organic, non-kill method, where you politely ask the snakes to consider leaving on their own, to the violent and the toxic. Ted Nugent's website suggested a modified flame thrower, which, coincidentally, he had for sale, free shipping included. Without a doubt, the best method involved hiring someone else to do the dirty work, and I found a business in nearby Kremmling dubbed, "The Critter Ridder."

The Critter Ridder showed up on time, with an assistant, equipped with flashlights, ladders, and glue traps. When I explained the situation, the man quietly went to his truck and came back with a Tyvek jumpsuit, a respirator, and a miner's hat.

"Where's the crawl space?" he coolly asked.

I had to refrain myself from falling prostrate in worship at the feet of this savior, this Grand Countian who not only showed up when promised, but he also was actually sober and showing not the slightest hint of fear at the horrific task that lie before him: crawling on his hands and knees into a dark crawl space for the specific purpose of looking for snakes.

I took him to the first portal of hell, the entry to the crawl space under our living quarters with three full feet of headroom, the crawl space that I'd never been in and was certain that I'd never have any reason to enter, in spite of the possibility of it containing a fortune in gold coins.

Mr. Critter Ridder donned the jumpsuit, strapped on the respirator, and topped it all off with the miner's hat. He switched on the miner's hat light, switched on his halogen flashlight, and slowly descended into the first portal of hell. Off he crawled into the inky darkness, without as much as a "wish me luck," in search of this nest of vipers.

Two things immediately occurred to me as that brave soul disappeared beneath the floor joists. One: Suppose he finds the snake nest? He appears to be totally unarmed; what will he use to eradicate them? He had no flamethrower, no AA-12 automatic shotgun, no light saber — what in the hell would he use to kill these slinky little buggers? Two: How much was he going to charge us to do what he was in the process of doing? We didn't discuss this before his descent into the abyss, and it quickly occurred to me that I wouldn't climb down there **AND LOOK FOR SNAKES** for a penny less than $500,000. While I didn't have that sort of ready cash, it wouldn't have surprised me if he were to have emerged from beneath the floor, the flashlight between his teeth and hundreds of writhing, tiny snakes clutched in his fists, saying through tightened jaws, "You owe me *$500,000!*" Let's be honest; any guy that would be man enough to crawl under your floors and capture live reptiles would have no problem shaking you down for cash.

After about twenty minutes that seemed an eternity, the Critter Ridder emerged from this subterranean snake farm empty-handed. No writhing, slithering masses were clutched in his clenched fists, nor did he triumphantly hold up a squirming gunnysack.

"I can't find a single snake. I looked all the way back into the deepest corner — no live snakes; no dead snakes. Whatever problem you had is gone now."

"Well I suppose that's good news," I said. Now for the tough part. "How much do I owe you?"

"One hundred and forty dollars."

"Per second?" I asked, praying that he would say, "No, per minute."

"No, I charge ninety dollars per call, plus any materials, and there's a fifty-dollar fee for driving over from Kremmling."

As I wrote the check I worried that perhaps crawling around in the dank, moldy darkness had terribly skewed the poor man's cognitive ability, and during his drive home reality would reinhabit his skull, the car brakes would be slammed, and he'd scream, "*Wait just a minute.* I only charged that reptophobic pansy $140 to crawl around in the dark, under his house, and look for snakes?" Never have I written a check so quickly, and never have I been happier to write one. Julie went back to sleeping in the house, and never again did we find a snake in The Riverside — at least not a thin one that slithered along the floor.

* * *

My most memorable encounter with the first section of Portal Number Two could not have occurred at a more inopportune time from a financial perspective.

It was January 2nd, 2009, the butt end of the busy holiday week. I was back in our living quarters taking my shower and getting ready for the evening when I noticed the shower drain wasn't draining so well. Out of the shower, I then noticed the toilet was also backed up. Our newly remodeled and replumbed living quarters had already had a few issues with the plumbing, so I cursed the plumbing issues and the jackleg contractor who did the jackleg job, quickly got dressed, and told Julie I'd plunge later, as the dinner rush had started. I wasn't long in the kitchen when I saw that one of the sinks, the sink that was supposed to be used only for washing hands but was also frequently used by our cooking staff as a dump sink for foodstuffs, had standing water and wasn't draining. I threw my first bona fide fit in front of the help since owning the hotel — cussing, throwing things, yelling, "How many times have I told you not to dump food in the sink!" at everyone but no one in particular. They weren't impressed. I then noticed the floor drain wasn't draining. I was then quick to deduce that there was a pattern, a pattern that I'd seen once before — I knew we had a clogged main sewage line.

The State of Colorado Department of Public Health and Environment — the folks who oversaw the safety and sanitation of our restaurant — had a pretty basic rule about not preparing or serving food without access to free-flowing water and a waste disposal system. I had no choice but to close the restaurant, a nearly full restaurant with a nearly full bar waiting for tables as well as numerous reservations for tables later in the evening. My hope was that I could get this problem solved in time to at least reopen in an hour and accommodate the evening's second seating. But wait a minute … I suddenly remembered that we weren't in Kansas anymore. I remembered that you can't get a plumber in Grand County to show up for a scheduled job at ten o'clock on a Monday morning (unless maybe it's to fix the dispensing valve on your beer keg), let alone answer an after-hours emergency call on a Friday night on a holiday weekend. I tried my best, going alphabetically through all of the Grand County plumbers, all of whose ads touted "24-Hour Emergency Service," and got not one, not a single one, who could make it to The Riverside that evening.

(Shortly after moving to Hot Sulphur, one of my neighbors told me a story about how they went to one of the local plumbers who lived across the street from them on a Saturday and begged him to come fix a plumbing emergency. They promised double the amount, in cash, that he would usually get for such a job. "Please, Please, Pleeeeze," they begged of him. His simple and direct reply was, "I'm just not feeling it today." I came to learn that this was pretty much the working man's mantra in Grand County.)

I was left with no other option than to call my friend Tony who lived up the street and was an excellent plumber, but whose good and reliable nature I hated to take advantage of. Unfortunately, Tony was ninety miles away in Denver and unable to help. Fortunately, Tony's company had a plumber, Ron, on call, and he also lived in Hot Sulphur. I called the number but it went straight to voice mail. I left my pleading message with Ron and then went to my second-to-last resort.

I sent my son, Scott — home for the holidays from college — up to the Barking Dog Pub in search of another local plumber who was known to frequent that bar. More to the truth, he lived at the Barking Dog and was occasionally known to frequent his house. Scott triumphantly returned with good news — no, the plumber that I sent him for wasn't there, but there was another plumber sitting at the end of the bar who volunteered his services, and he would be down shortly. And who says only the Irish have such fine luck?

In walked our Johnny-on-the-spot plumber, Ron — this would be Tony's Ron who was on call that evening. Did I say "in walked"? Perhaps I should say: in reeled, in staggered, in swayed, in teetered, in lurched, in weaved. Mr. Roget doesn't yet have a synonym for the one word you would use to aptly describe Ron's mode of locomotion. I'm pretty certain that the only reason Ron had agreed to vacate his stool at the Barking Dog and journey to The Riverside was that he had drank the place dry and hoped there was still booze to be had at our place.

I directed Ron, with great effort, back to the kitchen, where he immediately spotted the backed-up hand sink. Without saying a word, he plopped himself down on the floor and began to attempt to dismantle the P-trap under the sink. I said to Ron — and I was being very dramatic at this point by raising my voice, waving my arms about, and pointing in all directions — "It's not the P-trap! We're backed up in our bathroom; we're backed up in the bar; we're backed up in the kitchen; WE'RE BACKED UP EVERYWHERE. THE MAIN IS BACKED UP!" Ron looked up at me and, uttering his first words of the night, said, "Shlow down a minute, will ya?" He then turned his glazed eyes back on the P-trap, which he successfully dismantled and then watched as the turbid water rushed from the sink drain into his lap.

I helped a very wet and still very drunk Ron up from the floor, and led him to the main hotel lobby, to the entrance of the first section for Portal Number Two, where the main plumbing lines are located. Down into the space we went, and I pointed out the main sewage discharge line. Ron looked all around the crawl space as if he were looking for an "Easy" button, or perhaps a detonator that would blow this plumbing problem into the next county. Remember, he was having a tough time with his equilibrium. So the sight of this man half hunched over in the five-foot-tall crawl space looking and pointing at the pipes all about him took on the appearance of a drunken sailor swatting at bees below deck in a violent sea.

Ron finally got his bearings and faced me with his assessment of the situation. He also delivered this assessment in a dramatic fashion, similar to my aforementioned dramatic outburst in the kitchen. "Everything's backwards down here. Thish pipe ish running backwards; thish pipe should be goin' th'other way. Whoever built thish thing got it all screwed up!" He then proceeded to crawl slowly and carefully up the steps, and sat on the edge of the crawl space, his legs dangling over the abyss, his elbows on his knees, and his face buried in his hands. He didn't move for fifteen minutes. When he finally did stir — I wasn't there to see this but heard it secondhand — he got up, said not a word to anyone present, then reeled, staggered, swayed, teetered, lurched, weaved his way out the front door and into the cold, dark, January night.

In walked one of our kitchen employees, who happened to have a drug connection who was also a plumber. (This drug-connection thing was not uncommon in Grand County, or in the restaurant business.) I previously mentioned that the resident Barking Dog plumber was my second-to-last resort — this drug connection plumber was indeed my last resort. That story about "I'm not feeling it today," — that might've also been this guy. But then I figured: What did I have to lose? At the very least I'd have more fodder for a book.

Enter Plumber Number Three, the most unreliable plumber in Grand County. That's like being the biggest gambler in Las Vegas, or the biggest drunk at Mardi Gras, or … you get the point.

Not only am I stunned that he showed up when summoned, but he was bright eyed; he was clean; he was sober; and he was ready to tackle the problem. All those present, at least those who knew this gentleman and his predilections, could've been knocked over by a puff of bong smoke.

Four hours and $400 later our local hero had the lines flowing free. He worked down in that fetid crawl space from 8:00 p.m. until midnight, flushing the line with a high-pressure jetter and then cleaning up the offal responsible for the clog. This was a job so nasty and so incredibly filthy that the *Dirty Jobs* guy on TV would've hired it out; and our man did it with a smile. No matter what Plumber Number Three didn't do before, or what he yet may not do in the future, the night of January 2nd, 2009, will forever be known in local lore as the night that Grand County's most infamous meth-head, slacker plumber actually plumbed and, in doing so, saved our bacon and allowed The Riverside to continue to serve some of Grand County's finest food in a sewage-free environment, per the state code.

* * *

As mentioned previously, the space under the kitchen was original to the hotel's 1903 construction. It had a shorter head clearance than the crawl space under the hotel lobby by maybe a foot. You were in a serious crouch in this space, and in most cases to get done what you had to do when you were down there, you had to kneel on the four ten-foot pieces of 2 x 12's that ran the length of the space. The two kitchen drains ran under this section, both ultimately leading into the infamous grease trap, a 16" square box that collected … well … the sorts of things that would not only turn you into a vegan, you'd possibly never eat again if you saw what it contained. The exit side of the grease trap consisted of a three-inch pipe that ran into the main sewer line in the crawl space in the first section of Portal Number Two, where it joined with the three-inch exit pipes from the toilets, sinks, and showers.

It was the end of the Easter weekend, 2009, when we were shutting the hotel down for both a vacation and a kitchen reconstruction. The plan involved a big-bang, farewell Easter brunch, two weeks away from Hot Sulphur, then a return to gut and replace the old, inherited equipment we'd been dealing with the past year, replace the existing slippery linoleum floor with some primo commercial floor tile

I'd scored from an old adhesive-business contact, and be ready to fly by Memorial Day, 2009.

I can't remember why our chef went into Portal Number Two shortly before our two-week vacation, but he did, and he reported something pretty wretched.

"The pipe from the dishwasher and disposal has a crack in it, and the crawl space is flooded with … uh … well … some pretty bad stuff. There's, like, a foot of really bad water down there."

This was one of those rare times when procrastination seemed the wiser option. There was a basement full of fetid water that wouldn't be added to while we were on vacation. We'd rent a pump when we got back from vacation, drain the crawl space, fix the pipe, the floor, the kitchen, etc. No point in delaying our much anticipated and much deserved vacation to deal with this seamy little issue. Unlike us, it sure as hell wasn't going anywhere.

Two weeks later, we're back at The Riverside, ready for one hell of a floor ripping-up, crawl-space draining good time. I didn't even bother to look in the flooded crawl space before heading to the local equipment-rental place for a portable sump pump. Money down, pump in hand, I took a deep breath and opened the crawl space to find … no water! Closer inspection found a substance that, much unlike water, was thoroughly unfamiliar and indefinable. Several months' worth of restaurant flotsam and jetsam — discharging out of the dishwashing system through the crack in the exhaust pipe in small dribs and drabs over the past few months into the dirt floor of the crawl space to sit, stew, and percolate — had turned into a gel, a goo, an all but living, breathing, writhing clot. There is really no better way to describe this substance other than it being a grayish, rubbery, subterranean pudding, smelling like no pudding you could imagine.

'Crap!' I thought. 'I planned on being able to pump this problem out of my life.' No, it would require a shovel, some plastic bags, and me kneeling and crouching in the cramped quarters of the Second Portal of Hell. While my chef honorably offered to do this dirty beyond dirty job, I couldn't reasonably ask anyone that I was paying less than $140 a second to perform this horrific task.

I previously might have mentioned that it smelled really bad, and it most surely did. But when the gelatinous smelogma was actually disturbed, i.e., turned and probed by the peak of the spade, the odor that was unleashed from this custard of a thousand previous Riverside dinners was beggaring description. It was very quick duty: throw a plastic trash bag in the hole, hold my breath, descend and scrape two or three shovelfuls into the bag, stick my head above the crawl space for a breath of air, hold my breath, and repeat. There were a few times I had to exhale and breathe on my way back up, and the gag reflex was major, as just a momentary whiff of what I was excavating was potentially lethal.

It took a while, but the job was completed. The puddinous spoosmata collected, a layer of lime was deposited upon the crawl space floor, eliminating any of the remaining odors and slaying the resident microbial villains that had been wrought from the no-longer-festering foodjamma. I might have imagined this, but I don't think so, as the trash dumpster, containing the bags of crawl-space sploojisma, emitted a fluorescent-greenish glow from beneath the lid as it sat in our side yard waiting patiently for the second Tuesday of the month pickup.

CHAPTER ELEVEN

Paying Customers, Our Raison d'Être

While there were a multitude of reasons why we were attracted to the life-style of a mountain innkeeper, the fact that we thoroughly enjoyed entertaining and cooking for our family and friends was the foundation upon which we built our western folly. The notion that we could do something we absolutely loved — really, entertaining was our primary hobby — and actually earn a living at it was appealing enough to blind us to the downside of what we were undertaking. One of the realities of our situation that we failed to recognize as being a potential problem involved us not entertaining and cooking for family and friends but entertaining and cooking for total strangers. While Julie and I would each have categorized ourselves as being a "people person," we never would have imagined how quickly into the venture our good nature would be challenged when it came to dealing with our fellow human beings.

We had been official residents of Hot Sulphur Springs for a little more than a week on the Fourth of July in 2008, and we were anxiously anticipating what would be the first time that the hotel was nearly sold out with Julie and I as on-site propri-etors. We were also excited about spending our first night in our new bedroom, as the previous ten nights we'd slept in a variety of guest rooms due to our remodel being forty days beyond the promised date of completion. Up to that point (with the exception of having to live out of a suitcase while all of our worldly possessions sat stacked in a hallway waiting for their new home), all had gone reasonably well for us as innkeepers. But that "had gone reasonably well" feeling disappeared in an instant for me when another of the issues that I had failed to consider being a problem in my quest to be a hotel baron reared its disgusting, foul-smelling head.

That issue was vomit.

Those who know me well know that I would rather face a pack of hungry lions while wearing rib-eye underwear than deal with vomit. The only thing that possibly would be worse for me than dealing with a vomiting human would be dealing with a vomiting big, hairy, tropical spider. Oh Lord, let us not go there.

On this holiday night, the restaurant was extremely busy. Fortunately all of the diners and hotel guests ate early, and all but one couple departed for the fireworks extravaganza at Grand Lake — a good forty-five-minute one-way drive from The Riverside. This would also be the first time since moving to the hotel full time ten days earlier that I would be able to sit quietly in the lobby, gather my thoughts from the whirlwind of our first week of residence at the hotel, and enjoy a cocktail in peace, as the couple that remained went quietly to their room. They were the last to check in that evening, not having had a reservation and taking our only available room. When I was showing the gentleman the room, he asked if we had an elevator as his wife wasn't in good shape and would be unable to go up and down the steps. When I said no, I felt certain that he would leave and I wouldn't see any more of him; but I was wrong. A few minutes later, he and his wife were standing in the lobby, asking to check in to our last room. They'd flown to Denver from Illinois that morning, driven through Rocky Mountain National Park over the 11,000-foot summit of Trail Ridge Road, and were hungry, tired, and ready to settle in, elevator or no elevator. His wife, who was sixtyish and not able to wear slim dresses, felt that she could make it up and down the stairs, although she admittedly was having difficulty breathing, she felt, because of the altitude. She had me just a little worried.

Our visitors from Illinois were the last to be seated for dinner, and after getting over the crankiness that often comes with traveling, they seemed to begin enjoying themselves and The Riverside. The wife had our pan-seared scallops with asparagus tips in a *buerre blanc* sauce, while the husband ordered prime rib, and both shared a bottle of wine, then desserts, resulting in a hundred-dollar restaurant tab on top of an eighty-dollar room rental that I didn't think I'd get for the evening. Off they went to bed; off everyone else went to the fireworks; and off I went to my quiet lobby and cold martini. Even Julie had decided to pack it in early, anxious for a rest in our own king-size bed, the bed that had been sitting for ten days in the unfinished bedroom of the unfinished living quarters.

I'd had less than an hour of uninterrupted bliss when the guest from Illinois appeared in the lobby with a concerned look on his face.

"Can I help you?" I asked with a smile that tried to hide what I really wanted to ask: "What in the hell are you doing down here?"

"Your scallops made my wife sick. She's thrown up all over the bedroom. Can you call 911?"

'Oh My God!' I thought. 'I forgot about vomit. How in the hell could I have forgotten about vomit? Who in the hell is going to clean up the vomit? There's no way I can clean up the vomit! I doubt I'll ever even be able to go upstairs again, let alone head up there now to clean up the vomit!'

"You're serious?" I asked. "You really need me to call 911? I mean, the vomit is about the worst thing that could have happened at this point in my life, but I don't need 911!"

So I called 911, which would have to come from Granby, some fourteen miles away. I stood out in front of the hotel and waited anxiously for help, hoping the lady didn't die in our hotel, but more importantly hoping that she'd be well enough to help clean up her vomit.

Within fifteen minutes that seemed like the proverbial eternity, the ambulance showed up and I pointed the paramedics in the direction of the vomit-filled room. A few minutes later the two male paramedics (there was a third female paramedic) came down to retrieve the stretcher.

"How is she?" I asked.

"Severe altitude sickness," one answered. "A really bad idea for someone her age, in her shape, to come from sea level to 11,000 feet in an eight-hour period."

"How bad is the room?" I asked, cognitive of my being polite to ask first about the lady's condition before asking the paramedics about what really concerned me.

"Pretty bad," was the answer.

'Pretty bad! These guys are used to dealing with all sorts of nasty stuff, and he said, "Pretty bad." Oh my God, what awfulness awaits me?'

It was another thirty minutes before the ambulance crew started to descend the stairs with the stretcher that contained our guest. It is tough work to slither up and down those stairs with a box of donuts — imagine transporting a two-hundred-and-fifty-pound human cargo on a seven-foot, wheeled gurney. My hat's still off to those dudes, who were making something that I would have considered impossible look easy. Our guest didn't look well; She was pale, sweating, and strapped to the gurney with much-needed oxygen tubed up her nostrils. She gave me a sad look, a faint wave, and mouthed, "I'm sorry!" I know she felt sick and, worse, badly for me and the situation.

By this time guests had begun to return from the fireworks and were milling around the front of the darkened hotel. Off went the ambulance, followed by her husband in their rented Ford Taurus, that being followed by the $180 that went unpaid for the room and the dinner, the seafood portion of which was left behind in the "Linda" room.

When I finished dealing with the guests and locking the place down — and thanking my daughter, to whom I will forever be eternally grateful, for her courage in cleaning up the vomit — I went back to spend my first night in my old bed in my new room. I believe it was 2:00 a.m.

Julie awoke from a deep sleep to mumble, "How'd things go?"

"Would that be before or after the ambulance left?"

* * *

We were soon to find that not only were we entertaining and feeding strangers, but for the most part we were entertaining and feeding strangers from Colorado, in general, and Boulder, Colorado, in particular. And believe me, there ain't many strangers stranger!

As Boulderites are also children of God, they shall go unnamed in this tome to protect them from scorn, from ridicule, from the certain disdain and disparagement normal people would heap upon them if they knew them and suffered their eccentricities and outlandishnesses as we have. Nor will I single out the best or worst of them. Some of these multinamed unnamed guests (for example, Laura Light Temple Bluebird; and I won't say if she was on the best or worst list), while deserving of a full chapter in this book detailing their oddities and assaults on normalcy, will quietly and respectfully flow into the pools and eddies of what makes Boulder, Boulder.

Boulder, Colorado, can simply and adequately be defined as "twenty-four square miles surrounded by reality." As the suspected but undefined magnetic power field of the Bermuda Triangle so surreptitiously draws in unsuspecting airplanes and ships, the force of Boulder seeks out and sucks in, from all over the civilized world, the weird, the green, the soy-obsessed/gluten intolerant, the radically vegan, the granola crunching, the pot smoking, the humorless, the intellectually arrogant liberal East-Coast Ivy-League reject trust-funded, the men who all look like Allen Ginsburg, the women who all look like Allen Ginsberg, and variations and agglomerations of all of the aforementioned. Boulder is a beacon for all who live on the fringe, providing a safe haven where they can be amongst those with similar neurosis and experience a sense of normalcy that isn't available to them anywhere else in the civilized world. Boulder is indeed "twenty-four square-miles … surrounded by reality."

Having exposed all of these truths, it is important to note that a large percentage of our guests were from Boulder, and they loved The Riverside (or loved the old Abner-owned Riverside) because it so typified the fringe of what is acceptable as a hostelry. It's old, it's eclectic, it's funky, and it's … **IT'S SO BOULDER!** Or at least it used to be so Boulder. We constantly had to defend ourselves personally (we're not ultraliberals, vegans, 60s radicals, or native Coloradans) as well as defend the improvements we'd made to the hotel and restaurant to those we referred to as "old Abner people," i.e., loyal customers of Abner's.

Abner had three types of customers: 1) those that liked and patronized the place because of Abner; 2) those that liked the place and patronized it in spite of Abner; and 3) those that liked the place but never came back because of Abner. If you put percentages on that clientele, my guess is it was 10 percent for the first group, 20 percent for the second, and the remaining 70 percent we tried to recover and win over.

I got one of these calls weekly:

"Are you the new owner?"

"Yes, along with the bank."

"What happened to Abner?"

"He sold us the hotel two years ago and moved to Phoenix."

"Oh, we just loved Abner. We miss him so!"

"Wait a minute. You loved Abner, you miss him so, but you haven't stayed here for two years, and you didn't even know that he was gone?"

"Well, mostly we stayed at the hot springs. But we loved Abner. He was such a character! Do you have any rooms available this weekend, and do you still take pets?"

"I have some queen rooms that we allow for pet owners. What type of pets?"

"Oh, we have a husky and two labs, but they're small for their breeds. But Abner always let us bring our dogs."

"Sorry, but single dogs only, less than thirty pounds."

"OK. Well how much are the rooms?"

"Queen rooms are seventy-six dollars plus tax."

"WOW. Seventy-six dollars? You've raised the rates!"

"Yes. We've made some improvements — new beds, new sheets, light bulbs that actually work, toilets that flush — and these things cost money, but I think you'll find the place a little more welcoming. Oh, and other stuff has gotten more expensive since you last stayed here in 1994 for thirty-five dollars: electricity, water, gas — you know, the stuff that puts this place a step above camping out."

"Oh my! Please don't tell me you got rid of the mismatched, paisley, loudly striped, cartoon-character sheets. They gave the place such a unique feel."

"Well, unfortunately we did. They were, uh, threadbare, and to quantify them as acceptable bedsheets we would have had to develop a new process for thread grafting. We found it cheaper to buy nice, new, white, high-thread-count sheets. They're really comfortable. You should try them at your home."

"Oh, that's what we have at our home. But I'll miss those old sheets. Do you still have the restaurant? Abner's food was so good!"

"We have a very nice restaurant, and I think the food is as good as or better than what Abner used to serve."

"We loved the old chalkboard menu. Do you still use that?"

"No, we have a paper menu, and, in most cases, all of the stuff that's on the menu is actually available."

"We loved the way Abner used to be out of everything and he'd yell at us and tell us what we were going to eat, whether we liked it or not."

"I think there are probably restaurants in Hell where you can get that experience."

"We're gluten-intolerant vegan soy-addicts, and *no ice in our water*! Can you accommodate our dietary needs?"

"Wait a minute! Abner served fried trout, steak, or Cornish game hens with Spanish rice. What part of *that* accommodated your diet?"

And so it went, with predictable regularity. They usually ended up giving us a try, arriving late in the day in their late-model, bumper-sticker laden (COEXIST; Impeach Bush; Go Green; blah, blah, blah) Subaru, ready for a soak, a meal, and a bed. We bent over backwards to win them over. In most cases, we did. But this goes back to the fact that The Riverside is exceptional *because it is* The Riverside. It wasn't about us, our personalities, or our politics. It wasn't about comfortable beds and new sheets. It wasn't about whether you're from Boulder, Colorado, or Shawnee, Kansas. All you needed to "get" The Riverside was a heart, a soul, and an appreciation and understanding of what makes life unique and special. Twenty-four square miles surrounded by reality is Boulder, Colorado; and fortunately for us, it was loaded with people that got it.

* * *

While a significant percentage of our guests were from Boulder, and we'd come to recognize, accept, and cater to the vagaries that most of these Boulderites shared, we were to find that there were a select few Boulder residents that would, even in Boulder, stand out as being positively *peeeeculiar.*

It was late in August, and we were winding down our first summer season at The Riverside. It was a warm, sunny Sunday afternoon, and we were getting ready for dinner in the restaurant. The hotel had more than half of its rooms booked, so we were hoping that would translate to a busy evening in The River Room. We needed all we could get as we headed into the slower fall season.

As the restaurant was opening and the crowd was starting to drizzle in, an attractive couple in their mid-40s came into the lobby inquiring about a room for the night. Upon showing them one of our full rooms with a river view, they gladly took the room, registered, and paid in cash. I scurried back down to the restaurant, and all seemed Colorado, Grand County, and Riverside normal.

The night's dinner business was brisk, and it included our newly registered guests, who were from Boulder. I'll call her Jane, but she had four names that included a normal first name, then three surnames that covered the animal, vege-table, and mineral spectrum. I'll call him Jack, and he had but a first and last name; however, his last name was, I believe, a Native American derivative. Jack looked about as Native American as Andy Warhol, but he didn't look like Andy Warhol. During dinner, Jane gathered up several of Julie's knickknacks — a plate her mother had brought her from Italy, some colored votive candles, and a small statue — and put them on their dinner table for adornment.

'Hmmmmm,' I said quietly to myself. 'Probably need to keep an eye on this one.'

After dinner Jane took the knickknacks and put them back on their original table, slightly rearranged from how Julie had them, and then produced from her purse some rather beyond-ripe oranges and added them to the mix — sort of a still life sans the canvas and frame. She beckoned some of the remaining dinner patrons to view her display.

They all joined me in a quiet 'Hmmmmm.'

(A note to future guests of our home. Don't ever, ever mess with any of Julie's stuff. There are very few shit lists to be included on worse than Julie's "You Messed with My Stuff" shit list. [Wait a minute … I just remembered that Julie's "You Minimized My Birthday" shit list is pretty bad, too!])

After their meal and Jane's attempt at still-life art, she came into the kitchen while I was doing dishes. She walked right into the kitchen — we don't have a "Welcome" sign on the kitchen door — and came up to me for a chat. When I say came up to me, I mean she took the art of being a "close talker" to a whole new level, a very uncomfortable level. She talked about all of the energy she was feeling in the building and how blessed she felt that she and Jack had stumbled on to this marvelous place. She was very nice, very complimentary, and very well meaning — in spite of all this, she made me very nervous.

Monday morning started with the normal parade of departing weekend guests, followed by bed stripping and room cleaning. Not among the departing guests were our friends from Boulder, who had yet to surface. I was outside on the front walk, sweeping, when Boulder Jane greeted me with a bright good morning smile and asked, "Can you marry Jack and me?" I think I said something like, "Huh?" She and Jack had decided the previous evening that they wanted to get married, today, and spend their honeymoon night in the "John Lennon" room. Jack pulled out a hundred-dollar bill, handed it to me, and said, "This should cover our room for tonight and our dinner last night." It actually covered about 80 percent of the room and dinner for the night before, but Jack didn't stay around to hear about that. I informed Ms. Jane that I could not marry her, but as luck would have it, the Grand County courthouse was right up the street, and my guess was that would be a good place to start inquiring about marriage today and probably divorce later in the week. Off the happy couple went, followed shortly by Julie and I leaving for an always exciting trip into Granby and the City Market.

Back from the store an hour later, we pulled up to The Riverside, and what greeted us but Jack and Jane, sunning in front of the hotel. All of their belongings from their car were set out on the front walk, as if they were having some sort of yard sale: Jack's shirts hanging from our shutters, Jane's skirts and tops draped over the open car doors and on our table and umbrella.

'Hmmmmmmmm,' I said quietly to myself again.

Jane happily informed us that in fact they were to be married that afternoon at the courthouse and were going to spend their honeymoon night in our hotel! The next question was, 'Did I have enough liquor for Jane & Jack's honeymoon night?' Jane didn't ask that question — I asked it of myself. The rest of the day involved the two of them behaving oddly throughout the hotel. Jane burned sage to get rid of evil spirits. Jack made sage tea for some of our other guests; luckily no one who drank it sued us. They both were sunning themselves — not naked, but close — on our back porch, coming in and out of the hotel in various states of undress. Jack had that natural BO that people who disdain chemicals and corporations have — the kind that's real, as if it spews out of his pores from the bowels of his soul. He reminded me a little of the characters in Kerouac's *On The Road*, a throwback to the Beat, hipster days when everything was cool — he seemed like he was sensing everything around him for the first time, in a feral sort of way. Hipster Jack told me that we were cool, unlike the hotel operators in Winter Park, who'd booted them out the night before. "They were so uptight," he said. Perhaps "uptight" is a Boulderism for "concerned about their other guests and their property."

Jane was as nice as she could be, but she had no boundaries and absolutely no sense of propriety. I made sure I locked the bathroom door in our living quarters if I had business to do, because she would have tracked me down, barged in, and had a conversation with me as I sat on the throne, if the mood so struck her. I always told our guests to make themselves at home — and I sincerely meant for them to — but to take it to the literal context that Jane and Jack did had me rethinking my policy of liberal hospitality.

The restaurant wasn't open that night, so we didn't have to endure any more of Jane and Jack's antics in the dining room. I don't know where they ate — maybe down at the river where they caught fish with their hands and cooked them over a sage-stoked fire.

During this respite from their loony presence, I welcomed a French family of four, two adults and two small children, who spoke not a word of English. The mother had a French/English dictionary and pointed to English phrases: "We would like a room"; "We are very tired"; etc. We had only one room with two beds, and it adjoined the "John Lennon" room (which would be occupied that evening by our honeymooning Boulderites) but was separated by a door. "I'll put you in 'Phyllis,' our room with two full beds," I told them. They wanted a room with two beds — they were absolute about this, as absolute as someone can be who can't verbalize but can only point at phrases in a book. Not even having to read further, you know what a cataclysmic boner this was, putting these poor, tired Frenchies in the room next to our sage-smoking honeymooners, protected only by an uninsulated, one-hundred-plus-year-old wooden door. I could later picture the mother frantically paging through her French/English dictionary in the middle of the night looking for the English equivalent of "When can I expect you to quit howling like a dog?" or "Yes, we too wish God would help us!"

I was up and out in the lobby very early the next morning, maybe 6:30 a.m., and I saw a note on our check-in desk from our French guests that said, "We are eating breakfast, we will be back to pay." Very shortly, they were in our lobby, looking as if not only had they not slept, but they had been up all night experiencing hell and anguish known only to the souls of the eternally damned. I'm certain that they had experienced no less. The woman pointed to a phrase in the book that said, "Our neighbors were noisy; we did not sleep." (I swear this phrase was in the book, as if this is something that foreigners commonly experience when traveling in the U.S.) I apologized profusely, saying *"Sorreee, sorreee,"* using my best French accent. I also didn't charge them for their room. My biggest regret was that I didn't speak French, as I would have loved to have heard their description of the carnal carnival that was occurring throughout the previous night in the adjacent room. I'm also grateful, and still a little surprised, that the family, including the two infant children, didn't try to gang strangle me.

Jane and Jack finally checked out after a joint shower in one of our bathrooms. If you'd ever seen the showers in our bathrooms, you'd now be scratching your head in wonder as to how anyone could, or would want to, share a joint shower in one of them. You might also be wondering how I knew they took a joint shower? Trust me, everyone within three blocks of the hotel, because of their sexual hooting and hollering, knew that they took a joint shower.

I actually stood outside and watched them drive off, waving not so much a "good-bye" wave as a "shoo-fly" wave, as I wanted to make damn sure that they were indeed gone from our hotel, our town, and our lives. But they aren't totally gone from our lives. Their memory lives on in our psyches with every mention of Boulder, and every whiff of someone else's BO, and, in reality, through the permanent sage essential-oil stain that they left on the pillow sham in the "Lennon" room.

* * *

We had just made it through our first holiday season as owners of the hotel, and we were headed into the slow, bitterly frozen months of January and February, unsure as to what we could expect regarding paying customers. While we had virtually no business during the week, we were pleased to find that the weekends still offered decent revenue from room bookings and steady restaurant business.

Our bar wasn't generally open to the public in that we didn't actively pursue the business of those who made it their habit to stumble into a bar at its opening hour and drink themselves into oblivion on a nightly basis. Rather, our bar was there mainly to augment the revenue from the restaurant and serve the occasional nightcap to our hotel customers. However, that doesn't mean that on more than a few occasions, and usually with negative consequences, someone didn't stumble in off of the street looking for a bowl of loudmouth soup.

One such occasion occurred after one of those busy Friday, January restaurant nights at The Riverside. Julie had already scooted off to bed, and Damien, Rachel,

and I were in the bar closing things down, when in walked a very large man —
I'd say at least 6' 6" — with shoulder-length wispy gray hair, wearing a ball cap
and a filthy Arctic Cat jacket, and reeking of cigarettes and not particularly good
hygiene. He wasn't overly inebriated, but you could guess that we weren't his first
watering-hole stop of the evening. He was friendly, a little loud, and said his name
was Brian and this was the bar where twenty years earlier he had met his second
wife. Damien looked at him with that serious mortician look that Damien uses
and said, "We're closed"; not exactly what tall, friendly, loud, slightly intoxicated
Brian wanted to hear. In fact, this information quickly transformed him into an
unfriendly, much taller and louder, and very threatening and intimidating Brian. I
immediately became concerned for our safety, as none of us were physically able
to deal with this individual, but it wasn't yet to the point where we could justify
calling 911. So my brilliant solution was to placate him. I'd simply calm him down,
give him a drink, and befriend this big, furry, lovable Arctic Cat. This was, I was to
learn, far from a brilliant solution. (The best solution would have been never to get
in the bar business in a small, alcoholic-laden town in the first place — but way too
late for that.) Brian's requests started off simply enough — Jack Daniel's and Coke,
with the normal Grand County request of "light on the ice, heavy on the Jack, and
a little Coke for color." Like that isn't a recipe for disaster.

Brian held court, getting louder and more physically fluid by the minute, his
arms starting to flail wildly as he made his inane points and observations — it's not
as if any of us wanted to engage him in conversation. He was after daughter Rachel,
until he found out it was my daughter and somehow summoned the wherewithal to
think there might be a problem with his hitting on her (I'd have guessed Brian to
be north of 50 years of age), at which point he took up pursuit of young neighbor
Cassie, who had come in for a late-night visit. He then became overly fascinated
with my lingering chest cold — I'd had a Grand County-sized dose of phlegm and
mucous hanging around in my lungs for three weeks, making for that machine-gun
staccato sound when I tried to clear my airways. Brian was quite certain that a
shot of Southern Comfort would clear that stuff out of my bronchia once and for
all, or perhaps numerous shots if one didn't work. I don't do shots — ever! But
then, I found myself doing a lot of things in the hospitality business that I hadn't or
wouldn't have done previously. To show me that it wasn't as big a deal as I seemed

to make it out to be, Brian graciously offered to join me in this curative treatment — and he's paying! After two shots of Southern Comfort — exactly two more than my normal limit — I decided that this surefire home remedy cure-all was in fact not what the doctor ordered. "The phlegm's still here, but we're out of Southern Comfort," I told Brian. He reared his arm back and came straight at my chest — the important part where the sternum, heart, and lungs are — with a fist that looked, as it was coming at me, like the fat end of a large veal shank, as he shouted, "This'll knock that shit outta ya." Thank God that Brian was an experienced enough drunk to be able to maintain a modicum of motor skills after consuming excessive amounts of spirits; his flying osso bucco fist came to a screeching halt just as it was about to find pay dirt in the center of my congested chest. "That would've worked if I'd have actually hit you," Brian told me, laughing loudly at his attempt at brainless, bully humor.

We were now starting to edge towards that 911-call zone, as a drunk, intimidating Brian was bad, but a drunk, intimidating, *violent* Brian was the absolute last thing I wanted to deal with. I'd need someone with a uniform and a sidearm to get through to this mountain of a mountain man. A few shots later, Damien and I started to suggest to Brian that his night in our bar might be coming to an end. In this regard, Brian was no different than any other drunk at closing time; it's never news they look forward to receiving. Closing-time drunks get ugly, argumentative, profane, and, quite frankly, not persuasive to the point where you would ever want to placate them by giving them more booze — the only thing they're persuasive about is making the case for why God came up with closing time.

Naturally, Brian was angry and more than a little argumentative when he found that his fount of Jack Daniel's shots had dried up. His lack of gentility only increased when Damien gave him his tab, which totaled over a hundred dollars. By this time Brian was drunk enough that he was losing his ability to think clearly, which meant that he was more receptive to my calm nature and soothing voice — I'd seen enough 1940s monster movies to know that a serene demeanor will help tame the most savage of beasts. I told Brian that I'd walk him across the bridge and see that he got safely to his camper.

His camper? What else does it tell you about Brian to know that he was camping out in January in Pioneer Park, on the banks of the frozen Colorado River, on a night when the temperature would easily hit minus-fifteen degrees Fahrenheit. It tells you that he was tough, probably not terribly bright, and that he was definitely crazy. That was a really dangerous combination of attributes to combine with a hundred dollars' worth of alcohol, and here I was about to walk across the bridge with this sodden dynamite keg. All of my sane and sober associates tried to get me not to do this. But my goal went way beyond concern for Brian. We had a hotel full of peacefully slumbering guests, not to mention a few rooms containing people that I loved and cared for, principally my wife and daughter.

I thought I'd gotten Brian calm enough to where he'd go quietly, and this would be the end of the story. And it started out that way as we left the hotel and he reeled his way towards the river. I got him to look at the stars — brilliant beyond what most of you city dwellers have experienced, especially on that crystal clear, subzero winter night, ninety miles west of the nearest star-robbing metropolis. The details of the next few minutes are now, as they were that night, still blurry to me. It had nothing to do with the Southern Comfort, as I was pretty much stone-cold sober. I think it was the total surrealism of the situation — me on a bridge in Colorado, seven hundred miles from what had been my home for fifty-plus years, late on a bitterly frigid night with a gargantuan, drunken, human time bomb; him starting to discuss life in prison and how he'd been raped by bigger, tougher guys than he. Yes, you read that correctly. Out of nowhere (we'd been talking about the stars), he started talking about his life in prison, and how he'd been raped in prison, and how he'd killed a man in prison, asking me if I'd ever been in prison and, if yes, was I raped in prison. I was definitely not in Kansas anymore.

Then he sat down on the bridge railing and dangerously teetered back and forth a little bit. I was thinking there was a pretty good chance he'd fall backwards and break his neck on the frozen river that slumbered twenty long feet below the surface of the bridge, bringing a tidy and painless end (for me at least) to the night and to the problem at hand. Nope, even *really* drunk, he maintained enough coordination to not make what would surely have been his final drunken sway. Again, out of nowhere — as I can't remember any specific trigger words on my part — he erupted at me, swinging his big paw towards me in a roundhouse sweep, saying something like, "Well, I'm gonna show you what it's all about." But he missed the connection and fell flat on his face on the icy road. Finally, after a night of near hits and misses, that innate ability to manage his drunken motor control thing eighty-sixed itself. He went down in slow motion, and I began running, in what certainly at the time felt like slow motion to me, as fast as shank's pony would carry me back to The Riverside. One quick look back over my shoulder revealed Brian's lifeless form lying face down in the middle of the bridge, spread-eagled over the icy Colorado River.

When I told the assembled crowd — which now included an awakened and very upset Julie — that had been watching from the safety of the restaurant windows what had happened, they immediately called 911. We were told it would be forty-five minutes before anyone could get there — after all, it was Friday in Grand County, and a Friday in Grand County to those with DUI duty is busy like Christmas Eve to Santa Claus; maybe even busier. When the police did arrive, I was told I'd have to press charges of assault before they'd go bother with our friend Brian. He was no longer lying in the middle of the road, having gathered himself enough to get up and stumble towards his pop-up camper and, thank God, not towards the hotel to find the pipsqueak that took his hundred-dollar bill and left him lying in the street, prison-sex deprived.

(Another funny, after the fact, sidebar to Brian's swing, miss, and face-first street dive was one of my local friends, Tony, the sober, reliable plumber in Grand County, being dumbfounded that I didn't take the opportunity to kick the living hell out of Brian as he lie face down and helpless in the middle of the road. I hadn't lived long enough in Grand County to have that be a cognitive natural reaction to a fallen drunk. Tony had.)

I didn't want to press charges, mainly because I didn't want to prolong this incident any longer than necessary, as my post-meeting-Brian goals for the evening were satisfied: Brian was out of the hotel, and I was still a virgin from male ex-con rape. The police took a statement and then chastised me a little at having served an inebriated patron in the first place. Easy for them to make that call — they were swaggering around town with Glocks on their hips!

Even though I decided against pressing charges, the officers decided to mosey down to Pioneer Park and see just exactly what our friend was up to in his homey little Big Chief pop-up camper, just kickin' it in January in the middle of the frozen tundra. We all watched the officers' progress from the safety of the River Room. It was too dark and too far away to see any details of what was transpiring beyond the lights of the parked police cruiser, which included the omnipresent police car spotlight on the subject vehicle. But after about twenty minutes the lights went off, and the police car drove by the hotel and away towards whom knew where. We all went to bed in different states: me, glad that the event was over without me having to go for a late-night swim and pretty sure that Brian was in such a drunken slumber that I damn sure didn't have to worry about him anymore that evening, and remotely confident that he probably would have no recollection of what he'd done and who he'd threatened the night before; Julie, in bed for the second time that evening, very upset with me at the fact that I'd so stupidly put myself in harm's way.

We later found out that Brian's night didn't end in a drunken slumber followed by a Grand County-sized hangover. No, our friend wasn't only in the mood to tangle with this pint-sized bartender/hotel owner, he was after any swinging Dick who came his way, including two of Grand County's finest. He had gotten more than a little belligerent with the two officers, and after an ID check with the local authorities, they found that our friend had several outstanding warrants from the Great State of Wyoming — outstanding assault charges and numerous parole violations. Brian was wanted, and not for unpaid traffic tickets!

Needless to say, I learned a few new lessons that evening. First, when you're closing down the bar, the first step is to LOCK THE DOOR! Second, when you're escorting someone from the bar, let them go out the door first, then quickly shut it behind them — don't ever, ever take a walk with them. But back to sur-reality; we lived in a public building with a bar that people felt they had the right to enter because it had an "Open" sign on the door. Fair enough; that's the life we chose. Most often the visitors were some Seth and Sonya from Boulder who wanted to see what lie behind the doors of that charming old façade. Once it was 6' 6" Mr. Arctic Cat, January-camping Brian; drunk, horny, and wanted in Wyoming on assault charges.

CHAPTER TWELVE

The Big Night and the Big Day After

October 22nd, 2008, two short weeks before the presidential election, a late afternoon message on the answering machine told me that Rebecca, of the Obama campaign, wanted to verify when we would be closing on the following day as the governor and U.S. senator of Colorado wanted to stop by the hotel for a meet and greet on their way to Steamboat Springs, where they would spend the night. The governor and senator of Colorado — she said this so casually and nonchalantly, as if it were a daily occurrence to have people of their ilk stop by your business. I listened to the message numerous times, wondering if in fact it was a prank. I didn't recognize the voice; I didn't recognize the area code; and I knew for certain that I had no female friends that were capable of pranking to that level, so I decided to bite.

I called Rebecca back and she verified that indeed the governor and senator were on a tour of rural Colorado — the part of Colorado that was overwhelmingly Republican, due in large part to the gun issue — trying to gain support for the Democratic ticket. The plan was for the entourage to eat dinner in Idaho Springs and then head west on Highway 40 to Steamboat Springs, where they had a morning get-together with the Steamboat Springs ROTC, a group typically comprised of Republican gun owners. They wanted to stop in Hot Sulphur Springs, viewing it as a halfway point to "stretch their legs." I'd think traveling in a thirty-five-foot RV would give you the opportunity to continually stretch your legs — that's why you'd take the RV instead of a green-themed posse of Toyota hybrids. We're talking about a three-ish hour trip from start to finish, Denver to Steamboat Springs. These same people would comfortably and without complaint sit on a 767 for twelve hours on a fact-finding junket to China and not have one-tenth of the leg-stretching room afforded in a thirty-five-foot RV. (Oops, maybe in first class they would.) Anyway, the plan was to pull up at The Riverside at 8:15 p.m., meet with us and the locals for thirty minutes, and then RV on to Steamboat Springs.

Imagine my excitement! Not only would we be meeting and hosting the governor and U.S. senator of our newly adopted home of Colorado, but we would also be getting the greater-than-gold opportunity for press and publicity that was way beyond our financial ken. I envisioned the pictures of us with these two political icons, plastered on the front page of the *Sky-Hi Daily News* and forever hanging in our lobby for the future generations, adding a heretofore never written chapter to the history of this building — *"Governor and Senator Visit Hot Sulphur's Historic Riverside."* In fact, I was so excited that I began to feel the familiar burn of excess stomach acid slowly crawling up my esophagus. What would I say to a sitting senator and governor without looking like a total idiot, on-the-spot glibness not being one of my strong suits? Worse yet, would I have to make some sort of small speech to the assembled throng, a throng that would feature people who'd cut a fat hog doing nothing but making speeches to throngs? The acid went from crawling to sprinting up my esophagus at the thought.

The next day was spent preparing the hotel and restaurant for the big night as well as making a few well-placed phone calls to notify some key Grand County contacts of the impending event. (I was told by Rebecca that the visit was low-keyed with no press being notified, but I might want to let a few locals know so there would be someone to meet them beyond Julie, me, and the dog.) Those notified included Damien, who had close connections with the *Sky-Hi Daily News*, and a few friends in the business community known to have numerous important contacts with those who would at least come and support my political side of the fence. It wasn't long before the phone started ringing with queries from all manner of friends and strangers asking for the details of the evenings' visit. I told three people, and that mushroomed into a call from the mayor of Grand Lake, who heard about it from Mary who owned the Dari-Dine, who heard about it from a lady at the Grand Lake post office.

As the time approached for the opening of the restaurant, and all of the last minute details were being attended to — including a protracted deliberation with myself over what shirt I should wear in which to be photographed for posterity's sake — I took a phone call from Rebecca, the organizer. Rebecca casually informed me that the group had "way overspent" their time in Denver and at subsequent stops, and wouldn't be able to stop by the hotel until "way after" 10:00 p.m., and was therefore cancelling the visit. She said this as though it were in fact just Julie, me, and the dog that they had planned to drop in to see. I was stunned, devastated, and really, really, really sick to my stomach. I had all of these people coming to The Riverside; what manner of fool would they make me out to be? I told Rebecca, "Oh my God! I've got quite a crowd on their way here as we speak, and what in the world do we do?" A casual "sorry" was about all she could muster. I didn't offer, and she didn't ask for, my support in the upcoming election; that, along with our photo op, our front-page story, and our credibility with the locals, went the way of the delinquent RV.

* * *

As the governor and senator's thirty-five-foot Obama "Hope and Change" RV Express rumbled west on Highway 40 through Hot Sulphur Springs, way later than 10:00 p.m., the expectant and disappointed crowd who'd assembled under false pretenses to greet them had long since departed The Riverside. No one who made the trek to the hotel that night was too upset, as we turned the evening into a bit of a party, complete with food and liquor sales that would have been nonexistent on a normal Thursday night during the off-season. Besides, shame on us all if we actually expected a politician to deliver on a promise.

The next day brought a private luncheon for a group of ten retired Grand County high school teachers, for which our morning preparations helped us quickly forget about the big night that wasn't. About halfway through the luncheon I was summoned to the phone to speak with … Rebecca of the Obama campaign. It seemed that they might have some time on their way back from Steamboat Springs to stop at The Riverside after all. And, as luck would have it, they were only a short thirty minutes away. The fire drill necessary to prepare for our distinguished maybe-they-might-actually-show-up-this-time guests was once again set in motion. This time I didn't have the opportunity to give a damn about what shirt I was wearing.

I quickly learned that there is an underground Morse code notification system between the seven democrats in Hot Sulphur Springs, as they were all assembled at the hotel within five minutes of my warning phone call from Rebecca. How did they know, as Rebecca seemed to have been winging things from the RV? Their leader came with a few large Obama signs that she asked if we would hang in the windows of the hotel, perhaps to serve as a beacon that would signal the Obamamobile in this hostile, right-wing environment. It was bad enough that I'd have this rolling campaign advertisement parking in front of our building without also having our hotel window honking validation of what was not the political preference in a town that is not only not on the donkey team, but were an actual donkey to wander into Hot Sulphur, the line to shoot its brains out would be long and all but rabid.

So after a mad scramble, we were ready for the arrival of the previous night's politically celebrity-laden RV. And it arrived. There wasn't a senator or a governor on the bus, at least not a sitting senator or governor. The sitting senator, Ken Salazar, left the group in Steamboat in the early a.m. and headed on to Denver — more important business to be dealt with. We were left with a visit from only a governor — and not even the real governor, Bill Ritter, but Roy Romer, the old Democratic governor from a few years back. Holy Crap! I about had stroked out for a few days thinking I would have to match wits with a sitting U.S. senator and the current hot-property state governor, but instead I got the epitome of political sloppy seconds.

The big RV didn't park in front of The Riverside but pulled around the corner and parked in front of Rusty Pipes Plumbing Store & Meth Emporium. The group — mostly young political types — entered bug-eyed and wondering just what the hell Rebecca was doing when she scheduled a stop at this out-of-the-way shithole-in the-wall. I was certain they were thinking, 'Thank God we didn't make time last night to get here!' Ex-Governor Romer and his lovely wife, Bea, sniffed about the place with moderate interest as to what we did here and what transpired here before we did what we did here. The rest of the crew seemed intent on getting the ex-gov and his wife out of there as quickly as they'd gotten them in there. No press was present as there were very few votes to be had. Really, what was the purpose of their visit, I wondered — they didn't even need to use the bathroom.

As I showed our guests around The Riverside, I spoke to Governor Romer with passion of the pride in our venture: We weren't just entrepreneurs who chucked it all to buy this historic outpost in this beautiful state; more importantly, we were stewards of Colorado's history. His vacant look told me that as there were no votes to be had, he wasn't interested in being governor anymore, and he wasn't interested in us being historical stewards of his state. He just wanted to get back on that RV, use a clean bathroom, and stretch his tired old legs all the way back to Denver.

CHAPTER THIRTEEN

The River Room: Part I

As the new owners and proprietors of The Riverside Hotel, Bar & Restaurant, we'd just enjoyed/suffered through our first week of operation. During the previous week we'd experienced pulling a 9' x 12' U-Haul across an icy I-70, a major Colorado blizzard that filled our hotel and restaurant on our third night of ownership, a hair-raising encounter with the otherworldly inhabitants of The Riverside, and an outdoor vomiting incident that still has some of the local fauna shaking their heads in disbelief. This doesn't even begin to cover the emotional roller coaster that we were riding, without seat belts, over the life-altering signatures that we'd just affixed to paper.

I casually noticed on the evening of December 31st, 2007, that our restaurant license expired on December 31st, 2007. 'Damn that Abner!' I thought, as he'd told me the license was good until the next September. But I didn't sweat it too much, as in amongst all of the little caveat emptors that I'd discovered the last few days regarding Abner and — let's kindly refer to it as — his lack of forthrightness, this one didn't even raise an eyebrow, just a "Damn!" On I went with business as usual, not thinking that it was a big deal to temporarily operate the restaurant without a license. Plus, I knew that I would be heading back to Kansas City in a few days to what at the time was still my real job, where I would then make time to straighten out this new little administrative wrinkle.

Back in Kansas City, I searched the Web and made a few phone calls to find out where I needed to go and who I needed to talk to regarding renewal of the license. I finally was able to get a name and number, and I called, got his voice mail, and left my message saying something like, "Mr. Green, this is Richard Paradise, new owner of The Riverside Hotel in Hot Sulphur Springs, and I'm calling to see what I need to do to get the restaurant license renewed. The man we bought the hotel from told me it was good until September of 2008, but it looks like it actually expired at the end of the year. Please call me at your earliest convenience to discuss. Thanks!"

Within the hour, Mr. Green called The Riverside — I believe my nephew Thomas, who was our cook and chef, took the call — and said something like, "You will immediately and indefinitely cease operations of the restaurant, and I need you to have the new owner call me ASAP!" Thomas mentioned that Mr. Green seemed just a little "pissed."

So I called Mr. Green, and here's what was discussed, to my best recollection.

"Mr. Green, I'm Richard Paradise, the new owner of The Riverside in Hot Sulphur Springs," I said proudly.

Mr. Green did not respond warmly to my proud proclamation. "Mr. Paradise, you are in violation of the law by operating your restaurant without a license. You had a list of the things that needed to be done to that kitchen before we would consider granting a new license, and you were told to contact me for an inspection when all of the items were addressed. The quickest I can get up your way to inspect is the week of January 15th, so until then, you had better not open that restaurant!"

Thomas was right; Mr. Green was not happy.

OK — so I had to take a deep breath and stop and refocus on what I had just heard. I was a little dizzy, and the surrounding world seemed to be floating away from me.

"Uh, Mr. Green," I began, "I have to plead ignorance here and say that I don't know what items you're talking about. I was told by Abner that his restaurant license was transferable — I knew the liquor license wasn't, but he told me the restaurant license was. I'm kind of at a loss for words right now. We just bought this hotel and I've got my life savings tied up in this thing, and now you're telling me I can't operate the restaurant? Good God, what am I going to do? What do I need to do?"

Mr. Green, now calmer and his demeanor noticeably changed for the better, said, "Are you telling me that before selling you the place Abner didn't go over with you what needed to be done to get that kitchen up to code?"

"No sir," I replied. "The man that did the mechanical inspection showed me a few small things that he said would need to be addressed, and I planned on doing those after we purchased the place. Nothing really seemed to be that big of a deal, except for the walk-in cooler that I knew was going to cost me some money, and I've got a guy coming to look at that this week."

"Well let me mention just a few things for starters. Did you know that you need a new fume hood?"

"Uh, no. Do we need a new fume hood?"

"Darn right you do! Your current hood is made of galvanized metal and it has to be stainless steel. It doesn't even have a functioning fire suppression system. How about a commercial dishwasher; did you know you need one of those instead of the old three compartment sink you have in there?"

"Uh, no. I've still got the sink. I want a dishwasher, but I didn't know I needed one."

"How about all of the wooden prep tables? Do you still have those, or did you get stainless steel tables?"

"No stainless; still got the wood," I said, softly. My proud-new-owner-of-The-Riverside voice had disappeared. I was now all but whispering my responses.

"Well, Mr. Paradise, I'm thinking that maybe Mr. Renta didn't give you the full story about his kitchen."

"No, Mr. Green, apparently he didn't, and had he, chances are you and I wouldn't even be talking right now."

* * *

Mr. Green, who was an inspector for the Colorado Department of Public Health and Environment, had the responsibility for all food safety in the counties of Grand and Routt. Area-wise, these are the two largest counties in Colorado, but population-wise, they are the two smallest counties. Mr. Green's job entailed going into every commercial kitchen — restaurants, hotels, bars, grocery stores, schools, and hospitals — and making sure that all facilities met the *Colorado Retail Food Establishment Rules and Regulations*, a one-hundred-sixty-three-page document that Mr. Green suggested I make myself intimately familiar with if I intended to operate a restaurant in his jurisdiction. He also had the responsibility for dairy farms, of which there were more than a few in Routt county, as well as grocery stores, convenience stores, hospitals, jails, food warehouse and distribution centers — anywhere that food was grown, made, stored, handled, prepared, served, sold, and eaten.

Simply put, Mr. Green had a pretty daunting job; while not densely populated, his physical area of responsibility was massive. While this was bad for him, it was good for most of the restaurant owners as his surprise visits were few and far between. Upon entering any small mountain burg, such as Granby, Kremmling, or Parshall, the sight of his green Mazda station wagon would get the phone trees buzzing from diner to diner. If you owned a restaurant, the mere mention of his name, let alone the actual sighting of his visage as he appeared at your doorstep, would cause your day to quickly turn south.

During my initial phone meeting with Mr. Green, after peppering me with the brapp-a-papp assault of necessities for legal operation of The Riverside restaurant, his tone calmed, and my quest for his sympathy seemed to have gone fulfilled. Mr. Green relented and told me that we could operate the restaurant — today, tomorrow, whenever we chose. He would get the paperwork started for renewal of the restaurant license; all I needed to do was send a check for $150 and we'd get everything legal.

I also got the real story from Mr. Green. He told me he had visited Abner in September of 2007. It was "the first time in years" he'd been able to find the place open and Abner on the premises. He didn't hide the fact that his feelings for Abner were less than fond, as I'm sure Abner was a constant foil to Mr. Green and the rules and regulations that he was sworn to enforce.

"I went through that kitchen with a fine-tooth comb, as I hadn't been in there in a long time," he began, "and I busted him on twenty things — major things. I knew there was no way he had the money to get that kitchen up to code, so I just held him to things that he and his help could fix and clean."

"What were some of the major things?" I asked.

"I've already hit on a few of them with you. The biggest one is that fume hood. It's not stainless steel and it has a dry-powder extinguisher system that's not only out of code, it doesn't even work. I'll be real surprised if you make it through your insurance inspection."

Great to know that as well, I thought. "What is it going to cost me to replace?"

"Oh, I'd say, installed, you're probably looking at $50,000 to $60,000."

"Oh…My God! That is huge money that I simply don't have right now."

Mr. Green continued. "Then there is the walk-in cooler. Sounds like your mechanical inspector caught that one; must've been the duct-taped box fan that got it on his radar. And the list goes on. You need to get rid of the refrigerators and freezers, and replace them with commercial models. You need to get rid of every wood prep surface and replace it with stainless steel. You need a commercial dishwasher. You need to replumb the pipes, get some drains in the floor, and put in a new grease trap. You need new FRP walls that can be cleaned — no drywall like you've got now. You need to lose the old asbestos tile floor and replace it with ceramic tile. Shall I go on?"

"If you had to guess, what do you think it's going to cost to get everything done to where it'll pass code?" I asked, not really wanting to hear the answer.

"Conservatively, if you buy the stuff right and you do a lot of the labor yourself," then a pause, "I'd say you're looking in the neighborhood of $150,000 to $200,000."

"Good God, there's no way I have that kind of money."

"I figured as much, and I knew Abner didn't have that kind of money. That's why I let him off the hook on all the major things. But I told him, 'Abner, I'm not gonna make you fix all of this, but before you sell this place to someone else, you've got to let me know and have them get in touch with me, because *they're* gonna have to fix all of this before I give them a license.' And do you know what he said to me when I told him that? He said, 'Mr. Green, I have no intentions of selling The Riverside. I haven't given the first thought to retiring.' That's what he told me in September of 2007. When did you approach him about buying the place?"

"It was February of 2007. But do you know when we signed the papers and there was no going back without losing our $40,000 worth of earnest money?" I asked Mr. Green. "That would have been August 30th of 2007, the month before your visit. The month before he stood there and told you he had no intention of selling the place."

So let it be known that good old Mr. Green, the man who struck mortal fear into the meanest and toughest of Grand County restaurateurs, had a beating and empathetic heart after all. He could have shut Abner down years ago but chose to leave it be. He could have shut me down immediately but instead chose to take pity on me and leave me be. He said there were a few things I had to address immediately, the principle one being the walk-in cooler — as much for the energy savings it would net me (the old compressor ran 24–7 and still didn't properly cool the walk-in) as for the obvious health aspects of not being tempted to cook and serve food that dwelt in the nonfunctional cooler. He also was adamant about the commercial dishwasher but gave me a contact at a company that rented and maintained them for eighty bucks a month. He then asked that I make an effort, year-by-year and bit-by-bit, as my funds allowed, to start replacing the old, out-of-code equipment with new stuff. He said, "As long as I see continual improvement on an annual basis, you and I will be OK."

Perhaps it's like I've said before: God seems to have a soft spot for idiots like me. It's apparent that Mr. Green did as well. For as God, Mr. Green, and hopefully now you know, you'd have to be an absolute idiot to get into the restaurant business.

* * *

There were very few restaurants in Grand County that would qualify as fine dining establishments. Most were bar and grill-type places with burgers, chicken fingers, and fries; there were a few meat emporiums, a couple of pizza joints and sandwich shops, a handful of pretty good Mexican restaurants, and a dozen or so breakfast and lunch family diners. The market for the upscale dining experience seemed to be limited, and so were the choices, which included the tony eatery at Devil's Thumb Ranch, the Tabernash Tavern, a French restaurant in Grand Lake that I thought was awful the one time I dined there (however, he was still in business while I was writing about going out of business), and, last but not least, The River Room restaurant in The Riverside Hotel. Obviously I am interjecting from a strongly subjective point of view, but I felt that for a combination of ambience, food inventiveness, quality, and value, The River Room had all of the others beat. We also had our share of signature dishes, certainly unique to Grand County, that I'm proud to say brought loyal customers who knew excellent from mediocre back to dine with us again and again. I'll take this opportunity to share some of these recipes for posterity's sake as, like The River Room, they are now unattainable pleasures, available only in the memories of those fortunate enough to have experienced them.

* * *

My father, Alfred J. Paradise, loved to cook, and he passed that passion for good food and entertaining on to all of his children. I also place partial blame on both of my parents for helping to get me into the Riverside mess, as they both knew how to cook and entertain, and ended up instilling this trait in all of their children. It was rare that a week went by without some sort of get together in the Paradise house involving food and drink with either our large extended family or agglomerations of friends, neighbors, or business associates. I grew up around food and fun, and tried to turn those wonderful childhood memories and experiences into a respectable career at The Riverside.

Dad was an empirical cook, and rarely did he consult a cookbook or magazine for a recipe. He flew by the seat of his pants, often re-creating dishes from only the gustatory memories of food he'd had in restaurants. He took great delight in messing with people who'd ask for recipes of his original creations. "Oh, there's no recipe," he'd say. "It's just a few tablespoons of this or a cup or two of that." Or he would go to the other extreme, saying things like, "Boil the potatoes for seventeen minutes, then immediately douse them in forty-two-degree water for six minutes, making sure the water maintains the forty-two-degree temperature." He would delight inwardly as his unsuspecting dupes would diligently write down his culinary canard, always to come back at some later point and complain that although they followed the instructions to the letter, they were unable to re-create his recipe.

The Riverside Garlic Salad was our signature salad, developed from a recipe handed down to me and my siblings from my father. This is no canard; this recipe should make enough dressing for four large servings of garlic salad. You'll need a large, round-bottomed, wooden salad bowl - the rougher the texture of the wood, the better - and a hefty wooden spoon.

The Riverside Garlic Salad
4 fat cloves of garlic
1 tablespoon coarse kosher salt
2 teaspoons Dijon mustard
½ lemon, juiced, seeds removed
½ cup of olive oil
4 ice cubes

Press the garlic, or mince extremely fine, and place in the bottom of the salad bowl with the kosher salt and Dijon mustard. With the back of the spoon, make a smooth paste, grinding the salt into the garlic. Add the juice of the lemon to the paste, then slowly add the olive oil, whisking to a smooth consistency. Add the ice cubes and stir well until the ice has started to melt. You don't have to totally melt the ice at this point; you can pour the mixture into a cup and use it within the hour. The ice does three things: it emulsifies the mixture to help prevent it from separating, helps cut the potency, and obviously cools the dressing.

This salad should be served very cold, with chilled, crisp lettuce, shredded mozzarella, and croutons. No store bought croutons; here is our standard Riverside croutons recipe.

The Riverside Croutons
4 slices Farm to Market Sourdough Bread
¼ cup olive oil
2 tablespoons butter
1 teaspoon garlic salt
A few dashes of cayenne pepper

In a large sauté pan, heat the olive oil and butter until the butter is melted. Add the garlic salt and cayenne pepper, and then add the bread (which you've cut into ½" cubes). Keep tossing the croutons until they're coated with the oil/butter/salt mixture and toasted to a crunch — maybe 10–15 minutes. Don't multitask while you're tossing the croutons over the heat as they're not nearly as good if they're burned.

Toss the lettuce with the croutons and the shredded mozzarella. (Use whatever type of lettuce you like. We used a mixture of romaine; fresh spinach, when available; and mixed spring greens. This salad is also excellent with good old hand-shredded iceberg lettuce — that's all we had growing up as poor white children in Johnson County, Kansas.)

Add the dressing a little at a time and keep tossing until all of the mixture is coated. SERVE COLD on chilled plates, and top with fresh cracked pepper.

CHAPTER FOURTEEN

Words of Warning, Painfully Forsaken

Early in my discussions with Abner regarding our purchase and subsequent operation of The Riverside, he took the time during one of our inspection visits to sit me down by the fire and give me some unsolicited advice — the do's and don'ts of running The Riverside, if you will, the benefit of his twenty years of experience. I should have paid better attention.

"Ricardo" Abner began and then paused, as if he were waiting for me to scribe these edicts for eventual inclusion on stone tablets: "You do not, *under any circumstances,* want to open your bar to the locals — only to the hotel and dinner guests."

"Abner, are you serious? You've got this beautiful bar and you want me to keep it closed up? I'm going to be looking for every bit of revenue I can get from this place. I've even got a decent amount of bar revenue factored into my projections."

Answering me in his high-pitched, sing-song falsetto, and for added dramatic effect halting for half second intervals between each word, *"You ... do ... not ... want ... to ... open ... your ... bar ... to ... the ... locals! Trust me on this. That's all that I'm saying. Take it or leave it!"*

I didn't trust him and I didn't take it. I left it, which would be yet another bad decision in what would be an endless string of bad decisions that I would make during the next two years.

It took less than twenty-four hours of our ownership of The Riverside before Abner's admonition regarding opening the bar only for hotel and dinner guests — no local, walk-in, bar-only business — was put to the test. Late afternoon December 28th, 2007, our first full day of ownership, in barges one of the locals (and when I say barges, I mean barges; had we had old-west saloon doors they would have been off of their hinges and airborne after this grand entry). And then, bigger than life and louder than a Mars Volta concert, Patty exploded into the lobby and yelled, "I hear you bought Abner out. Are you guysh gonna open the bar to localsh? I sure hope sho, 'cause I could sure use a rum and Coke about now!" She meant to say *another* rum and Coke, as it was obvious that this wouldn't be her first of the day, or hour, for that matter.

Patty was not the owner of a size-four dress; in fact, I doubt very much that Patty had ever worn a dress of any size. She was a cowgirl to the max, rough and tough, with coarse, thick, dark hair and massive pigtails that resembled those gym ropes that you used to straddle and inch up towards the top of the gym upon, your eyes shut tight from fear while in a state of constant prayer. Possibly the only feminine attribute of this women was the artfully delicate way in which she braided her chest hairs.

"My name's Patty and I've been coming here for yearsh. You got a room up there named after me. Could I get that rum and Coke?"

Whoa, I thought. If Abner had only mentioned *this* local, I would have possibly taken more heed of his advice. In fact he said "locals," in that there may be more like this that would descend upon us in their quest for rum and Coke. Oh my, what have we gotten ourselves into?

Patty was served a rum and Coke, and Gabe, who quickly stepped in as both bartender and bouncer, charged her five dollars for a shot of bottom-shelf Old Jamaica rum and a hefty pour of Coca-Cola. Patty rummaged through her jean pockets until she came up with the cash, and said, "If you guysh wanna get the local trade, you gotta charge lesh than five bucks a drink for housh booze. Jusht a friendly pieshe of advische, shince you're new around here … hic!"

Unlike my educational session with Abner, I took stern notice of the advice I'd just been given by Patty. The price of a rum and Coke was immediately raised to six bucks.

* * *

The first three months of operation went fairly smoothly, mostly because I wasn't there to anal-ize over the details or agonize over the defeats. Julie and I were still working in Kansas City, and my only involvement with The Riverside was through nightly updates from my daughter Rachel or the American Express card statements, monthly evidence of the daily "going to the store for supplies" thing. I'm thinking things were especially good for our two chefs — limited work, as we were only open for dinner Thursday thru Sunday, and copious amounts of downtime for snowboarding, Nintendo playing, guitar plucking (Chef Gabe is a player of professional quality), and late night partying that led to late morning wake ups. There didn't seem to be much time left for hotel fixing and cleaning, which was one of the things I'd hoped our chefs would do to round out the forty hours per week of pay that they were receiving versus the eighteen hours of work they were doing in the kitchen. I didn't stress too much over it, as I viewed this whole period as a dry run before Julie and I arrived at the beginning of the summer season. I was still getting a paycheck that allowed for the funds to fuel this fantasy.

The only discordant note in this scenario involved the personal interaction between the three young participants, which was understandable considering we'd thrown three family members into a haunted mansion located in an isolated mountain town. Picture a low budget version of *The Real World;* this whole ordeal damn sure would have made for some fine reality television. One of the issues involved Rachel ratting out the chefs for playing music loudly enough in the kitchen that it would drown out the lilting strains of the classical music that we featured in the restaurant. I don't know if you've ever tried to enjoy a fine meal while listening to The Mars Volta, but if you haven't, you'll have to trust me that it would play serious havoc with both your mood and your digestive tract. The Mars Volta is what you would listen to if you were trying to set a speed record for chopping apart a large house with a hatchet.

Gabe, who was my second cousin, and I didn't promise each other much in terms of commitments, as he wasn't sure how long he wanted to stay and I wasn't sure how long I'd need him once I got to the hotel full time. It worked out well as I was glad to have him there as a referee between the two first cousins, and he gave the place an air of uniqueness — like it needed any more of that — for Gabe truly was a character's definition of "a character." About two months into the arrangement he informed me that an opportunity for some sculpture work (he was also a sculptor amongst his many other talents) was opening up in Washington, D.C., and he was planning on leaving the hotel in mid-March. After that he might pursue some travels with his band, or do some cooking for a Mississippi Blues Cruise, or whatever, for Gabe was bound by no calendar, reliant upon no clock, and responsible only to himself.

The middle of March coincided with our spring break visit to the hotel. We'd planned on being there all week to work our asses off: painting, cleaning, decorating, hauling trash, installing new beds and tossing out the old, and on and on and on. Friends from Kansas City were coming with us to help in the effort, and in a dizzying display of the illogical, they remain friends to this day, most probably out of pity. A few weeks before our trip, Gabe called to ask if he could have a farewell concert at The Riverside, as two of his bandmates were coming to pick him up and he'd promised some of the locals that he would play for them before he left Colorado.

For a fact, our Property, Casualty, and Liability insurance strictly prohibited us from having live music, due to either the increased risk of people drinking to excess and getting rowdy when exposed to live music, or to the one-in-a-million chance that The Mars Volta would show up, play, and the ensuing potentially lethal effects that exposure to their live music would incur upon a tort-hungry public. But I relented, thinking, 'What harm could come from a little concert for some close friends?'

I didn't give it another thought until I stopped for gas at a station in Winter Park, some thirty-five miles from The Riverside, on our way into Hot Sulphur for our spring-break visit. Plastered in the window of the gas station/convenience store were several posters advertising, no, SCREAMING:

"THE RIVERSIDE HOTEL BLUES FEST"
Featuring
The Flood Brothers
Sunday, March 19th, 8:00 PM
$10.00 Cover Charge
All beers 2-for-1!!!
$5 Jaeger Shots

The Historic Riverside Hotel
Hot Sulphur Springs, CO

'Holy Shit!' I thought; not only did our insurance policy prohibit live music, but it also prohibited any type of drink specials, especially the men's bathroom cleaner's worst nightmare, the dreaded two-for-one beer special. The situation became more dire the nearer we came to Hot Sulphur, for on every store window in every town — Fraser, then Tabernash, and finally Granby — the posters were everywhere, loudly and clearly pointing the way to every Grand County drunk in search of an "Open on Sunday" place to pound down beers at half price. If I've not mentioned it prior, excessive consumption of alcohol was Grand County's national pastime; it was something that came as naturally to Grand Countians as getting out of bed in the morning, albeit late and terribly hungover. They damn sure didn't need an excuse, or an invitation, and here were both everywhere we looked. Possibly even the churches in Grand County mentioned the two-for-one beer and music fest in their weekly announcements on that Sunday at the end of their service.

While I had to give Gabe an A+ in the art of self-promotion, I also quickly had to figure out a way to delicately rain on his parade without his losing face with those thirsty locals.

* * *

Upon our arrival at the hotel, I was immediately approached by Thomas, who nervously informed me of his trepidation regarding the impending blues/booze fest that I'd fallen prey to the old Hannibal double-shuffle into allowing to happen.

"Uh, Uncle Richard, I'm a little worried about this concert we're having here Sunday night ... "

"Why's that, Thomas? Because there are five hundred posters plastered all over Grand County advertising free music and cheap booze on a Sunday, when all of the other bars in Grand County are closed?"

"Oh, so you saw the posters? Yeah, I thought it was a little excessive. Could be a good time, though."

'Nice ... ,' I thought, picturing buses pulling up in front of the hotel, the doors springing open, and Patty and hundreds of her ilk barging out and reeling into The Riverside. Next would come a small flood of wadded up dollar bills being fished from dirty dungarees and flying through the air as the din from the calls for two-for-one PBRs and rum and Cokes were drowning out Gabe's Marshall-amped up bye-bye to Grand County. The only upside to this scenario was that the whole sight and sound of it might possibly, once and for all, vanquish the hotel of the prank-sterous spirits that wreaked havoc upon our person and our plumbing, providing we made it through the evening alive and didn't end up joining them in permanent, eternal residence.

So I girded my loins and stocked up on cases of cheap beer and cheaper hooch. Gabe and his band buddies set up stage in the Green Room, the large, garishly green painted gathering room located between the main lobby and the restaurant, moving this and that to form an impromptu stadium, in the smallest sense of the word. Gabe prayed for a crowd; I prayed that my insurance agent and all of her office staff, relatives, and neighbors were vacationing out of state.

God kind of answered my prayers ... with a blizzard.

At about 4:30 in the p.m., an all-out, Grand County humdinger of a blizzard unleashed from the heavenly skies, a blizzard so intense that not even for cheap beer and free music would a Grand County drunk venture out in this weather. Oh, don't get me wrong; they'd break a sweat, they'd pace around their house and suppose, they'd think that maybe it might be worth the risk. But at the end of the discussion, they'd lose out to a wiser spouse, a pleading child, or the sober voice in their head that would say, 'Are you out of your mind? It's a Grand County blizzard out there! Plus, it's not like you don't have a jug of vodka in the cupboard.'

When I said God "kind of" answered my prayers, I meant that the blizzard neutered all of the Grand County drunks that would have to *drive* to the Riverside Blues Fest. Unfortunately, there were those in Hot Sulphur that could get there by walking, blizzard or not, and, for a fact, there's no worse kind of drunk than a Grand County drunk that has unlimited access to booze and doesn't have to worry about driving.

At 7:30 p.m., in walked Patty, in walked Jane, Isaac, Brad, Jim, and fifteen to twenty more of the Hot Sulphur locals. They'd braved the weather, and they were in the mood for some live music and Sunday night bar booze because, after all, the Barking Dog wasn't serving.

"What'll you have?" I asked in cheerful bartender fashion to the first young man who sidled up to the bar.

"Gimme a rum and Coke — heavy on the rum and a little Coke for color!"

"Done deal," I said. "That'll be six bucks."

About four minutes went by, and the same young man came back and said, "Gimme another rum and Coke, and go lighter on the Coke, heavier on the rum this time."

"Here you go! That'll be seven bucks."

Pockets were searched and wrinkled bills were proffered. "Much better! Now pour me another one of those 'cause I'll be back in a minute."

This pattern would continue for the next few hours with no regard to my on-the-spot efforts at temperance through price-fixing.

Gabe and his group got things going at 8:00, and he was fast ripping it up — great music, good time. But the locals were only perfunctorily interested in the music as a means of having access to a walking distance Open-on-Sunday bar in a blizzard. Gabe was rocking his little heart out, but for all that the locals cared he could have been playing a Jew's-harp solo in the Green Room, so long as the rum and Cokes were flowing in the bar.

At 10:00 p.m., as proprietor and owner of The Riverside Hotel, Bar & Restaurant, I'd decided that I'd had about enough. Our rum and Coke dude was all but having sex with one of the local maidens on one of our rickety bar tables. Some of the others in the bar were throwing darts — not at a dartboard but at each other. The rook pieces on our chess table had found their way into one of the patron's nostrils along with a pawn into each of his ear canals. His attempt at bad bar humor was going unnoticed, as most of the patrons were cheering on the carnal performance of Captain Morgan and his table wench.

One of the locals that I'd previously seen at the post office — she was a sweet, grandmotherly looking lady that more than surprised me by her attendance at this affair — asked me to total up her tab, and would I take a personal check?

"Not a problem," I said. "That'll be thirty-two dollars."

"Thirty-two dollarsh," she slurred, "how many beersh d'I have?"

"Sixteen beers," I replied. "Two-for-one is eight times four bucks apiece, equals thirty-two dollars, assuming you don't want to add a tip."

"Sixteen beers! Thash crazy! I coulda shworn I only had fourteen ... hic."

It's 10:07, and I loudly announce, "Last call folks! The music's winding down and the bar is closing!"

At this pronouncement, our rum and Coke guy disengages himself from his local Hot Sulphur hottie and staggers up to the bar, steadies himself, violently slams his fist on the bar — as much for ballast as for exclamation — and says, "BULLSHIT! Last call in Colorado is two a.m. It's only ten o'clock!" I was truly surprised that he could tell time at this point. He had a look of wildness in his eyes that, never before being in the bartending business, I'd never seen in a human and wasn't quite sure how to deal with. But I'd really had enough and decided I'd have to grow a pair and put this mess to bed. I looked him squarely back in the eye with a little wildness of my own and calmly but with a little bit of an edge, sort of Clint Eastwood-like, said, "Last call in *this* Colorado bar is 10 p.m., and that's right now. So what'll it be?"

Shrinking back a little, he said, "Gimme six rum and Cokes — heavy on the rum, a little Coke for color."

As I began lining up those six rum and Cokes, Abner Renta seemed to me, at that moment, the wisest man in the entire world.

CHAPTER FIFTEEN

The River Room: Part II

The morning after what most would consider an epic display of alcohol-fueled debauchery but in Hot Sulphur Springs was just another Sunday night at the local watering hole, the damage was assessed and, fortunately, there was no significant physical damage, only psychological damage at the reality of what lay ahead of us in this Colorado "adventure." On the upside, there was a big fishbowl full of dirty, crumpled up bills of all denominations. Nice, but had the sum been tenfold I would have made the same post-game decision to follow Abe's advice; *not in hell* would we have a functioning bar in Hot Sulphur Springs, selling cheap booze, for the purpose of catering specifically to the local trade.

We said our good-byes to Gabe, and shut the hotel and restaurant down for two months while we installed the new dishwasher and began the first few steps of rebuilding the kitchen. Thomas and Rachel took some time off and came back to Kansas City, and the plan was for them to both go back to The Riverside in mid-April. Thomas would start working on the kitchen; Rachel on painting rooms, cleaning, and getting the hotel ready for the summer season and our eventual arrival. The last day of our stay we also hired the aforementioned Grand County-reliable contractor to redo our living quarters before our arrival, and someone needed to be there to oversee the remodel — in reality, to report daily that NO remodeling was going on as it should have been.

With Gabe gone and me having seen what a busy night at The River Room entails, I knew we'd need some additional kitchen help for the summer, especially when we threw a summer lunch shift into the equation. A mention of my need for additional help was made in passing to my brother in Kansas City, who thought that a good friend of his had a son that worked in a restaurant in high school and was looking to move to Colorado. He offered to mention The Riverside to his friend.

One phone call and two weeks later, Chef Danny shows up at The Riverside with a suitcase full of bad clothes, a guitar, and a few boxes of books and LPs. His prior cooking experience included summers working at a country club golf course bar and grill, and a stint at Garozzo's, a Kansas City Italian eatery famous for Chicken Spiedini, a dish that we stole and made our house specialty. I had no idea what Danny could do in a kitchen as his first month was spent redoing ours. I had not a clue if he could cook, but, damn, the kid was handy and a hard worker.

The place reopened on Memorial Day weekend, 2008. Julie and I were in Kansas City watching from the sidelines. We had most of the rooms booked for a wedding party, and the place was hopping, bar and restaurant both. Thomas took Danny under his wing, and, quickly into the deal, we had two of the best chefs in the mountains, putting out heretofore unheard of fare in Grand County.

A beautiful white linen dining room with soothing music, thanks to Julie and the iPod playlist, complemented by food and presentation that were off the charts — by my standards, and I had some damn high restaurant standards — and The River Room had become a fine dining destination.

Don't get me wrong. We had some bumps and bruises along the way as well as our fair share of assholes.

"How is everything this evening?" I asked a table of four, two couples in their early 60s. The obvious alpha male looked like a cross between an angry bulldog and Oliver North.

The bulldog replied, in a bulldog sort of way, "OK."

"Just *OK*?" I asked.

"Yeah, just OK!" he said, the chip on his shoulder growing like a bag of microwave popcorn.

Chipper and cheerfully from me, "What can we do to make it better than 'OK'?"

He held up a small piece of the grilled bread that we served — grilled bread that Thomas sliced on the bias; painted with butter, olive oil, and garlic; then grilled with burn marks to a crunchy, crispy finish — and said, "How about serving soft dinner rolls, **NOT BURNED BREAD!**"

His wife cowered and looked at me apologetically, as without question she'd suffered through scenes like this for the sad past forty years of her life. It is important to note that the foursome had choked down three FREE orders of this burned bread; but no matter.

This was my first lesson in "Opinions are like assholes. Everybody has one but some are bigger than others!" I think that's how that saying goes.

Summer went on … good food, decent business, and the establishment of the building blocks of a place that could actually become a dining destination in Grand County. People started calling about Christmas parties, fall weddings, and group events. But in spite of the successes, there was some unrest with one of the major cogs in this seemingly well-oiled machine — Chef Thomas was ready to blow this pop stand for bigger cities and greener pastures.

His discontent may have coincided with our return in mid-June, as when we arrived we put demands on *all* of the employees that weren't existent while we watched from afar in Kansas City, demands like getting out of bed before 2:00 p.m. and actually working. But more importantly, he was getting pounded by his former employer with opportunities in Chicago, Charlotte, and everywhere other than Hot Sulphur Springs, for way more than we could pay. No question, the young man could cook.

It wasn't but a few weeks into our full-time, late-June arrival that Thomas told us he was planning on leaving at the end of the summer. The fun meter had dipped to near the empty level, and Thomas told us that we'd need to find a replacement. Although Danny was picking things up well, there was no way he could singularly manage the kitchen going into the fall, especially with all of the specialty business we'd booked.

There is a quote from a classic 1980s movie, *Once Upon a Time in America* — great cast, great director, and this bit of simply, wonderfully expressed profane profundity from Burt Young — "Life … (dramatic pause) … is stranger than shit!"

Now for a fact, life is stranger than shit, because not one day after Thomas gave us the devastating news that he was checking out of The Riverside, I got a call from an old contact at our favorite Kansas City restaurant. "Hey, how's it going? I want to move to Colorado, and I'm wondering if you've got any openings in your kitchen?"

Life ... is stranger than shit.

"Richard, I hope you remember me. Joe Amato gave me your phone number. My wife and I are in Colorado on vacation, and I wanted to stop by and see your place. We're in Grand Lake right now planning on heading your way."

His name was Dhoubi Nhutjob, and he was a strapping 6' 2" Iranian whirling dervish (figuratively, not literally) full of cooking energy and enthusiasm. He was planning on moving his wife, dog, and cat to Colorado at the end of the summer, and when I told him that Thomas was leaving in August, he said, "No need for you to even look .... *I'm your new chef!*" We knew him from when he'd worked as a waiter at Il Trullo, our favorite restaurant, Italian or otherwise, in Kansas City. I didn't know he could cook, but he promised me that he could; they just wouldn't let him in the kitchen at Il Trullo. (Red flag!)

"I've worked in the kitchen at Room 39, and for the past six months I've been working the pasta station at Lidia's" (both top-end places in Kansas City). "This will be *incredible*. We'll make this into the best restaurant in the mountains."

I couldn't help but love his attitude and had enjoyed him as our waiter — always full of energy and passionate about the food he was serving. So I figured, what did I have to lose?

And so it happened. Mid-August, Dhoubi showed up with Brody, his border collie mix; a suitcase; and a beat-up Toyota truck pulling a really sketchy trailer full of hardwood: oak, hickory ... the good stuff from the Midwest. He made this trek without his wife and the cat, as they would arrive a few weeks later after Dhoubi got settled. He claimed that he'd been stopped and hassled a little by the Kansas Highway Patrol because of the lack of tags on this trailer thing he was pulling. It was basically an old 1950s pickup truck bed that had some wheels cobbled onto it and a cheap camper top affixed to it. It looked like something ten-year-old boys would have assembled, bored, with nothing better to do on a summer afternoon. Couple this vision with a wild-haired Iranian driving this unlicensed contraption through the flatlands of western Kansas, *and there's a question why he was pulled over?* Knowing him, he was probably driving this prairie schooner at ninety miles per hour plus.

"Dhoubi, welcome to The Riverside. You've had a long drive today ... perhaps a shot of Johnnie Walker Red would make things right for you," I gladly offered.

That first shot disappeared down his gullet in less than a blink of an eye.

"Ok, sure, maybe two or three shots ... " And in rapid-fire succession, the second shot, then the third, and on and on followed until the ensuing part of the bottle disappeared.

'Hmmm,' I thought, 'he'll certainly have no trouble fitting in with the Grand County locals.'

Dhoubi's first day of work was a lunch shift. We had a menu with about six items: Kansas City barbecue brisket, a hamburger that we made from daily fresh-ground rib eye steak (cheaper butcher cuts from the end of the roasts), a chicken sandwich, a soup of the day, and a few lunch salads.

"No problem with any of this," he said as I showed him this and that about what we served. "I'm also gonna have a pasta special today. Some of the veggies in the walk-in are about out of time. I'll make a vegetarian dish, say maybe fettuccine with red peppers, celery, maybe some snap peas and finish it with a champagne cream sauce — very light, but *fantastic* flavor."

"Uh, gee, that sounds great." I was stunned, almost speechless. Here he was, excited about cooking lunch. Thomas and Danny had lost their zest for the lunch shifts midway through the first week.

We sold every order of the pasta special. It was out of this world; there were literally moans and groans of ecstasy from the patrons as they ate. I honestly hadn't eaten anything that good in forever — and that's no slight to the Riverside crew that was already there, as they put out terrific food. But this sauce was in another league. Honest to God, we had lunch patrons come back that evening and request the same dish for dinner, it was that good.

The plan was for Thomas to show Dhoubi the ropes that held The Riverside kitchen together during Dhoubi's first dinner shift as a new member of the staff. In fact, Thomas agreed to stay with us for two weeks for the sole purpose of training Dhoubi. I think it was only three days later that Thomas packed up and headed for his next gig in Charlotte, North Carolina; Dhoubi clearly didn't need any training. He took over that kitchen without any hesitation as his presence during the heat of the rush was a commanding one — saucing here, searing there, and barking orders all the while.

The only person in this mix who was less than thrilled was Danny, as he'd had aspirations of taking over the head job, but he quietly stepped into the supporting role. He didn't need to have it spelled out for him that Dhoubi intended to take a backseat to no one. And that "no one" included me.

Things seemed to be going well, especially with regards to the originality and quality of the food. Every day Dhoubi made fresh pasta for a nightly pasta special — fettuccine, tagliatelle, raviolis — and the sauces were beyond better than any you could imagine. He made his own fresh mozzarella cheese from curds. His lasagna was unlike any you'd ever had; it was the béchamel sauce that he layered into the mix. The oak and hickory he'd brought from Kansas City went towards making "dirty steak," a rib eye thrown directly on the glowing coals, which seared a smoky flavor into the meat. It was then finished inside on the flattop, sliced on the bias, drizzled with reduced balsamic vinegar, and served with an arugula salad tossed with a hint of truffle oil. It was, as they say, to die for. His soups were spectacular and his desserts … magnifico!

There was a period early in Dhoubi's tenure that I would have put us up against any restaurant in Denver, and most visitors from Denver who ate at The River Room agreed that there wasn't a better restaurant in the Mile High City.

So you might wonder: Why then, seven short months later, was Dhoubi storming out of the hotel amidst his hail of insults, threats, and F-bombs, after being fired?

It started in late September on a beautiful fall Monday, the sky a blue that could only be imagined, the aspens at the peak of their golden majesty. The kitchen was closed and the hotel unoccupied, and Angela, one of our friends and neighbors who ran the bar at Dead Pines Golf Club, gifted me and Dhoubi a round of golf. As Dhoubi got in the car with me to head to the golf course, he was accompanied by a king-sized reek of marijuana. It was as if he had smoldering bongs stashed in each of his pockets.

I didn't think much about it other than that I hadn't realized he was a stoner. He never acted stoned; he never looked stoned. His manic behavior was the polar opposite of stoned, and he'd never even mentioned anything about pot or drugs. It just kind of surprised me because there had been zero behavioral traits exhibited that would cause me to connect those dots.

Dhoubi's fondness for weed connected the dots for me as to why he would suddenly move to the Centennial State, as it's even known to surviving Japanese World War Two cave hermits on Iwo Jima that smoking weed in Colorado is as prevalent as those big, pointy mountains that they've got there. (While it is fully legal now for recreational use, during our Riverside tenure the medicinal use law had just passed.) All you needed was an ailment — from tennis elbow to toenail fungus — and a prescription from a Pot Doctor, and you were good to blow. Couple that with the proclivity of those in the restaurant industry to abuse drugs and alcohol, and you've got yourself a genuine reason for an Iranian kid who's about as outdoorsy as Truman Capote to pack up and move to the remote mountains of Colorado.

But we were soon to find out, the problem with Dhoubi wasn't when he was stoned — it was when he wasn't.

* * *

The Great Mississippi Flood of 1927, the Dust Bowl of the 1930s, the tsunami of 2004, Hurricane Katrina — natural disasters of biblical proportion, events that define disaster and epitomize human suffering at the hands of Mother Nature.

Colorado was also witness to a natural disaster so profound, so horrific, that the elders will only mention it in hushed tones, while the contemporaries tremble and turn ashen at the memory: The Great Colorado Pot Shortage of November, 2008.

No one knows for certain who or what sinister series of events conspired to cause the shortage. Was it the prolonged Mexican winter of 2007? Some thought it was the recent locust infestation on Maui, while others suspected the Jamaican drug embargo. More than likely it was none of the aforementioned. Rather, the shortage happened to coincide with the 2008 state election that legalized medicinal marijuana in Colorado, causing most of the 4.8 million unhealthy Coloradans to flee to their doctors for some much-needed relief. Just like that, overnight, the demand for weed far exceeded the supply. There wasn't a joint left to be had in the state.

Dhoubi took the pot shortage hard … very hard.

His carefree, fun-loving demeanor took a nasty turn for the worse as he became quiet, sullen, and quick to temper. His alcohol consumption, already epic, went off the charts. During the dinner shift, whenever I was out of the bar in the dining room, he would go into the bar, grab a bottle by the throat, and swig gulps from either the Sauza Hornitos Reposada tequila or the Johnnie Walker Red — his brands of choice. On a positive note, Dhoubi was very picky about the booze he'd chug, preferring not to drink if we were out of his favorites. This knowledge caused me to begin hiding the Hornitos and the Johnnie Walker in my bedroom closet. While it made for a bit of a trek when someone ordered a top-shelf margarita, so be it, as hidden away in the bedroom, I'd at least have top-shelf booze to serve.

Dhoubi began all but accosting people — anyone and everyone, including our guests — asking whether or not they had any pot he could buy. At the slightest rumor of there being pot anywhere, he'd hop in his truck in pursuit. There was a spontaneous midnight run to Aspen, next a three-day trek to Durango. I swear he would have climbed the nearest fourteener in a raging blizzard at a hint of the possibility of scoring a roach.

To say this lack of weed had a negative effect on his job performance is a few kilos short of an understatement. His kitchen deportment was horrific to the point of everyone threatening to walk out if he didn't get some self-control. His food preparation became so sloppy that I'm certain it cost us our third Michelin star. I strongly considered firing him, but with the holidays coming up — sold-out weekends, group Christmas parties — I had no other choice but to put up with his god-awful behavior.

In mid-December, Christmas came early, not only for Dhoubi but for all of the ailing Coloradans — weed had suddenly reappeared. Like a Times Square New Year's Eve, the smoky streets of Boulder were filled with revelers (although they were like way more laid-back than those New York Times Square revelers), a healthy, hazy fog hanging over the pie-eyed throngs.

I was glad for this change in fortunes as I felt it would get Dhoubi back on an even keel — but such was not the case. The constant combination of a freshly stoned-again Dhoubi and a liquid diet of pricy tequila made for a brand of intoxication heretofore unknown to the consuming public. Even some of Grand County's finest drunks were aghast at his perpetual high-level state of self-medication. And if your level of intoxication is noteworthy to Grand County drunks, you have accomplished one mean feat.

His menu choices, while already a little on the eclectic side for Grand County, became so over-the-top that the Iron Chefs would have been perplexed. "Yes Dhoubi," I'd say when looking over the evening's specials, "perhaps if I were stoned to the ceiling and hadn't one solitary functioning brain cell, I would then be tempted to order the Ox Tongue Stew with Candied Jicama and Hot, Buttered Groat Clusters. Honestly, where do you come up with this stuff?" He would then try to tell me, through a tongue that was as thick as a 4" x 4" and eyes that were glazed like a fat man's dream donut, that the reintroduction of pot into his life had awakened his senses and expanded his mind and his culinary imagination to unimaginable levels of creativity.

The last night Dhoubi worked at The River Room was Saturday, February 14th, 2009 — Valentine's Day. The hotel was booked solid, and the restaurant was essentially sold-out with reservations. Dhoubi had a special menu full of Italian-themed obscurities that were guaranteed to furrow the brow of every Grand Countian who would dine with us that evening. Try some of these on for size:

Capezzoli Mucca con Limoni e Salsiccia

Brasato di Rana Pescatrice con i Piedi Maiale e Broccoli

Zuppa di Lumache, Noci e Fagioli Lima

Mmmmm. Makes you hungry, doesn't it? It was one thing trying to read it, having to pronounce it and explain it to our patrons that evening was next to impossible.

A sample of one of my many exchanges with the paying public that evening: "The Zuppa di Lumache, Noci e Fagioli Lima is a soup of snails, walnuts, and lima beans. I know it sounds a little unusual, but our chef told all of the staff that it is sublime."

"Have you tried it?" the patron asked.

"Uh, no, I actually haven't. But I hear it's really good if you like snails!"

"Think I'll pass on that. What is the Brasato ... . How do you say the rest of it?"

"The Brasato di Rana Pescatrice con i Piedi Maiale e Broccoli is a delightful little dish of braised monkfish, known as 'poor man's lobster,' with pig's feet and broccoli. Again, an unusual combination, but I'm told by the chef that it's quite tasty!"

"Whoa! Could maybe I get like an Italian hamburger or something?"

And on it went.

At the evenings' conclusion of Dante's Valentine's Day Inferno at The River Room, and in true post-pot-shortage fashion, Dhoubi was absolutely, positively 100 percent popped to the gills. I asked him a simple question — "Hey Dhoubi, can you get up off of the floor and help Danny and Anthony clean the kitchen?" — and he looked in my general direction, with an insane grin plastered across his face and a small river of drool flowing from the corner of his mouth, made a pained effort to open his mouth and form words, and said something like, "Plawd mullied gippo roaberdy."

I simply couldn't take any more of it, and however difficult for all of the parties involved, I knew what had to be done. Danny had the Sunday night dinner shift, and we were closed the following two days, so I had to agonize over the inevitable until Wednesday morning when Dhoubi arrived at the hotel. He seemed moderately sober, as I was able to understand a "morning" as he flew by my office. I was quick to track him down and give him the news that I no longer required his services. Simply put, he did not take the news well. I recall that "F-you" was possibly the nicest thing he said to me as he exited our hotel for the final time. The honeymoon and the marriage had come to an end — thank God.

The mantle of "Head Chef at The River Room" was finally passed on to its rightful heir, Chef Danny. He'd worked for a year now under two capable trainers, and he'd soaked up all of their good habits like a sponge and fortunately hadn't seemed to have picked up any of their bad habits. But he was going to need some help in the kitchen, especially on busy weekend nights. Enter Chef Carrie, a hippie chick from Minnesota who had come to Colorado in the 70s looking for snow, slopes, and … have I mentioned the Colorado weed thing?

* * *

We brought our signature dish, Chicken Spiedini, to The Riverside from a storied Italian eatery in Kansas City, Garozzo's Ristorante, which built a bit of an empire on the back of this grilled, garlic-laden fowl. The first time I ate at the original location on 5th and Harrison, down near the Kansas City Farmer's Market, the waiter suggested the Chicken Spiedini over a pasta dish I had been tempted to order. I took his advice and found that I'd never tasted anything quite like it. It was one of those seminal degustatory moments that jarred you into the realization that there was a whole culinary world beyond your mother's meat loaf. Mr. Garozzo went on to open three more restaurants, all of which were fueled by the success of his spiedini. Chicken Spiedini was so popular amongst Kansas City diners that it even wrought new competitive restaurants from former Garozzo's employees, including the original Garozzo's chef who'd invented the dish.

At The Riverside, we never claimed Chicken Spiedini as an original recipe but gave due credit by referring to the dish on our first menu as "Chicken Spiedini a la Garozzo." I do steadfastly believe that our version was better than Garozzo's, an opinion that was shared by numerous Kansas Citians who had eaten the dish in both Kansas City and at The Riverside. The only restaurant review that we ever received in the local paper, good or bad, was a one-line mention in a "what to do this weekend" column from the *Sky-Hi Daily News* entertainment writer, saying, "Try the Chicken Spiedini at The Riverside — it's incredible!"

While it was immensely popular, it was also very labor intensive to prepare, and in our last few months of operation, down to a single chef, we decided to scrap the dish in favor of easier preparations. Make it at home, and you'll get a feel for what our kitchen help had to do on a daily basis for the throngs of dinner guests who ordered, and adored, Chicken Spiedini. I'm proud that we threw very little uneaten food away at The Riverside, and when we did, never was it spiedini.

The Riverside Chicken Spiedini a la Garozzo
(Serves four.)
4 large boneless, skinless chicken breasts
¾ cup flour
¾ cup olive oil
2 tablespoons dried sweet basil
½ cup grated Parmigiano Reggiano
1½ cup Panko bread crumbs

Amogio Sauce
¾ cup olive oil
¾ cup vegetable oil
1 medium-sized head of garlic
1 lemon, juiced
1 teaspoon red pepper flakes
1 tablespoon finely chopped fresh basil
1 tablespoon finely chopped fresh parsley
A few hefty grinds of fresh black pepper and a few stout pinches of Kosher salt

You'll need kabob skewers and, in a perfect world, a nice, hot bed of coals over which to grill the spiedini. If you can't grill, you can also cook the skewers indoors on a hot griddle. Spiedini is an Italian term with the loose translation of: skewers of meat or fish, grilled over a flame; the direct translation is: skewers of meat that are slowly prepared to the sound of blaring heavy-metal/bad rap music by highly paid kitchen staff.

Pound the chicken breasts thin, about a quarter-inch thick, and cut lengthwise into one-inch-wide strips. If you've pounded the breasts thin enough, you should get sixteen strips from the four chicken breasts.

You'll also need three prep bowls, one that will contain the ½ cup of olive oil, one the flour, and the third a well-mixed blend of the bread crumbs, the grated parmesan cheese, and the basil flakes.

Lightly salt and pepper the chicken strips; grab a strip, dredge it in the flour, shake off the excess, dip it in the olive oil, drip off the excess, and dredge it in the bread crumb mixture. Place the coated strip on your work surface and roll it into a pinwheel. Stick this onto a skewer, jamming the business end of the skewer through the entire diameter of the pinwheel, and repeat the process with all of the strips. Dependent upon your dredging, dripping, and shaking skills, you may end up needing more flour, oil, or bread crumb mix, but you'd have hopefully figured that out on your own, as any cook knows that a recipe is but a ruler, not a micrometer.

Let your skewered, spiedinied chicken sit patiently on your cooking sheet and begin preparing the Amogio sauce. Peel your garlic cloves and chop to a fine dice. Don't use a garlic press; there is a profound difference in how garlic tastes and reacts to other ingredients when it is chopped versus pressed. Throw your finely diced garlic in a mixing bowl along with all of the other ingredients and stir the mixture gently with a spoon every so often. Don't whisk it, as you don't want to emulsify the lemon juice into the blend.

You can make the Amogio sauce the day before, but, needless to say, the longer it sits, the more potent it gets. If you do make it the day before, I'd leave out the freshly squeezed lemon juice, adding that closer to mealtime. Stir gently after adding the lemon juice.

Grill or griddle your chicken to doneness — and you have to be careful about this, as the rolled-up chicken will need to cook through, but be careful not to burn the crap out of the outer portion of the chicken in the process. Grilling is a skill not to be maligned, chided, or laughed at by those who don't practice the art but only eat the fruits of the hot iron grate. The first time we had the dish at the newly opened restaurant of the chef who had invented the recipe, the inner part of our spiedini was RAW — not undercooked but stark naked RAW! The waiter was flustered and actually said, "Uh, keep this quiet, and the tiramisu is on the house!" Mmmmm, raw chicken and tiramisu, one of my favorite Italian delights! What wine goes with that?

To plate, liberally spoon one-third cup of the Amogio on a plate, unskewer the properly grilled chicken onto the pool of sauce, top the chicken and rim the plate with a little finely chopped parsley, spoon another tablespoon or two of the remaining Amogio over the top of the chicken, and accompany with sides. I'd suggest a nice penne pasta with a light, slightly sweet marinara sauce as an accompaniment, as you'll want something all but bland to offset the punch in the nose you'll get from the Amogio sauce. Nicely prepared fresh green beans or broccoli will seal the meal.

Listen to some Sinatra and quaff some Chianti, or Amarone, if finances will allow.

CHAPTER SIXTEEN
The River Room: Part III

Dhoubi's exhaust fumes hadn't left the front parking lot of the hotel before Damien showed up with a replacement for Dhoubi. Her name was Carrie Trent, and she was as sweet as Steen's Cane Syrup.

Carrie had worked at restaurants all over Grand County and had even tried her own little pie/diner/café place. She was in the process of attempting to open another take-out-only place that would serve to-go breakfast and lunch, but, in the interim, would love to help us out by putting in a few hours here and there. Once again, I viewed her appearance at the doorstep of The Riverside as a serendipitous event. At the worst of it, if things went bad, I didn't see myself fearing for my life if I had to let her go, as was the case with my last chef.

Carrie was a baker extraordinaire; bread was her specialty and pies were a close second. The first day she was at the restaurant she whipped up about a dozen loaves of the most airy hard-crust baguettes imaginable this side of Paris. She finished the day with a few apple jalapeno pies for dessert — flaky crust and sweet apple cinnamon filling with just enough of a hint of a peppery attitude to let you know that this wasn't your mama's apple pie. Like Dhoubi's first day in the kitchen champagne cream sauce, I'd never had anything quite like it.

Carrie also helped do some of the food prep for Danny — mostly chopping, slicing, and dicing. What Carrie couldn't do — and what we needed the most — was to help Danny on the frontline during the dinner rush. So basically, to sum it up, Carrie would show up early afternoon, make all of the bread for the evening, and leave before the dinner rush when we really needed help. She would then give me a bill for her services for $300–$400 at the end of every week.

Have I mentioned previously that we gave bread away for free?

So here's the reality of the situation — here I was, nearly broke, paying someone $350 a week to make something that didn't make me one nickel. And it gets worse! As her bread was so awesomely good and free, people ate tons of it, creating the need for Carrie to spend more hours baking it for us. Those $350 labor bills were growing to $500–$600 per week. Couple this cost with the black olive tapenade spread that Danny spent thirty minutes every day making by the gallon, which accompanied this awesome bread, and I would estimate that I was spending $700–$800 per week in labor and materials on something that I gave away in unlimited quantities for absolutely free.

Have I mentioned previously that I went broke in the restaurant business?

Thankfully, Carrie left of her own accord to open her business, a successful one where she charged people money for the bread that she baked.

Carrie's last day was March 27th, 2009 — Easter Sunday brunch — our last day open before shutting the hotel down to take two weeks' vacation back to the Kansas City area. Waiting for us when we got back was a kitchen that we intended to gut, put in a new floor, and re-equip with up-to-code stainless steel prep tables, a new cold table, a new freezer, a new flattop, a new oven with a six-burner cook top, and new piping, plumbing, and electrical systems. Danny and I would dismantle and dispose of the old tables and equipment, and install the new tile floor; our handy friend Tony the Sober Plumber would do the plumbing and electrical; and Damien supplied all of the new tables and equipment, which he'd purchased at an auction in Denver.

Hopefully any of you who are potential restaurateurs have picked up this nugget of wisdom from reading about The River Room: You work your butt off when the restaurant is open, and you work your butt off even more when the restaurant is closed.

For the next six weeks we flat worked our butts off, our first chore being to dismantle the wooden work surfaces and shelving. Next we took apart and hauled off the 1920s-era god-awful piece of crap stove, oven, and flattop combination that was about the size and weight of a small locomotive and about as functional as a locomotive in a kitchen as well. Everything else was then moved out of the kitchen and we got on with tearing up three layers of old flooring: scraping up the top layer of 1980s asbestos-reinforced vinyl tile; pulling up the mostly rotted, moldy, one-quarter-inch plywood deck to which it was attached; then ripping up sheets of 1930s asphaltic linoleum that were tacked (and tacks were apparently plentiful, cheap, and really easy to hammer back then) to the original 1903 tongue and groove 1" x 4" wood floor. To this original floor we affixed, with screws, twenty-five 3' x 5' sheets of three-eighths-inch backer board (picture thin sheets of plywood made out of concrete). All of this was topped off by approximately 3300 hexagonal, industrial-grade ceramic floor tiles that were adhered with quick-curing epoxy onto the backer board. This was possibly the highest-end and highest-priced floor system you could purchase for a commercial kitchen. I received it for free from a friend in the business, an overage on a large food storage freezer job in New Mexico; it was cheaper for him to give it to me than to ship it back to Indiana. The net result was a floor that will probably still be intact after the wrecking ball and bulldozer have had their way with The Riverside.

The new equipment was then installed, and by the end of May, just in time for our Memorial Day weekend reopening, we had ourselves an honest-to-God functional and mostly up-to-code commercial kitchen. Only one thing was missing, and that was kitchen help for Chef Danny. Once again, who stepped up to the plate for us in the personnel department but our good friend Damien.

Damien placed an ad on craigslist: "Assistant Chef Position at historic hotel located in the beautiful Colorado Rockies. $10/hour plus room and board. Prior cooking experience required. Must pass drug test."

Even with economic times being what they were, Damien got very few hits on the ad (might have been that drug test requirement). But all he needed was one, and he did get one. A young man from the Great State of Alabama was in his 1974 Cadillac Sedan Deville and heading west to Colorado at the end of his three-minute phone interview (Red Flag!), ready and anxious to assist in the newly remodeled, almost up-to-code kitchen at The Riverside for ten bucks an hour and room and board at Damien's house, which Damien was kind to offer as he had the space and I'd made the stand that I didn't want employees living with us as it made the act of employment termination a tad messy.

Enter ... Chef Stinky Butt.

This poor guy had something seriously wrong with his intestinal tract that caused him to continually emit the foulest of foul BM odors with unheralded regularity. And to make matters worse, they were silent emissions. Without any noise to serve as a harbinger to the impending assault, you'd find yourself suddenly engulfed, overwhelmed, and olfactorily assaulted if you were anywhere within ten feet of the dude. The fact that he wouldn't profusely apologize after besmirching not only the immediate air but more than likely the ozone layer as well, told me he was possibly oblivious to his condition and certainly devoid of a sense of smell.

That wasn't the half of it. When Chef Poopy Pants used the facilities in the lobby to expunge his system of the viral monster that created the gas, he would clear the room. The first few times he did his business, before we knew what "doing his business" wrought, there would be me and whomever else — my spouse, Riverside employees, hotel guests — innocently occupying the lobby, and then WHAM! It was as if a lethal stink bomb, the kind they used in World War One in deadly combat, exploded and sent those assembled diving for the nearest exit. I AM NOT EXAGGERATING!

After those first few tear-inducing, eye-popping bowel movements, we knew to head for the fresh Colorado mountain air the second that he made a move for the commode door. How in the world did *he* live through it? Again, he absolutely had to have no sense of smell, nor, I'm certain, a sense of touch, as the heat from the act had to have been searingly intense.

On a positive note, he really didn't have any kitchen experience either. It turns out that the only thing he had cooked professionally was crystal meth on the summer concert festival circuit. And as far as being able to pass a drug test, he did that with flying colors. Ask him anything you'd want to know about drugs, illicit or otherwise, and he'd know all of the answers.

I will say this for the young man: He worked hard and gave it his all. But if hard work and giving it your all made you successful, I would be King of Hot Sulphur Springs, sitting riverside on a pile of gold. One week after arriving at The Riverside, Chef Poopy Pants was back in his beater of a car, heading to and fouling the air in parts unknown.

Damien, thank you for the new kitchen equipment, but no longer will you oversee human resources at The Riverside.

The final addition to The River Room staff, before we gave up the ghost at the end of 2009, was a friend of a friend who lived in Winter Park. Enter Chef Ryan, one massively large human being. Our friend played baseball with him in a recreational, all blood and guts, Sunday league (fast-pitch and serious hardball played by twenty-to-thirty-year-olds who were good enough to have played some small college ball). Ryan was the pitcher, and the sight of this seven-foot-tall human being on the mound with his wild hair, thick glasses, and control problems would put the bravest of hitters into the fetal position before stepping out of the dugout. This dude was huge! When looking through the food service window into the kitchen, you could see Chef Danny's torso and the lower half of his face; Chef Ryan, you could see only his stomach.

No funny stories or odd habits from Chef Ryan — he was big, quiet, and steady as a rock. He wasn't in Danny's league for being able to cook but was more than adequate in helping Danny put together stellar meals night after night.

After the personnel roller coaster ride in The River Room of the previous two years, in Danny we finally had a stable, able, and mostly sober employee who was willing to put his heart and soul into our kitchen, and he made the most of this opportunity. His menus were sophisticated but accessible to the type of clientele that lived in Grand County or would visit a historic hotel in an out-of-the-way locale. You didn't need a degree in ancient colloquial Italian to select an entrée. Herewith follows the final official menu of The River Room restaurant, courtesy of Chef Danny.

RIVER ROOM
Winter Menu, 2009

APPETIZERS

Wild Mushroom Bruschetta $8

A plate of our house made crostinis topped with black olive tapenade, shitake, oyster, and cremini mushrooms sautéed with garlic, fresh basil, and freshly squeezed lemon juice

Roasted Garlic Hummus $7

*A mixture of smashed chickpeas, roasted garlic, freshly squeezed lemon juice,
and spices, finished with a touch of black truffle oil, served with warm pita bread*

Smoked Salmon $9

*Fresh salmon, brined then slowly smoked over apple & cherry wood,
served with our house made crostinis, lemon wedges, capers and truffled aioli*

ENTRÉES

All entrées served with either a house salad or soup of the day.

Trout Almandine $20

*A filet of ruby red trout, pan seared, topped with sliced almonds and finished
with Triple Sec, served with Riverside mashed potatoes and seasonal vegetables*

Swai Jardinière $17

*A delicate white fish filet, pan seared with garlic, shallots, roasted tomatoes,
and fresh thyme, finished with white wine, fresh lemon juice, and a splash of cream,
served with Riverside mashed potatoes and seasonal vegetables*

Chicken Picatta $18

*A tenderized 6 oz. chicken breast, pan seared in butter with garlic, Capote capers,
and fresh thyme, deglazed with white wine, and finished with a splash of cream
and fresh lemon juice, served with Riverside mashed potatoes and seasonal vegetables*

Pork Chop with Port Sauce $21

*An 8 oz. bone-in sweet brined pork chop, pan-seared and finished with roasted shallot
raisin port sauce, served with Riverside mashed potatoes and seasonal vegetables*

Braised Lamb Shank $23

*A 20 oz. lamb shank, slowly braised and served fork-tender, set upon a
bed of Riverside mashed potatoes in a rich gravy, served with seasonal vegetables*

The Dirty Rib Eye $26

*A Riverside tradition, this 16 oz. cut of choice rib eye steak is cooked directly on a bed
of hardwood coals, sliced on the diagonal, and drizzled with a balsamic reduction,
served with Riverside mashed potatoes and seasonal vegetables*

DESSERTS

Crème Brûlée $7

*The classic French dessert custard, made with fresh cream and vanilla beans,
finished with a delicate layer of caramelized sugar*

Riverside Tiramisu $7

*A twist on the classic Italian dessert, made with fresh cream, mascarpone cheese,
marsala wine, fine-ground coffee, cocoa powder, and finished with
espresso- and brandy-dipped ladyfinger cookies*

Mocha Pot de Crème $7

*A French mousse, made with a mixture of chocolate, espresso,
rum, and cream, served chilled*

All of this wonderful food was prepared superbly and presented impeccably, with touches in taste and visuals that Danny had gleaned from his predecessors. To the end, broke and fighting heaven and earth for ways to pay the bills, we never compromised on quality or ingredients. As previously stated, we went belly-up but we did it with elegance, our chins held high. I can say this with all honesty and without bias, prejudice, or subjectivity: I still have a hard time finding a restaurant in The River Room's price range that equaled Danny's consistent output in our last few months of operation. This includes Kansas City, Mississippi, New Orleans, and a dozen other cities and restaurants that I've dined in during the past few years. As I taught him most everything he knew, I'm proud to report that Danny left The Riverside and, after knocking around Denver for a few months, wound up being Chef de Cuisine (second in charge) in one of Kansas City's finest restaurants, which led him to his current gig in the major leagues at a Michelin-starred restaurant in New York. And to think he cut his teeth in The River Room!

Our venture was categorically a financial failure, but my dream for what I envisioned in a restaurant was a rousing success, first and foremost in my mind, and also in the minds of most everyone else who dined with us, exclusive of a couple of nameless, raging jackasses. If I had a plethora of restaurant choices tonight, I would pay good money to eat one last time at Chef Danny's nearly up-to-code River Room Restaurant.

* * *

One constant with Christmas and me, be it Hot Sulphur Springs or Shawnee, Kansas, is the art of the feast. The menu has been unchanged for years: a standing rib roast on Christmas Eve, and Thanksgiving dinner redux on Christmas night. The standing rib roast recipe was also handed down by my father, and all of the prime ribs made at The Riverside were prepared in this fashion. Prime rib was our standard offering on all of our holiday and special-event meals: New Year's Eve, Valentine's Day, wedding meals, and large group dinners.

What makes this roast special (beyond the fact that you've just spent more than a hundred dollars on a piece of prime, marbled beef) is the panko-crunchy, garlic-laden, butter-infused outer layer. As this crust bakes and mingles with the marbled fat exterior of the roast, it takes on a life of its own, almost eclipsing the flavor and splendor of the smoky beef, kind of like finding cash inside of a gold nugget. By last count — I swear to God — we had eight full bore, dining-room conversions of vegans who jumped ship as they rediscovered the wonders of carnivorousness. It brought tears to my eyes watching the color return to their cheeks as the smiles resurfaced on the faces of these ill-humored, wan, sallow jicama junkies while they scarfed down these blood-rare bits of roasted goodness, shouting "Amen, brother!" and "Hallelujah sweet Jesus but this is tasty!" between mouthfuls.

Prime Rib for Vegans
(Serves eight — or four reformed vegans.)
One 4-bone prime rib roast (6–7 pounds)
½ cup Dijon mustard
1 stick unsalted butter
6 cups panko bread crumbs
8 cloves finely minced garlic
1 cup finely shredded Parmigiano Reggiano
3–4 healthy sprigs of fresh rosemary leaves, finely chopped
½ cup Kosher salt
¼ cup freshly ground coarse pepper

Melt the butter in a saucepan and whisk together with the Dijon mustard. Using a pastry brush, paint the exterior of the roast with the mixture until all is covered.

Mix all of the remaining ingredients in a large dish and roll the coated roast in the mixture until all is covered. This can be done early in the day, storing the roast uncovered in the refrigerator. (The "store in the refrigerator" part wasn't necessary at The Riverside, as room temperature was typically in the mid-40s.)

Preheat the oven to 500°F. Put the roast on a V-shaped roasting rack (they sell these at Walmart for six bucks) and put it in the oven for 30 minutes. This will sear and crunch-up the crust.

Reduce the heat to 300°F and slowly roast until the internal temperature hits 125°F — that's the high side of rare. Remove the roast, tent with foil, and let rest for thirty minutes. The roast will still be cooking, and the internal temperature should get to 135°F — medium rare — at the end of the resting period.

Slice to a thickness of ¾", serve with a Gruyère and Black Truffle Potato Gratin and a robust red wine, then stand back and watch whilst even the most strident of the anti-red-meat crowd quiver in anticipation before caving and succumbing to that which must be enjoyed.

ABOVE: *Riverside 1910* - *One of the earliest known pictures of the newly built Riverside Hotel & Livery Stable. The stable, with its turreted façade, is on the right side of the structure, and was originally built in 1867.*

ABOVE: *Kids on horseback* – *Another early picture, circa 1910, of some local cowpokes with the hotel in the background*

ABOVE: *Hot Sulphur Springs, 1918* - *A 1918 view of the town of Hot Sulphur taken from above town, from the road which leads to the Parshall Divide.*

LEFT: *Riverside, 1920*
This picture, taken in the 1920's, shows the hotel with one common façade, the livery stable going the way of the horse and buggy. With the high altitude winds we experienced with regularity, it is a mystery to me how they were able to secure that awning.

ABOVE: *Old Riverside dining room* – *The original narrow dining room, with attending staff.*

Omar Qualls – *The second owner and proprietor of the Riverside, Mr. Omar Qualls of Hot Springs, Arkansas, leans proudly in front of his newly purchased Brunswick Bar, seen in the back, left. The glass display cases upon which Mr. Qualls is leaning were still present and in use when we owned the hotel, as was that beautiful back bar.*

ABOVE: *1935 addition – Construction of the western-most addition to the hotel, which added four upstairs guestrooms, and doubled the size of the restaurant.*

ABOVE: *1935 Riverside dining room – The enlarged 1935 dining room with wait staff. The waitress on the far right is Margaret McLean, wife of US Ski Hall of Fame member and Hot Sulphur native, Barney McLean. We had the pleasure of knowing Ms. McLean during our ownership of the hotel.*

CHAPTER SEVENTEEN
Local Government

Hot Sulphur Springs, Colorado, is a little itty-bitty town situated halfway between two little bitty towns, Kremmling and Granby, on U.S. Highway 40. Both Kremmling and Granby are home to about 1500 people, while Hot Sulphur boasts a population one-third of that, with roughly 500 inhabitants. Other than being the county seat for the county of Grand, Hot Sulphur doesn't have a lot to offer beyond the hot springs; two diners, The Depot and The Glory Hole; one bar, The Barking Dog; a seasonal hamburger stand, The Dairy Dine; two motor court motels, The Canyon Motel and The Ute Trail; and an auto repair shop. Before the crash of 2008 there were also a gas station/convenience store, a liquor store/Laundromat/bait and tackle/DVD rental store all rolled into one, and a funeral home. Sadly, Acme Savings & Loan foreclosed upon all three of the latter businesses in 2010. Having that bank for a business partner was about as comforting as having a nest of asps in your pants.

Having a sparse population and few businesses leads to a serious problem that Hot Sulphur Springs has encountered: Such a tiny tax revenue base begets tiny tax revenues, which further begets a town that, while it does have a river to piss in, doesn't have a pot to piss in. It is virtually broke. I've been broke, and it is not a good way to be. It is an especially difficult situation when you are broke and the state's Department of Public Health and Environment tells you that you need to spend $2 million immediately to upgrade your water department and the associated infrastructure or they will shut off the water supply to the town. A small town may not need a funeral home or a DVD store, but it damn sure needs drinking and washing water. We sure needed water at The Riverside — in fact, our picky customers demanded it!

The town council of Hot Sulphur Springs, the brain trust that was charged with finding a solution to this dilemma, consisted of six members and the mayor, and met publicly on the third Tuesday of the month. I was sensitive to being critical of small-town public servants, as they donated their time and weren't able to profit from graft and perks like our public servants on the state and national level; however, the Hot Sulphur Springs town council's resolution to this cash crunch was ill-advised. No, that's not accurate — it was insane, idiotic, and borne of fools.

As it stood, everyone paid a flat fee for water without regard to usage, which was a bad practice as it didn't promote or reward conservation. The Hot Sulphur Springs homeowner paid a flat fee of $30 per month, regardless of the amount of water used or wasted. I don't know what other businesses paid, or how this sum was arrived at, but our water bill at The Riverside was $150 per month. I thought that fair, as we used a decent amount of water, what with a commercial kitchen and dishwasher and eight toilets, six showers, twenty-five sinks, and two washing machines.

In an effort to forestall the actions that were threatened by the state health department, the town council got together, most likely at The Barking Dog Pub, and came up with some sort of inexplicable formula for determining the new water rates, rates that would help them chip away at that $2 million water tab. Based upon I have no idea what, our monthly water bill was raised to $750, and we were billed quarterly, which meant that instead of having to come up with $450 every three months, I now had to come up with $2250. The rest of the businesses in town had to bear the brunt of this as well, as the town council, in its infinite wisdom, incorrectly assumed that if you had a business then it would follow that you had to have money somewhere, somehow. They had not the first inkling of the principle of cash flow, or of what cause and effect would be required to make up the delta between $450 and $2250 every quarter.

The homeowners were equally put upon by the council, as their bills arbitrarily went from $30 per month to $95 per month. There was out-and-out outrage in the community, and the best place to take the pulse of the community was at the monthly town council meeting, open to the tax-paying public. As a business owner, I felt it my duty to attend this particular meeting; it would be my first town council meeting and it would also be my last.

Imagine a small room in the small city hall, the town council at tables in the front facing an angry crowd of perhaps fifty Hot Sulphurites, the majority of whom were inebriated. What eventually made it even worse was the fact that we didn't get around to discussing the water issue until two hours into the meeting, nearing 9:00 p.m. This is important to note as now most of those who had on a pre-meeting buzz were now coming down from the clouds, and they were really grouchy.

After the mayor and the town council member who'd drawn the short straw in having to spearhead the water issue had their say, the crowd was quick to start harrumphing and a roomful of shaky hands shot into the air. The first to speak was Ed, one of the most serious of contenders for the title of Town Drunk. Many in the crowd were impressed when they noticed that Ed's pre-meeting buzz had yet to wear off.

A wobbly Ed slowly stood, steadied himself, and raised a clenched fist into the air. "Thish ish a absholute traveshty! What I wanna know ish whoosh reshponshible for getting ush in thish messh?" garbled Ed, who then all but fell back in his seat and promptly began to doze off before getting an answer.

Next up was a local businesswoman who was getting severely pounded by the blighted real estate market as well as getting severely pounded while dining with us every so often at The River Room. "There is no way I can come up with the additional sixty-five dollars a month," she said — the net result of the increase to homeowners. "Thirty dollars a month, maybe, but no way sixty-five." I quietly agreed with her, at least not if she was going to continue to be able to afford dinners and ten dollar Grey Goose martinis at The River Room.

On it went, one irate Hot Sulphurite after the other, each getting more inane than the next in trying to make a more salient point than the next, while all essentially saying the same thing, i.e., "This stinks; we're mad as hell, and we can't afford it! Oh, and we want this meeting to be over so we can get back to our bottles."

The best was saved for last, as one of the town's true characters stood before the crowd and paused dramatically, as if he were about to recite the Hot Sulphur Springs version of the Gettysburg Address. "My fellow townspeople," he began, "I understand the concerns about the rising price of water; I don't like it much either. But you gotta realize, we gotta do something to get all of the poisonous metals out of the water. They're not good for anybody, but that lead in the water really plays havoc with the metal plate that I got in my head during the Korean conflict. I know that's what's causing me to hear accordion music all the time." And then he began to laugh, low and slow at first, then building to a hysterical wail, all over the course of a very uncomfortable ten-second span.

The meeting was abruptly adjourned without any sort of resolution, and as it stood, all of the other businesses and I were left with the task of figuring out how we were going to pull a monetary rabbit out of the hat when those new water bills hit the mailbox.

Obviously those on the town council or whoever refigured this new rate had no concept of cash flow as it relates to running a business. That $600 a month increase translated to an additional 103 room rentals per year — and that was just to maintain our current levels of income versus expenses. Multiply that by five, which was the total number of hotels in town who would also have similar rate increases, and that required an additional 515 room nights spent in Hot Sulphur, with these increases needing to occur in a depressed economy where average bookings were down in 2008 by 40 percent. Even my infantile knowledge of business, cash flow, and the hotel industry told me that churning these numbers was an impossibility. It's a nice premise but, unfortunately, *wishing and hoping don't make it so!*

One of the town council members actually said, "If the business owners aren't smart enough to figure out how to come up with the extra revenue, they shouldn't be business owners." Smacks a little of Marie Antoinette's "Let them eat cake" attitude, doesn't it? It was my suggestion back to said town council person, "If you're smart enough to be on the town council, you'll be smart enough to figure out where to come up with all of the money you'll need to run this dump of a town when all of the tax-revenue generating, stupid business owners go belly-up!"

When the first round of elevated water bills hit our mailboxes in mid-July, the much discussed "what-ifs" became reality for all of the business owners, complete with an August 15th due date. One of the other problems with the increase was that the water bills were quarterly, so you needed to come up with three months' worth of $750, or $2250, all at once. That's a big unbudgeted check for a business struggling to meet payroll, buy supplies, and keep the lights on, especially when it's for water that flows by your business unabated at the average rate of 650 million gallons per day.

This spurred several of the business owners to band together for a meeting — not a town hall meeting but a meeting of business owners only — to discuss what could be done to stop this municipal cash grab from all of what the town council thought were the Hot Sulphur businesses' million-dollar war chests. I was informed that we were to meet on Wednesday night at 7:00 p.m. at the Barking Dog Pub. Unlike the last town meeting I attended, where the participants had to stoke up on hooch at home before spending the next few hours at the Hot Sulphur Springs town hall, the meeting planners decided to skip that formality and just have the meeting in the town bar. Anybody yet see a potential problem with that? Let's get a bunch of people together who are already fuming mad, put them within arm's reach of alcohol so they pound down brews before and during the meeting, and then have a heated argument. That should make for a productive evening.

When we entered the Barking Dog for the meeting there were only a few of the business owners present, and only two that I had previously met. There was one man whom I didn't recognize holding court down at the end of the bar. He was a tall, slim fellow made all the taller by his outlandishly conspicuous white cowboy hat — not a ten-gallon hat, but maybe a 7.5-gallon hat. He wore a gray tank top, the armpit areas of which were truncated with dark sweat stains. He was wildly waving his arms about as if he were below deck in a rolling sea swatting at bees.

Wait a minute ... it was Ron, the drunken plumber who tried unsuccessfully to unclog our pipes on New Year's night. What in the world was he doing here? What kind of a business did he own? I didn't know being the official Hot Sulphur Springs Town Drunk qualified someone as a business owner. Can Town Drunk be some sort of a new franchise opportunity I'm not aware of?

After a few inquiries I found that Ron was at the meeting not because he was a business owner but because he lived at the bar, and the meeting *was at the bar*. WHY IN THE HELL DID WE HAVE THE MEETING AT THE BAR? Perhaps that town council member was right after all to question the intelligence of the local business owners.

At about 7:30 p.m., when all of the owners had arrived, we ordered one more round for the discussion and moved from the bar to a large table to begin the meeting. Including Cowboy Hiccup, there were eleven participants at the table, representing three of the five hotels, owners of most of the town's apartment units, and the owner of the Barking Dog. The meeting started badly, as Ron the plumber was dominating the conversation with inane drunken babble about how he personally ran the water treatment plant for twenty years, and how he was the town's master plumber, and how everything in this town was screwed up, and blah blah blah blah blah. If any of this were in fact true, that certainly explained the current FUBAR status of the town's and The Riverside's water and plumbing.

After about five minutes of this, the meeting organizer asked that we limit our responses to two minutes and then suggested that we appoint a sergeant at arms in the event that participants got out of order. How many informal business meetings have you attended where the first order of business was to appoint a sergeant at arms?

We went around the table with everyone getting their two minutes to state their issues, offer solutions, ask questions, etc. Except everyone's two-minute allotment turned into five minutes as the Popped Plumber kept interrupting with his nonsensical blather, which would then bring the sergeant at arms around the table to shake a finger in his face and threaten to throw him out. Several times the sergeant actually grabbed Ron in a bear hug and tried to pull him out of his chair. Again I ask, ever seen this sort of thing in one of your neighborhood meetings? But then I don't suppose you have your meetings in a bar.

One of the apartment owners, a lovable old curmudgeon named Lou, barked so loudly that he scared the bejeezus out of all in attendance. But he was able to get Ron to shut up and then make the two most essential points of the evening's discussion, point one being that they should no longer officially refer to the town of Hot Sulphur Springs as the "county seat of Grand County"; rather, it should henceforth be known as the "toilet seat of Grand County." His second point, the highlight of the evening, involved the importance of water conservation and environmental stewardship, and he suggested a citizens' awareness campaign with a slogan of: "If it's yellow, let it mellow; if it's brown, flush it down!"

It was at this point that Julie and I excused ourselves from the proceedings and headed back to The Riverside. The end result of the group meeting was a decision to show a united front as business owners and write a formal letter to the town demanding to know specifics on forthcoming stimulus money, educating the council as to the catastrophic end this town would come to — on *their* watch — if they ran all of the businesses off, and, finally, a strong suggestion that all future town hall meetings be held at the Barking Dog and Ron the Plumber be installed on the town council as its voice of reason. He couldn't have done any worse and would have been a damn sight more entertaining while running a town meeting.

CHAPTER EIGHTEEN
Local Color

While Memorial Day is generally acknowledged to be the start of the summer season in the rest of the United States, Grand County waits until the second weekend of June to kick off the summer. The two prominent reasons for this two-week delay are: most Grand County schools aren't out until that second week in June, and, most importantly, more often than not it's still snowing on Memorial Day in Grand County, the snow and subfreezing temperatures making for very small opening-day crowds at the swimming pools and picnic grounds.

The second weekend in June is also home to "Hot Sulphur Days," a three-day festival to celebrate the town, its history, and its citizens current and past. These festivals are common to small-town America in the summer, and Hot Sulphur's line-up of activities reads like most other towns of its size: kiddy carnival rides, Friday night street dance, pie-baking contest, craft fair, softball games, pancake breakfast, Saturday night fireworks, etc. Unique to Hot Sulphur Days, and one of the weekend's highlights, held at high noon on Saturday a few short yards from The Riverside at the intersection of Grand and Aspen, is the reenactment of the Texas Charlie Shoot-out.

It is difficult to get to the real story behind Texas Charlie, as I've read several accounts of the incident all differing on some major details. What seems to be a common thread in the story is that 19-year-old Texas Charlie — Charles Wilson — came to the Hot Sulphur-Grand Lake area in 1880, most directly from Colorado Springs. It's not known if he actually was from Texas, but he most probably got the name from the oversized, white sombrero that he wore. He also carried a large knife with a deer-foot handle and two Colt .45 revolvers with gold nameplates inscribed "CW." His prowess with those revolvers was quick to become the stuff of legend in Grand

County, invoking fear in the local residents, as Charlie loved to play the role of bully and bad guy. In December of 1884, Charlie got into a gunfight with a local, W. L. Veatch, with Veatch getting shot in the shoulder. A warrant was sworn for the arrest of Texas Charlie, and when he was served with the papers, he tore them up and headed for the courthouse, located in a log cabin just across the street and up the hill from where The Riverside is now located. He intended to confront the local law, bragging that there wasn't a man in this town big enough to put him behind bars.

The locals had by this time had enough of Charlie, and much like the citizens of Skidmore, Missouri, did some 100 years later to Ken Rex McElroy by taking the law into their own hands, they quickly and quietly banded together in The Springs Hotel, and anonymously hidden behind the safety of the hotel's room windows, doors, and roof façades, gunned Charlie down as he walked across the street on his way to the courthouse. The stories vary from Charlie being shot by a single bullet to the extreme of fifteen guns blazing and hitting him multiple times. After an inquest into the shooting, the jury's verdict read: "We find that said C.W. Wilson came to his death by gunshot wounds at the hands of some person or persons to us unknown."

The annual reenactment of the Texas Charlie shoot-out that you'll see at every year's Hot Sulphur Days follows the single-shot theory, probably more for the fact that they can't find fifteen reenactors with fifteen guns shooting fifteen blanks than for the actual historical bent. It is a sight to see if for no other reason (actually, specifically for this reason) than it is amateur drama played out and hammed up at its best. You might see one or two of the participants decked out in period regalia; most of the others simply wear cowboy hats along with their Harley shirts and camouflage pants (a rather common clothing ensemble in Grand County). Most of the actors have a difficult time keeping a straight face. The crowd doesn't even try. After Charlie is "shot," his body is put on a pallet and he becomes the focal point in the Hot Sulphur Days parade; "Charlie" is required to lie lifeless (save the occasional wink and wave to friends and family) as he is carried along the parade route.

It goes without saying, but I'll say it anyway: Hot Sulphur Days and all of the fun and festivities could, to the erudite and overly educated visiting city dweller, be considered low-rent, small-town hokum. It also goes without saying that this low-rent, small-town hokum was another reason we gave up the grind and moved to a town like Hot Sulphur Springs.

* * *

Fred Wallace "Wally" Reynolds was our first official dinner customer at The Riverside. I say "official" in that the restaurant had been opened two previous nights as we catered to an influx of snow-stranded travelers who were waylaid at the hotel. Our first official opening night in the restaurant was New Year's Eve, 2008, and we didn't know when Wally walked through the door at 6:00 p.m. that a Grand County icon was in our presence. As Wally strode in with his daughter, son-in-law, and oxygen tank in tow, I could immediately tell by his purposeful gait that he knew where he was going and what he was after. He'd obviously been to The Riverside before.

Julie and I stood in the lobby and nervously greeted our first dinner guest. Wally asked, "What'd you do with Abner? Shoot him?" "No, we bought him out," was our proud reply. "You should've shot him," was Wally's response. I laughed at the thought at the time, but I now concur.

Wally's first dinner with us was a portent of dinners to come: difficult, mildly tense, and causing us to ask ourselves at what point do we throw the notion of "the customer is always right" under the bus. Wally ordered a Beefeater Gibson, which I liken to Nolan Ryan throwing a first-time big-league batter his spiciest curveball: Let's see what these new proprietors are made of. Did we have Beefeaters? Did we know what makes a Gibson a Gibson? Not only did Abner not stock Beefeaters Gin in his bar, he usually didn't even keep rot-gut gin around, and he damn sure didn't have cocktail onions for a Gibson. In fact, Abner's bar was stocked with a limited amount of the most god-awful, low-end hooch that you could imagine. A patron once ordered a scotch from Abner and asked, "What kind of scotch do you have?" Abner replied, "The kind that I'm going to bring you!" In other words, Abner knew that if the scotch drinker had actually heard of and known of this low-rent swill, he would've passed on the before-dinner cocktail and Abner would've missed out on six bucks.

Anyway, Wally got some gin — not Beefeaters — and no cocktail onions. He then suggested that if we wanted his continued patronage we had better get some Beefeaters and cocktail onions in the place. We did, and I bent over backwards to make sure that Wally had the best Gibson in Grand County when he dined at The Riverside. Julie made sure that Wally had company whenever he dined with us; she waited on him, traded barbs with him, sat and drank wine with him, and thoroughly enjoyed his company, all the while mining Wally's knowledge of local people and places to fill in the missing historical blanks of the town and the hotel. He became something of a regular during our first year; not only was he our first customer, he was also our best customer.

Grand County, Colorado, because of its altitude, its isolation, or the often brutal living conditions, is home to more than its fair share of characters, and Wally Reynolds stood out amongst them. Wally was as tough as they came, and not only was he not one to walk away from a fight, legend has it that he was also the one responsible for starting most of them. In his early years, he drove freight down to Denver and back for McLean Transportation, whose garage was located next to The Riverside. There were some rough places in Denver in the 1950s (as there probably still are today), and Barney McLean, one of the trucking company owner's sons and a U.S. skiing legend, commented that he wouldn't deliver or pick up freight in these areas unless he was accompanied by Wally, as nobody who knew Wally messed with him, and anybody who messed with Wally once never did it again.

Wally had a notorious hatred of hippies. As there was a disproportionately large influx of them into Grand County in the 60s (Does the phrase "Rocky Mountain High" ring a bell?), Wally had ample fodder on which to vent his ill will.

This is a true story.

Wally walked into a bar in Kremmling and saw a gentleman with a waist-long ponytail sitting at the bar with his back to the door. Wally walked back outside to his pickup truck, grabbed his hunting knife, and came back into the bar. Without saying a word, Wally walked up to the man, grabbed the ponytail, and cut it off, holding it up for all to see as proud as a conquering warrior on Last Stand Hill. Needless to say, the newly shorn bar patron wasn't as thrilled with the haircut as Wally was and stormed out of the bar. Wally sat down on the vacant bar stool and calmly ordered a drink, laughing a little at what he'd accomplished. The hot-tempered, short-haired hippie came back into the bar with a hatchet, and before anyone could react to the possibility of what might happen next, he cleaved Wally right in the center of his back with a blow that would have killed most men. It didn't kill Wally, but I believe it did slow him down enough to allow the hatchet-wielding hippie a hasty exit from both the bar and Grand County.

There's another story — less violent, more comic — about Wally walking into another bar in Kremmling during an early winter storm and asking loudly, "Who's the son of a bitch with the peace sign on his car?" The guilty hippie proudly and loudly fessed up, and the two headed outside for what turned into a badly performed boxing ballet on ice, both of them chasing and swinging at each other, neither to strike a solid blow as they kept slipping, sliding, and falling on the icy pavement, much to the delight of the bar patrons who'd assembled at the window to watch.

On January 16th, 2009, Wally came to The Riverside with friends to have dinner, but Julie and I were in Denver, on our way back from a visit to our home in Kansas City. Our daughter, Rachel, was minding the hotel in our absence and called, in hysterics, to say that Wally was having a heart attack in his car in front of the hotel. Damien was quick to come to Wally's aid, but even quick was too late. Wally died parked in front of The Riverside. His car sat there for the next few days as an empty reminder of his final visit.

When we attended Wally's memorial service in Kremmling a few days later, we learned of another side of Wally. There was a lot more to Wally than the larger-than-life, Gibson-drinking, hippie-hating, hell-raising cowboy that I've described. One after another, family and longtime friends and neighbors described a man with a heart as wide and strong as his roundhouse. Life can be hard in Grand County, and it's often tough to go it alone. Wally made sure that those he knew didn't have to; he was always there when they needed him — without hesitation, without a complaint. The list of those he helped included his country; Wally was a proud and decorated veteran of the Korean War. I'm certain every last one of his platoon mates were glad he was on their side.

We also found out that Wally was cheating on us. Every night of the week he was at a different bar or eating establishment, and at each place he had a special drink — it was CC and water at The Parshall Inn; margaritas at El Sambre in Kremmling. As he was a bachelor — three times married and three times divorced — and didn't cook for himself, he had to rely on the local eateries for his sustenance.

Wally was obviously not in good health, what with the oxygen tank that was always at his side and his worn and broken-down body being barely able to walk across the room. He'd told Julie that he had cancer and he didn't feel that he had too much time left. It was, in retrospect, maybe a bit of a good thing that he died in his car before beginning the fifteen-mile trek back to his home in Kremmling, as the first five miles of the journey snakes through Byers Canyon, and in January on snow-packed, icy roads, with sheer one-hundred-foot drops to the frozen Colorado River below, I shuddered to think of Wally coding out as he rounded a corner and flying into the canyon to ultimately be found by whom and who knows when.

We missed Wally after he died — his company, his cantankerousness, his stories of the old days, and his regular revenue — as I'm certain did the other restaurants that he frequented. While his passing was sad, it was also inevitable and swiftly and safely accomplished, and Julie and I considered it a badge of honor that this most colorful of locals, who single-handedly had done his best to keep the local food and beverage outlets in cash, had his last hurrah at The Historic Riverside Hotel, Bar & Restaurant.

* * *

The first ski jump in the United States was constructed on the southern hill over-looking Hot Sulphur Springs and The Riverside in 1911 by a transplanted Norwegian named Carl Howelsen. (Howelsen went on to build his next, and more famous, ski jump in Steamboat Springs in 1921, where The U.S. Olympic Ski Jump Team still trains on the hill that bears his name.) The lodgepole pines that blanket that hill are all now dead from the pine-beetle infestation, but it is still worth a long and enjoyable sunset gaze when compared to the relatively flat (yet not unbeautiful) suburban view of oaks, hickories, and two-story plat homes that we left behind in Shawnee, Kansas.

But the most prominent view from the front porch of The Riverside was our across-the-street neighbor's house, aka, Grandpa's. Grandpa lived in a 1960s ranch house on a half-acre lot, the dominant feature being two magnificent fifty-plus-year-old, forty-foot tall spruce trees that overshadowed the house and completely hid the property from the west, especially during the winter. However, they did not, from our unfettered southern vantage point, hide the exposed eastern yard, which contained a disabled 1986 Chevy K5 Blazer, couches and chairs that not too long before had displayed "Free" signs that this time didn't get a bite from the locals, several old buckboard wagon wheels, tires (not new), trash cans, yard furniture, an old chest of drawers, and the general demeanor of a trash heap. As badly as some may have thought Grandpa's yard looked when we owned the hotel, it was actually much less cluttered than when Abner owned the place.

Grandpa and Abner hated each other — this probably stemming from Abner's constant haranguing about all the junk in the yard. I'm certain this only pushed Grandpa to call family, friends, and neighbors in a quest to help him assemble the largest collection of useless and visually offensive odds and ends in Grand County. The town has no restrictions against using your property as a dump site, so what the heck — especially if it went towards as noble a cause as antagonizing Abner.

Some hotel guests suggested that we go to the town council about the blight and demand that Grandpa clean it up. Some even suggested that we buy Grandpa out, raze the house, and clean the place up. What would we have put there? A lemonade stand? An amusement park? A high-end mountain furniture/Native American art store? Quite frankly, Grandpa's house, yard, and the associated visual effluvium typified this town more than anything else that would come to reside in its stead. Grandpa's yard daily reminded us, and all of our visitors who got why they enjoyed coming here in the first place, that we'd truly left the grind behind. Much as you'd like to, you can't even attempt to get rid of your unwanted stuff in Boulder or Cherry Creek by putting it in your front yard with an attached "Free" sign, hoping that someone will value this thing more than you, pull up with a truck, and have it out of your life for the price of a cardboard sign and a Magic Marker.

Grandpa, whose given name was Harry — but NOBODY, not even his wife, called him Harry — moved to Hot Sulphur Springs in 1970 after retiring from the U.S. Army. He was the embodiment of the stereotypical old Colorado miner: small, wiry, stooped over, and long bearded; a pack mule and a pick axe would complete the picture to perfection.

Grandpa was a demolitions expert in the army and used that skill to work for the nearby Henderson Mine company, blowing holes in the Rocky Mountains in search of molybdenum. The gold and silver that brought fortune seekers to this brutal environment in the 1860s was long gone, with the mountains now yielding a much less glamorous treasure. Grandpa also had a brief career in the restaurant business, managing a group of small diners and hash houses around Grand County, and these experiences gave him the right to question and criticize the food that we put out of The Riverside kitchen. He brought us samples of concoctions that he'd cooked up — Three-Ingredient Chicken, Fried Bacon Poppers, Grandpa's Famous Beans, etc. — some appealing and edible, and some otherwise. When the ingredients were discernible, I'd sample his fare, but when they weren't (as in Three-Ingredient Chicken), I'd politely take his offering and tell him I'd try it later. Truth be known, Grandpa probably looked at some of our more eclectic menu offerings (Pan-Seared Swai with Arugula Pesto and Balsamic Reduction) and politely pulled the same "I'll try it later" stunt with me as I did with him.

In the summer Grandpa sat outside of his house, facing north and The Riverside, and sipped scotch and beer for most of the day. (In the winter, which started in mid-October in 2008, Grandpa hibernated. He didn't come out of the house for anything, ever. I hadn't seen him since October. Not once. I'm not kidding.) When we were out front working (sweeping, tending flowers, cleaning windows), he was always thoughtful enough to take the time to yell profane chides alluding to the fact that he was sitting in the shade sipping scotch and we were working our butts off. My occasional sit-downs with Grandpa always involved a recitation from him on the sorry state of the world in general, the utter worthlessness of most of the residents of Hot Sulphur Springs in particular, and the joys of being able to sit on your porch and sip scotch all day.

We all know and have seen lots of people who've worked hard all their lives and are now enjoying their golden years to varying degrees, but I've never known one to rub the deliciousness of total retirement in your face like Grandpa did. I admired him for that, as so many of those other retirees are still trying to figure things out, still trying to succeed at something or put one more dollar away out of either greed or need. Bluntly put, Grandpa didn't give a shit. He had two modes of existence — sitting outside sipping scotch in the summer, and sitting inside sipping scotch in the winter — and his level of contentedness was rarely approached by others and certainly not yet by me. My guess regarding the real motivating factor behind Grandpa's demeanor was that if you had spent your career down in a hole playing with dangerous explosives, and were able to walk away with a pension and all of your digits intact, you'd leave well enough alone, sit on your porch, and sip scotch all day. And you'd do it in a place like Hot Sulphur Springs.

CHAPTER NINETEEN
The Colorado River

It was May 8th, 2009, and I was looking out of our dining room window at the Colorado River. The sun was setting behind Mt. Bross, and the river glowed, as if Hollywood's higher technical powers had grabbed hold of it. I knew that when gazing upon this iconic river of rivers — one that ranks with the Nile, the Amazon, and the Mississippi, not because of its size or length but because of what it has wrought, namely the Grand Canyon, as well as its being the aorta for the American West — I was viewing, from my dining room, a living, flowing entity about which songs were composed, books were written, and from which our history was forged. Imagine that; we lived on a piece of land — which was for a short while our property — that John Wesley Powell, Kit Carson, John Fremont, and numerous other historical luminaries had paddled by and camped upon, not to mention the Native American tribes, particularly the Ute Indians, who'd called this area home for four thousand years. I acknowledged that I was blessed to be here but was also humbled enough to realize that I'd never be a speck of what makes this ground relevant to human history.

When I think about living on the banks of the glorious Colorado River, it is more than just a little awe-inspiring, as civilization was built on and around rivers. Most of our great cities are built on rivers, and these rivers are our lore, our past, our present, and our future. They are more famous and more vital to our survival than mountains, buildings, streets, cities, and people. A river is why Paris and London will remain a world destination, and the lack of a river is why Los Angeles or Houston will never be anything more than a population center. Here's the A-list river roll call — Seine, Danube, Thames, Ganges, Zambezi, Congo, Rhine, Rhone,

Rio Grande, Indus, Volga, Niagara, Yangtze, Amazon, Nile, Mississippi, Missouri, and Colorado. I might have missed one, but not the one that I lived upon, owned land akin to, and into which I occasionally peed.

The Riverside Hotel is possibly the oldest existing nonagricultural business on the Colorado River. The fact that for a short while I owned that little piece of history still puts a lump in my throat. By the time we'd moved in full time to The Riverside in June of 2008, the river had thawed and was flowing freely. In 2009, our first winter and spring living on the Colorado, it was also my first time of seeing the river frozen, then thawing, then flowing, then bursting and roiling. I will liken the witnessing of the transformation of the Colorado River from solid to liquid as experiencing the grandeur, spectacle, wonder, and awe of seeing fireworks as a child for the first time. Out of my kitchen window, I watched daily as this thirty-yard wide, snow covered, and dormant piece of river turned into a boiling, rushing, and violent living thing that popped, cracked, and screamed its way into a new season. It was an "Aha!" answer to my question: Why did we give up what we had to move to a place like this? One answer: To witness the once-in-a-lifetime liquid fireworks show that lasted for the better part of a month. Two-hundred yards south of what was our river property, the Colorado bends at a ninety-degree western dogleg and then S-curves another three or four times until it flows into Byers Canyon. At the height of its spring thaw, at that first bend south of our property, the river thrashed and railed like a whitecapped sea, not accepting of the fly fishermen who typically probed its languid pools during the summer months. In its spring-thaw state, no caddis, no midge, no wooly bugger would find respite in this tumultuous stew, nor would a hungry trout have the strength to indulge.

It was my first, and sadly it was to be my last, spring gaze upon the seasonal transmogrification of the Colorado. As that was the case, I can say that I witnessed a sight so spectacular and significant that it will be remembered and cherished like the first view of my newborn children, or the first glimpse of my beautiful wife. It will forever be as essential to my being as water.

If you have the chance, if even it's for a short while, live on a river.

* * *

It was Saturday afternoon, June 6th, 2009, and I was walking our border col-lie-corgi mix of a beautiful yet funny looking rescue mutt, Lucy, along the south river road, where we would eventually turn west and begin the slow 1000-foot ascent up the Parshall Divide. It is a fabulous walk, one that takes you on mild switchbacks past open-range cattle fields, up through heavy pine forests, and even-tually onto a vast, treeless plain that overlooks Byers Canyon and the Colorado River. The plain is blanketed in the summer with golden lupine, yellow daisies, bluebells, and fire-orange devil's paintbrush. The climb sucked your breath away, and then the view at the top rendered you speechless. I loved living there.

New to me that day on a walk that I took quite regularly was what seemed an inordinate amount of people fishing the Colorado. They weren't the usual genteel, split-cane rod, Orvis wader-clad crowd that usually flicked and pecked at this sec-tion of river. They were, well, a little rough, rougher than I'd ever seen fishing the Colorado. I felt for a moment that I was back in Missouri, down on an Ozark trib-utary watching locals angle for mud-feeding blue catfish with a large rod, a larger reel, and a treble hook full of stink bait. I walked past one of these anglers and was impressed by his fighting what appeared to be a very large fish that he had hooked downstream, as I'd seen many of the aforementioned classical fly fishermen do nothing more than go through the motions — cast, retrieve, cast, retrieve — with rarely a trophy to be had. Further downstream I witnessed another fisherman who was hard at landing what appeared to be a huge fish that he'd hooked upstream. 'Wow,' I thought; I saw fly fisherman by the hundreds who did nothing but dab their dry flies at this water, never to fight, never to land, and here were two of the most unlikeliest-looking trout fisherman fighting trophy fish within twenty yards of each other.

Lucy's reticence to progress on our walk, and her insistence at sniffing the riv-erbank black sage, allowed me the opportunity to watch both of these anglers land their respective catches. Except neither had hooked a trout; rather, they'd hooked each other's weighted night crawler rigs and were now cursing each other back and forth, engaged in a heated piscatorial pissing contest. I then noticed that the upstream fisherman had a serious pile of empty Rainier beer cans at his feet, while the downstream fisherman had a 1.75-liter bottle (in Grand County it's referred to as an "week-ender") of Seagram's 7 resting at the base of his folding chair. My mind suddenly clicked onto the realization that the first weekend in June was "Free Fishing Weekend" in Colorado, i.e., "no fishing license necessary weekend," a weekend that apparently tends to bring out a different and less-refined crowd to the banks of this storied waterway.

This got me to thinking. The week following Free Fishin' Days is Hot Sulphur Springs Days — which is just a bit of a redneck fest. Hot Sulphur Springs Days is followed the next weekend by Kremmling Days — Kremmling being the next major town west of Hot Sulphur Springs. Kremmling is lovingly referred to by many in Grand County as "Kremtucky." I'm not entirely sure why, except that it might have something to do with the shooting, hunting, drinking, and cross-pollination habits of many of the town's constituents.

Trout fishing on the Colorado isn't the only outdoor pursuit that brings sportsmen from all over the world to Middle Park; deer, elk, and moose hunting are all but a religion in Grand County. Ergo, another "oh, by the way," funny little thing about our neighborhood involved a stretch of state land between Hot Sulphur and Kremmling — the largest state-maintained shooting range in Colorado, a veritable Candy Land for gun-toting, trigger-happy Coloradans. This thing stretches on for a full half-mile — plenty of parking spots for the Ford F-150s, and endless racks for the hanging of torso targets, paper enemies just waiting to be obliterated by Coloradans armed with the firepower necessary to make continual hay upon these faceless phantoms. These were my neighbors and, like the view from atop the Parshall Divide, I loved them, in spite of the fact that they rarely spent a plugged nickel in my establishment.

Being the natural-born entrepreneur and marketer that I was, my thoughts ran to developing a big, weeklong, start of the summer Grand County festival involving free fishing, the two city historical celebrations, alcohol, and guns. Let's be honest with ourselves, Grand Countians! Hot Sulphur Springs Days and Kremmling Days are nice, and usually well attended by the locals, but if you want to make a big splash and draw not only people from Grand County and the Front Range but also people from all over the U.S. — nay, I say, from all over the world — you'd combine all that Grand County has to offer, throw in the booze and Beretta factor, and you've got the potential for a genuine Redneck Woodstock.

Just imagine it! At Hot Sulphur Days they have a couple of crafts booths, a Hot Sulphur Chamber of Commerce booth, and some local churches selling hot dogs, kettle corn, and kiddy face painting. Nice, but where is the maximum benefit for the city and the county in a deal like that? Just imagine it! In my vision of what could be for the "Fish, Shoot & Swill Fest" in Grand County, picture Mr. Jack Daniel himself putting on a big old soiree right next to the Remington Shotgun booth, across the way from the Seagram's tent, around the corner from the Ruger .44 Magnum exhibit, which happens to be next to the Bacardi & Coke Pavilion — light on the Coke, please.

Face painting? Nice, but we'll go that one better with the Hustler Body-Painting Contest. Kiddy carnival rides? Sure, we've got those, but how about muddin' over the Parshall Divide in a monster Dodge Ram 4 x 4 while you're blasting away at off-season trophy elk with an AA-12 Super-Auto shotgun?

It would have meant big food, beverage, and lodging revenues for all of the merchants in Hot Sulphur Springs, not to mention a long-term financial boon to all of the vendors who would be able to build a lifelong customer base right here in the heart of guns and guzzle country. Local taxidermists could've gotten fat as well. The county probably would have generated enough extra revenue from the festival week's DUI convictions that they could have afforded to pay their fair share of the Hot Sulphur water bill.

The only downside I could see was that the county might have had to budget for bringing in some extra EMTs from neighboring counties. We might have also needed some Centers for Disease Control people to help clean the hot springs pools. However, those potential downsides would have been but a small price to pay for having "Fish, Shoot & Swill" become a part of our national lexicon.

Sadly for The Riverside and the other Grand County businesses, our premature departure from Grand County never allowed me the opportunity to see this dream of a worldwide event, an event that would have rivaled the Hot Sulphur Springs Winter Carnivals of old, through to fruition. Alas, "Fish, Shoot & Swill" was tossed upon the scrapheap of a hundred other dreams that never materialized for us, along with the dreams of wealth, dreams of fame, and dreams of simple contentment.

CHAPTER TWENTY

The Hot Springs

Central to the establishment of Grand County, the town of Hot Sulphur Springs, and ultimately The Riverside Hotel, Bar & Restaurant was an eternal geothermal pool of 300°F water, boiling and steaming under intense pressure more than a mile beneath the earth's surface, which for untold centuries at a steady rate of two hundred thousand gallons per day had been fighting its way upward to a small fissure at the surface. This fissure is located roughly smack dab in the middle of Middle Park, Colorado. Water wrought in the fires of hell and exposed to unimaginable pressures and forces ultimately ended up providing respite to the visitors of this verdant valley, this earthly paradise.

Sources say that millions of years ago the Colorado River valley that holds the town of Hot Sulphur Springs in its protective hands was a violent, exploding cacophony of molten lava, sulphurous fire, and poisonous gases, with massive jagged boulders hurtling through the air like wayward missiles, only far more deadly. Riding herd over this grand opera of hellfire and brimstone was mighty Mt. Bross, at that time not the peaceful, slumbering slug of a mountain that it is today but an active volcano, at times unleashing a fury at the surrounding area that can only be imagined, as no one would have survived witnessing the actual experience.

All of this ancient seismic activity has now distilled itself down to a single pool, the actual size and depth of which is still specifically unknown, that is percolating gently (especially compared to its prior self), comfortably, and profitably under the property of Mr. and Mrs. Sunil Guptha, owners and proprietors of the Hot Sulphur Springs Resort & Spa.

Following is a review of the Hot Sulphur Springs Resort & Spa posted in March of 2012 on TripAdvisor, an online travel site. (Grammatical and spelling errors have been left intact in all reviews quoted.) This is a five-star — out of five stars — review.

> *Nice and clean room. The train woke me up like 4 times at night but I went right back to sleep, didn't bother me at all. I actually like watching trains. I would stay here again. We paid $118/ night including tax and the pass to the pools for the day of check-in and check-out for both of us. The pools were great and the staff were friendly. My personal favorite was the Ute pool (I think that's how it was called) with the fountain. It has a small cave to the right of the fountain if you are facing it. The temperature in that cave is the hottest of all the pools. So I loved it! I would recommend exploring all the pools with their locations and temperatures in the daylight because they don't have the map of the pools. We did that on the second of our 3 days and we found a very neat pool from which you can see the passing train. That was fun. There is also a magnesium pool in the building with the lockers. The lockers by the way are 50 cents for every time you open them or you can bring your own and use it. The towels are $2 or bring your own. Also, some people had robs on which I think was really helpful in winter. It was cold to run from on pool to the other. Eventually the robs and the towels freeze and stiffen and you can't use them anyways. I would not take your best bathing suit because the smell stays after washing.*

I'm thinking that robes would keep you warmer than robs, but that's just me.

* * *

Much of the historical information contained in this book was gleaned from the definitive tome on the history of Grand County, *Island in the Rockies: The History of Grand County, Colorado, to 1930*, faithfully written by Robert C. Black

III and published in 1969 for the Grand County Pioneer Society by Pruett Publishing Company. The sulphur springs were central to the formation of civilization in Grand County, and they are equally the central theme of Mr. Black's book. Every bit of growth or progress in Grand County seems to begin at the springs, located in the center of the county, and spokes out from this hub to the rest of Middle Park.

Robert Black sets the known human origins of Middle Park to "during the warm phase of the 'post-Pleistocene' (about 4,000 B.C. to about 2,000 B.C.)." The volcanoes were gone, and it was probably colder than a Swedish hermit, so it was only natural that the early inhabitants of the region would be drawn to warm water, not only for drink but also for relief from the brutally cold Middle-Park winters. It would also follow that the animals of the park would seek out the water and the warmth as well. It was a match made in heaven — water, warmth, and an endless supply of food for the party with the best weapons.

This love affair with the springs continued for the next four thousand years, the principle benefactors of the warm, healing waters and the ensuing faunal banquet being the Ute Indians, who traveled from their native region (what is now Utah) during the winter to take up residence some two-hundred-plus miles from their dry, frozen home to the hot, sulphur springs and the resultant supply of winter water and fodder. This sulphurous nirvana, this place of warmth and wellness, was considered sacred ground to the Utes, and well it should have been, as it no doubt kept generations alive through the vicious Rocky-Mountain winters, winters that still try the souls of current inhabitants, those with creature comforts unimagined to the Utes and all others who trod these hills from time immemorial.

* * *

It wasn't warmth, water, or food that brought Mr. Guptha and his wife, Rahji, to this mountain magnet, this eternal source of life and divine largesse. Nor was it an altruistic or spiritual mission — the desire to tie into this historical font of healing and well-being for four thousand years' worth of preceding generations. No, it was cash money, the same cash money that had my wife and me stumbling blindly up the mountains into this town and towards these springs.

The Guptha's, some fifty-plus years of age, were both immigrants from Pakistan, moving first to San Francisco, then to Denver. Sunil met Rahji in 1979, and in 1980 they married and, with Rahji's dowry, bought a few liquor stores along Denver's notorious Colfax Avenue. Betting on success in the liquor business in Colorado is as certain as betting that the sun will eventually set. The Guptha's hit it big, parlaying the profits of two liquor stores into four liquor stores, then six liquor stores, and finally ten liquor stores — all low-rent places in bad neighborhoods, selling mostly malt liquor, MD 20/20, and rolling papers. No money was spent inventorying Petrus Bordeaux or Johnnie Walker Blue Label as that wasn't on their preferred clienteles' radar.

In 2003 the Gupthas decided that they'd had enough of being the alcohol slumlords of West Colfax Avenue and put the stores up for sale. They quickly had a line begging to buy them and sold them all in a flash for a serious pile of money. They next aspired to a peaceful existence in the mountains, away from the bustle of Denver's seedy heart, and with but a little coaxing from an anxious real estate agent and the current owner, settled upon the acquisition of the Hot Sulphur Springs Resort & Spa as their next cash cow.

Here is another TripAdvisor review for the place, this one also five stars out of five, entitled "Fun Evening!" from November of 2011:

> After reading many negative reviews on all hot springs within driving distance of Denver we went with this as it was the closest. We had a great time! It was 12 degrees and snow on the ground at about 6pm when we got there. Not crowded, friendly staff, and great pools. We actually loved the train! There is a small isolated pool when you are directly across from the track. We stayed there for almost an hour just waiting to see a train. Wouldn't you know, 2 minutes after we change pools we heard the train! It would have been really neat to watch it go by while laying in the isolated pool.
>
> We spent most of the time in pools by ourselves because there were so many pools and not many people. Maybe it was the time of year, but we wouldn't have needed to pay for a private pool. It was a great experience! Next time we want to go for a few days and stay in the cabin, from the outside it looks really cute and would be a fun weekend trip with friends.

* * *

The hot springs and the surrounding grounds were purchased by William Byers in 1863, but the first commercial structure wasn't built until some forty years later at the turn of the century. As mentioned previously, this roughly coincides with the construction of The Riverside. The springs and the area brought tourism to Grand County, which included the immensely popular Winter Carnival, the first one occurring in 1912. It was reported that as many as twenty-five thousand people crammed into the valley to celebrate the skis, cold, and snow that to this day are celebrated by millions of annual visitors to Colorado, albeit in tonier mountain towns like Aspen and Vail. In the 1920s a large bathhouse was constructed — wooden and resembling nothing like the marble palaces that you find in Hot Springs, Arkansas. The building was still standing yet was shut down, having been abandoned in the mid-1970s, when we made our first venture to Hot Sulphur Springs in the summer of 1993. Sitting silent and boarded-up, and continually deteriorating against the foot of Mt. Bross, the bathhouse had an intensely high creepy factor, even in broad daylight. That foreboding was amped-up all the more when passing on our moonlit strolls along the railroad tracks and the adjacent Colorado River, the distant barks and yelps of the coyotes adding to the otherworldly aura.

In 1996 a local mover and shaker, Charles Nash, bought the springs and demolished the existing structure, replacing it with the current iteration, the central feature of which is a log cabin/Swiss Chalet-looking building that houses the entryway, offices, massage rooms, and two private hot spring pools. Once you exit the main building, you wander along a series of concrete walkways to twenty other pools of various sizes and temperatures, most being small two-person fiberglass tubs that were culled from backyard saunas gone badly. The crown jewel of the property is dubbed the "Ute Pool" and is large enough for ten soakers. It's about four feet deep and has a small waterfall that pours into the pool from the surrounding rocks above, resembling a small grotto, a kind of "Lourdes" for the Boulder agnostics.

None of the twenty-three pools are natural in that the natural spring water is harnessed at its single point of entry from below, collected in a central pool, and pumped to the other pools, all of which were man-made and placed there by

Charles when he remodeled in 1996. Also included in the complex is a swimming pool with a slide, containing not spring water but chlorinated fresh water, which is open only during the short summer season.

The hotel structure of the hot springs resort is a separate building, a long rectangle made of cinder block that looks as if it were built in the early 1940s for single-residence housing on an army base. It is anything but quaint. I never went into one of the rooms, but I'm told they were small with cold linoleum floors, void of any decoration or personality, and austere beyond the standards of a monastery, with showers that would cause a small child to cramp when turning around in them and toilets that were in a tiny room with no door. I've been told by some that possibly there are minimum security Federal prisons with swankier accommodations.

And then there is the infamous "1840s Cabin," a single-room log cabin on a hill overlooking the complex, accessible only by a lengthy run of wooden steps. This cabin is notorious amongst the locals for being absolutely, positively, and sometimes violently haunted. Too many disparate people have told about similar incidents of haunting and experienced the same frightful traumas for there not to be some truth to the stories.

As you cross the train tracks and enter the hot springs complex, there is a welcoming sign that states in bold letters: QUIET ZONE. NO ALCOHOL. NO SMOKING. NO PETS. It pretty much sets the tone for the visit.

This TripAdvisor reviewer eloquently sums up the opinions of the vast majority of reviews on the Hot Sulphur Springs Resort & Spa. Dated January 23rd of 2011, with a one-star rating, it is entitled, "Worst place I've ever stayed."

> *My fiancé and I rented the cabin on the hill. We were intrigued by the fireplace and thought the complimentary Champagne might be a nice post-soak treat.*
>
> *When we checked in, we were greeted by one of the rudest women imaginable. She treated us like garbage, despite the fact that we were renting the most expensive room the hotel had to offer. After this terribly unpleasant check-in, we went up to the cabin to get settled.*

To be fair, the cabin was quite clean. However, the Champagne turned out to be a complete joke: two half-liter bottles of no-name sparkling wine. There were also several small, but important, details of the cabin that were overlooked. For example, the lighter they provided to start the fire was out of fluid and the bed was made such that the tags on the corner of the duvet were at the face instead of the feet. How hard could it be to get these details sorted? In addition to these small things, the cabin creaked and moaned all night long, which, in addition to the train going by, made for a terrible night's sleep.

The pools themselves were alright, but the locker rooms were disgusting, with slimy and moldy floors. Despite this, the hotel charges extra for sandals — even if you're renting a room. Ridiculous.

The town shuts down at 9pm and even before then it has very little to offer. We ordered dinner from "The Depot," which turned out to be of extremely low quality, although we were served by one of the kindest meth-heads I've ever met, so that was a plus. Kind of.

All in all, this is the worst place I've ever stayed. And I've stayed in some bad places. Like, bad for 3rd-world countries bad. And this place is worse. Do not, for any reason, patronize this establishment.

* * *

During our two-and-a-half-year tenure as owners and proprietors of The Riverside Hotel, located adjacent to the trout-laden Colorado River, I fished only once. And I love to fish. When the weather was good for fishing, I never had the time to fish. Only during the dead of winter, with three feet of ice and snow on the river and no guests in the hotel, did I have time to fish — something like a cruel twist of fate.

While I fished only once, that is one more time than I soaked in the hot springs, they being but a long stone's throw across the river from our establishment and open 365 days per year, including the time when the river was frozen and fishing was out of the question. There was a variety of reasons behind this blatant gap in our being well-rounded citizens of Hot Sulphur Springs: lack of time and lack of money, but most importantly, a profound lack of interest.

While I stated that we'd not once been to the springs as owners of The Riverside, we did visit the springs as tourists during one of our late 1990s Christmas visits. The place had just been newly remodeled but already the men's locker room had a collection of mold, mildew, and gelatinous who-knows-what on the carpeted floor. I couldn't scream "ICKY" and "EWWW" loudly enough.

And then there were the pools themselves. If you could get beyond the smell — imagine sticking your head in a box in which someone had just simultaneously struck a thousand matches for the purpose of cooking the dozen rotten eggs also contained within — you would then be put off by the white scummy stuff that floated on the surface and glommed onto your skin as you exited the water. When I asked what on earth this unidentifiable nasty stuff was and could they clean it up, I was told simply, "That's the minerals." Again, I have to counter that claim with a hale and hearty, "ICKY" and "EWWW." Couple this with the fact that after you have soaked in the springs, you, your hair, and any article of clothing that you wore to and from the spa smell as if you've been an important cast member in the campfire scene of *Blazing Saddles*. Come home and put those clothes in the washing machine, and every other piece of clothing that you put in with the tainted hot sulphur clothes ends up smelling like Beelzebub's ass, and I'm not referring to his pet donkey.

I'm aware of the fact that I was raised in the middle of the country, in the state of Kansas, in the county of Johnson — a place that defines the ultimate vanilla existence. I am in the minority when it comes to understanding and appreciating the joys of sitting in a mineral-lading pool of hot, sulphurous, and floogisma-laden water. Coloradans, Europeans, and many of those in between thronged to the town for that water, that smell, and those white, scummy floating minerals, as did the Utes from centuries before. Secondary to most of them was a gourmet meal, a stout pour from the bar, and a quaint room without a private bathroom, all of which we offered but was not accepted often enough for our survival.

* * *

And finally from our friends at TripAdvisor, this one-star review from September 16th, 2008, written during our tenure as owners of The Riverside, while offering props for our efforts, did little to forestall our inevitable downfall.

"Horrible Experience! So much for a RELAXING spa!"

The owners are terrible! Extremely rude, loud and obnoxious even though they want quiet. Came for a relaxing spa treatment and left crying. Mrs [Guptha] would not let me pay with credit cards, even though they accept them. Her employees were embarrassed as was I, considering she yelled at me and told me that I had to pay cash to her right away or I couldn't have my treatment. Then she yelled at me that this was a holiday weekend so no discounts. She then proceeded to yell at other customers as well! They couldn't even get a tour of the place before they decided if they wanted to stay all day. Mr and Mrs [Guptha] provide no water, cheap towels and absolutely NO customer service. In fact, while I was there, a therapist quit because of the rude treatment he received. Their staff was as accomodating as possible but I would not recommend going there ever! On the other hand you can go to The Riverside Hotel and receive excellent service, quiet rooms that face the Colorado River and outstanding meals! So worth the trip to Hot Sulphur for that reason alone.

While our classy, quaint little venture went belly-up, the Hot Sulphur Spring Resort & Spa endures, as it has for the past million or so years, in spite of the foibles of Mr. and Mrs. Guptha. Apparently that which has always been is meant to be — filthy floors, cantankerous owners, and fetid water be damned. C'est la vie!

CHAPTER TWENTY-ONE

More Paying Customers

I come from Kansas, a languid little piece of flyover country. We're a bit behind the socioecological curve and, for the most part, prefer it to be that way. When I moved to Colorado, the state that houses the city of Boulder, without knowing or asking for it, I immediately upgraded to a place that was way ahead of that curve. For example, in Kansas, going to the bathroom and emitting bodily waste is hopefully a regular part of daily existence; how passé. I learned, however, that in some parts of Colorado, defecation is considered "ungreen" and an affront to the environment, fouling the soil and releasing excessive amounts of ozone-depleting methane, and those who are truly sensitive to our mother, Earth, hold it in out of respect for the planet. Perhaps that is why many of them are so full of shit. (Sorry; I couldn't resist.)

I stumbled onto several concepts in Colorado that were heretofore unknown to this Midwestern, suburban boor. A prime example of being a few yards short of a well-rounded mile was my not knowing of the condition of being "gluten intolerant." Shortly after we arrived in Colorado, I was given a graduate-level primer course on not only what gluten is but also that there are those who are intolerant of it, and I was dumbfounded by the subject matter. Basically, no grains or grain products of any type — no wheat, barley, rye, oats, nor pasta — can be ingested. How do you survive in this world without being able to eat bread and pasta? Does this also mean no beer?

Another new reality to me, one that I didn't run across living on the desolate plains of Shawnee, Kansas, was that there actually exists the certified and paid profession of "Life Coach." A life coach? How in the world did society advance to its current iteration without the aid of this profession? And isn't that the role of a parent, a spouse, a sibling, a boss, a teacher, or a friend? I soon learned that possibly there are those who had no parents, no spouses, no siblings, no bosses, no teachers or no friends to coach them, and, by God, these individuals needed to be coached. Fortunately for them, there now exists a cash-only solution for that.

We entertained a group of ten people for dinner who had signed up with a Certified Life Coach for a mountain weekend of life coaching. They paid $1000 for the two-day experience. This fact alone told me that they did indeed need some sort of coaching — maybe financial-responsibility coaching, and certainly common-sense coaching. As the group entered our establishment, I thought about having the life coach arrested. Taking money from these people for needing to be life coached was no different than a professional pickpocket hosting a cash-only vacation to Las Vegas for a bunch of blind billionaires who'd also lost their sense of touch. A more obviously dysfunctional group I'd never seen. Again, that probably explained why these individuals felt they needed coaching. My guess is that if you think you need a life coach, you probably do.

I explained to the assembled group that we'd be having a set small-course menu, including a salad, a gluten-laden ravioli appetizer, a fish dish, and Smoked Chicken Penne Pasta with Vodka Cream Sauce. Immediately half of the group fidgeted noticeably and murmured amongst themselves. One member finally stood up and said, "Some of us don't drink, and we'd prefer to not have vodka in our sauce!" I assured them that the vodka is cooked off in the preparation and that there is absolutely zero alcohol content in the final sauce. Their collective bodily shaking and continual looking back and forth at each other for support told me that the vodka was still an issue, so I then assured them that they'd have no vodka in their sauce, cooked off or otherwise.

The group sat for dinner, and to describe them as an eclectic mix would shame any other group that would want to be described as an eclectic mix. We had women who you might see working at the Clinique counter at Nordstrom, and we had women you might witness lustfully putting an axe to the Clinique counter at Nordstrom. There was a young, shy, heavily tattooed Goth girl that weighed maybe eighty pounds, and another woman who could have been a high-round NFL draft pick for linebacker. You'd have made the Goth girl jump through the roof if you had said "Boo" to her; the lady linebacker would have thrown you through the roof if you'd said "Boo" to her. It made for some interesting table waiting.

As Damien and I were delivering a course, one of the guests loudly made a point to the rest of the table, saying, "If all males were castrated at birth, there would be no violence in the world." I wanted to chime in with my opinion that unsolicited castration might be considered a violent act, but I thought better of it and kept to my seen-but-not-heard table waiting. I also surreptitiously took the yet-to-be-used knife from the speaker's place setting. Damien quickly excused himself and crept back into the kitchen, where I'm certain he slipped into his custom-made Kevlar codpiece. I got so nervous when waiting on this prospective pecker-whacker that I almost dropped the vodka-free chicken pasta down her back. Fortunately, had I actually made that mistake, the hair on her back would have kept her from noticing my spill and sending her on a frantic search for her missing table knife, with which she most certainly would have attempted a retaliatory castration.

Dinner concluded with little fanfare, and the group huddled together and moved out into the night. I will give the life coach credit, as she seemed to have all of her charges in sync, functioning as a group, supporting each other, murmuring amongst themselves, mutually avoiding eye contact with strangers, etc. The way they banded as one and moved out of the hotel reminded me a little of the minimalist animation used in the TV show *South Park*. In fact, now that I think about it, I think I've seen this group on *South Park*.

So, one more lesson I can chalk up on my Colorado life-experience board: There are people that feel the need to be coached, and there are those who, for a not-so-nominal fee, will coach them. My guess is that if this particular life coach were to read this book, she would gladly and at no charge coach me as to how I can take my opinion of her chosen profession and shove it up my you-know-what. Not a problem, as here in Colorado we don't use our you-know-whats for you know what.

* * *

It is purported that John Lennon slept at The Riverside Hotel — not exactly sure when, obviously before 1980. I was told this by Abner Renta, who even claimed to have a copy of the signed registration receipt. Abner further mentioned that we would ultimately own this important little piece of history when we bought the hotel, but, regretfully, that promise was never fulfilled. This story was verified as truth by some of the older locals, who also boasted of celebrity visits by Janet Leigh and Dennis Weaver, who at one time supposedly was interested in buying the hot springs.

Abner didn't have a lot of details to pass along regarding Lennon's visit but did say that he had stayed in what is known as the "Mil" room, which is located at the southwest corner of the hotel. The "Mil" room is nice in that it is one of the larger rooms and has the best views of the river, Mt. Bross, the town, and the hills south of town. It is generally also the brightest room in the hotel.

When we bought the hotel and were in the process of redecorating, we thought it important to recognize the importance of this historic visit by hanging a picture of Mr. Lennon and a plaque detailing a short story of his stay in the "Mil" room. Julie scoured the Internet for just the right Lennon picture but nothing obvious stood out as the one we had to have, until we stumbled on a print in a dingy old shop on Chartres Street in New Orleans of John standing in front of the Statue of Liberty in 1974, waving the peace sign. You've probably all seen the picture. We chose it because it seemed to sum up the John Lennon we loved and wanted to remember — still the boyish and fun-loving Beatle.

Julie was in charge of the picture, and I was in charge of the plaque. Tough to come up with an informative plaque when you have no information; I knew absolutely nothing other than: "John Lennon slept here." So I did a little research, and the first tie that I found to John Lennon and Colorado was that the Beatles played at Red Rocks Amphitheater on their first U.S. tour in August of 1964. That Denver show was preceded three days earlier by a show in Los Angeles at The Hollywood Bowl. There it had to be! Here was Lennon in the Denver area, with three days unaccounted for. Surely he must have taken some tourist time to visit the majestic Rocky Mountains, Grand Lake, the National Park, the Colorado River, and, naturally, The Riverside. But I needed a story for the wall, not just a string of dates when this could've happened. So I made one up.

Borrowing a little from Mr. Kerouac, the story went something like this:

On August 23rd, 1964, after the conclusion of the Beatles concert at The Hollywood Bowl, John Lennon left the touring party and with two friends drove east across the great American West, en route for the Beatles next show on August 26th at Red Rocks Amphitheater in Denver, CO. On the evening of August 25th, he pulled into Hot Sulphur Springs in search of a meal and a bed, and found The Riverside Hotel & Restaurant. He stayed in this room.

I printed it, framed it, and hung it in the room next to sink — the sink he would have washed in.

We always took visitors to this room when they toured the hotel and watched with delight as they smiled at the thought of John Lennon at one time habiting the space where they now stood. Many would get their picture taken in front of the plaque, while a few even went as far as to wash their hands in the sink. I often even offered guests the opportunity to vacuum the floor upon which he trod, or clean the windows through which he gazed, but never had takers.

Everything was going smoothly with the fabricated John Lennon legend until the arrival of Ms. Janet, a guest who stayed in the John Lennon room one night while visiting the Rocky Mountains from California. Janet called immediate and total BS on the story, saying there was no way that Lennon left the group and drove across the desert with his buddies. She informed me that, in fact, the first American Beatles tour was planned down to the second, and nowhere on the agenda would there have been a day away from the group for open time.

All right, so she caught me. But she was intrigued enough by the legend of his visit to do some research. Her job as a consultant in historical buildings and landmark preservation bent her towards a proclivity to get to the bottom of things and places. It wasn't long after Janet's visit that I received an e-mail from her detailing her best guess as to when and why John Lennon would have visited The Riverside.

In the summer of 1974, four years after the breakup of The Beatles, John Lennon traveled to Caribou Ranch, a music studio in Nederland, Colorado, to record a few songs with Elton John: among them was Elton's cover of "Lucy in the

Sky with Diamonds." Lennon was accompanied not by Yoko but by May Pang, Yoko's personal assistant who at the time happened to be assisting Yoko by taking care of John's personal needs.

After the recording session, John and May struck out on their own for a few quiet days in the Rockies. They were spotted buying a pair of cowboy boots in Boulder, and there are a couple of snapshots in May Pang's book, *Loving John: The Untold Story,* of John in a mountain meadow and John lying in a mountain stream. Beyond that, not much else exists as a record of their Colorado visit. Being the internationally famous icon that he was, odds are he traveled the back roads, visiting quiet, out-of-the-way places, all the while keeping a low profile.

When you say things like back roads, out-of-the-way places, and low profile, what on earth would spring more quickly to mind than Hot Sulphur Springs, Colorado? And Lennon wouldn't have wanted to stay at a busy summertime hotel, one with a bunch of nosey, autograph-seeking tourists. Again, what better spot for solitude in a deserted hotel than The Riverside? It makes perfect sense to me.

So did he or didn't he stay at The Riverside? And if he did, did he play "Imagine" on the piano in the bar, that same bar piano that I had for sale on craigslist? Did he eat in the restaurant, and did he really use the utensils that I sold for $600 on eBay? We might never know for sure, but I'm going to "Imagine" that he did.

* * *

There were two absolutes about our management of the hotel that were given to me by Abner before we signed our lives away on that cold December night in 2007. Absolute #1, which I have mentioned previously, was: "Don't under any circumstances open the bar to the local drinking trade!" I thumbed my nose at that absolute and ended up suffering through a night of debauchery that would take high-dollar, intensive therapy to fully erase from my memory.

Abner's Absolute #2 was delivered to me in the lobby, him standing with his arm pointing skyward, reminiscent of Moses on the mountain, sans those pesky numbered and scribed tablets: *"Don't ever,* under any circumstances, *no matter how badly you need the money,* rent rooms to the elk hunters! You will regret it eternally!"

"But Abner," I countered, "Middle Park is rife with trophy elk and, ergo, elk hunters with money. Don't they come here from all over the country and pay big bucks for a license?"

"I'm telling you one last time," said Abner; "no matter how much money they have to spend and how badly you might need it, you will never break even on the deal! *Never,* I tell you!"

As was the case with Absolute #1, I failed to heed Abner's warning regarding Absolute #2 and did, in fact, rent a room to an elk hunter.

It was late summer 2009, and the first few notes of our swan song were wafting through the air — nah, those notes were barking, bleating, honking through the air. I knew that I was out at the end of August, heading for my paying job in Mississippi, leaving the dregs of our dream to be dealt with by my wife and daughter. Needless to say, my heart wasn't in it anymore, but my mind knew that we needed every nickel we could squeeze from whatever source of revenue that sometimes literally stumbled our way.

Enter Larry and Heidi Olafsson, elk hunters extraordinaire, visiting Grand County all the way from Langdon, North Dakota. They had been camping up at high elevation in the Gore Range for the previous week, each successfully bagging a trophy elk with bow and arrow (as was the early season weapon of choice) but unsuccessfully practicing good hygiene. They seemed to be nice people, but the aroma that they brought into The Riverside had me longing for the days of Chef Stinky Butt. And without question, Larry was not only terribly stinky, he was also terribly stinking drunk. As I stood watching them check in, breathing lightly through my mouth so as not to whiff myself into a gag, I was reminded of Abner's warning and then began to worry about how I would be able to con Julie into cleaning their room the following day.

They checked in at 4:00 p.m., and I showed them to their room, "Mary," the haunted room at the end of the hall, the room our dog, Lucy, wouldn't enter, not even if there were a juicy rib eye sitting in the middle of the bed. I put them in this room for no other reason than it was the last available room. For some unknown reason we were all but booked this weekend, possibly the only weekend that summer that we were fully booked.

I mention this now because it's ultimately germane to the story. The room adjacent to "Mary" was "Betty," a room of pastel greens with all of our pictures from France: photos we'd taken at Montmartre and Versailles, and travel posters purchased at both locales. "Betty" was a serene room, very calming, but for some reason it seemed to be the last room we put people in, which I found odd as were I a guest, it would have been one of my first choices. In the "Betty" room that evening was a couple from Denver. I'll be judgmental here and call them high-enders. Were there a Ritz Carlton in Hot Sulphur, they would have forsaken our homey little hostel and opted for the luxury. But one nice thing about these folks was the fact that while they knew the amenities they normally sought in a hotel were screamingly absent at The Riverside, the charm of our place served as an adequate substitute. The husband had an early tee time at Dead Pines Golf Club with some buddies, so their plan was to do the spa, eat dinner, sleep, and the husband would bolt early with his sticks and the wife would sleep in and leave at her leisure. This was our idea of perfect clientele.

In the next room, "Mary," were Larry and Heidi Olafsson, our idea of the clientele we'd pursue if we were in the process of going broke.

Larry and Heidi headed to the hot springs shortly after checking in. I wondered if they'd bother to shower before entering the springs, as the fetid stench they were exuding from their personage might actually help deaden the smell of the spring water. I was also giddy at the fact that their first shower in more than a week would be taken anywhere but The Riverside, as I would for certain have had to high-pressure wash any of our bathrooms that they would have fouled prior to any other guests' utilization of our facilities.

Not much more thought was given to the Olafssons, as the restaurant was packed that night with a full hotel and a crowded town. Near closing time at The River Room, the Great White Hunter and his wife sauntered into the restaurant looking for dinner, their hair wet and reeking of sulphur from the springs. Showing up in our restaurant in this fashion was neither unusual nor unacceptable — like it or not, the raison d'êtres of our town, our hotel, and our restaurant were those smelly hot springs and the denizens who'd pay good money to park their bottoms in the sulphurous stink of those healing waters.

Larry and Heidi had the prime rib special, a couple of beers, and a glass of wine each, then scuttled out at 9:00 p.m. for one last go at the hot springs, which closed at 10:00 p.m. We closed The River Room at 9:00, cleaned up, and started to wind down for the night. The hotel was full, but full of a genteel tourist crowd, most of whom had toddled off to bed by 10:00. I was shutting the bar down when Larry and his wife came in from their last soak in the heated dung water.

"You're not closing the bar down, are ya, eh?" asked Larry.

"Well ... maybe. Would you like a drink?" I asked with a sense of trepidation so obvious that the least observant person would've immediately known that the last thing on earth I wanted to do at that particular moment was keep the bar open and serve drinks.

"*Hell yes,* we want a drink! We came here to party! It's only 10:00 o'clock!"

"Dad, you go to bed. We'll take care of things," my daughter, Rachel, offered. She and Chef Danny were decompressing from the busy restaurant night and had no intention of calling it quits at 10:00 p.m.

Without question, that was the best offer I'd had all day, and I accepted it as quick as a hiccup.

As I slinked out of the bar and headed towards our living quarters, feeling as if I'd just gotten away with stolen money, I heard Larry loudly proclaim to no one in particular, as if he were exhorting the Huns before a slaughter, "Life on the trail was tough, and the pursuit of the beast even tougher. But the waters have revived me. We will party tonight, and the drinks are on me! *Owweeeee!*"

Our bar featured a famous print, entitled "Custer's Last Fight," gifted to us by a favorite cousin. This print was supplied to bars throughout the west in the late 1800s by Anheuser-Busch to commemorate the Battle of The Little Bighorn — a slick marketing piece, with violence and mayhem about, our blond-haired hero standing tall amongst the savages and above the words: ANHEUSER BUSCH BREWING ASSOCIATION, seemingly oblivious to his impending doom. Brevet General Custer has stood stoic and valiant in that print for more than 120 years, but I'm certain that his neck hair bristled at Larry's pronouncement that evening. Mine certainly did. I slinked out even faster, and double locked the door between the lobby and our living quarters.

Fast forward to 6:30 a.m. as I crawled, with a drugged reluctance, out of bed and made myself ready to face another day of living life Riverside. As it was still summer, my first chore didn't involve starting a fire; the only heat I needed to administer was to a coffee pot. That task accomplished, I headed to the bar out of curiosity about the preceding evening's events, which, fortunately, I had slept through soundly.

While I have made mention of the beautiful Brunswick bar at The Riverside, I have not described its history or the room in which it resided, and will take this opportunity to do so. It was a smallish twenty-foot by twenty-foot room, dominated by that ornately carved, oaken/cherry wooden masterpiece of a bar, which was in my estimation the star of The Riverside. The Brunswick Company, famous for pool tables and bowling balls, made ready-to-order back bars and bar counters to complement the sale of their pool tables from 1895-1905 in Dubuque, Iowa. You could order them in the Sears & Roebuck catalog. Word had it that this particular Brunswick bar was originally in a bar in Leadville, Colorado, and was moved to The Riverside in the early 1920s at the behest of Mr. Omar Qualls, the second owner of the hotel. The back bar consisted of four six-foot tall, one-foot diameter oak pillars holding up an ornately carved headpiece, encasing a six-foot by eight-foot mirror, dulled from the ages but still holding the faces and stories of the past century. The bar was solid oak, weighing God-only-knows how much, with the original brass foot rail fronting the base. It was spectacular. Lord knows, I've been in more than a few bars, and I've seen few bars to compare. And for a while I owned this regal piece of history.

The rest of the bar contained six small three-foot by two-foot tables with two chairs each; a busted, out-of-tune piano in the corner (certain to be the one that John Lennon composed "Imagine" upon during his 1974 stay); a moderately functional jukebox; and a wild boar's head, slain and stuffed in Georgia, hanging on the north wall.

The walls had dark-stained 1" x 4" cedar slats running vertically every two feet, with the most god-awful green and orange striped wallpaper between. We were quick to have our painter, Crazy Mike, mud-stucco over the wallpaper and paint it celery green. The ceiling was a heinously dark-brown corkboard. In our dream world, we would eventually replace the cork with a pressed tin ceiling,

typical of the type of ceiling in a turn-of-the-century bar. That dream, along with a plentitude of others, never materialized.

My first sight as I walked into the bar that morning was an estimated fifty empty bottles of beer, upright, judiciously distributed on three of the six tables, and an obviously empty bottle of Jägermeister lying on its side atop the bar. Wow! The businessman in me made a quick calculation that we grossed $150 on beer after I went to bed. But at what ultimate cost?

I was surveying the scene quietly, imagining what in the hell I'd thankfully missed out on, when over my shoulder, causing me to jump full out of my boxers, Larry appeared, asking, "Hey! What the hell does it take for a guy to get a Bloody Mary around here, eh?"

"All you gotta do is ask the bartender. I make a pretty good Bloody Mary," I replied, a forced smile breaking the plane of my weary face. This is what I said, but what I was thinking was, 'Are you kidding me? You're standing amongst fifty dead soldiers that you helped obliterate but a few hours ago, and you're now wanting more alcohol at 7:00 a.m. in the morning?'

"And I'll take a beer chaser with that Bloody Mary!" said Larry.

While making the Bloody Mary for Larry, I decided that I'd make small talk as a way to stop me from screaming at him about his near epic alcoholic excesses.

"So," I asked, certainly with an edge, "out of the sack at 7:00 a.m. and thirsty for a Bloody Mary?"

"*Hell no!* I was up at 5:00 o'clock, and I've been fishing out there for the past two hours. I caught me a few nice ones too, eh!"

"Wow. Up at 5:00? What time did you guys finally close it down here last night?"

"The wife and me headed upstairs at 2:30 when your daughter told us she'd get in trouble for keeping the bar open any longer. We'd 'a made you a bunch more money if she'd have let us keep at it, eh."

'Oh my ... ,' I thought, 'for the love of a buck.' Abner had duly warned me.

I produced the Bloody Mary, with the beer chaser, and left him in the bar to go start my morning rituals: checking people out, stripping beds, washing sheets, checking people out, making more coffee, stripping more beds, checking more people out, etc., etc., ad nauseam.

About 9:00 a.m., Larry's wife, Heidi, came down, bags in tow, ready to check out. They'd paid cash as they went — for the room at check-in, for the hot springs tickets, for dinner and drinks — and, after a quick check with a sleeping-like-the-dead Rachel, I learned they'd paid cash as they went for their depravity in the bar. I even had a warm, crumpled ten-dollar bill in my pocket for the morning's Bloody Mary and beer chaser. They were good to go.

"We had such a wonderful time. We just love this hotel! The food was great, and your daughter is lovely. We can't wait to come back!"

OK, so then I felt a little crappy for thinking the bad things that I had thought about these folks. They were moderately friendly people (*real* friendly by North Dakota-Swede standards) and the absolute salt-of-the-earth. And they'd spent a big chunk of change, CASH MONEY, at a time when we were desperate for CASH MONEY. I gave a heartfelt wave good-bye as they roared off in their loaded-down Ford Double-Dog Diesel Monster Truck, replete with two massive elk racks protruding from the canvas covering in the bed of the truck.

Still kind of half waving good-bye, I sauntered back into the lobby of The Riverside, and who was standing at our checkout desk but the Denver golf widow who had stayed in "Betty" — the serenely appointed room next to "Mary," where Larry and Heidi had shared a quiet, relaxing getaway after a week in the bush.

"How was everything, and how did you sleep?"

"Well, we were sleeping very well until about 2:30. The people in the room next to us were, uh, really loud. Well, I'm sure you had to have heard them too." She looked more than just a little pained as she relayed this information. "And it didn't let up for two hours. *It was like we were being tortured!*" The look on her face as she said this showed the anguish of one who had been tortured. I was thinking that an online review that described one's hotel stay as "it was like we were being tortured" wouldn't exactly be good for future bookings.

I apologized profusely, but our guest couldn't have been nicer about it. After all, it wasn't me that had been up there putting the wood to the spouse in the wee morning hours. I didn't have to say, "Come back and see us again," because I knew that the only way this lady would visit us again would be in her nightmares.

I plodded upstairs to assess the damage in the Second-Honeymoon Suite — it was a sight that would have put the second generation of any Hilton or Marriott out of the hotel business and into pig farming for the purpose of seeking a clean-er, more wholesome occupation. I cleaned more than five hundred guest rooms during my two-year stint at The Riverside, and only once did I feel the need to don rubber gloves and a mask.

Strewn about the room — on the bedpost, on the windowsill, on the sink, and on the dresser — like so many trophy mounts of slaughtered prey, hung the spent condoms of this hunter's night's conquest. The bedsheets, quilts, pillows, towels, and signature Riverside flannel robes were thrown about the room as if the occupants had been having a contest to see how far and wide they could scatter the bedding and such from their original places. One dozen empty Budweiser bottles decorated every level space in the room upon which you could stand a beer bottle, and an empty fifth of Captain Morgan had almost found its way into the trash can. And for the sake of sheer decency, I won't go into a graphic description of the olfactory funkiness that hung in the air like a stubborn layer of brown fog. On a positive note, I was certain that the ghost that previously had inhabited this room was now screaming towards, and excited about, the alternative prospect of living out the rest of its days in hell and eternal damnation. Had the ghost room for another passenger on its southbound train, I would have considered tagging along as opposed to having to execute the clean-up task that lay before me.

On with the gloves and mask, and out with the bleach. The CASH MONEY that came with this deal was dearly earned, but it wasn't nearly enough — as Abner had duly warned me.

CHAPTER TWENTY-TWO

Ghosts of the Riverside

All of the hallways in The Riverside, of which there were four, were dark, even in the broadest, brightest hour of daytime. The high ceilings and the closed guestroom doors, coupled with the absence of light fixtures in this structure built before the advent of routine, affordable electric wiring, contributed to the ever pervasive feeling of gloom.

It was March 17th of 2007, and my wife Julie and I were guests at The Riverside, staying in the western wing of the hotel. I'd already had a few phone calls with Abner regarding our interest in buying the hotel, and we'd come out over spring break to "kick the tires" before getting down to making him a legitimate offer for the place. We were the only guests; not only in the western wing, but in the entire 16 room structure. A few of the local townspeople had joined us for dinner in the hotel restaurant – a St. Patrick's Day feast of corned beef, cabbage and boiled potatoes, the corned beef so rubbery that were it not pink and fatty, I'd have thought it to be cut from a tire – but no other out of town travelers would bed down at The Riverside that evening. After dinner and a few minutes of small talk with Abner in the lobby, we climbed the stairs into the dark upper hallway, with stone-cold silence being the only bit of ambience to be found in this ancient hostelry.

I woke from a sound sleep with a start, and found myself staring at a small digital alarm clock that told me it was 3:33 AM. Concurrently, my bladder told me that it was time to urinate. This was a bit of an issue, as the rooms in The Riverside – save for one – didn't have private bathrooms, and I was hesitant to take the walk down the darkened hallway to the community toilet. Hesitant for a variety of reasons, most of which having to do with my relative state of coziness as I lay comfortably cocooned under a pile of quilts in the chilled, heatless room. But there was one other issue that was keeping me in bed, with me reasoning with myself over the degree of which my bladder needed emptying.

I was afraid. Afraid of what lay beyond the closed guestroom door, out in the dark hallway.

The owner of the hotel had told numerous stories about the ghostly goings-on that occurred with regularity in The Riverside; stories that I had summarily dismissed as nothing more than window dressing for some of the tourists, lipstick on this pig of a hotel, if you will. I didn't for one second believe in ghosts, and I gave no credence to the possibility that the owner was being forthright with his ghoulish descriptives. Yet, I continued to lay in bed, all but frozen in fear at the thought of walking down that long, dark, silent hallway.

And then it happened.

The old door handle to the room began to turn, the creak audible, even above the noise of the fan that Julie had used to add white noise into our nighttime routine for the past 20-plus years of our married lives. My breathing stopped, seized actually, frozen in my chest and throat.

The door began to slowly and deliberately open, and the contrast of a faraway hall light appeared in the vacant doorway. For although the handle had turned, and the door had opened, there was no visual evidence of any one or any thing that could have performed those tasks.

I could not move. I could not breathe. I could not look away. I actually tried to make a sound, form words, make any sort of utterance to address this unseen intruder, but was unable. I just lay there, paralyzed by fear. And then after a few seconds, seconds that seemed to tick away as if they were awash in molasses, the door slowly and deliberately closed, all with a silence that transcended the gentle hum of the fan, a silence that you could hear.

I did not get up to go to the bathroom, nor did I sleep for the remainder of night. Perhaps I had only been dreaming. That is what I told myself.

* * *

Are there ghosts at The Riverside?

Probably ... or so the infamous FAQ sign in The Riverside lobby answered to that oft-asked question.

The first time I walked into The Riverside Hotel in June of 1993, the first thing that struck me was a two-foot by four-foot, heavily scripted wooden sign hanging on the north wall of the lobby. (OK, that's a bit of a lie. The first thing I noticed was the *Little Shop of Horrors* plant collection that threatened to eat you as you walked into the lobby. Then I noticed this creepy little man sitting in a rocking chair. Then I said to myself, 'My, how quaint; how charming. How much will I have to drink to get through the next twenty-four hours of my life?')

The FAQ sign grabbed your eye as you walked in the door, and it answered most of the questions that people would want to ask about the hotel, the town, the river, the weather, the hot springs, etc. My guess is that some unknown Riverside owner (someone prior to Abner) who put the sign up had gotten sick and tired of answering the same questions over and over and over and over and over. It wouldn't surprise me if on a larger level, he'd also gotten sick of talking to and dealing with people in general.

Some of the questions and answers were:

When was The Riverside built?....................1903

What is the elevation of Hot Sulphur Springs?...7763 feet

How cold does it get in the winter?...................-30°F, sometimes colder

Are there fish in the river?................................Yes, mostly trout

Can you eat the fish from the river? ....Yes, if you can catch them!

How far is Boulder?...Not quite far enough

And so it went. The sign was written in a colloquial, folksy sort of way; i.e., the answers were given in the form that a friendly, old-timey, homey hotel owner might give them. I immediately loved the sign, and it was one of the little things that made me love The Riverside. Knowing this, you can imagine how I felt when I walked into the hotel on the December day that we were to close the sale and the first thing I noticed was the empty space on the wall where the sign used to be. Abner was sitting in his rocking chair, and I didn't say, "Hello, Abner," I said, "Abner, where the hell is the sign?" I was, to put it mildly, more than a little irritated and on edge. Abner kind of cleared his throat and nervously said, "I, uh, er ... I gave it to a friend in California" — an obvious lie, but the best thing he could come up with at the time. It was a portent of other surprises to come, much bigger and much costlier surprises, relating to shady things Abner did and didn't do in his transfer of ownership of The Riverside.

Two wonderful happenings came from this bad missing-sign surprise. My sister-in-law found a picture of the sign on an old website and re-created it whole, right down to the original font. Julie and I all but cried when she gave it to us as a housewarming gift, a labor of love I've not seen equaled. We also found out that in fact the original sign wasn't given by Abner to a friend in California (certainly not a surprise) but sold to a man in Boulder for $350. We befriended that man, and I'm glad that he has the sign, but sorry that he had to pay for it.

My sister-in-law took some literary license when re-creating the sign in that she updated it and added a few new FAQs. In particular, one of the newest most-often-asked questions was, "Are there ghosts at The Riverside?" and the answer given on the sign was, "Probably."

I would now answer that question, "Absolutely!"

During my first weekend as an owner of The Riverside, I got smacked square in the face by the unnatural, my spine frosted with the chill of the unexplainable turning off of my shower, followed by the totally inexplicable appearance of a fresh bath mat. With unequivocal absoluteness, I physically experienced these events — with my eyes wide open and my senses sober as a working nun — unlike the blips, flashes, and squeaks that you see on the Travel Channel's *Ghost Hunters*, and the memory of this unaccountable phenomena still makes my skin crawl.

I'd be lying if I said that this first otherworldly encounter didn't temper my bearing towards the unseen and unknown every future day that I was to spend in The Riverside. From that point forward, there wasn't a time that I was in the hotel — the Green Room, the bar, the restaurant, the kitchen, and especially the upstairs hallways in the west wing of the hotel — when I was alone yet was not mortally aware of the presence of another. Certainly for me — and I was quickly to find that for many others as well — The Riverside definitely had a *feel*.

Very early in our ownership we were visited by a young lady who was in charge of marketing for the Grand County Tourism Board, selling us on the idea of joining the Chamber of Commerce and advertising in a variety of their venues. Contracts were signed and checks were written. Then after the deal was consummated beyond the point of no return, with expectant bright blue eyes, she asked, "So tell me about the ghosts? Everybody says this place is like totally haunted!"

"Who is everybody?" I asked, more than a little annoyed.

"Like *everybody*! That's why most people are afraid to come here! Have you seen anything?"

I smiled politely at the young lady and left it alone, as this ghost thing was most certainly a double-edged sword. There were many who wouldn't set foot in The Riverside if they thought they would encounter something otherworldly, and there were those who were fanatic believers that you wouldn't want staying in the hotel and scaring the nonbelievers. A successful séance would definitely be both good and bad for business.

Before my first encounter I would have fallen into the category of an aggressive nonbeliever. No way did I believe in ghosts or the ghostly; in fact, I chided those who subscribed to this folly. While ghosts and ghouls have been feared by many from time immemorial, they are also unproven and substantively undocumented.

I was among the most skeptical. I am now among the most fervent of believers, because I both physically experienced and witnessed things beyond blips, blurs, and flashes of light. Sitting in a chair once, resting quietly sober under a brilliantly starlit sky and a three-quarter-full moon that illuminated the darkened night as if it were still dusk, I watched in awe, then in terror, as something that was clearly not of this earth walked before me, stopped and scrutinized me, and then moved on into nothingness.

* * *

I was told the story of a woman who saw something as she sat soaking in one of the hot spring pools across the river from our hotel. She didn't announce herself as a seer, a visionary, or a ghost hunter, and she was discreet about her vision, quietly revealing what she had seen to the manager of the hot springs when asked about the quality of her visit. Her disclosure was totally unsolicited and seemed sincere, offered more out of curiosity, wondering if others had seen and reported what she'd witnessed. She told the manager:

"I saw a train, an old train, a steam engine; it stopped at the junction in front of the springs. I saw a crowd get off the train, maybe twenty people — men, women, and some children — all of them dressed from the early 1900s. I saw this so clearly, as if it were happening at *that* moment, right before my eyes. For a minute I actually believed that it was happening, maybe some sort of a reenactment. Then they all walked across the bridge towards that big white hotel across the river and entered the building. They looked happy, as if they were going to a picnic or a party … chatting, laughing."

* * *

It is said that animals have a profound second sense when it comes to rec-ognizing spirits and ghosts, sniffing and calling out those from the otherworld. In January of 2009, beginning our second full year of ownership, we drove to Denver and scored ourselves the finest rescue dog, ghost hunter of a mutt that fate would allow us.

Our family pooch of fifteen years, Lucky, the ultimate rescue mutt, gave up the ghost in dramatic fashion on Thanksgiving Day, 2006. Julie and the kids had stumbled upon Lucky in a park in Nevada, Missouri, in 1991. She was being abused by a pack of Nevada toughs — kicked, roughed up, and thrown in the small-town lake. As she struggled to paddle back and finally swim onto the shore, they'd grab her up and toss her back in the lake. Lucky never much cared for water again.

Julie put a quick stop to this and rescued the pooch from these brutes, on the spot adopting her and naming her Lucky. She was a small, sweet, blond mutt of what lineage we never had a clue. When Julie called me back in Kansas City to tell me that we now had a dog, the conversation went like this:

"Great news! Guess what?"

"You're pregnant!"

"No, we found a dog!"

"I wish you were pregnant!" I was not a "dog person."

As a kid I had a dog that I loved, but my dad was cold about dogs, as was his mother; she was cold about both dogs and humans. Sadly, I latched on to my dad's proclivity only to tolerate dogs, and tolerate them as he did, only on his rigid terms. Loving the dog wasn't in the deal — merely tolerating, feeding, and disciplining the dog were allowed. Dogs had their place, and while they had a regimented place in our house when I was growing up, they didn't seem to have a place in my father's heart.

I adopted this skewed worldview and but barely tolerated Lucky, our rescue dog, for her fifteen years of life: feeding her, cleaning up after her, but rarely loving her. Had I life to live over, I would alter that equation and love her first and foremost.

Fast forward to January, 2009. From the first day of Lucky's passing, Julie had been working on me subtly to get another dog. I'd muted myself to her continually increasing groundswell of, "We need a dog … we need a dog!" and I believed I had successfully driven her away from the idea, especially once we were up in the mountains dealing with the mountainous task of running our business.

Finally she figuratively jerked the steering wheel out of my hands, pushed me aside, and informed me that she had procured a rescue dog in Denver. And that pretty much was that. On a Monday in late January, the hotel closed and no guests on the books offered us the opportunity to head east and pick up our new little charge. I was silently pissed, as I was so engulfed in my world of dealing with the hotel and the business that the notion of bringing the wild card of a dog — a puppy, no less — into the equation had me grumpy beyond reason.

As we were preparing to leave the hotel to pick up the dog, one of our neighbors came in for a brief visit. He was the manager of the Hot Sulphur Springs Resort & Spa, working for and constantly cleaning up after the deficient social skills of the Gupthas, the owners. Rick and his wife were also relatively new arrivals to the mountains, chasing their Grand County dreams as had we. Rick had been a pig farmer in Illinois and a radio personality as well. He was a character, and he called them as he saw them.

"What's going on today?" he asked.

"Oh, we're going to Denver to pick up a dog," I answered in a grumpy, hang-dog fashion. "Julie pretty much went behind my back and had her sister pick up a rescue dog for us."

"You don't like dogs?"

"Nah, I'm not crazy about 'em."

"Are you kidding me? What kind of an asshole doesn't like a dog?"

I took this as a challenge, and within a few short days, our new puppy, Lucy, had this same asshole wrapped tight around her little paw. She was a Border collie mix, and we would eventually find out that the mix was with a corgi, as we watched her grow horizontally but not vertically. Lucy was smarter than most humans I knew (certainly including me), wicked quick, and a long, lean low rider. She was also a four-legged barometer when it came to sensing and occasionally calling out the unseen and the unknown that inhabited the halls and the rooms of The Riverside.

With the exception of the kitchen and the dining room, Lucy had the run of the hotel. She would follow us everywhere and would always keep us company when we were upstairs cleaning rooms. Here Lucy found a solution to the problem of not being able to bury bones outside due to the frozen ground that was usually covered in snow. She would bury bones in the decorative pillows that adorned all of the beds in the hotel rooms; that is, all of the rooms except for "Mary," the far corner room in the east wing, and "Mavis," the far corner suite in the west wing. These were two areas of the hotel that she wanted no part of.

"Mary" was a brightly decorated room, flooded in pinks and whites with the occasional dash of yellow. Lucy wouldn't enter this room — not for any reason — regardless of how much coaxing and pleading. Of greater note was her disposition when waiting for us outside of the room; she would sit with her head down and ears pinned back, looking as if we were about to smack her with a newspaper. This behavior was noticeably and consistently peculiar.

One particular day Lucy was sitting outside of "Mary" looking intently into the room, though neither Julie nor I were in the room. I was in the hallway, at the other end, putting bath towels on the towel rack, and stopped to watch her as she began cocking her head from one side to the next, much like the RCA Jack Russell terrier. She then quickly sprung onto all fours and arched her back in attack mode, growled, and then began viciously barking at something in the room.

Her abrupt change in demeanor and her sudden, piercing bark frightened me, and I barked back at her, "LUCY! Stop it!"

Stop it she did, as she then looked at me and shot down the hall towards me, her ears pinned back, and then raced right by me, flying down the stairs into the lobby, as far away from the "Mary" room as she could get.

I stood silent for a second, listening, hearing nothing but afraid to go down to the end of the hall, down to the "Mary" room, to see what Lucy had seen. Remember, I'd already had some unexplained events happen, and I was now predisposed to consider the paranormal first whenever something out of the ordinary like this occurred. I headed down the hall with trepidation and then caught myself a little, stepping up the pace and thinking, 'Come on, get a grip; it's probably nothing.'

And it was indeed nothing — at least nothing that I could see.

What did Lucy sense in that room that would preclude her from entering? And what did she see in "Mary" on that particular day that had turned her into a vicious sentinel, acting as if she wanted to attack the demon, just not enough to cross the threshold?

As a witness to the whole affair, I can say with certainty: Lucy saw something in that room — something that no one else could see — and that something posed a threat to her.

* * *

As previously mentioned, The Hot Sulphur Springs Resort & Spa includes a cabin that rests at the foot of the first gentle rise of Mt. Bross, some fifty feet higher in elevation than the rest of the resort; a long wooden stairway is the only access to this cabin dubbed, "The 1840s Cabin." It has a fireplace, a queen bed, a small kitchenette, and comes with a bottle of cheap champagne when rented for $225 a night.

One would assume that if indeed the cabin was built in 1840, some twenty years prior to the official founding of the town of Hot Sulphur Springs, that it was very possibly the first structure built by white visitors to the valley. One would also assume that the cabin has some history.

I listened to a story told by guests who stayed with us at The Riverside one evening that had spent a night in the 1840s Cabin — two women from Boulder who loved the springs but would now be unable to recommend the 1840s Cabin as an accommodating spot for a peaceful night's slumber.

"We'd been sleeping soundly for a few hours ... it was maybe two a.m. ... and the fire had pretty much died down, when we were both awakened by a roar of flames from the fireplace, like someone had shot lighter fluid on the fire. There was an old antique lantern that hung from the fireplace that started swinging back and forth, like it was being blown in a strong wind, clanking loudly against the mantel. We were both so petrified we couldn't even speak. And then I realized that there must be a massive storm going on that was causing all the wind through the chimney, causing the fire to roar and the lantern to swing. I got up to look outside, wondering if it was just a windstorm or if it was snowing a blizzard, actually hoping that we might get snowed in. But when I looked out the window, the night was as still as it could be. I opened the cabin door and it was a crystal clear, starry night — no storm, no wind, and no blizzard. The fireplace went back to flickering and the lantern hung still. We were freaked! I was so afraid that I got nauseous. We grabbed our stuff, got out of there as quick as we could, got in our car, and got the hell out of Hot Sulphur."

* * *

It was June 22nd, 2009, a Monday after a slow weekend, only but a few rooms rented, a few tables served. I was upstairs that afternoon, cleaning the two rooms that had been let that prior Sunday evening — the "John Lennon" room at the south end of the hall, and the "Mavis" suite at the north end of the hall. Both of these rooms were in the extreme west wing, the one that was added in the 1930s as an afterthought, the wing that many said "had a feeling."

I can't say why, but I was always most ill at ease in this part of the hotel when it came to sensing that I wasn't alone. Julie felt the same, as often when she left one of the rooms in this section after cleaning or tidying, she would announce out loud to what was unseen but she perceived was there, "See ya later! Take care of us!" She wasn't doing this to be cute; she really felt that she wasn't alone, and was being seriously cordial to the eternal, unseen but existent cohabitants of our house.

On that Monday afternoon, I was doing my normal cleaning routine: strip both beds and take the dirty linens downstairs to the laundry room, then load the washer and head back upstairs, clean sheets in tow. Make the bed in the "Lennon" room, then shoot down the hall to the "Mavis" suite and make that bed. Back to the "Lennon" room with the vacuum, vacuum the "Lennon" room, then down the hall to the "Mavis" suite with the vacuum, and vacuum. Store the vacuum, then grab stuff to clean the sinks and the mirrors, which I did first in the "Lennon" room, then swiftly headed down the hall to the "Mavis" suite.

This new west wing that was added in the 30s gave the upstairs a cobbled feel — no straight lines or hallways, only left turns, right turns, and a few cut-up little passageways. There were guests who claimed to get lost between their room and the bathroom. One of these little side hallways was home to the linen closet, and across from the entry to the linen closet was Abner's magic haunted mirror. The haunted mirror was an antique with which Abner forgot to abscond, coming back later to ask if he could have the mirror. We knew it was old, classic, and had value, and told him that we'd … uh ... given it to the same man in California to whom he'd sold the FAQ sign, and to go pound sand. There was no love lost at this point with Abner.

Anyway, I was zipping down the hall from the "Lennon" room to the "Mavis" suite, minding my own business, when I saw in my peripheral view, in the small hall with the linen closet and the haunted mirror, a man standing with his hands crossed in front at his waist, as if he were patiently waiting for a train. He was attired in late 1800s dressed-up cowboy clothes. Honest to God, he looked a lot like Sam Elliott, that quintessential, droop-mustached cowboy. Maybe that's what my mind wanted to see, and, in fact, that was what it saw, enough to make my knees buckle.

Two quick steps past the little hallway I stopped, frozen, now deathly afraid to step back and see if what I thought I saw was still there. I stood for a second, then headed quickly away from the vision down the hall to the "Mavis" suite, where I started cleaning the sink and the mirror, acting as if nothing had happened. But every thought I had as I absentmindedly sprayed, cleaned, and wiped was consumed by the vision that I'd just seen — my heart was pounding away like a jackhammer. I also knew that I would eventually have the room cleaned and, assuming I didn't want to take up permanent residence in "Mavis," I was going to have to walk back down that hallway and face my fear.

I took a deep breath and walked as fast as I could, looking quickly to my left into the short hallway where I'd seen the cowboy. He was gone, but that didn't slow the tempo of my gait or the pace of my heart.

* * *

The "Mavis" room, the other room with which Lucy had issues, was a two-room suite: a queen bed and sink in one room, a loveseat and overstuffed chair in the other. It was our most popular room, even though it had no bathroom and was in fact the farthest room from the bathroom — the 3:00 a.m. trek to the toilet from "Mavis" was a bit of a haul. What "Mavis" did have were two large windows, one on the western wall that presented the best view of the Colorado River and Mt. Bross, and one on the north wall that offered a pretty decent view of the tire mountain in the back of Joe's Garage and Auto Repair, our neighbor across the road to the north.

Rumor had it that there was a murder at The Riverside during the wild hey-days of the Eisenhower Tunnel construction. The first story, which was told to me by a wild-eyed, raging drunk during one of the few nights that I had the bar open to locals, had a man coming up behind the victim, who was standing at the Brunswick bar, grabbing his hair to pull his head back, fully exposing his naked neck to the blade of a large knife, then violently slitting his throat; mortuus patronum.

I asked Grandpa, my neighbor who had lived across from the hotel for the past forty years, suffering through the reliving of the Wild West during the Eisenhower Tunnel construction, what he knew about the vicious throat slashing in The Riverside's bar.

"That's a bunch of bull! That's not what happened at all!"

With relief at not having had such a horrid deed happen in the place where I worked, where I lived, and that I owned, I asked Grandpa the next stupid question: "So was anyone ever murdered at The Riverside?"

"Yep, sure was. During the Eisenhower Tunnel build, one of the workers staying at The Riverside got a little too friendly with one of the local women. He was living in that back room that looked over the river (the "Mavis" room), and the woman's husband came in the hotel during the middle of the night and stabbed him to death. These guys building the tunnel were all transients from someplace else, so nobody was keeping track of them. He didn't show up for work and nobody thought any different. It was a few days before they found the guy, and only because of the smell."

* * *

It was Monday, August 4th, 2009, and I was sitting on the back porch at The Riverside. The moon was a few days shy of being full, but it rose brightly from the east in the clear summer night, fighting for acknowledgement in the evening sky with the panoply of stars that brilliantly painted the heavens, the rising moon bathing Mt. Bross in a lustrous, luminescent glow and making the river look as if it were a rolling jumble of diamonds and fireflies.

While I miss very little about living in Hot Sulphur Springs, the stars and the sky at 7800 feet in the middle of an inky-dark nowhere were a sight to behold. I do desperately miss the nightly display of the Milky Way in season, the planets as they screamed with their brilliance, and the shooting stars that blasted across the evening sky for what at times seemed like minutes, me almost expecting the sparks from their trails to fall from the sky and land in the yard.

Monday was our off day; the restaurant was closed and we usually tried not to book rooms on Mondays. As badly as we needed the money, we needed the break more, physically and mentally. Mondays are the bane of the average working person; they quickly became our favorite day of the week.

It was relatively early, maybe 9:30 p.m. Julie had already trundled off to bed, and Rachel and Danny the Sober Chef were sitting in the lobby watching TV. There were no paying hotel guests and, of unusual note, no nonpaying local guests — friends and neighbors who hung out at the place, always, ad infinitum and ad nauseam. That night, just the four of us were all doing our own thing.

I chose to spend this time alone out on the back porch, thinking and brooding about the ills of dying a slow financial death, apprehensive about the near future of me packing up and heading south in an effort to earn enough money to keep the place afloat.

Those who know me well will call BS on this one, but, I was not nursing a glass of gin. I'd had my requisite two martinis before dinner, and a glass of wine with dinner, but that had been three hours prior. I was as sober as a Southern Baptist - not while fishing or hunting, but at Sunday service.

The back porch at The Riverside was about five hundred square feet of cobbled stone laid in cement, built by Abner's enslaved Mexican illegal. It had a three-foot-high wall of cemented river stone around it, broken by a small fire pit on the western wall, facing towards the Colorado River. On the north side of the patio was a cedar structure that housed a collection of junk — yard debris, a busted-up camper shell, rotted wooden bed frames, fractured clay pots — basically a trash dump ensconced within a nice wooden shed, for which we had paid good money. Bless Abner's heart; he took the valuable antiques, pictures, furniture, and kitchen equipment, but he was kind enough to leave us with this trash.

On the other side of the patio wall bordering the river was a string of lilac bushes — big, healthy lilac bushes, the perfume of which ensorcelled the attendant bees and rendered them sufferable. These bushes all but hid the river as you sat looking west, the only gap being a six-foot stretch on the west side of the fire pit. There was also a three-foot gap between the most northerly lilac bush and the cedar junkyard — a sliver of sight that afforded you a terrific view of both the river and the foot of Mt. Bross.

On this beautifully serene night with a golden moon rising at my back, my attention was focused on this three-foot window, the river flowing, the mountain rising. This glorious vision was helping ease the angst of my turbulent existence, numbing me to the reality of my bleak situation. I was suddenly at peace with the stars, the moon, the river, and the sky. I was blissfully enjoying one of my last unencumbered Monday nights while living at and owning The Riverside.

As God is my witness, what I am going to describe next absolutely happened.

As I sat on the back porch watching the sky, the river, and the mountain, with only the sound of the rushing water, which was pervasive and comforting, beyond the fireplace in front of me appeared a large, dark figure that walked slowly south to north on the outer rim of the patio wall. One would describe its walk as processional. The apparition had no features except a head and a torso, its lower half obscured by the fireplace and the patio wall. It appeared as more of a dense shadow than a living thing. I would have guessed it to be as tall as seven-foot, and I still can envision its head as large and misshapen; I would almost describe the figure as that of a Minotaur, sans the horns.

The specter disappeared briefly as it passed behind the two large lilac bushes, and then it reappeared in the short little three-foot gap between the last lilac bush and the cedar junk shed, the gap that afforded me the best view of the river; a view that was now totally obscured by this vision. Here the phantom stopped, turned its massive head toward me as if intending to stare me down, froze for a second or two, and then turned and walked on into the nothingness behind the cedar shed. All of this in stone silence — no footfall; no rustling of leaves, pebbles, or grass.

I was absolutely paralyzed with fear; I literally couldn't breathe. I remember all but instinctively — as if my inanimate body moved by innate motor skills grabbed hold of me in spite of what my mind was still trying to process — shooting from the chair and running inside, quickly locking the door and staggering into the lobby where my daughter and Danny the Sober Chef were watching TV.

They paid no attention to me as I sat, pulse racing, trying to breathe. I was having a difficult time reckoning with what I'd just seen. I wasn't doubting what I'd seen, because I knew I'd seen it as clearly as I'd seen the moon and the stars, but I was trying to come to grips mentally with what I'd just experienced — seeing this illogical, unexplainable, and all but indescribable phantom.

I'm now going on several years after the fact, several years of introspection and mental dissection, far away from the scene of the crime, far away from the stress of the venture, and far away from the magical aura of the mountains, the river, and the stars at but a hand's grasp away. Several years of soul searching later, seven hundred safe and sober miles away, while I have no explanation, I know and stand by what I saw. What I *saw*.

* * *

The owners of the Hot Sulphur Springs Resort & Spa could not get locals to clean the 1840s Cabin. This town of five hundred residents, most that relied upon the meager tourist trade for employment — working in the few restaurants, cleaning the few hotel rooms — wouldn't for love or money clean that notably haunted cabin.

The stories of ghostly shenanigans were all consistent among those who had worked at the springs and had cleaned the cabin — flying kitchen utensils, the suddenly roaring fireplace, gale-force wind in the cabin. No locals would subject themselves to the gates of hell that seemed to have their foundation in that 1840s Cabin for the thirty dollars that the owners would pay them to clean the place.

Whatever the unearthly presences in our place were, they didn't seem to have the angry disposition of the spooks that inhabited the hot springs. Our spirits were pranksters, at their worst messing with the plumbing infrastructure at inopportune times at the expense of us. And there was also the quiet spirit, standing off to the side, just visible enough for me or the dog to see but certainly not a physical threat. The black phantom on the patio: I've not a clue as to what that was or what it represented — perhaps a thousand-year-old Ute spirit, long dispossessed of this river, these sacred springs, that feudal mountain, and this magnificent valley that ensconces them all.

Are there ghosts at The Riverside?

Yes, absolutely!

CHAPTER TWENTY-THREE

More Local Color

Early in the summer of 2009, The Riverside hosted the inaugural Hot Sulphur Springs Chamber of Commerce Meet & Greet. In a town of 500 people, obviously there were very few businesses — two motels on Highway 40, the hot springs resort, two small diners (The Glory Hole and The Depot), the seasonally open Dairy Dine, The Barking Dog Pub, a gas station/convenience store, a liquor store/video rental/fishing tackle/Laundromat, a mortuary, and The Historic Riverside Hotel, Restaurant & Bar — and perhaps the need for a Chamber of Commerce was questionable. Hot Sulphur Springs is also the county seat for the county of Grand; ergo, you had the courthouse, drivers' license bureau, county treasurer, appraiser's office, building department, and the crown jewel of the public trust — the Grand County jail.

None of the aforementioned businesses were represented at the HSS Chamber Meet & Greet, with the obvious exception of yours' truly. In place of the real brick-and-mortar town businesses were friends and neighbors who had small businesses on the side — Amway, Avon, Pampered Chef, and Aveda sellers; four certified life coaches; and an income-tax service, to name but a few. Mostly it was a good excuse to get together and eat the appetizers that we had prepared, and belly up to the typically "not open to the locals" bar at The Riverside; the appetizers were free but the booze wasn't.

One interesting thing about the get-together that I noticed immediately: I'd never before seen any of these people enter The Riverside as paying customers. A few I'd recognized from seeing them at the post office, which was located across the street from the hotel, but otherwise none of them had dined with us in our restaurant — you know, that room overlooking the river where we were trying to earn our living. This speaks to one of my major miscalculations when I was projecting revenue for our business venture; I'd made the incorrect assumption that locals would dine in our restaurant. But nada, as very rarely did that happen.

One of the strangers I met that evening was a tall, pleasant young man named Justin Tiem (pronounced "time"). That's right; twenty-five years ago Mr. and Mrs. Tiem had a baby boy and decided to make him the poster child for peer abuse. Really, what were they thinking? Justin was pretty good-natured about it, even using the misspelling in the title of his business; his business card read: JUST-IN TIME WOOD SERVICE, Justin Tiem, Owner. His mission statement, or motto, was, *"I'll Put the Wood Wherever You Like!"*

In the land of eternal winter, the need for a steady source of firewood was profound. This profound need was ratcheted way up at The Riverside, as the two main rooms in the hotel had no source of heat — gas, electric, forced air, or otherwise — other than two small fireplaces with nonfunctional Heatilators (blowers to disperse the heat). It wasn't unusual to get up first thing on a frigid morning and find the inside temperature of the lobby to be hovering in the high thirties. On killer-cold nights I might leave an electric heater blowing, always weighing the notion of frozen pipes versus the potential fire hazard. But then, unlike Abner, I had insurance.

More often than not, by morning the late-nighters at the hotel would have expended all of the wood that was brought in throughout the previous day and night. This would generally be the reason people actually went to bed: no firewood; getting damn cold in here and way too damn cold to go outside and get any more wood. Oh, and we're out of beer. Most all of my days started with a trip through the bar and out the back door to the woodshed, in a biting, dry cold that stung any exposed skin or appendage with the fury of an angry wasp. It was the norm for early morning, first-light temperatures on clear days, December through February, to average twenty below zero.

The woodshed was roughly ten feet wide and fourteen feet long with seven feet of clear headspace. That's roughly one thousand cubic feet, which will house about nine cords of wood. We filled that space to the brim both winters we owned The Riverside, with an additional five or six cords stacked outside under a tarp.

We used the outside wood first, as the eventual snowfalls would make anything exposed to the elements positively unattainable without the aid of a backhoe, and I didn't have one of those. All the wood stacked to the gills of that shed in late October was a little like a big paycheck: sitting full in the bank on day one, that deposit seemed like a lot and looked like it was more than you could spend; come mid-February, that paycheck had dwindled down to pennies in your account, and you wondered how you were going to get to the next payday (spring and warm weather, in our case) intact.

Here's one other little thing about that wood. It wasn't the oak and hickory hardwoods of my Midwestern life experience, the kind that was a dense, heavy, slow-burning wood, generating hotter heat and prolific glowing coals. It was pine — dead pine — from the dead pine trees that dominated the Grand County landscape, courtesy of the dreaded mountain pine beetle. Vast expanses of forests that were for centuries Christmas green from the curtain of a million evergreens — blue spruce and ponderosa, piñon and lodgepole pines — were now dominated by the deathly ashen-brown pallor of these heretofore regal emerald titans.

There is good and bad associated with dead-pine wood. The good is that it's relatively easy to split. Chef Danny, one of his buddies, and I chainsawed into eighteen-inch lengths and split every stick of that firewood with a maul — thousands of pieces of firewood cut, split, and stacked. That would have been an impossible feat for this fat old man were we dealing with hardwood, and next to impossible for the youngsters. The bad news is that the easy-to-cut-and-split, dead-pine wood burned faster than a gasoline-soaked firecracker fuse. You could stoke a hot fire with three or four stout logs, and within fifteen minutes it would be as if you'd stoked the fire with a sack of cotton balls. Where in the hell did it go? On an average night, with guests in the hotel and a small crowd in the lobby, you could easily burn forty to fifty logs in a five-hour period. On a night when there weren't guests in the hotel, in an attempt to conserve our wood resources, we kept the fire low, dressed in our warmest sweaters, and froze our asses off. The others at the hotel cursed me on those nights quietly under their frigid, visible breath, as I was the keeper of the firewood.

* * *

Our first batch of wood at The Riverside in the summer of 2008 was delivered gratis, courtesy of our good friend and neighbor, Tony. I've mentioned Tony before and have festooned him with adjectives such as sober, reliable, able, talented, and stable; for a fact, these were adjectives that were seldom used to describe the working male in Grand County, Colorado.

Tony and his father were the kind of guys that if they weren't doing something highly physical and potentially dangerous, they might as well have been getting a pedicure. Tony had a friend who gave him access to all of the dead lodgepole pines you could want — all he had to do was cut them down and haul them off. That might sound easy to you flatlanders, but it involved driving a truck and trailer up a fifteen-degree incline, whacking down one-hundred-foot-tall dead pine trees — *TIMBERRRRR!* — shaving off the branches, cutting the trunks into twenty-foot lengths weighing one thousand pounds apiece, and then manhandling those adult-sized Lincoln Logs onto the trailer. After this blistering display of high-elevation derring-do and mountain-man machismo, Tony drove to the backyard of The Riverside and left us twenty of these logs, without even expecting a thank you. He was that kind of a guy.

Whilst we were winding down our stay in Hot Sulphur as it coincided with the demise of the Grand County economy, Tony's "new construction" plumbing business — along with all other construction-related businesses — had gone straight down the toilet. Not one to sit around and feel sorry for himself, Tony bought an old diesel truck and a log-hauling trailer, and employed himself hauling dead pine logs out of the mountains. His summertime hobby of felling and gathering those logs for friends and neighbors was mere child's play compared to his new winter profession. Imagine driving a diesel truck with tire chains, pulling a forty-foot log trailer up the side of a newly hewn, snowy mountain path in the middle of the freezing Colorado night. Logs loaded, Tony would then carefully traverse his way back down the hill, his foot all but always jammed on the brake, as the slightest bit of unchecked downward motion could cause the trailer to jackknife, upending both the cab and the trailer and sending them down the steep mountainside in a grisly, cacophonous pas de deux. Once safely down the mountain, the real trek began, as the final destination for the load was a sawmill in Rifle, Colorado, 170 miles west-southwest of Grand County, and the target time was always 4:00 a.m.

The quickest route that a normal person would take to Rifle from Hot Sulphur Springs during the winter was Highway 40 west to Kremmling, a flat, easy, seventeen-mile track, and then south on Highway 9 along the floor of the Blue River valley. During the fall, this forty-mile drive is as beautiful as any on Earth, with golden aspens ablaze against the jagged peaks of the Gore Range. In the winter, while still beautiful, you had better not notice the view; you'd best keep your eyes squarely on the often windy, sometimes treacherous, two-lane stretch of highway. At the end of the road you will find yourself on I-70 in Dillon, Colorado, at which point you head west another 115 miles until you hit Rifle.

That is the route I would travel (it is the route MapQuest would suggest as well), and I would be cautious and generally white-knuckled as I gently maneuvered my 2003 four-wheel-drive Chevy Suburban along the curvaceous, snow-packed lanes of Highway 9 during the winter. If you wanted to cut thirty to forty-five minutes off of the drive, and if you had no regard for your life or limb, you would jump on the "Trough Road" just south of Kremmling and be deposited about fifty miles further west on I-70 in Eagle. The Trough Road is a mostly gravel, barely two-lane, narrow road that snakes its way along the Colorado River, sometimes adjacent, sometimes five hundred feet above the river as it hugs the side of some of the Rockies' finest granite. This is also the route that the Amtrak's California Zephyr takes midway on its trek from Chicago to Los Angeles. (If you ever get the chance to jump the train in Denver and take the six-and-a-half-hour trip to Glenwood Springs, take it, as you'll believe you've died and gone to heaven.) This drive is an attention-getter for tough guys in summer in a small car. To me it was an unimaginable feat in the winter while pulling a trailer loaded with forty thousand pounds of logs in the wee hours of the morning. The only possible upside to this predawn journey — and I'm stretching hard here to find one — would be the total lack of any other fools on the road.

The only time I took the Trough Road was in late spring for a brief trip to Glenwood Springs. There was still some slickness and the occasional snow and ice patch. A few points in the journey — narrow curves overlooking deadly drop-offs into the majestic Colorado River — I had to fight hard not to wet my pants from fear. On that return trip I didn't even for a second consider taking the Trough Road back; I simply opted for the additional time and mileage of Highway 9.

Tony made this nail-biter twice a day, six days a week, at night, often in blinding blizzards with gale-force winds. He had some close calls and more than a few scares — once when his brakes were smoking hot and nonfunctional as he flew uncontrollably down, thankfully, a relatively straight stretch of road — and he was fully aware of and not enthralled with the danger he faced every night. More often than not, upon his return home around eight to nine a.m., dog-tired from both the physical labor of maneuvering his belching diesel mammoth and the stress associated with keeping his load intact and himself alive, he would have to do one repair or another to either the truck or the trailer. You'd assume correctly that a guy who would buy a truck and do this sort of thing for a living would have the wherewithal to repair his own rig.

After trying to live a fragment of a normal family life, and after four to five hours of sleep, Tony was back up and in the truck, heading for another load of logs at 12:00 a.m. He did this for eight hundred bucks a load. While that may sound like a lot — $4800 a week — the reality is that he spent $300 per trip on fuel and untold more on repairs, plus he had the truck payment and insurance. At the end of the deal he might clear $200 a day — before taxes. So he was risking his life, working his tail off, and barely surviving. Sound familiar? I've stated previously, times were hard, and living and surviving even harder, in Grand County.

I made certain that I wouldn't play to Tony's good nature for free logs our second season, as the mere suggestion of our neediness would have had Tony working on his weekend off to bring us logs, and I simply couldn't heap that guilt on this giant of a friend.

* * *

At our Meet & Greet, Mr. Justin Tiem, the provider of both wood and unintended mirth to the fine folks of Hot Sulphur Springs, was quick to offer me his wood for The Riverside. He was a young newlywed with another mouth to feed on the way, and, free appetizers and decently priced booze notwithstanding, he was at the premiere HSS Chamber event to rustle up some new business.

It pained me to ask, but I had to. "If the baby's a boy, will he be named Justin Jr.?"

"We already know it's going to be a girl. We're thinking of naming her Precious. Get it? Precious Tiem?"

Obviously the nut had not fallen very far from the Tiem family tree.

"So what do you charge for a cord of wood, delivered and stacked?"

"Normally I get $175 a cord, but that doesn't include stacking. I can get $200 a cord if it's stacked. Now if you bought maybe at least ten cords, I could deliver it and stack it for $2000. How's that sound?" The concept of the volume discount had not yet made its way to the thin mountain air between Justin's ears.

"Wow! That seems kind of steep. I paid maybe $150 in Kansas City, delivered and stacked. Let me think about that, Justin. That kind of cash is pretty hard for me to come up with in one chunk. What would you charge to dump some ten- to twenty-foot logs in the backyard, and I'll cut them down and split them myself?"

"Hmmm ... I'd have to think about that for a minute. Everybody wants it cut already."

I could see this new wrinkle to his wood business had thrown him for a bit of a loop. Justin may have been many things, but a savvy marketer wasn't one of them. I came up with a better idea.

"How about this, Justin? You bring me a load of logs, and I'll treat you and a guest to dinner in our restaurant, not including drinks. You gotta pay for your drinks." (An extremely important caveat in Grand County when bartering goods and services is that not on any deal would you break even if unlimited free drinks were offered in exchange for anything.)

"And every time you bring me a load of logs, you get a dinner for two." A worst-case cost for a dinner for two without alcohol, if each person ordered rib eye steaks and dessert, was a sixty-dollar tab, with an actual out-of-pocket cost to me of twenty dollars. If they ordered alcohol with dinner, that profit would help offset the twenty-dollar expense. I'd be getting loads of uncut wood for fifteen to twenty bucks a pop. You couldn't beat that deal!

Justin was quick to accept, as his wife's birthday was fast upon him and he'd promised her a birthday feast at The Dairy Dine. The Riverside would be quite a step up on that promise. It would really work out well for both of us, as I needed wood, had limited funds to buy wood, but had the nicest restaurant in town and plenty of food to serve. Justin wanted a nice meal, had limited funds to buy a nice meal, but had plenty of wood to deliver. It was a Hot Sulphur Springs version of "The Gift of the Magi."

The following Monday, I was up early taking Lucy outside to do her morning business. There were no guests to check out and nobody checking in, and the restaurant was closed on Mondays, so it was as much of a day off as we got at The Riverside. It was 7:30 a.m., cool, crisp, and I was in my Riverside signature flannel robe, leaning on the woodshed, watching and waiting as Lucy sniffed her way to where she ultimately wanted to be. The morning stillness was broken by the loud rattle of a rickety truck coming down the alley between our neighbor's apartment building and Joe's Auto Repair, which bordered the north, back end of our property.

Enter an old, beat up, coughing, wheezing, barely running Ford pickup truck (Google research tells me it might have been a 1965) rusted out with bald tires, and a short bed to boot, a goofily grinning Justin Tiem at the wheel. In the back of that short bed were eight six-foot pine logs, each with a diameter of less than eight inches. (Tony's free logs the summer before were twenty feet long and eighteen inches in diameter.) Justin didn't go up into the woods and lop these logs down; I think possibly he found them lying in the streets of Hot Sulphur, or in the woods of Pioneer Park ... maybe even on the riverbank next to our property. They were like big twigs, the stuff you'd gather up at a city park if you were going to roast weenies.

"Here's the first load," Justin said, proudly beaming. "Where do you want me to put the wood?"

"Uh, just toss them right there on the ground. They shouldn't get in the way of anything." I don't think Justin picked up on my sarcasm.

"What time does the restaurant open?" Justin asked.

"We're closed on Mondays, so it'll have to be tomorrow night if that works for you."

"No problem; we'll see you tomorrow. I'm coming hungry!" Off chugged the oldest still-functioning piece of commercial wood-hauling equipment in the lower forty-eight states. Possibly there were older ones in some Third World countries ... possibly.

Justin and his pregnant bride showed up promptly Tuesday night — actually early — waiting in front of the hotel for us to open up. I sat them at the corner table, the best one with the best view of the river. Of course, as expected, they both ordered appetizers, salads, and the Dirty Rib Eye, plus desserts. But Justin decided to be a teetotaler that evening — no revenue-producing booze for which I could charge him, only the endless glass of free iced tea. (Perhaps he was being thoughtful of his wife, with child and probably not drinking, as he wasn't the least bit shy about pounding down the discounted hooch at the Meet & Greet.)

Justin and his wife had a lovely dinner, but unfortunately they ended up being our only customers that evening. I fired up the kitchen, paid a cook, and gave out two free meals for eight logs that I could have cut, split, and burned before I'd served Justin's rib eye. So far that "How could you go wrong with a deal like that?" deal was tilted in the favor of Mr. Tiem. Within a few short days that favorable tilt would turn to a ninety-degree landslide of inequity, and, true to previous form, it was certainly not tilted in my favor.

Two days later I awoke to find a load of ten logs, some but three or four feet long and all skinny as fence rails, deposited in the backyard. Twelve short hours after I'm thinking he must have been the one to deposit them in the yard and who shows up at The Riverside but Hot Sulphur's version of Jack Haley, this time with his mother. Two more rib eyes with all the trappings and an endless river of free iced tea refills later, my good humor was starting to wear a little thin.

The following Tuesday, the third "pile" of logs was delivered by Mr. Tiem. While there were a few more logs, they were still of the same quality with regards to their length and diameter. My good humor had now disappeared completely, to be replaced by a state of pure pissed-offedness, more at myself than at Justin, for once again I'd let myself fall prey to the old Grand County bait & switch.

Justin showed up by himself that evening, and I took the opportunity to have a frank man-to-man discussion with him about our previously agreed-to business arrangement.

"Hey, Richard! How're you doing this evening? Did you see the load I left this morning?"

"I saw a few small logs in the backyard that I hadn't noticed being there yesterday," I answered, somewhat icily. "Was that the 'load' you're talking about?"

"Sure was. That's why I'm here for dinner. I sure could use one of those rib eyes. I love the way you cook those steaks."

The attempt at flattery flew right by me, finding no purchase upon my frigid façade.

"Justin, I gotta be honest with you. Those aren't exactly what I'd call Dirty-Rib-Eye logs. I'd even be stretching it to call them Chicken-Spiedini logs. If we served hot dogs here at The Riverside, those logs you brought me today would be hot-dog logs. Get it?"

He cowered a little. "My equipment isn't set up to bring big wood ... you've seen my truck!"

'Yes, I've seen your truck, and I'm surprised that it would haul a case of toilet paper,' I thought but didn't say.

"But Justin, your business card says ... well ... I assumed you had a real wood business. Hell, you've even got a slogan! Are you telling me you can't actually put the wood where I'd like it?"

"I can ... I have to split it into eighteen-inch lengths, deliver, and stack it, one cord at a time. And for fifty dollars a cord and a few more of those Dirty Rib Eyes, I can deliver all the wood you want ... JUST-IN TIME!"

"Still want that Dirty Rib Eye, buddy... extra-well done?"

Eleven extra-well done Dirty Rib Eye dinners later, and an extra few hundred bucks to boot, I had my wood for the final winter of living life Riverside ... à la Justin Tiem.

* * *

Without question, our signature dish at The River Room was our Dirty Rib Eye, a twelve-ounce cut of choice steak from the rib section of the cow, which we would purchase in fifteen-pound Cryovac hunks and hand cut. We'd buy these slabs of beef for about $125 each and sell the resultant twenty steaks for $500, served with a starch, a vegetable, and a salad. With that sort of markup, you'd think that any idiot would be able to make a living in the restaurant business — except, of course, for this idiot.

This manner of preparation, i.e., "dirty," came from Dhoubi, our stoner chef from Kansas City, who got the recipe from my favorite KC restaurant , Il Trullo, which sadly is no longer in business. Il Trullo shut down shortly after we moved to the mountains, and I swear its demise was due in large part to the loss of our revenue, as I'd dropped bucket loads of money there both with business dinners and personal meals.

One advantage to the Dirty Rib Eye was that we could make a steak taste exceptional without using a wood-fired grill — good for us, as the kitchen in The Riverside didn't have a wood-fired grill, only a flattop griddle upon which a steak could be cooked. Another nice feature of the recipe involved the ability to "dirty" the steak — which gave it such a superior flavor — early in the day and finish it quickly to order during the dinner rush. This became a necessity as our cooking staff dwindled to one during the last six months of our operation.

The Dirty Rib Eye was accompanied by our poor man's Aceto Balsamico Tradizionale, officially known at The Riverside as Balsamico a Basso Costo delle Montagna, which we drizzled on the steak; it is essential to the dish.

The Riverside Dirty Rib Eye
(If you buy four steaks, this will serve four.)
1"-thick, nicely marbled rib eye steaks — choice for certain, prime if you can find them
About one dozen hardwood chunks — mesquite, hickory, apple, cherry, pecan — roughly the size of a five-year-old's fist
A cast iron skillet

In a charcoal chimney, get the wood to blazing, then dump it in your grill. Let it simmer down for a minute or two, until the flames are mostly gone and you're left with glowing, red-hot chunks of wood. Throw the meat directly on the glowing embers for no more than two minutes per side. That's it! Take them off and set them aside. They'll have some ash, some burn marks, maybe even a little grit on the exterior — no worries, as that also is digestable. Most importantly, what they'll also have is a seared, smoky char infused into the buttery fat inherent in the cut. (You can do this step early in the day, then cool them covered in the fridge.)

When you're ready to eat, make sure your cast iron skillet is hot — not white hot as if you were blackening redfish, but pretty hot. Finish the steaks in the skillet to your liking, no more than two-minutes per side, which shouldn't be any more than medium rare. (If you like your steak cooked beyond medium rare, I would suggest you skip the first three steps of this recipe, as I see your journey to Belly Blissville involving a trip to a Golden Corral.)

Slice the steaks on the bias into ½"-thick strips, fan out on your plate, and drizzle generously with the balsamic. We rested the steaks over a small mound of arugula; the smoky meat, the sweet tang of the balsamic, and the peppery arugula resulted in an exceptional marriage of flavors, as if it were always meant to be.

Balsamico a Basso Costo delle Montagna
One 16-oz bottle of inexpensive balsamic vinegar
2 teaspoons cornstarch
2 tablespoons corn syrup

Empty the balsamic into a saucepan, whisk in the cornstarch, and simmer until reduced by half. Stir in the corn syrup, let cool, and pour into one of those plastic, pointy-tipped condiment dispensers that chefs use to make drizzles and spiky swizzles on plates.

This stuff can also be used in salads, over fresh tomatoes when making caprese, and anywhere else you use a good balsamic — possibly even over Little Debbie bars, or Cheez-Its.

Better yet, if you can afford pricey, aged Aceto Balsamico Tradizionale, dispense with the aforementioned culinary skullduggery and enjoy the real thing, imagining while you enjoy this feast that you are dining Riverside.

CHAPTER TWENTY-FOUR

Damien the Mortician: Part II

In November of 2008 our first Thanksgiving arrived, and with the restaurant closed, we had a large meal for family, close friends, some unattached single townsfolk, and whatever guests were staying at the hotel. I gave the chefs the night off and did all of the cooking, with the exception of Sober Chef Danny deep-frying a turkey to go along with the monster bird that I had brined and roasted. Dhoubi didn't have to worry about anything beyond whetting his appetite and chowing down when the dinner bell rang. By the time the dinner bell did ring, Dhoubi was so wasted that he literally couldn't find his mouth with a fork, his first attempt at plowing mashed potatoes into his pie hole landing straight northeast, just missing his left eye but not missing his left eyebrow, his mouth still flopping, carp-like, waiting for that first bite of food.

The Thanksgiving feast was possibly the seminal point of Damien transitioning from good friend to a part of the family, as his family was all back in Nebraska. He never went into the details, but there seemed to be a hint of estrangement, particularly from the paternal side of the equation. No worries, as he melded into the Paradise clan as if he'd grown up next door.

The Christmas season arrived with several group Christmas parties: one of the local banks (not the thieves to whom we owed money); the *Sky-Hi Daily News* staff; and, my favorite, the Granby chapter of the Experimental Aircraft Association, EAA 1267, a bunch of high rollers, mostly Air Force and commercial pilots who'd retired to Grand County and flew daredevil around the mountains in small single-engine planes that they'd built from kits. Anyone that would risk his or her life for a thrill flying over the Indian Peaks, the winds churning a plane on a good day as if it were in a blender, would probably be the type of person that would raise hell at a Christmas party. And raise hell and spend lots of money they did.

Each of the parties was a hit, due in large part to another Dhoubi contribution that he lifted from Il Trullo, my favorite Kansas City restaurant: an efficient method of serving large groups known as the "Feed Me." It involved a six-course meal, all small plates, in which everyone was served the same food. The Feed Me was very easy on planning, ordering, preparing, plating, and serving, and people loved it. We would start with an appetizer, then follow with a salad or soup, a pasta course, a fish course, a meat course, and a dessert — all elegantly plated, and all culinary treats that few of the patrons had ever sampled, certainly never anywhere in Grand County.

The other constant of the successful Christmas bashes and the Feed Mes were Damien's desserts. He outdid himself with elegant ingredients and artistic plating, the bread puddings and berry cobblers of his October River-Room-dessert efforts taking a backseat to the likes of Sugar-dusted Mint Chocolate Ganache Cake with Cherry Coulis. Damien was quickly becoming a local star as the newly renowned pâtissier of Grand County.

As the restaurant was now starting to get legs with locals, we were excited about the prospects of the upcoming New Year's Eve crowd. We were completely sold out with three seatings of forty-five diners, two weeks before the end of the year. We would be having a special yet easy to prep, plate, and serve menu of Riverside Prime Rib, Roasted Cornish Game Hens over Leek Polenta and Porcini Sauce, Dhoubi's killer Lasagna with Béchamel Sauce, and Hearty Cioppino … and Damien was in charge of the dessert. What would his special talents bring us on this most special of evenings? We could only dream and imagine.

The first seating was at 5:00 p.m., and all was ready by 4:00, The River Room aglow with beautiful centerpieces on every table, the lights glistening, and the music sublime. I was in my tuxedo, with a festive bow tie of cardinal red, and Julie dressed to the nines as hostess and proud creator of this festive atmosphere. There was only one glitch in the evening proceedings: our maître d' and dessert maker, Damien, was nowhere to be seen.

We'd been busy all day: checking out guests, cleaning rooms, doing laundry, making beds, cleaning bathrooms, checking in guests, hauling in firewood, setting tables, doing dishes, stocking the bar, stoking the fire, helping the chefs, getting dressed, fixing drinks for guests ... just another busy day at The Riverside. I hadn't given a thought at any point throughout the day to Damien and his essential duty of having a fabulous dessert to send our guests off to their New Year's revelries. It was assumed that he would punctually show up, dessert in tow, and be nattily attired as I was counting on him to direct traffic in the dining room while I worked the bar and glad-handed diners, as was my owner-given right and most necessary duty — I referred to it as "working the room," and it gave me an immense amount of pleasure.

I said out loud to no one in particular, "Oh my, but where is Damien? Has anyone talked to him today?"

Daughter Rachel offered, "Wow! Now that you mention it, I haven't heard from him all day ... which is weird. He always calls me sometime during the day."

Then it dawned it me, and I shared my insight with the group. "I'm guessing that he's been so busy all day making dessert — making a really killer dessert — that he's been totally out of pocket. That's gotta be it. He'll show up here any minute with something that will blow us out of the water!"

I believed I had succeeded in both lifting their spirits and hyping them up, almost working them into a chant of "Damien ... Damien ... Damien," each successive Damien getting stronger, louder.

And then as if on cue, Damien came slinking into The Riverside, hunched over like he was trying to hide E.T. in his coat. He rushed by us all, wordless, back into the furthest reaches of the kitchen near the walk-in cooler, adjacent to the two out-of-code, frost-proliferate freezers where he normally assembled his masterpieces.

All were excited, aglow, and agog about the possibilities of what Damien had brought for dessert, quietly hustling in as if he had just stolen the crown jewels and was about to use them in his dessert presentation.

All except for me. I was as nervous as the proverbial whore in church, as I'd noticed a couple of big, fat, hairy, unusual things, things that totally belied the proclivities of the reliable Damien that I'd come to know. First off, not only was Damien not clad in a tuxedo — as was the discussed and previously agreed-to dress code for the evening — he was wearing his everyday slum-about jacket and looked as if he'd been sleeping in a cave for the past few days, unshaven and unkempt. Second, every past fancy Damien dessert, particularly the ones that were served with such aplomb at the recent Christmas parties, involved not much less than a caravan to transport and assemble: platters, trays, plates, coolers, flambé torches, silver service; i.e., they were a production. Whatever was for dessert to-night, this most special of nights, was in a bundle that fit neatly against Damien's belly and under his winter coat. And thirdly, Damien never slunk, or snuck, into The Riverside — or Starbucks, or City Market, or Ace Hardware, or anywhere else he frequented in Grand County — he always walked into the room as if he were announcing himself. I often wondered why this man of means hadn't hired one of the unemployed locals, of whom there were many who would work for but a thimble of gin, to proceed him into a room and proclaim to those in attendance, "Please welcome," as he entered with a flair and a grand dose of panache, "the one and only Supreme Mortician of Grand County, Colorado ... Mr. Damien Farmer!"

So I was unnerved. 'Hmmmm,' I thought, trying to reach for the positive, 'may-be the dessert involves truffles, possibly even white truffles, and small gilded wafers of Belgian chocolate. That's why he had them under his coat, protecting them, nurturing them.'

And then another pep talk from me to me, 'This dessert is so fantastic, so over-the-top, that it explains why he hasn't shaved and showered for a few days, why he didn't have time to put on the tuxedo we'd talked about, why he's wearing the same clothes that we saw him in when he was here two days ago. In fact, this dessert is so awesome that he hasn't even talked to us the past two days.'

At this point I decided to quit having internal one-on-one pep talks and get to the truth, as it was zero hour and forty-five humans with money were minutes away from having dinner with us, followed by another forty-five humans with money, followed by another forty-five humans with money. This was some serious busi-ness coming at us, and I needed to know what was for dessert and why our maître d' looked as if he'd been on a Denver street corner holding a sign and collecting quarters for the past two days.

"Alright, Damien, what's going on?" I asked. "Where have you been all day, and what in the hell's for dessert?" I tried not to be testy, as this was ultimately an uncontracted, uncompensated, employee-at-will relationship. But dammit, we'd had up to this point an unspoken understanding, a gentlemen's agreement: We gave him food and booze, and he showed up on time, clean, and brought dessert and welcomed people to the restaurant. Here we were on our biggest of people-seating, dessert-needing nights, and he showed up late, sans the previously agreed-upon tuxedo, and, as far as my eyes could see, dessertless.

A whole new level of testy shot back at me, one I'd not seen before from our friend Damien. *"Ice cream! Ice cream is what's for dessert!* Chocolate and vanilla, with Hershey's Syrup if they want it, and sprinkles, assuming you have some sprinkles, and you should because I left some here when I made the Fantaisie Desserts Français avec les Paillettes for the newspaper people, which incidentally, went totally unappreciated!" Tears were beginning to well up in Damien's eyes.

Seeing that Damien was obviously fighting some demons unknown, I quickly backed down and tried to assuage his angst with a different tone. "Not to worry, Damien. If you brought ice cream for dessert, then that's what we're having for dessert! Who in the hell doesn't like ice cream anyway? Uh ... were you still planning on being maître d' this evening — you know, wearing a tux and maybe shaving?"

Damien answered, much calmer. "No, sorry ... but I can't. I'll pretty much have to stay out of sight in the kitchen. I can help the chefs and do the desserts."

"Damien, I don't mean to pry, but what the hell is going on? I thought you were excited about working the New Year's crowd and making something a little more upscale than scoops of ice cream for dessert."

And then Damien opened up and unleashed those demons from his tortured soul as well as a wellspring of tears from his reddened eyes. "I've been hiding in my house from the sheriff the last two days. They've been sitting out front waiting for me to come home — they think I'm gone because I haven't answered the door or the phone, and my car isn't out front; I've got it parked in the garage. I had to sneak out the back door and walk here when the sheriff finally left about an hour ago. I couldn't get to the store to make anything for dessert!" His eyes were a flood, his self-esteem a barren desert.

Now profound sympathy and concern came from me. "I can't believe this, Damien! Are you serious? What in the hell is the sheriff after you for?"

He was indeed serious, as he explained that there was an issue with him re-investing money from some pre-need accounts that he'd bought as existing assets of the funeral-home business. Unbeknownst to me at this point, Damien had an extremely contentious relationship with the county coroner, and she was looking into every possible nook and cranny of his business to bring him to ruin. The relationship was so rancorous that it was her intention to have Damien arrested on New Year's Eve so he would have to sit in the Grand County Hilton for a few days, court being out of session until the fifth of January, before he would get his first opportunity to plead his case before the judge … unless, of course, some kind soul ponied up $5000 cash to bond him out of jail. The coroner, a female unnamed, was pretty certain that Damien had no friends with that kind of cash, and she chose this lull in the legal process to make his life, and his holiday, at best a short-term hell. Her long-term dream for Damien was a prison term and the loss of his funeral home — the funeral home at which she had previously worked, the funeral home which she had aspired to own, and the funeral home from which Damien had fired her after his purchase of the business. Possibly vengeance was at the root of her actions versus a greater concern for the public cause?

So Damien spent the evening hiding out in the kitchen, helping the chefs, artistically plating his scoops of ice cream with Hershey's Syrup and the occasional sprinkle, and, most importantly, continuing to escape the long arm of the Grand County law. My memory is foggy as to where he ended up spending the night, but I do recall that there were no brushes with the authorities that evening — not with Damien, our kitchen help, or any of the assembled New Year's Eve patrons of The Riverside.

* * *

New Year's Day dawned bright and beautiful. The morning sun and the brilliant blue of the Middle Park sky brought the repentant revelers down for a 10:00 a.m. breakfast and a robust head start on the new year. A day of good-byes at the checkout, room clean up, and the occasional glimpse at the football games were followed by a slow dinner crowd, which afforded us the opportunity to sit down to dinner with our visiting friends from Kansas City on their last night at The Riverside. Damien, now seemingly free from the threat of arrest for a few days as he felt the sheriff would be home enjoying his holiday, assumed his role as maître d' and part-time waiter, and demanded that we sit, relax, and enjoy the experience and cuisine of The River Room Restaurant. Perhaps this was his attempt at

216

recompense for his dessert and tuxedo no-show of the previous evening. The wine and the accompanying good times flowed, and the hectic holiday week was indeed ending on a sweet note.

I can't remember who came and told me that the Grand County police were in the lobby waiting to serve a warrant for Damien's arrest, but the timing couldn't have been worse as Damien was in the process of serving our hot entrées. Couldn't I have had an opportunity to quaff the fine wine and savor the rib eye before having to deal with our friend being handcuffed by civil servants that made Barney Fife look like the paragon of law enforcement? It was not to be. As our hot entrées sat before us, delivered by Damien as his last act as a free man, he began removing his turquoise jewelry and handing it to Julie for safekeeping, looked mournfully at us, and said, "I must go." The scene in the Garden of Gethsemane must have looked and felt much like this, except they'd already gotten to drink their wine and eat their bread!

The county coroner really outdid herself in getting her judge buddy to set a $50,000 bond on some minor embezzlement wrap for a local business owner who probably wasn't very likely to bolt the county and leave his life's investment sitting fallow. Three hours and $5000 on my American Express card later, coupled with a session with a slick, neon-orange-business-card bail bondsman that made me feel, well, icky, and Damien was sprung from the Grand County Jail. Grand County is slightly notorious for its ability to generate revenue from speed traps at the bottom of mountainous stretches or unlicensed, defective-car-owning neo-criminals that drink, drive, and wind up spending quality time at the county lock-up — thus the saying: "Grand County — Come on Vacation, Leave on Probation!"

Then throw this little detail into the mix: The bond contract I filled out and signed not only stated that I was giving them $5000 but also that I was responsible for a surety bond for $50,000. If Damien were actually guilty of all of these nefarious charges and decided to bolt to Cancun, we'd be out some serious money.

'Wait just a minute!' I thought. This guy showed up at our hotel/restaurant first as a good customer, then as a friend who wanted to help us by waiting tables and making desserts, which gave him something to do and someone to hang with when nobody in Grand County was busy giving up the ghost. We really didn't know him at all; we didn't know his background, his foreground, his above or below ground.

We didn't have a clue about this guy, and I had just signed a $50,000 surety bond to get him out of jail for charges we didn't know the first thing about. Could've been murder, terrorism, kidnapping, hotel/restaurant embezzlement charges — we had no real idea why those cuffs were slapped on him. And I willingly stepped into this deal for fifty grand — fifty grand that I damn sure didn't have. It was my legs they'd break if in fact the Damien-off-to-Cancun scenario turned into reality.

Let's be honest. This whole Riverside ordeal at its essence was about us taking a leap of faith. Buying a business in which we had no experience, in a town that didn't have any customers, in an economy that we didn't know would start turning south as soon as we signed the purchase papers, and with a predator for a banking partner — with this track record, why wouldn't I put $50,000 on the line that a virtual stranger wasn't really a felon and would stand true to face charges of I wasn't sure what and not put me into default for money I didn't have with Vito the Mile-High Bounty Hunter?

Like it or not, every aspect of living and dying, including getting out of bed in the morning and going back to bed at night, is all about faith.

CHAPTER TWENTY-FIVE

Surviving Damien: Part II

While the funeral business in Grand County was deadly slow for Damien, it wasn't nonexistent, and striking up an unlikely friendship with the local mortician had its, uh … death benefits.

If you had told me that our new life in the mountains would involve me helping to lift coffins into a hearse on a few occasions, not as a pallbearer but as a much-needed second set of arms and muscles, I would have scoffed at you. If you had suggested that I would spend a spring afternoon at a cemetery on a mountainside, in a sleet blizzard that felt like an AK-47-fueled BB attack, helping set a tombstone as it was craned from the back of a truck onto the top of a newly occupied grave, I would have complimented you on your wildly fertile imagination. And if you had proposed that I would have a friend that had a hot tub in his two-car garage, surrounded by frozen corpses that would be unable to find their way into permanent underground repose until the Colorado May spring thaw, I'd have thought you mad beyond reason. But all of this I did (stopping short of entering that garage and soaking in that hot tub), and it was obviously I who was mad beyond reason.

Second to the obvious first choice of big, hairy tropical spiders, death is what we mortals fear most — third would be morticians. I never discussed the mortician business with Damien, although I couldn't help but be curious about it. Anytime there was ever a discussion even headed in that direction, however, Damien was always matter of fact and nonplussed about the issue of dying and dealing with the dead as, of course, this was his job, hard as it is for us nonmorticians to imagine.

Once when describing to Damien the crawl space below the kitchen that required a clean out of the most god-awful stuff — that twelve-month collection of fouled dishwater and bits and chunks of old food, the smell of which was beyond one's most brutal imagination — at the end of my dramatic narrative, Damien looked at me with a deadpan face, thoroughly unimpressed, and asked, "Ever had a dead, bloated body blow up in your face?" He pretty much had me with that one, and that was the last time I attempted to impress Damien, the only mortician I'd ever befriended, with one of my kitchen unpleasantries.

* * *

Entering into our second season of operation of The Riverside, we decided to close the hotel in early April after an Easter brunch, take a few weeks' vacation back to Kansas City, then return and put in a much needed new floor, using high-end industrial food-service rated tile that I'd scored for free from an old customer from my previous life, the life in which my business made money and I only worked forty hours a week.

One day near the end of March, out of the blue, Damien called me, excited to the point of being out of breath, and said, "Richard, I'm at an auction in Denver that is loaded with restaurant equipment — some used, some new, but all stuff that you need!"

"Stuff like what?" I asked.

"Like a new commercial freezer; like a new stove, grill, and flattop; like a new cold station; like all of the stainless steel tables you'd ever need! And all of it's going to go for pennies on the dollar!" Again, Damien was all but breathless with excitement.

"That sounds great, Damien, but I don't have pennies or dollars. I could maybe come up with $500–$600 to get some of the stainless steel stuff, and we can replace the wooden tables while we're ripping out the old floor … maybe, if the price is right. That would go a long way to making the health department happy."

"Don't worry about it. I'll buy it all! Pay me back whenever you can."

Now I was breathless and blathering. "But ... but, Damien, I can't … I don't know what to say."

"Don't say anything. You need it, and I'm sick of working in that dump of a kitchen. Oops, gotta go. They're starting the bidding for the stove. I'll let you know how it goes." Click.

Within a matter of a few hours, the plans for a new floor also included new stainless steel work tables; a new oven, grill, and flattop; a new refrigerator and freezer, both commercial grade; a new cold table; a new warming station; and a varied assortment of serving items, pots, and pans. The only out-of-pocket cost to me, upfront, would be the rental of a truck and the excruciating round-trip to Denver to load and haul all of this stuff back to The Riverside.

I'll condense three weeks of backbreaking labor, much of it donated by friends and neighbors, into a Memorial Day grand opening of Season Two of The Riverside Hotel, Bar & Restaurant under the proprietorship of Julie and Richard Paradise, featuring the glistening new, Damien Farmer-supplied, almost up-to-code River Room kitchen. It was a glorious feeling to have a new six-burner gas grill with six working gas burners; a freezer that didn't grow layers of frost that would technically qualify as a glacier; a cold station right in the middle of the kitchen, where we could keep salad stuff cool without running back and forth to the walk-in during the dinner rush to get salad stuff for every entrée order; stainless steel work surfaces to replace the old wooden tables that contained a century's worth of old food jam hiding in their cracks and crevices; and a floor so beautiful, so clean, so solid that it made us feel as if we were actually striding across a surface that ran concurrent with blessed terra firma.

We were proud; we were rejuvenated; and we were ready to tackle our second season. We were also indebted to Damien way beyond any level that I wanted to think about at that particular time. But think about it I did. What was behind this unsolicited, profound act of largesse, executed as efficiently and casually as a mortician embalms a corpse? I started to believe the answer to this question may actually lie in comments that Damien had made over the previous few months — mostly offhand comments, but certainly insinuations that were possibly meant to plant seeds in my overstressed, cash-starved mind.

Damien started by making generic comments, or insinuations, that he would like to get into the hospitality business; it was where his true heart and skills lay, and, after all, the mortuary business in Grand County offered very little opportunity for either toil or revenue. Then the comments began to get more specific, such as, "If I owned The Riverside, I would have freshly baked cinnamon rolls every morning; the guests would smell them as they lay in bed," or, "If I owned this place,

I would move the Brunswick bar into the Green Room, with polished wooden floors, and brass and mirrors. I'd turn this into every Grand Countian's Friday night dream destination." Couple this with Damien's all but full-time involvement in the restaurant and hotel. He installed, again gratis, a hospitality software system, light years beyond the spiral notebook, pencil, and calculator that I had been using to calculate dinner bills, room bills, and bar bills. He even once admitted referring to himself, to a disgruntled customer while Julie and I were away for a weekend, as "the soon-to-be new owner of The Riverside." And so it went.

Then it hit me. Damien had put new equipment, gratis for the time being, into The Riverside kitchen because he intended to eventually buy the business from us. That had to be it. Julie and I talked about this and weren't sure that we were ready to throw in the towel. We'd just been there a little more than a year and were excited about the prospects of our second season, having a year of hard-won experience under our belt. But the possibility gnawed at me to the point that one day in early June of 2009, out of nowhere just standing in the Green Room, I looked him in the eye and asked, "Damien, do you want to buy The Riverside?"

Without hesitation and as resolutely as if I had asked him if he'd like the rarest of white truffles delicately shaved atop his steaming, cream-laden parmesan risotto, he looked me squarely back in the eye and said, emphatically, "Yes! I want to buy The Riverside!"

So there it was. We'd owned The Riverside but a little more than a year, experiencing the life of mountain hotel proprietors but for one summer season; we were four years ahead of our five-year plan, which was only half of our ten-year master plan; and we already had a buyer for the business. To make matters fall into place all the more seamlessly, my old employer, the large conglomerate to whom I'd sold my business, had called me in late May asking if I would consider consulting on a few projects. When I told them that I would be interested in consulting (not telling them that I was so desperate for cash that I would have considered cleaning their toilets for minimum wage), they then went one step further and asked if they could put an offer together to get me back full time — not right away, as they knew I still had the hotel to run, but maybe within the next two years, with the ultimate requirement being relocation to the corporate headquarters in Mississippi.

I'd like to tell you that I had serious soul-searching talks with my wife and business partner, with family, with friends and neighbors regarding this once again life-altering decision that was staring us in the face. Should we really consider giving up on our dream so quickly, selling out, and heading back into the corporate world that I'd just abandoned one short year prior — abandoned with glee, in fact? What about the five-to-ten-year plan of building up the business to the point where we could pay off the bank and the SBA, then sell it and make a sizable-enough return on our investment to fund a comfortable retirement? Selling now would merely allow us the opportunity to get whole by getting our original investment back.

All of this introspective soul-searching was avoided with one subjective look at The Riverside's financials. The reality of the situation had me looking at a willing and able buyer for the hotel that I might not stumble upon again in the next twenty years, a way out of the financial quagmire that engulfed us, and a high-paying job waiting for me after we crawled out of the hole, albeit in Mississippi working for a conglomerate. I was quick to give Damien the news that the negotiations for the sale of The Historic Riverside Hotel, Bar & Restaurant should commence. Concurrent with this, Julie and I totally and absolutely checked out mentally as proprietors, and all but turned the keys over to Damien and his hotel and restaurant financial software program, which was conveniently linked to our bank account. The program made things so easy for us, especially considering that I didn't have to learn to operate the system; Damien took full control of things, leaving Julie time to look for homes in Mississippi and me time to start traveling for the old company, travel that was accompanied by a regular paycheck and health insurance.

* * *

With a new kitchen and a new unofficial General Manager and soon to be new owner, our second season started off with a resounding "THUD"; The Riverside was all dressed up with no place to go. The effect on tourism and the lack of discretionary income due to the downturn in the economy was so profound in 2009 compared to 2008 that it seemed as if an impenetrable bubble had been placed around the perimeter of Hot Sulphur Springs. Our first year, tourist traffic was a steady, constant flow of cars driving through Hot Sulphur Springs, many stopping at The Riverside, most staying and leaving money. The start of this second season, business for us as well as all others in Hot Sulphur was reminiscent only of the ghostly visages that were purported to exist throughout our little burg. It was bleak at best, yet I didn't get too discouraged as I knew my ticket out of this business and the town was all but waiting for me at the will-call window.

Business was down but employment and expenses at The Riverside were up. Damien had hired two high school girls to wait tables for the lunch crowd (although there was no lunch crowd) and an absolute shark for a dinner waitress, highly efficient and greedy beyond belief — there went my daughter's occasional attempt at tips and some small semblance of an income. Add to that the burden of payroll, payroll taxes, and unemployment insurance, necessary items that Damien's fancy hospitality software didn't address but that were still on my plate as owner of the hotel and the hotel's checkbook. I was writing our dinner waitress checks for $400–$500 every week, on meager dinner business that because of the new software I had no way of substantiating. I'd just get a visit from Damien after service on a Saturday, during which he'd hand me a ticket and say, "You owe Jeanette $480 for the week; she's outside waiting for her check." That was $480 dollars that I could have been paying my daughter, or my wife, or me! Jeanette would grab her check and then retire to the bar where she would eat her comped Dirty Rib Eye and pound down her comped vodka martinis — all part of the deal between her and Damien, my new unofficial GM. Good work if you can get it!

The high school lunch girls were even worse, as we were doing NO lunch business whatsoever. I could have sat buck naked in the lobby waiting on lunch diners and, more days than not, never have to worry about putting my pants on to wait the tables. Yet, I sat and watched these young girls sit, waiting for business that never came. Typically, the only lunch the chef would prepare on most days was the meal for the high school help, included in the deal. And at the end of their shift they got a handout of thirty-two dollars in guaranteed salary — guaranteed by Damien; paid by me. But again, I was pretty cool about things as I knew that the end to this financial bludgeoning was but a sales contract away.

And I felt good about this because of things that were happening all around me, things that I felt were all but days away from pushing the exchange of our hotel for cash money from a dream to being a reality. Things like Damien telling me he met with the bank to make certain that his CDs would be acceptable collateral for his loan to buy the hotel. Things like Damien bringing in friends, bringing in architects and engineers, bringing in potential business partners to stand in various parts of the hotel and ask, "What do you think if I were to tear out these windows and put in French doors?" or "Is this a load-bearing wall, and, if not, can we get rid of it and open up the whole area?" Not to mention the big things like Damien buying all new restaurant equipment and bringing in a fancy hospitality software system. And the all-important biggest thing: Damien looking me in the eye and telling me, *"Yes! I want to buy The Riverside!"*

* * *

I don't have to tell you that Damien did not buy The Riverside. One night in mid-July, 2009, he and I had one of those face-to-face reckonings, much like the earlier one in which I point blank asked him if he was going to buy the hotel. I asked him about it point blank again, this time eight weeks after all of his aforementioned posturing about buying the place.

"So, Damien, I've shot you a number, to which you've given me no counteroffer. Are you still interested in buying The Riverside? Julie and I are at a serious crossroads for planning our next life steps, dependent upon what you and we do together. I've really got to know something!"

His response was silence for an uncomfortable ten seconds and a shaky stare back at me. And then it came forth, and it wasn't really a surprise as I'd truly known, deep down, all along, that this dog wasn't going to hunt.

"NO, I'm no longer interested in buying the hotel. I've got some other things going on in my life, like my lawsuit against the county coroner, and it's best for me to concentrate on those things right now." He looked ashamed and a little frightened as he waited for my reaction, and frightened he well should have been.

I all but exploded. "What the … ? You had people in here *yesterday* talking about remodeling the place. You told me you met with the bank last week to cash in your CDs as a down payment. You loaded up our kitchen with new equipment, which you know I haven't the funds to pay for. We haven't even seriously talked money. Can't you at least make me a counteroffer?" It was now I who was sick to my stomach with the fear of what this new reality was offering, acting business-like and nonplussed even as I saw my lifeline slipping away before my eyes.

My ticket out of Hot Sulphur and financial ruin, to this point held for me in waiting by Damien, was now being ripped up and thrown to the wind by this mysterious, fickle, underemployed body embalmer.

Simpering, then defiant, he said, "I'm just not interested anymore." Like that was a reasonable excuse to end this two-month ruse and scam to which we'd so gullibly fallen prey.

That little outburst made me lose my business-like, nonplussed demeanor. It was now time for F-bombs — never fashionable but occasionally so necessary. There is absolute magic in the well-articulated F-bomb, as I'd learned in my previous thirty years of business experience. As a little guy that posed no physical threat to people, and as a notably nice guy who posed even less of a threat, I'd successfully used the F-bomb, with exacting and calculating timing, tenor, and inflection, to cause individuals who could knock my block off with a flick of a finger to cower and recoil from me in fear, all but eager to succumb to my wants, full of dread of the ultimate consequences of further pissing me off.

A few words of advice regarding the use of the F-bomb: Before you go ripping them off indiscriminately, know that the F-bomb has to be used judiciously, as using it all of the time renders it meaningless. Using it selectively — maybe once or twice a year in a formal business or personal conversation at a pivotal time and in a serious situation — makes it lethal; it really has to get people's attention.

First, practice at home by yourself. Then, after making sure there aren't any kids or grandmas around, let one or two of those babies fly the next time you feel that you're in a desperate situation involving important human interaction. Remember, serious stuff has got to be on the line. For instance, don't use it at the dry cleaners when someone has cut in front of you in line. There has to be a lot more on the line than your being inconvenienced or unconsidered.

Back to Damien ...

I exploded. "Well fine, then!" I began, as if the cork had just erupted from an old, foul bottle of cheap champagne.

I continued, and not calmly, "I want that *fucking* software system and that *fucking* computer out of this lobby by noon tomorrow, and you had better get me hooked back up with my credit card machine and my bank before you leave tonight, *fucking pronto,* or I'll be up at the courthouse tomorrow to discuss theft charges. I believe that just might *fuck* with your current probation situation a bit. Am I not correct?" Smoke and steam were wafting from my blood-red eyeballs, my ears, and the surface of my ruby-red visage. I then turned and stormed off to our living quarters, not giving Damien the chance for a rebuttal of any type.

The F-bomb tirade brought the desired result, as not only did I hear Damien's asshole pucker, I heard it loudly snap shut like a mousetrap. For whatever reason he backed out of our imaginary deal, he was now contrite and in the lobby early the following a.m., unplugging USB cords and other Internet stuff, packing up his computer, and shuffling out of The Riverside with his figurative tail between his legs. I was still smoking at him, not saying anything like, "Sorry it didn't work out," or "Maybe we can still feed you free rib eyes." I said not a word, but my glare blasted a novel's worth of feelings towards him, mostly ill.

When my heat subsided, I was as distraught at the loss of a buyer for the hotel as I was at the loss of the friend who was supposed to buy it.

* * *

You've just metaphorically witnessed a spark, then a promising smolder, then a fire, growing and roaring into a full-fledged conflagration of friendship and family; next the tragic dampening then drowning of those passionate flames, the flames abating, then disappearing, the fire ending up a mound of smoking coals, eventually dying with nothing remaining beyond a pile of ruined ashes, left only to be sifted through by the fueling parties hoping to recover but a semblance of the good feelings that had once existed substantially between them.

Damien stayed behind in Grand County, plea-bargaining his way out of the theft charges that took him from our New Year's dinner service but brutally suffering the bad PR that came from the county coroner's trumped-up allegations against him and his business. The death business in Grand County was slow at the best of times; it was nonexistent when your customers had the supposition — false or otherwise — that the guy that was going to prep and plant them was a crook. Damien and his mortuary went tits-up shortly after we headed for Mississippi.

While I never got the full story from Damien of why one can't now journey to Hot Sulphur Springs and spend a relaxing getaway weekend at Damien Farmer's Historic Riverside Hotel, Bar & Restaurant, I have more than a few suppositions. I really do believe that Damien both wanted and intended to buy the hotel, but I also believe that he was clinically delusional regarding his financial ability to pull it off. He was already in debt to Acme Savings & Loan with his funeral home mortgage, and Acme Savings & Loan was well aware of what a dog The Riverside was when it came to producing loan-repaying revenue. He'd also made numerous references to family wealth, as they'd helped him get into the mortuary business; however, I'm guessing that the phone call back home requesting additional money to get into now another line of work was icily received and the request summarily dismissed. While Damien's intentions of purchasing The Riverside may have been pure, his means of a successful acquisition were purely nonexistent — at any price that we might have been able to negotiate.

Per his instructions, we ended up selling Damien's loaned kitchen equipment for nickels on the dollar in an auction, the meager check then forwarded to him shortly before the kind folks at Acme Savings & Loan swooped in and took possession of the remaining furniture, fixtures, and foundation of our Historic Riverside Hotel, Bar & Restaurant. They tried to make a case that Damien's kitchen equipment was part of the original loan and secured property. I once again judiciously used the F-word and gleefully told them what they could do to themselves, and sold the stuff with prejudice.

Even after the hotel sale fall-through and all of the bad feelings and bad words that ensued, Julie and I eventually forgave Damien, Julie hugging him with moist eyes immediately prior to pulling out of Hot Sulphur for the final time late on the Sunday afternoon of March 21st, 2010. Lucy barked viciously at Damien one last time … part in hate, part in love.

We have a long list of rues from our Grand County midlife transgression, but the friendships that we fostered and grew, and even those that we made and lost, are not on that list. We left Grand County without a nickel; the only things of value that we took and have left to spend and enjoy are the memories of the friends that we left behind.

CHAPTER TWENTY-SIX

The Wheels Fall Off

During our first weekend of living at The Riverside full time I received a couple of harbingers of things to come that would unfortunately validate my already nervous self-examination about: Have we done the right thing?

On June 25th, 2008, as I was driving into Hot Sulphur Springs following the truck belonging to the jackleg moving company that I had hired on the cheap, I took a deep breath and drank in the moment. The sun was setting over Mt. Bross and the spacious valley that was carved by the Colorado River, the valley that is Hot Sulphur Springs; it all lay before us in spectacular fashion as we drove in for the first time as residents.

"Ahhh," I exhaled, then said out loud to both Julie and myself, "It's June 25th, and we're arriving at our new home and our new life. It's hard to believe that we're actually going to live here! Let's never forget this date!"

No sooner were the words out of my mouth when that date and the factoid part of my brain collided, and I said to myself, as loudly as one can talk to oneself — 'JUNE 25th!! YOU IDIOT! THAT'S THE ANNIVERSARY OF THE BATTLE OF THE LITTLE BIGHORN! YOU KNOW, CUSTER'S LAST STAND?! HE WAS A FOOL, RUSHING BRAZENLY INTO A VERDANT VALLEY NEXT TO A RIVER — FOR GLORY, FOR HIS EGO — AND HE WAS SLAUGHTERED ON THIS DAY, 132 YEARS AGO. BRUTALLY SLAUGHTERED FOR THE SAKE OF VAIN GLORY! DO FOOLS NEVER LEARN FROM HISTORY?'

As I instantly recognized the obvious parallel between the blond-locked General and my headlong rush into the unknown, I remembered a quote that offered me temporary comfort, this from Teddy Roosevelt in an 1899 speech fighting for the establishment of the U.S. National Parks Department and brought to light in reference to General Custer in the definitive tome on the subject of the General and the battle, *Son of the Morning Star: Custer and The Little Bighorn,* by Evan S. Connell.

> *Far better it is to dare mighty things, to win glorious triumphs,*
> *even though checkered by failure, than to take rank with those poor*
> *spirits who neither enjoy much nor suffer much, because they live*
> *in the gray twilight that knows not victory nor defeat.*

Dare mighty things, indeed! The content of this fine quote gave me great comfort as I chastised and felt superior to you poor spirits, you that live in that gray twilight — you that still have your 401Ks intact in the bank.

So much for the pursuit of glory …

… and on to the bigger harbinger. Our first weekend had us hosting guests in six rooms, and one of the couples were old-time Abner guests, i.e., people that had stayed at The Riverside for years and knew both its charms and its failings. They were celebrating their wedding anniversary and were staying in the two-room suite, "Mavis," overlooking the river; a wonderful couple who were very supportive of what we'd done to improve the hotel. They had a lovely dinner that they raved about, complete with wine and champagne, then retired to the bar for a "final-final." Through bar chatter I learned that the gentleman was a circuit court judge in Denver — a very distinguished, intelligent man; a man whose opinion would hold some weight.

After I shared our story of quitting our jobs, packing it up, and moving to our brave new life in the mountains, he looked at me earnestly and said, "I really admire you for what you've done. You've done great things with this place, and I really hope that you're able to make a go of it. But I can tell you, Grand County is a damn tough place to make a living. I can only wish you the best."

When he told me this, the economy was still robust, or as we know now in retrospect, was still robust on the surface to us idiots. The bubble had yet to burst, and this guy who dealt with the day-to-day reality of making a go of it in Colorado had looked me in the eye, with a face that showed genuine concern, and said, "Grand County is a damn tough place to make a living. I can only wish you the best."

After our first weekend in our new venture, it began to occur to me that a carrion of Kobe Beef might stand a better chance against vultures than we against our ultimate demise.

* * *

Our first five months of operation, January to May of 2008, were not indicative of the financial struggles that lay ahead. First of all, Julie and I weren't there to experience the experience; rather, we were relying on three unsupervised innkeeping novices under the age of twenty-five to manage our life savings. The business still had a decent amount of money in the bank, and Julie and I both still had jobs and incomes. I'd sit down monthly to pay bills and payroll for the distant business without feeling much of a sting; I went along as happily as if I had good sense.

Things started to get a little hinky when we hired the previously mentioned bar-tender/building contractor to redo our living quarters. Again, this was an instance of me ignoring the fact that I was all but being beat to within an inch of my life by red flags, as prior to engaging Jack Legg Construction to tackle the big job of renovating our quarters, I hired them to redo our walk-in cooler that the State Department of Health mandated be redone. That job went 40 percent over budget and took two weeks longer to complete than promised; yet, armed with this knowledge, I went ahead and rehired Jack Legg Construction for the living quarters. Their proposal seemed sound, and while at the high end of what we could afford, the numbers still fell within my worst-case budget for the project. However, there was one important little fact that the contractors held from us in their proposal, a fact that would play heavily into the project taking five weeks longer to complete than promised.

In fact, Jack Legg Construction, while tackling The Riverside's renovation, were also in the midst of building a competing bar and restaurant in neighboring Silverthorne, Colorado — *their* bar and restaurant. The plan was for them to have their place open by Memorial Day weekend, 2008 — the same Memorial Day weekend that Julie and I had intended to take up residence in our new living quarters so we could manage our first sold-out holiday weekend on site. This didn't happen, as I strongly suppose that any extra of Jack Legg's workers, time, and efforts went to meet their restaurant's deadlines. The further fact that July 4th was the first night we were able to spend in our bedroom tells me my supposition is more than just such. I wouldn't dare insinuate either that the 25 percent overage they hit us with in labor and materials would have been due to any bad accounting or misallocated costs from their own restaurant project. Why, only a thief or a crook would do something like that, and there certainly weren't any of those in Grand County that hadn't already been signed on to work at the local bank.

While dropping ninety grand with these part-time room-remodelers for the renovation of our living quarters would be considered fiscally brain-dead by most, it still had a long way to go before it topped our primary financial f-up, that being the purchase of the property in the first place. The previous owner of The Riverside ran a cash-only business and, therefore, kept no reliable records as to the earning potential of the hotel and restaurant: no occupancy rates, no average number of diners per month, no monthly or annual revenue figures — nothing. So not only did we quit good jobs and leave friends and family to buy a 106-year-old haunted building in need of major repairs with fetid living quarters in an out-of-the-way town that smells like rotten eggs, in a climate that would freeze the ass off of Nanook of the North for nine months out of the year, we also invested our life savings into the textbook definition of a financial pig in a poke.

The business plan that I had developed for the bank was based upon some wild-ass guesses using formulas that involved days of operation, number of rooms, room rates per night, number of dining room seats, and price of the average meal ticket, all put against estimated monthly expenses — most of which came from Abner. I conservatively figured — or so I thought at the time — that our breakeven point was at a 20 percent occupancy rate. I actually took a lot of time putting occupancy numbers together, with bell curves trending during busy seasons along with expenses, and felt that I had a pretty good grasp of things. After all, I had run a successful business for the better part of twenty years, a large part of which involved the financial management of budgets and expenses, and the generation of revenues. So while I was a neophyte in the hotel and restaurant business, I certainly wasn't a neophyte in running a successful business. While purchasing and owning The Riverside ended up being nothing but an endless string of bad decisions, I had previously had a history of making mostly good business decisions. The bank relied upon that fact in buying into my 20 percent occupancy rate business plan, which included five-year cash flow and pro formas.

The first summer seemed to go pretty well, in spite of the fact that we'd done zero marketing or advertising. We ended up being at full occupancy every Saturday night from the middle of June until mid-September, with numerous near sell-outs throughout the weeknights. Our lunch traffic was steady to good throughout the summer, with bustling dinner business on the weekends. I was able to comfortably pay the bills, and even had the cash to make an extra mortgage payment in September.

However, in October and November our flow of business shut off like a haunted shower but the expenses held steady. I started eating through our cash like a victorious football team at a post-game buffet. A decent Christmas season helped to momentarily right the ship; then came the off-season — January, February, and March — followed by the dead season, or more commonly referred to as "mud season," which is comprised of April, May, and the first two weeks of June.

I also terrifically miscalculated the amount of business that was available to us during ski season; from a lodging perspective, it was virtually nonexistent, as skiers want to be on the slopes and we were twenty-five miles away from Winter Park. If not for Valentine's Day weekend and a couple of group events, our first full winter would have been disastrous. It was in March that I went to the bank for our promised line of credit that was ultimately denied. If not for me raiding and ultimately depleting my 401K, we wouldn't have made it to our second summer season.

We shut the hotel down in mid-April after an Easter Sunday brunch and headed to Kansas City for a few weeks. We still had our unsold, unoccupied home in Kansas City that we were making payments on — a situation that never even in my worst-case scenario plan occurred to me when we packed up in June of 2008 and headed west. Not only was I not budgeting in a house payment, I had budgeted in the income from the quick sale of that house at pre-depression real estate values.

There was another nasty little "What if?" I missed when I was running the business plan numbers on this venture that was now strangling us to a slow, very intense, fiscal death — the depression. While I now have profound doubts about our ability to have been successful at The Riverside in a robust economy, I for damn sure know the state of the economy in 2008 didn't do anything but hurt our situation. As bad as things were nationally, they were far worse in Grand County, with the hub of the pain and suffering being centered in Hot Sulphur Springs — the county seat. The whole raison d'être behind Grand County is tourism, and tourism is fueled by discretionary spending, and discretionary spending is the first thing to dry up in a depressed economy.

The difference between our first summer (economy still robust) and our second summer (economy in the toilet) was profound and immediately discernible. Our bustling lunch business of 2008 disappeared in the summer of 2009. On many days not a single soul walked through the door, but a cook was paid and much of the prepped food went to waste. By mid-July I'd sent home all of the peripheral help, and it was down to Julie, our cook, and me to handle all of the chores. I had way too much 10:00 a.m. to 2:00 p.m. empty lunch time listening to the dining room playlists and reading books, whilst sitting, hoping and praying that a customer would walk through the door. Although I listened to a lot of good music, and read a number of excellent books, not one second of it was relaxing or enjoyable.

Our 2009 summer preseason hotel room bookings were nonexistent and the Saturday afternoon walk-in crowd of the summer of 2008 that filled the hotel every single weekend was hunkered down someplace else. Business was in the cellar but the fixed expenses were still in the penthouse. As mentioned previously on numerous occasions, our monthly water bill had been arbitrarily raised from $150 per month to $750 per month. By making improvements to the hotel, the newly assessed tax value was raised from $12,000 per year to $36,000 per year. Abner's professed monthly utility bill rates of $400–$500 per month (which I took at face value) were in fact triple that number, and his paying $2500 per year for PC&L insurance was a bald-faced lie. I found out that he had no insurance of any type on the property; knowing that I ultimately had to pay $10,000 per year for insurance told me why he chose to play the daily gamble of not insuring.

As we headed into our second summer season, we were bleeding; we were dying; and the coffers were bare.

Our only possible way out of this financial doomsday was to try and sell the hotel. It had been our plan to give the hotel business at least five years, and as many as ten, at which point we'd have the business soundly established, the place refurbished, the mortgage retired, and we'd sell the joint for two million bucks and move on to the next phase in our lives. Can you guess how far reality has taken us away from that scenario?

Next came proof positive that not only is there a just God, but, more importantly, proof of the existence of a God that seems to have a soft spot for idiots. In May of 2009, my old employer called, out of the blue, and asked if I'd be interested in working on some special projects for them. It had been a year since I'd left their employ, and I'd had virtually no contact with them during that time. Regardless of how dire my situation had become, my last expected source of relief would have come from a company that, with no warning, I had walked out on. There were some in the organization that were upset with me for leaving; they'd had plans to promote me and move me to their Mississippi headquarters, and my sudden departure put a bit of a hole in their organizational chart. I didn't figure they'd have me back if I'd come begging and crawling, let alone that they would initiate my return; I'd have never hired me back. Wonders truly never cease, and the sun occasionally shines on the simple-minded.

The offer was for me to work part-time for as long as the next two years, during which time we would sell the hotel, and then I would come back to work full time. And, no ifs, ands, or buts, that full-time thing would include me relocating to the corporate office in Jackson, MS. Some might have cautioned that I play harder to get, as it was they who contacted me, and in spite of the Business Boner of the Millennium that I had committed, they still placed a value on my services. Let me tell you, I was as coy with them as a Times Square hooker; a nanosecond seems an eternity to the speed at which I accepted their generous offer. The only one who moved faster than me at accepting their largesse was Julie in pushing me to accept; I believe I still have the bruises on my shoulder blades where she pushed me.

And then came Miracle #2: We had a buyer for the hotel in the person of the aforementioned Mr. Damien Farmer. It was at this point that Julie and I mentally checked out as the owners and operators of The Riverside. Julie immediately went from looking online for second income opportunities to looking for tony residences in Mississippi. We weren't going to sell the hotel for that gaudy dream sum I mentioned earlier, but we were going to recoup all that we had invested into the business, and that was enough to get us out of debt, refill the retirement accounts, and put us into a home in Jackson.

However, that "mentally checking out" thing ended up being critical towards our ultimate demise, as we would have definitely done things differently if we didn't think (actually, we were 99 percent certain) that we had the place sold to Damien. I'm not saying we would have been able to salvage the place, just that we would have put time, money, and resources in different areas that may have allowed us to ultimately sell the property and, at the very least, minimize some of the bleeding that ultimately occurred. I damn sure wouldn't have paid high school girls to eat lunch, and a dinner waitress $450 a week, plus her tips, to eat steaks and drink free martinis at the end of her shift.

I *really* checked out, as I started traveling a bit for the new job in early June, leaving Julie and Rachel behind to fend for themselves. I also quit paying attention to the business side of the business, the penalty for which I would later pay with some late, frantic nights trying to assemble for the IRS the gory financial details of a year in ruin.

When in the middle of July Damien backed out of buying the hotel, we quickly contacted a realtor — a friend who was confident that if properly marketed we'd be able to sell the hotel, even in the current economic climate — and we officially put the hotel on the market. In the first few weeks, we had a few people kick the tires but no serious buyers. What appeared to be our first real prospect was a young couple who flew down from New York to look at the place; it was their dream to own a B&B in Colorado. While they loved The Riverside, they were savvy enough (as savvy as your average five-year-old would be savvy, which was unfortunately savvier than I) to know what a tough go it would be to make a living in the out-of-the-way hellhole that is Hot Sulphur Springs. "Lovely place you've got here, but no thanks," they said.

Next we had a business owner from nearby Glenwood Springs, a man who'd made a good living in the construction supply business and was looking to sell that business and make a lifestyle change. This really had me excited, as here we had an individual who was a native, already accustomed to the brutal life and winters of small town, mountainous Colorado, which was the major put-off for our heretofore interested Yankees. More importantly, he had the money to actually make it happen. His first tour of the property had him salivating, envisioning then vocalizing the improvements he would make, including building a covered, heated deck overlooking the river, with French doors out of the dining room onto the deck. I watched with muted glee as he excitedly painted a picture of the life he was going to change and the business he was going to transform. As he left, he made arrangements to come back and spend the next weekend with his family at the hotel. I never heard from him again.

Then there was a woman from Iowa who'd inherited a large sum of money and "really wanted to do something crazy with the rest of her life," something that wouldn't ultimately define her as an Iowan, I suppose. It turned out she had met a man from Denver in an online dating forum, and he knew of The Riverside and knew that with the right people running the place, they could make a go of it. He actually told our realtor that we were idiots and had no clue about what we were doing, which was why we were failing so miserably. While his assessment of us was spot on, my hurt feelings would have quickly been assuaged when his check cleared. The woman was making the arrangements to visit us and her cyber-beau for the first time when she called to ask me some questions. It was maybe a few words into the conversation when it occurred to me that if there were someone on this earth with less sense than I, she was in fact now on the other end of the phone line in Des Moines. She told me that she was starting to have second thoughts, not so much about buying the hotel and moving to Colorado but about her boyfriend that she'd yet to meet face-to-face, as in their last few discussions he had become violent and verbally abusive towards her, and she wasn't certain if she still wanted to include him in the venture. 'Oh my!' I thought. She never heard from me again.

Finally, in December of 2009, a call came from a promising potential buyer — a chef from a restaurant in the Denver foothills who wanted his own place and wanted to raise his young family in the mountains, away from the gangs, the drugs, and the vagaries of city life. He also had a backer who was interested in buying the hot spring complex from the Gupthas. I felt that the stars had miraculously fallen into alignment with this combination of money, experience, and desire.

* * *

It was 10:00 a.m. on the morning of December 29th, 2009, and the last of our Christmas guests had checked out of the hotel. Our prospective buyer was to show up around lunchtime to tour The Riverside, so we basically had about two hours to bust hump and get twelve rooms turned, the bathrooms cleaned, the downstairs tidied up, etc.; we had to flat rock to get the place up to speed, and rock we did. All was going well until it hit me that I never really nailed down a time for our "lunchtime" visitors. And no sooner did I consider this than, lo and behold, at 11:00 a.m., there they stood, waiting for their tour.

All was well downstairs, and I knew Julie was wrapping things up upstairs, so no big deal. I even bought a little more time by getting them coffee and excusing myself to change from my work clothes. I sent word to Julie that the guests were here, and Julie sent word back to "show them the downstairs, and stall!" So stall I did, lingering in the dining room, stretching out my stories on the past history, taking every opportunity I could to let them examine while I explained. Inevitably, we headed upstairs, first to the east wing, which houses the main hall with the chandeliers, the bathrooms, and the bookshelves. Again I stalled, asking them a lot of questions, many a ploy to forestall what, I wasn't sure, as we headed to the west wing of the hotel, where I believed Julie was still cleaning, as I'd yet to see a sign of her.

We walked past the bathrooms into the short west hall (the hall where the ghost had been standing once, which parallels the long west hall), viewed the rooms, and headed into the sitting room in the "Mavis" suite. Suitably impressed with this room, as it is the largest with the best view, we headed down the long west hall towards the "Lennon" room. About halfway down the hall I encountered an olfactory sensation that was something akin to getting smashed in the face with a fungo bat; the smell took my breath away and all but buckled my knees. I continued to prattle on, acting like I didn't notice anything; I'm certain the first question that entered the guests' minds was, 'Is there a sewage plant that we didn't notice located immediately next to the hotel?'

We entered the "Lennon" room, and I hastily pointed to the plaque on the wall detailing his Riverside stay, laughing nervously as I said, "Yep, heh ... heh ... he stayed *here*, all right ... heh ... heh," the guests thinking, *'Stayed here?* He obviously *died* here, and we're certain he's still under the bed!'

I simply couldn't hide it any longer; I had to mention what was as obvious as the pea-green pallor of my complexion.

"Hmmm. Smells a little like *dogs* in here. We had guests stay in the room who had four dogs, and, *wow,* that smell is a little overwhelming; my apologies. We probably shouldn't allow dogs." (I'm thinking, 'Yah, the dogs stayed here, but I didn't know they pooped in here for the last two days and piled it all under the bed,' *because that's what it smelled like!)*

The guests were quick to say, "Oh no, this is Colorado; you've got to allow dogs!"

Downstairs we go, tour all but complete, and there stands Julie, looking lovely, calm, and collected. After introductions, she pulls me aside to tell me the raw truth. No, it wasn't the four guest pooches that fouled our attempt at selling the Riverside; rather, it was our own little hoyden Lucy that did potentially permanent damage to not only our relocation efforts but to our sense of smell as well. And this time she didn't do it outside the door, her usual modus operandi for saying good-bye to our big-dog guests, nor even did Lucy have the good grace to simply do it on the room's floor. Nope, she laid it right smack in the middle of the bed, on the comforter that Julie had replaced two minutes prior. This was the ultimate "Up yours!"–a two-day, fine-wine-aged poop, planted deliberately and skillfully, with love and obvious pride of ownership. When Julie discovered Lucy's contribution to our efforts to sell the hotel, her first thought was to throw the comforter out the window, but she heard us below outside on the west deck and thought better of it, as a flying, poop-filled comforter might have been a little tough to explain. Even in Grand County!

All involved had a good laugh when they heard the details behind the source of the smell. Then the chef went with me to ask some pointed kitchen questions, while his wife spent time with Julie getting details on the schools, the town, and life in the hotel. As they left we felt electric about the possibility of them actually being the ones that would save us from ourselves.

Twenty-four hours had barely passed when the chef called to tell me that as much as he loved the prospects of owning The Riverside and moving his young family to the mountains, the time simply wasn't right for him, what with the poor economy and the bleak state of the tourism industry in Grand County.

And so went our final attempted sale of The Riverside.

CHAPTER TWENTY-SEVEN

… And the Car Crashes

It should be no revelation to those who knew us and our situation that we were struggling to make a go of it at The Riverside; we were struggling hard. The deeper we went into the summer of our fiscal discontent, the more it became apparent that I was going to have to go back to work full time, way sooner than I had imagined; I was going to need every penny I could muster to help keep the sinking ship afloat. The plan involved me moving back to Kansas City, living in our unsold house and working at my old Kansas City office. When our house sold, I'd move to an apartment in Mississippi, and Julie would join me when the hotel sold. This solution to our problem, which involved us living apart, was beyond distasteful to us, but there was really no other available alternative. We felt in our hearts that someone would come along and buy the place within the next two years, and with my job, Julie getting a job, and the help of the bank in refinancing the loan, we'd be able to hang on long enough to sell.

After the Labor Day holiday weekend — the final thud to the 2009 summer from a revenue perspective — I packed some clothes, a few personal effects, a picture of Lucy, and my fishing rods and headed back to the old homestead in Kansas City. As luck would have it (or perhaps by dropping our asking price by 30 percent), we had two offers on the house after two days on the market and quickly selected what seemed the better of the two. This didn't come without some wringing of hands and gnashing of teeth, as even though the house was now priced considerably below its appraised value, it was, after all, still a buyer's market. To ultimately close the deal, we had to put in four new windows, a new furnace, cut down a tree, paint some trim, fix part of the roof, and throw in the brand new washer and dryer we'd just purchased.

But "woe is me" aside, we did everything we could to keep The Riverside afloat. Thank God for my old employer. And Thank God for the fine folks at Acme Savings & Loan, who promised to work with us in redoing our loan to make the monthly nut more affordable. In October of 2009, when we were struggling to keep up with our payments, the bank sent us an angel who promised that if we got current on our first mortgage and paid up another short-term loan they'd given us, our loan would be refinanced, allowing us a reduced monthly payment so we could make our mortgage with only my job revenue. This sweet-faced, seemingly innocent bank vice president — she could be mistaken for an ex-nun — looked us in the eye and promised us a sanctuary from the impending financial doom, provided we did our part in getting our loan out of its past-due status. Our part included depleting both Julie's and my retirement accounts, which we gladly did in an effort to satisfy the bank and pave the way for a new financial future. Even better news, in mid-December Julie called me in Mississippi to report that our ex-nun bank angel brought a savior to The Riverside to help us with our situation. Julie made them coffee, showed them around the hotel, and bid them off with the feeling that our fate was in the hands of these caring, helpful souls. There was a light at the bottom of this seemingly bottomless financial abyss, provided we kept up our end of the obligation.

As promised, with much effort and at the expense of vendors and creditors, we paid the bank every owed cent by year's end — a gut-wrenching process but what a relief when the bill was paid.

During this supposed refinancing process, in early November I received an e-mail from our realtor that brought news to which I was uncertain of its affect regarding our situation: Acme Savings & Loan had been issued a cease and desist order from the Feds in September of 2009, this little nugget of information finally making its way to me in Mississippi more than a full month after the fact. A modicum of research told me that this is what the Feds do before they barge into your bank unannounced and seize it at 4:30 p.m. on a Friday afternoon — a not-so-gentle last warning to get your financial shit together or you'll quickly have no financial shit to get together. This wasn't a surprise to me, as weekly I'd seen numerous foreclosures on $600,000 weekend-getaway homes, crumbling Grand County businesses, and a major financial sinkhole in a 36-hole golf course/fly-fishing resort on the banks of the Colorado River that went totally tits-up a third of the way through the development process — all on the balance sheets of Acme Savings & Loan. (Know for a fact that this primo, upscale development, located twelve short miles from the front door of The Riverside, with the national high-end clientele it would draw, played a big part in us taking our leap. Didn't happen for them; didn't happen for us.)

All of a sudden, it dawned on me that Acme S&L giving us a loan might not have been the vote of confidence I was looking for in higher financial powers having an educated insight into the potential success or failure of our dream. Throughout the process of our buying The Riverside, Julie would say, "I wish we could get a sign as to whether or not we're doing the right thing." I would respond, "The banks will give us a sign. If we can't make this work, they'll have smart people that will know the performance numbers I've given them aren't attainable, and we won't get a loan." I naively relied on the bank, knowing every last one of my intimate financial details and relying upon my worst-case-scenario five-year pro formas, to tell me whether or not we had a viable business venture. What a fool I was.

January came and went without news from our sweet angel at the bank regarding our refinancing. At the end of the month, I sent her a brief e-mail saying, "Waiting to hear from you re. our refinancing. Don't want to get another month behind." February came and went with no news from the bank. I was worried, but I knew our angel was working behind the scenes to make our path easier. Unfortunately, now I was coming up to being two months behind on the mortgage.

Monday, March 1st, the Acme S&L savior that had visited Julie at The Riverside in mid-December, Mr. Ray Schmutz, sent me an e-mail. "Mr. Paradise, you are two months behind on your mortgage. Make payment immediately or we will begin foreclosure proceedings." Wow! I'd never met or spoken with him, but Julie had said he was a nice guy who said he wanted to work with us; this e-mail was a little chilly. I called our new friend and explained that I'd held off making payments as I was waiting to hear from the bank regarding my promised refinance. If need be, I could make the January payment immediately and the February payment by March 15th.

This is where the story turned. This is when I realized there was more at play than us being late with the mortgage. Mr. Schmutz then proceeded to tell me exactly how it was going to be.

"Mr. Paradise, first and foremost, you need to take that money and hire legal counsel. Regardless of whether or not you get current, we are going to declare you in default. You have a clause in your loan that states if there is a material change in the ownership, management, or operation of the business — and with you living in Mississippi and not on site to manage the hotel directly, that certainly qualifies as a material change in the operation of the business — the bank can declare the loan in default. We are going to exercise that right."

"But what about the refinancing that your VP promised us? All we want to do is hang on to the place until we can sell it."

"Mr. Paradise, the cease and desist order that we are operating under doesn't allow us to refinance your loan."

"Wait a minute! Your bank VP promised us in October that if we got current, we would get refinanced, and you've been under the cease and desist since September. Did she just flat lie to us to get every last penny we had before you called the loan? She knew we couldn't refinance yet she strung us along until we drained our retirement accounts and handed them over to you? She seemed so sincere. How could anyone be that evil and not be doing time somewhere?"

"Mr. Paradise, that's past history. I'm only concerned with the here and now." (That is a direct quote.)

It was at this point that the disdain and vitriol that I usually reserved for the legal profession was now borne by those in the banking profession — specifically these lying bankers. In fact, I now needed to embrace the legal profession, as it was my only course for being able to deal with this den of thieves.

* * *

I called a good friend, who is an attorney, with my devastating news. The news was devastating on two fronts — the obvious one being my realization that all we'd invested, both financially and emotionally, and all that we'd accomplished the last two years at The Riverside was at the stool's edge, ready to topple into the bowl and be flushed down the toilet. But perhaps even more disturbing was my coming to grips with my naiveté regarding the bank's total manipulation of us and our money. I trusted them implicitly, viewing them as my most essential and necessary partner in this venture. Learning that they were anything but a partner — in fact, they were an adversary — made me question my core ability to accomplish the most basic of tasks that separate us from our animal brethren: reasoning, deducing, anticipating, obviating, etc.

I also always thought I was a pretty good judge of people; well, go right ahead and throw that notion to the four winds. To think that this bank lady that I trusted so entirely — I can't begin to tell you the information I shared with her, not only financial but personal as well — was probably the most devious, evil, dishonest person I'd ever encountered. I had sat in this woman's office and teared-up, as I recounted my financial situation, and in joy, as she promised me that everything would be alright. Little did I know that as I was pouring out my heart and soul, her hands were under her desk sharpening a scythe that would make the Grim Reaper envious, while her gentle demeanor was masking what she was really probing for as she looked at me with her comforting eyes — namely, the best part of my fleshy personage to whack away at with that machete she was honing.

My lawyer friend was fired up when I told him the situation, saying, "Just because the bank says it's so, doesn't mean it's so! Let's put these crooks on notice that you're not going to just sit back and let them have their way." His thought was that in these tough financial times, with the post-recession national and legal mood regarding financial institutions, there wouldn't be a judge in the world that would let them take our hotel from us if we were current on our payments. But first and foremost, I needed to go on record with the bank and write them a letter detailing some of the issues: the fact that they lied regarding a refinancing, and another heretofore unmentioned issue of them promising, and then reneging on, a line of credit.

When we were in discussions regarding our loan before purchasing the hotel, the purchase was discussed at length and I was promised a line of operating capital, which was to be secured by the equity we had in the hotel. This detail was spelled-out in every cash-flow statement and every operating statement, and also explicitly stated in my business plan, all of which were approved by the bank loan officer, the loan committee, and the board of directors. **I would never have considered purchasing the hotel without a line of credit**. Take that cash infusion out of my five-year projections and the venture would be dead after two years, as all of my numbers reflected, and as was now, in fact, the case.

When the time came to sit down and request the credit line, about ten months into the venture, the loan officer had me give him year-to-date financials and a write-up on the general state of the business, including improvements we'd made to the hotel and actual sales and expense numbers versus budgeted numbers. I complied, and off he went to the loan committee for what I was assured was a done deal. (I wasn't asking for much — less than 5 percent of the equity we had in the hotel — just enough to get through the end of the year until the busy holiday season refilled the coffers.)

When I received the news that, in fact, the line of credit had been denied, I said to the banker, "We're dead." And he didn't deny it. Every financial blueprint I'd come up with had that credit line being essential to our survival; I never figured it any other way.

So a letter was written that detailed what I felt were misrepresentations by the bank that were critical in the failure of the business. My job in writing the letter was to enlighten Ray Schmutz regarding some of the past history, regardless of his professed lack of interest in "past history." The letter was to be written in three parts, part one being, "We were promised this"; part two was, "You welshed on your promises"; and part three, to be completed by my lawyer friend, was, "Now here's what we're going to do if you don't make things right." I had not a clue as to the legal what we can do and what we can't do, so I let the lawyer have at that.

I wrote parts one and two, and when I got to part three, I decided to have a little fun and vent, as I knew my friend might get a kick out of it and it might make me feel a little better. In lieu of the legalese that my friend would supply, I started part three of the letter with, "So, Acme Savings & Loan, all I can say is: **BIG FAT HAIRY FUCK YOU!** You lying, thieving pack of bastards can rot in hell, assuming hell will have you!" Then I e-mailed the letter to my friend.

He sent me back an edited version, changing some of my text in parts one and two, and adding the all-important legal piece at the end of the letter. He used that Microsoft Word feature that lawyers use where the deletions are shown in red with a line through them, and the additions are in blue. I cleaned it up, or so I thought, and sent it on to Big Ray at the bank. I then went to lunch. After lunch, I decided I'd open the e-mail I sent to the banker and reread the letter, trying to get the feeling Mr. Schmutz would get when he opened and read this legal tour de force.

'Ohshit ohshit ohshit ohshit ohshit!' I said to myself as I realized that I had inadvertently e-mailed the original letter, the one where I ended with: *"So, Acme Savings & Loan, ... BIG FAT HAIRY FUCK YOU!"'*

I thought I had gotten rid of all of the colorful deletions and additions, especially that real colorful part at the end of my original letter. But no, unfortunately — and with very bad timing — there were still some applications in Microsoft Word that I'd had yet to master.

So really fast, I sent another version — this time as clean as our bank account — to Schmutz in an e-mail that said, "Please disregard the previous draft submission. Clean version attached."

And here it is:

March 4th, 2010

Mr. Ray Schmutz
Acme Savings & Loan
PO Box 6969
Denver, CO 80210

Mr. Schmutz:

I would like to take this opportunity to respond to you and Acme S&L regarding the loan status for The Riverside Hotel, d/b/a Riverside Paradise LLC. First and foremost, our experience in Grand County has been difficult at best and, without question, the most devastating two years of our life. My wife and I invested everything we had in our dream, and to watch it crumble before us has been demoralizing. Granted, we freely entered into the business venture ourselves, but I must go on record and tell you that Acme Savings & Loan [ASL] has played a large part in our failure.

Before we ever seriously considered the purchase of The Riverside, we had discussions with ASL officers concerning competitive financing and a line of operating capital; my five-year projections and a comprehensive business plan, which were submitted to and approved by ASL officers, forecast losses and negative cash flow for our first four years of operation. The line of credit, which was unconditionally promised to me by your representative, was essential for our survival during our start-up years. There was never a question in my mind that the business would be unable to remain solvent without the line of credit. Had there even been a chance that I wouldn't ultimately receive the line of credit, I would have never risked all for this opportunity. Unfortunately, ASL's blatant misrepresentations to me deprived me of the opportunity to exercise that alternative.

As we headed into our first off-season, with cash reserves starting to deplete, I met with your representative to discuss the line. At that time we had $200,000 worth of equity in the hotel and an additional $150,000 worth of equity in our property in Kansas City; your loan officer once again assured me that the promised working capital would be approved by the loan committee. When he came back with the news that in fact there would be no line of credit, I knew at that instant that the future success of our venture had been severely if not fatally compromised. I founded, managed, and was part owner of a successful business in Kansas City for twenty years — a seasonal business that relied on a partnership with our bank for its survival during the slow season. When I learned that I had no partner in ASL, I knew our venture had little or no chance for success — a very disheartening realization.

Over the next year we nevertheless struggled to make our payments to ASL and on our SBA [Small Business Administration] note. In fact, I don't believe we were ever late until midway through our second year. Because of ASL's failure to honor its commitment to provide working capital we had to operate the hotel and our lives on a shoestring budget throughout this period; we had absolutely no money to market and promote the business. In early April of 2009 I went to ASL to plead for a loan. Although one should have already been provided to me consistent with ASL's previous commitment to me regarding a line of credit for working capital, I agreed to collateralize the loan with a $26,000 tax refund, which I hoped to receive from the IRS by midsummer. Again, your officer said the loan would *be approved, and six weeks after our first meeting (your representative "forgot" to present it at two straight loan committee meetings; all the while suppliers, vendors, and creditors were screaming at me for payment) the loan was finally granted.*

Our inability to market the property, combined with an extremely depressed Grand County economy, made for a terrible 2009 summer season. It was at this point that I had to choose between paying employees and vendors or ASL. I stayed in constant contact with one of your representatives, who assured me that ASL would work with me to get us through this tough time; I did keep current with the SBA portion of my note. A new ASL rep, Ms. Mandy Lyde, kept in constant contact with me, as I provided her with weekly updates regarding our financial status. I pledged to Ms. Lyde that with either my tax refund (I still to this day have not received it from the IRS) or my wife's retirement account (I'd long since drained my IRA) that I would get current by year's end. Ms. Lyde's promise to me in return was that ASL would rework my twenty-year, 7.5% note to a more manageable payment — thirty years with a competitive rate. She promised this in every conversation with me; she promised my wife, and she also made this promise in front of other ASL employees — conditional only on us getting current and full repayment of the $25,000 note. Based on those explicit representations, we followed through on our commitments by repaying the $25,000 note in full through personal funds and bringing our payments on the original note up to date as of January 1, 2010.

Unfortunately, after we took these actions in good faith, ASL once again failed to keep its end of the bargain. The promised loan modification was never made. Instead, in our conversation of March 1st, you admitted that Ms. Lyde had, in fact, lied to me. You informed me that due to your bank currently operating under a "cease and desist" order, you were never able to rework any current loans or grant any new loans. When I made you aware of Ms. Lyde's bald-faced deception, as well as ASL's failure to make good on a promise of a line of credit, you didn't deny these bad-faith practices but simply referred to them as "past history." And now after you've had my wife and I drain every asset to make good on our note through 2009, and there are no more assets for you to grab, you now simply say, "ASL is tired of playing with you." Even though I outlined a plan to get current with you and stay current moving forward — even without ASL redoing the loan as was explicitly promised — you've threatened to call the loan.

During our last discussion, you suggested that I might wish to contact legal counsel. I have and will continue to do so to the fullest extent necessary to protect my legitimate interests. It is my hope, however, that we can resolve this matter without the expense of litigation by sitting down and working out an arrangement that is satisfactory to both of us. I am an honorable person and I keep my commitments. I think the actions I have taken over the past year, including repaying the note out of personal funds and moving heaven and earth to bring my payments on the other note current as of January 1, 2010, have conclusively demonstrated just that. I anticipate receiving a sizable bonus in the future as well as the proceeds from my tax refund, and I will either use those monies to keep current on my obligations to ASL or to pursue whatever legal remedies are available to me for the situation I have been put in as a direct result of ASL's inexcusable pattern of misrepresentations and failures to honor its commitments. I hope you will agree with me that the former alternative is the one we should be focusing on.

I look forward to hearing from you in the very near future.

Sincerely,
Richard Paradise

As Mr. Schmutz never said anything in our subsequent discussions like, "How dare you infer that hell won't have me?" I never found out whether or not he read the original unedited letter that I accidentally sent. (Or was it really an accident — is there such a thing as a physical Freudian slip?) After what they did to us, I would've loved to have had the opportunity to scream those nasty things to their faces. And for the record, I would like them to rot in hell. And I also believe that hell is too good for them. And *yes, Big Fat Hairy Fuck You!* It's not like they could do anything worse to us than they were already doing ("Oh yea? Well if that's how you feel about us, we're gonna *double* foreclose on your property!"), so why not let them know how we really felt about them.

Ray Schmutz's only response to the letter was a terse e-mail saying that there was no written record that I'd ever requested a line of credit, and, when questioned, Mandy Lyde told him she'd never promised us a refinancing, and, finally, that he was left with no choice but to proceed with the foreclosure process. Well, I had written proof of our credit-line discussions in the form of my bank-approved business plan. And as for Mandy Lyde lying to Ray Schmutz about not promising us a refinance — after her blatantly dishonest dealings with us, who would ever expect her to tell the truth about anything?

After reading the e-mail, the reality of our situation was paralyzing, suffocating; it literally took my breath away. And couple getting this e-mail prior to a meeting with my largest account while back at my new-old job, then having to sit all after-noon in a rather tense meeting, acting to the assembled crowd as if my entire world hadn't just come to an end. Oh yes, then I had to call Julie, still fighting it out at the hotel in Colorado, with the news that these two wonderful people from the bank that she'd openly put her trust in may show up at any moment and demand that she vacate the premises. I had no idea what to expect, as I'd never had anything like this happen before. Julie was only slightly hysterical beyond my ability to calm and console her.

Our next step involved finding a real estate attorney who was licensed in Colorado. I was led to a highly recommended gentleman with a pricey firm, whose first words to me, after I explained our dire situation, were, "Mr. Paradise, I want you to calm down and relax. They can't throw you out of your house or take your possessions. There is nothing about this situation that can't be fixed." So calm down I did as the attorney laid out the options.

Option #1 involved getting current on the loan; this lawyer echoed my friend's opinion that in this economy the legal system would look very harshly upon the bank if they tried to foreclose on a current loan. We could then fight them in court as to the validity of the "material change in the operation of the business" reason for calling the note. However, Option #1 involved us coming up with a lawyer-load of money for legal fees. This could ultimately cost us $50,000–$100,000, and we still had the potential for a downside if we didn't prevail in court. Well heckfire, if I'd had $50,000 or $100,000 I wouldn't have been in this mess in the first place. So, cancel Option #1.

Option #2 was to move heaven and earth, pull a rabbit out of my hat, part the Dead Sea, and then find a buyer for the hotel in the next sixty days. In the eight months the hotel had been on the market, we'd had one potentially serious buyer, and he had backed out due to the out-of-the-way location and the depressed economy. So I didn't hold a lot of hope for coming up with someone in sixty days, and certainly not someone who would buy the place for a reasonable sum.

Option #3 … Walk away. That's right … just walk away. Walk away from our investment, our equity, our labors, our memories, our friends, our dream, our successes, and, sadly, our failure. Walk away from a lot of good things, but, more importantly, walk away from a boatload of bad things. This is referred to in the business as a deed in lieu of foreclosure. You simply give the bank the deed to the property, the bank excuses the indebtedness, and you walk away clean.

No more $6000 a month mortgage payments; no more $1500 per month electric bills; no more $750 per month water bills; and, most importantly, no more Julie and I living apart.

When the lawyer explained this to me, and how easily it could be accomplished, I slowly and deliberately exhaled all of the air I'd been suffocating on since early that afternoon. I began to breathe normally again. The tightness in my jaw and chest relaxed; the massive weight and profound stress that had been burdening me for the previous two years slipped off of my back like a cheap kimono.

Just walk away.

But what about our equity and all that we'd invested? Equity is only equity if you sell X for Y. There wasn't a chance in hell of us selling X for Y anytime soon, yet the thousands of dollars in monthly expenses *would* continue indefinitely — the biggest percentage being never-to-be-recovered interest paid to those slime balls at Acme Savings & Loan. Realistically, how much longer could we continue to fund this financial waterloo, all the while living like paupers in Mississippi?

Knowing that all of the pain and suffering could be over and we could begin to live a normal life again, albeit broke, for the price of something that may never have existed or been attainable anyway, was almost too good to believe. When I explained the situation to Julie, I could hear her smile over a thousand miles of fiber optics. No question it was tragic that it ended the way it did. But of greatest importance: it ended, and the peaceful feeling of realizing that it was finally over was worth more money than you can ever imagine.

* * *

It was St. Patrick's Day, 2010, and we had an appointment with the fine folks at Acme Savings & Loan — Ray Schmutz, the heartless android that they'd brought in at the request of the government to oversee the cease-and-desist reorganization and weed deadbeats like us out of the bank's portfolio, and Frank DeVoleur, the distinguished bank president, who I met once at a Rotary meeting in Denver. Sadly, I never met him spending money in our restaurant, or dropping coin in our bar, or spending a buck in our hotel. Mandy Lyde, the sweet VP that played us like a pinball machine with a busted tilt mechanism, wasn't going to be at the meeting. (This was a good thing, as had she been at the meeting, very possibly I would be writing this book from a cell in Cañon City, Colorado, the Centennial State's permanent residence for convicted murderers.) The purpose of the meeting was to sit down with our high-powered real estate attorney and tell these dishonest creeps that we weren't going to play the game by the rules that they'd recently imposed.

We were to meet our attorney at a coffee shop in Granby thirty minutes prior to the bank meeting. It would be our first face-to-face with this man who had done so much with just a simple phone conversation in calming my fears of dealing with this next sure-to-be-brutal chapter of our western adventure. We pulled into the parking lot of the coffee shop, and parked there was a black 2009 Mercedes that was just slightly smaller than an aircraft carrier, bearing Colorado plates from the county of Denver — this had to belong to our hired gun. Into the empty shop we went, and there sat a smallish man, jet-black hair, fairly nondescript, wearing an ill-fitting blue polyester suit right off the rack from J.C. Penny, a white shirt, and a noticeably inexpensive red tie. Perhaps he'd spent too much for his car.

He was indeed a very pleasant gentleman — very calm, very knowledgeable, and very reassuring. He gave us the confidence we sought prior to this meeting in which our main role would involve crying, yelling, and unleashing the frustrations of our dire situation upon the bankers. "Let them have it!" he told us. "It will be your last and only chance." He then asked if I had the $1500 retainer check that he'd requested in our initial phone call.

Now fully prepped by our CLS550 Mercedes-driving, polyester suit-wearing attorney — he now on the positive side of $1500 towards his next car payment — I popped a beta blocker and headed off to have it out with the bank.

After arriving at the bank, we were seated by the receptionist in the main board-room, the surrounding walls covered with 8½" x 11" color photos of the board of directors — this room an obvious monument to themselves, the only monument on this earth that will ever honor this greasy lot of greedy hayseeds. Possibly there will ultimately be a monument to their accomplishments in the southern part of Hades, at which they will collectively be able to worship themselves.

In walked the inimitable Ray Schmutz, the self-important squelcher of dreams who now wielded the club for Acme S&L. Having corresponded but never having met Mr. Schmutz in person, he wasn't what I expected. I expected Lee Marvin, and instead I got Art Garfunkel. Next entered Mr. DeVoleur, he looking all but contrite as if he felt our pain and wanted to help. Last to join the meeting, via conference call, was our U.S. Small Business Administration liaison, Ms. Liz Whorely, she of Shaftum & Cheatum Investments, a middleman for the SBA. I still to this day can't figure out how they made their money from this deal, but I know for a fact that somewhere in the endless moving train of dollars, they had a prime seat in first class, certainly not in steerage. Historically put, I was having a meeting with the type of folks who would have been the first to grab a seat on the lifeboats — women and children be damned — to save their sorry asses as the *Titanic* was going down. They also would have expected meal service, and their only thought to a gratuity would have been pocketing the one that their neighbor had been kind enough to leave.

The bank and the SBA — who'd previously had meetings and already had a plan of attack regarding Julie and my future and how our next move would ultimately be to their mutual betterment — proposed that in lieu of a foreclosure we put The Riverside up for sale in an auction. Whatever proceeds were netted would first go towards retiring our indebtedness to Acme S&L, and whatever was left would go towards retiring the second loan to the SBA. If the bidders went crazy, there might even be a little left over for us at the end of the day. It sounded pretty positive to me, and my mood lightened.

And then, our distinguished counsel was quick to speak: "Wait just a minute. Who is responsible for the cost of the auction: the auction company's commission, the marketing costs, the closing costs?"

After a few seconds of uncomfortable silence from Messrs. Garfunkel and DeVoleur, Ms. Whorely, who'd briefly mentioned the idea of the auction to me prior to this meeting, spoke up with obvious reluctance. "Uh ... the Paradises would be responsible for all of those costs ... uh ... up front."

"And what would you estimate those costs to be, Ms. Whorely?" asked Mr. Mercedes CLS550.

"They would need to pay the auction company $10,000 up front for the marketing costs, and then 7 percent of the sales price as a commission."

"Really, Ms. Whorely, what sort of alternate universe are you living in? You better than anyone know that these people have drained their life savings and given it to you people to now find themselves in their horrific financial position, and you think they might have ten grand in up-front cash hidden somewhere to give to an auctioneer, on which you will no doubt make a percentage for marketing costs to sell their life investment for pennies on the dollar? Ms. Whorely, this isn't some sort of make-believe Renaissance Fair; this is the Paradise's bleeding, suffering lives. You can talk to me again when you're back on this planet!"

('Wow!' I thought. 'Maybe the $1500 was going to be well spent. Hell, that smack down alone was worth close to a grand!')

Ms. Whorely was quickly defensive and just a tad bit testy. "We're trying to help the Paradises; we're trying to offer them a way out of their suffering and help them do the honorable thing by paying their debts."

Our shark rebutted, "Ms. Whorely, the law allows these people options to relieve their suffering without coming up with ten grand, without putting another penny more than they've already put into this deal. Have you discussed those options with the Paradises?"

The speaker phone box sitting in the middle of the conference table, from which Ms. Whorely's voice had been emanating, sat silently.

"You know that the Paradises can declare Chapter 7, move to Mississippi, and be done with you, the bankers, and the SBA for the rest of their lives. Have you given them that option?"

Ms. Whorely replied, "We're hoping they do the honorable thing and own up to their debts."

Mr. Mercedes barked back, "Ms. Whorely, tell me one honorable thing in this deal that you, that Shaftum & Cheatum Investments, that Acme Savings & Loan, or that the SBA have done for the Paradises. Name me one honorable thing! Name them that and maybe they'll reciprocate!"

Again, and now with permanence, Ms. Whorely's speaker phone box sat silently.

* * *

Our attorney had made his plea to the honorable Messrs. Schmutz and DeVoleur for granting us a deed in lieu of foreclosure: We'd give them the title to the hotel; they wouldn't foreclose; and they'd now own the place and we'd owe them nothing. They said they'd take it under advisement and politely excused us from their nauseating inner sanctum.

Ms. Whorely and her suggested auction had been summarily tossed from the money train to lay fallow at the side of the tracks, waiting for some other broken fool to reach and grab up this one-sided act of congress.

But before I left the boardroom, it was then my turn to tell these gutless, thieving vultures how I felt. I'd slipped a pill that would give me strength — as if I'd needed it after what these greedy rubes had done to me, my wife, and my family. We'd pumped close to $600,000 into this deal, and only one of us was going to come out holding the short end of the stick.

Deep breath, and here I went …

"I just want to start by saying: We entered into this deal with our eyes wide open and of our own accord. I first and foremost blame myself for what I did and for where I am right now. But I have to tell you that based on what your people told me, *what your people promised me,* that we were in this deal together. We based our life savings on what we were led to believe was a long-term partnership with you, a partnership that we absolutely needed to succeed. We trusted you! That was the second biggest mistake that we made! Had I for one second known that you wouldn't back me up in the lean times — lean times that I forecasted in the business plan and budget that you approved — I wouldn't have on any day considered getting into this deal.

"As soon as things started going to hell, you totally disappeared. Then you sent Mr. Schmutz and his lying cur to steal all that you could steal under the guise of helping me reorganize. You had no intention of helping me reorganize; your only intention was to grab every available penny my wife and I had, right down to the last dime from my wife's retirement account — after thirty years of teaching Special-Ed kids — and now you've got that cash as well! I hope you choke on it!

"You're liars and you're thieves! How in God's name can you look at yourselves in the mirror and come to grips with what you do for a living? You've ruined my life; you've ruined my family's life; and you've deprived us of any kind of a future. *You* have to live with that! I'm thankful that I don't have to bear that sort of a burden."

I was now sated, feeling triumphant, feeling as if I'd just scalded these men's souls. I was now expecting these leeches to bend over, broken down and embarrassed at my call out, ashamed and contrite.

That was not the case. They looked at me smugly, with wry smiles on their faces. They'd obviously heard this rant before, daily, maybe five times daily, and more eloquently, from other broke, poor-hearted Grand County deadbeats whose life savings and investments they'd also wrangled and sucked into their portfolio.

The smarmy looks on their faces said, "Tough shit, Mr. and Mrs. Paradise. Oh ... and Big Fat Hairy Fuck You, too! Your best hope is that we don't sue you, and please send the proceeds of your short sale to our bank. The SBA second loan is yours to deal with after that!"

Thanks, Partner!

CHAPTER TWENTY-EIGHT

The Survivors are Pulled
from the Wreck

On March 21st, 2010, at 6:15 p.m., we closed the doors of The Historic Riverside Hotel, Bar & Restaurant, gave our local caretakers the keys, tearfully hugged our close friends good-bye, and drove out of Hot Sulphur Springs. The emotions that came with that action were a metaphorical flood — a massive, violent, lifting, rumbling jumble of both destruction and cleansing, washing away the old and clearing a way for our ultimate rebirth. A flood is the perfect metaphor for what occurred, as we stood back, helpless, and watched a force much greater than us sweep over and destroy our dream and, despite our protestations and earnest but futile efforts, take that dream away from us and leave us with little more than the reckoning of what would come next. What hopefully comes next after a flood, provided it doesn't kill you, is rebirth, reorganization, and the realization that you got smacked hard but you're still alive and, Thank God Almighty, you're still able to smack back.

What destructive force took us under? The list is as long as a Grand County winter, and it would be small of me to blame first and foremost anyone but myself for my bad business acumen. Couple that with a horrible economy in an out-of-the-way place whose sole existence is based upon tourism and discretionary income — the first type of income that goes south in a bad economy. Add to this volatile mix the local financial institution, the supposed backbone of this beautiful, rugged but financially strapped area, run by a bunch of wealthy ranchers who combined a lethal mixture of financial naiveté, avarice, and a moral compass that would make you opt for Somali pirates as your business partners. The final mistake would be our poor choice of location — a small town whose only reason for being is to draw a select group of clientele to a hot springs complex that ranks at the bottom of all hot springs complexes in the state, country, and world. We were catering to a very small, very select group, going to the (arguably) worst of all possible very small, very select places. No knock on those that love the place, but honestly, it's a very select group, and a depressed economy can be a financially fatal time to cater to a select group. Oh well, I'd been lucky in life way beyond my skills and efforts up to that point; odds dictated that there eventually had to be a bump in that road.

The packers were supposed to show up on Thursday, March 18th, and the moving van on the 19th to load us up and take us to our new world. But Colorado had a parting gift for us: a blizzard the morning of the 18th that shut down I-70, Berthoud Pass, and most of Grand County. To this point, it was the largest snow-fall of the year in this snow-and water-starved environ. Unfortunately, the ski slopes had closed the weekend before; no question, timing is everything. The blizzard put the move back two days, with the packers now scheduled to arrive on Saturday, March 20th, and the moving van on Sunday the 21st.

When I awoke early on the morning of March 20th — the first day of spring — the temperature in Hot Sulphur Springs was a robust eighteen degrees ... below zero. While there were innumerable things I would miss about living in Grand County and Colorado, the blissful memory of greeting spring with eigh-teen degrees below zero would be tossed quickly into the dustbin. As the packers had to have doors open to move in and out of the building, the temperature for most of the morning — in the hotel — was below zero; dustbin that memory as well.

I learned something interesting about the relocation industry that day, especially those involved in corporate relocations — the kind for which the company picks up the total tab. I would have assumed the cost of the move was based upon mileage and cubic feet of truck space. In fact, it is based upon gross weight. This would explain why a packer would use a 24" x 12" x 12" box, loaded with five to six pounds of packing paper, to carefully and thoroughly wrap a box of paper clips, a roll of Scotch tape, a small stapler, and a pencil holder from the top of our office desk. In total, the carton and its contents weighed eight pounds; the actual contents (things I would have thrown

away versus packing) weighed less than a pound. We had large moving boxes —
36" x 24" x 24" — containing two eight-ounce lamp shades, secured by reams of
packing paper, total weight approaching fifteen pounds. Oh, and they also charge
per box and per one thousand sheets of packing paper. They were nice people but,
sheesh, what a racket!

Sunday the 21st arrived, along with the moving van, and the 10 a.m. ther-
mometer read 30°F; that's a fifty-degree swing from the previous morning. It
took the movers until about 4:00 p.m. to load all of our furniture, appliances, a
1300-pound gun safe (cha-ching!), and 123 boxes of various weights, shapes,
and sizes. As the movers emptied a room, we cleaned behind them, as our intent
was to leave the place spotless for future sales showings, then get out of town
before dark. At 3:00 p.m. I did the final upstairs walk-through. We'd left all of the
furnishings in the rooms so there wouldn't be the empty feel that our downstairs
living quarters would offer. A sad, slow walk-through, room by room, filled me
with a thousand memories, such as, "I've made this damn bed a thousand times,"
and "I've scrubbed this damn toilet a thousand times." I said my final good-bye
— aloud, in case I wasn't alone — giddy in knowing that I'd made that bed and
cleaned that toilet for the last time.

I joined Julie downstairs, watching as she made her final pass with the vacuum. (Speaking of doing something a thousand times, Julie knew every square
inch of that floor from the handle of our Riccar vacuum sweeper, and I know for
certain that her vacuuming memories would soon be joining a few of mine in
the dustbin.) We were joined by a few remaining friends as we wrapped things
up, preparing to leave The Riverside forever as the owners. I needed to make a
final pit stop in our bathroom before departure, and I headed back to our spotless
living quarters for what I thought would be the last time.

Business completed, I gave one final flush and then watched in horror as the
water in the bowl began to rise. 'Oh my, how could this be?' I thought. After all, it
was business #1, not the number of business that typically clogs a toilet. I quickly
shut the water off and headed to the toolroom to retrieve the plunger. Needless to
say, I'd done this more than a few times in this plumber's nightmare of a house.

Plunge. Plunge. Plunge … nothing. Damn!

One other time during our ownership of The Riverside did the plumbing main back up — I've previously chronicled this après-New Year's Day night-mare. But that clog was the result of full hotel rooms for three straight days, which equates to pretty extensive number two-ing. We'd had no guests in the hotel for the previous two months; I couldn't imagine how — and why now, why today? — we could have a clogged main sewer line.

I checked another downstairs toilet and, sure enough, the main was backed up. I shut the water off to all of the toilets and stood looking at the throne in our bathroom wondering just what in the hell I was going to do about this. Then, as if a switch had been turned on, the water in our stool began to slowly rise. 'Holy crap!' I thought. I'd shut the water supply off. What could be causing this? In a matter of seconds, the water began flowing over the brim of the bowl, onto the just cleaned and disinfected tile floor. My neighbor came running when he heard my screams, and quickly surveying the situation, he ran to the toolroom to grab the wet vac. He began vacuuming the water out of the bowl — it took less than ten seconds to fill the five-gallon vacuum canister. I grabbed the forty-pound bucket and moved outside as quickly as I could, dumping it into the street in front of the hotel. Back and forth I went, filling the vacuum canister and dumping the water into the street, all the while the water continuing to slowly rise.

Where in the hell was the water coming from?

I'd made eight, ten, twelve trips — I'd lost count — back and forth in my Sisyphean effort to keep the water from flooding our bathroom, but to no imme-diate avail. The water just kept coming, but from where? During bucket-running trip number ten, I noticed the sound of running water as I ran past the laundry room. Instantly it registered with me, as I'd heard that sound before; the upstairs toilet in bathroom number two was running, as occasionally the flapper valve in that toilet would stick — not often, but occasionally. However, the previous occa-sions of stuck flapper valves had always involved actual humans being upstairs, actually flushing the toilet. No one had been upstairs for an hour.

I dumped the bucket and ran upstairs to fix the toilet. 'Oh Shit!' The bath-room door was locked. 'You've got to be kidding me! The bathroom door is locked!'

This would be the bathroom on the left, bathroom number two, for which we had no key. It wouldn't be the bathroom on the right, bathroom number one, for which we had a key.

'All right,' I said to myself, 'take a deep breath and gather your thoughts. Let's see. Five of us have been in the house for the past hour, and none of us have gone upstairs. I'm certain of this, as we were all downstairs together, and all within earshot as the water started rising in our bathroom toilet, water which I now know is from this running toilet. So within the last ten minutes, this toilet flushed, the flapper valve got stuck, and now the door is locked.'

I didn't have too much more time to stand around and talk to myself about the implications of obvious physical activity without the presence of physical beings. I ran downstairs and told my neighbor what was up, his wife stepping in to vacuum the water while he took over the bucket-running duties.

Three or four times during our ownership this bathroom door had been inadvertently locked by guests. You'd think that I would have gotten a new lock with an actual key. But no, I'd found a cheaper way around this problem, as I was able to pry the door molding ajar with a putty knife, then use a small saw blade to jimmy the lock. I would have run to get that prying tool and small saw, but I knew it would be a wasted effort as they were probably packed in a 36" x 24" x 24" box, with twenty-four pounds of packing paper, labeled "BATHROOM #2 LOCK JIMMY TOOLS." The box was certainly well hidden in the moving van; in fact, all of my tools, and anything that even resembled a tool, was in a box in the van.

At this point, I was running around pell-mell downstairs, resembling something like a wild-eyed, sweaty, fleshy pinball as I dashed from this room to that, looking for something, *anything,* that I could use to get in that bathroom. I'd run by a large silverware tray, which we were leaving behind for what we hoped would be the new proprietors, four or five times, a silverware tray that contained 150 knives, any of which would have worked beautifully for both the molding pry and the lock jimmy process, before it hit me like a punch in the nose. I grabbed a knife — a simple dinner knife — ran upstairs and, within a matter of seconds, pried open the molding, jimmied the lock, and silenced the toilet. The water stopped rising. The bucket brigade ended.

The ghost had to be laughing hysterically, proud as a peacock of his final Seinfeldian prank. If there were multiple Riverside ghosts, I'm certain there was backslapping and high-fiving as well. While they were no doubt humored, I'll hope that they were also heartbroken at our impending departure; we were not only good stewards of their domain but even better fodder for their ghostly folly.

* * *

The mysterious water flow had now ebbed, the car was packed, and the inevitable departure from our dream was now at hand. It was a beautiful evening—the kind that I grew to relish; the kind that made all of the pain and struggle inherent in living in Grand County worthwhile. All of my favorite Grand County early evening accoutrements were on display, particularly the emerald-blue eastern sky that starkly contrasted the pumpkin-colored alpenglow on the rise of Cottonwood Pass. Many an evening I sat in front of the hotel, regardless of the temperature or the crowd in the restaurant ("Have you seen our waiter?"), and drank in that had-to-be-seen-to-be-believed vista to the east. I guess I always knew that our stay in Hot Sulphur Springs would be relatively short-lived—five to ten years at best—and I took advantage of every opportunity to gaze at the surrounding spectra as if it would be my last. The moment for my last gaze had now come, albeit a lot sooner than I had either imagined or intended, and I witnessed that natural spectacle for the final time through eyes blurred by tears of both joy and sadness.

We'd succumbed to the forces that had been thrashing our dream—the economy, the bank, our ineptitude, and our newfound lack of desire due to all of the aforementioned obstacles. We were leaving good friends and a lifestyle in a vacation setting that most people only imagine realizing. The tears shed on the wings of such failings, such sadness, were expected and require no explanation.

However, there were also tears of joy shed at the immitigable delight of a fresh start, in a new place; another exhilarating go at embracing the unknown. This speaks to why we left our Shawnee, Kansas, comfort zone and did this crazy thing in the first place. We were the new pioneers, giving up the safety and security of our cushy life in the suburbs and packing up our belongings to head west into the unknown. And not unlike it was for the old pioneers, that unknown held the promise of a radically different, and a hopefully better, way of life. We knew there were risks, both in the journey and at the destination, but we looked beyond the rational and forged ahead. We focused on the challenge of change and the excitement of the unknown, concentrating on the glory of what could go right as opposed to the agonizing reality of what might go wrong.

I don't wish the feeling of failure and nothingness at the end of the rainbow on anyone, but I can tell you that the emotion you experience at the onset of a quest is an elixir that cannot be reproduced, bottled, or sold—not for any price. I also have many regrets about our midlife crisis and our westward transgression, but one of them isn't the indescribable sensation of stepping off the ledge into the unknown.

And here we were, two short years later, stepping off yet another ledge. I was short of breath; my head swirled and, yes, melded into the burnt orange and azure eastern evening vistas, there were indeed tears of joy.

The plan was to pull out of Hot Sulphur whenever we were able and drive as far as we could that evening. I didn't care what time we left or how far we got; whenever and wherever it would be, I didn't want to spend one more night at The Riverside. I even had discussions with myself all that day about the ultimate departure and not looking back. You'd have to have experienced what I'd gone through the previous eight months—with me living in Mississippi, Julie living in Colorado, the bank dissecting us and then throwing us aside, etc. etc. etc.—before you'd understand why I wouldn't want to look back. I loved the place; I had great times and better memories; but I was ready to get out of Grand County in the worst way!

It was 6:15 p.m.; we locked that door for the final time and said our good-byes to the few friends who had assembled to witness our departure. We climbed in the Suburban, backed out of the alley, and headed east on Grand Street. I hadn't driven thirty feet when, in spite of what I'd promised myself I wouldn't do, I looked back into the driver's-side rearview mirror. It was a spectacular vision as the magnificent white façade of that grand old girl was bathed in the luminescent orange glow of the setting sun. This was my favorite Grand County evening scene—alpenglow on The Riverside. I didn't take my eyes off of the place for the half mile up Grand Street that I could still see her. In my last sight of The Riverside, she looked as beautiful as I'd ever seen her look. It was a 240-volt jolt reminding me of why I shucked it all to move west to move here. The tears flowed unabated.

The rearview mirror view dissipated. We hit Highway 40 and headed east, and the tears instantly abated.

Eastward ho!

CHAPTER TWENTY-NINE
The Vultures Pick at the Carrion

On June 15th, 2010, I received a letter sent regular mail from the Grand County treasurer. It stated that "on August 13th, 2010, at 10:00 a.m. MST, on the steps of the Grand County Courthouse, the dwelling and real estate that is comprised of Plat # 23, 509 Grand Street, in the town of Hot Sulphur Springs, etc ... will be sold at public auction."

So this is what our dream had come to; it was as cold and impersonal as Grand County itself.

There was no adjoining letter from the bank, nothing from the SBA — not a phone call or e-mail to explain, describe, question, or quantify the process to which we were to be subjected. I had a lot of questions, but the only person who might be able to answer them would charge me $300 an hour, and, to this point, I'd have had more substantive results from my dealings with the legal profession regarding The Riverside by throwing away the money that I'd already given the lawyer on lottery tickets. While Mr. Mercedes had been able to pile a small amount of humiliation upon the bankers and the SBA representative, nothing else came from our meeting with Acme Savings & Loan except the bank's refusal of our offer of a deed in lieu of foreclosure. They were going to foreclose, own the property, and still expect the money owed them.

I didn't hear anything from anyone for the next few weeks, until I received a call from a friend who was watching the hotel. He had been contacted by Ray Schmutz Garfunkel, asking for a tour of the hotel. I guess Schmutz wanted another look at the property that they were going to foreclose upon and resell. When we left the hotel, we left it in stellar shape — show-ready condition for a sale. The only things we took were our personal furnishings, leaving all of the furniture we acquired from Abner as well as the bar and restaurant furniture, all of the beds and bedroom furniture, all of the kitchen equipment, our two leather sofas, and my favorite rocking chair.

We hadn't been gone a week when it was reported to us that most of the remaining furniture — certainly all of the good stuff — ended up finding its way to various residences throughout Hot Sulphur Springs. We'd left keys with three people and had given them permission to take something if they liked it and could use it, not stopping to think that they and their friends, families, and neighbors would ultimately like and use everything. Next went most of the pictures and decorator knickknacks, those same pictures and knickknacks that I had risked my life transporting one night whilst pulling a 12' x 9' U-Haul trailer over Berthoud Pass in the middle of a total whiteout blizzard.

So, as the banker was touring the hotel, my friend apologetically explained that we had left the place in better shape than it now appeared, and we had left quite a bit of furniture that was no longer on the property. The banker said, "I couldn't care less about the furniture; I'm only interested in the real estate." Upon hearing this, I asked my friend to clarify a few things with his contact at the bank, mainly, could we auction off what of value we'd left behind that hadn't been absconded with by the locals, including the original Brunswick bar? While the thought of that bar not being at The Riverside pained me — it'd been there for almost 90 years — the thought of maybe getting a good chunk of money for it and helping to salve a few of our financial wounds at least had to be perfunctorily examined. The answer I received back from the bank was, "We're not interested in the contents, including the bar. If they can haul it out, they can have it."

We only had two weeks before the foreclosure, so I quickly went about trying to find an auctioneer in the Denver area who would be interested in helping us unload what was left of The Riverside, sans the real estate. After a brief description of the property and the limited items we had to offer, not only was the auctioneer interested in holding the auction, he was most interested in the Brunswick bar, as he said the current demand for these was "through the roof." He was so interested that he drove to Hot Sulphur Springs the next morning, toured the hotel, stopped at the bank to discuss the auction, and had me a contract to sign by that next afternoon. Perhaps this was another of my missed red flags?

* * *

No sooner had the auction been advertised throughout Grand County and on the auctioneer's Web site than the e-mails from the bank's and the SBA's attorneys started flying — not directly to me, of course, but to my designated $300 an hour legal counsel. The auction was advertised as a "Foreclosure Sale," giving the public the opportunity to snatch up countless bargains on priceless antiques, antiques that were advertised as having inhabited The Riverside since the turn of the century. There were pictures of more than thirty pieces: dressers, armoires, tables, chairs, ornate clocks, beautiful wooden bed frames, and so on. In their e-mails, both of the attorneys claimed that all of these pieces were part of the property, germane to the operation of the business, and needed to remain at The Riverside. There was also the SBA's assertion that due to provisions in our loan, they had a security interest in the items; they were in fact encumbered. And as for that Brunswick bar, it took less than twenty-four hours after me hearing indirectly from Ray Schmutz, "If they can haul it out, they can have it," for someone at Acme S&L to wise him up on the value of the bar, at which point he reneged on his generous offer. I imagine the real scenario involved one of the cowboy bankers on the bank's board having found just the spot for that old bar in his $1 million log home on the 14th fairway of Dead Pines Golf Club.

However, there was one small issue that the bank and the SBA lawyers failed to consider before raising the hackles on their clients' backs to the point where they were asked to write expensive e-mails to my lawyer. Not one of the items advertised in the auction preview was ever a furnishing at The Riverside — they belonged to the auctioneer (who was also a dealer of fine antiques), who intended to cart them from his showroom in Denver to Hot Sulphur for the sale, using The Riverside as nothing more than a vessel to give what weren't probably genuine antiques in the first place a needed air of authenticity. Trust me; other than the Brunswick bar, Abner left nothing of value at The Riverside after selling us the hotel, and certainly not a valuable "antique anything," or he would have carted that off as well.

Back and forth the e-mails went between the SBA, the bank, and my attorney regarding this auction that was to be held for items that didn't belong to any of the participants. The SBA attorney was including terms such as, "in violation of the law" and "punishable by fines, imprisonment, or both"; I just wanted to sell the beds we bought for the hotel, not rip the tags off of them. What we were talking about selling in the auction that did belong to us — remember, most everything of value that we had left behind had already been pilfered — were principally the fourteen primo queen beds that we'd purchased for the hotel and were still technically paying for on our Master Card. I sat back, helplessly, and watched one e-mail after the other fly back and forth between my attorney and the attorneys for Acme S&L and Shaftum & Cheatum Investments, all the while envisioning the dollar signs mounting into an ever-burgeoning pile.

Finally, at about 10:00 p.m. that evening after the umpteenth e-mail, I could stand the legal raping and pillaging no longer. I sent all three attorneys the following e-mail. (I won't deny that alcohol might have helped fuel this rant.)

Gentlemen: Re. the auction of assets.

*We're talking about selling some beds, beds that I'm still paying for on my Master Card, that were purchased after the 2007, bifurcated, 504, screw-job loan that I signed without the aid of counsel. The auction company that we hired (after being given the OK by the bank to auction the furnishings) is bringing onto the site numerous items that are their property to sell, and using the old hotel as nothing but a backdrop for the sale of these antiques. **Pay Attention — the items being auctioned are not the property of your client, the bank, or either of my LLCs, and are not subject to your lien, or were ever previously at The Riverside; they are being trucked up from Denver to be sold at the site.***

My wife and I have left our $600,000 worth of life's savings in Colorado at The Riverside. We were trying to sell a few thousand dollars worth of personal effects to defray credit card debts — now it will be used to pay for expensive e-mails sent by lawyers. I don't know the definition of a bifurcated loan, but I do know the definition of carrion — that's all that I have left for the bankers and the lawyers.

Mr. Filchem, you threaten to come after my assets if we sell our personal items out of The Riverside; good luck with that, as I have no assets for you or anyone to come after. I'm broke! I live in a dumpy little rental house in Mississippi, living paycheck to paycheck, and as *of this writing, I have $242 in my bank account to get me to my next end-of-the-month payday. Had your client and ASL been as open, honest, and diligent about the X's & O's of loaning money as they are about collecting it, neither of us would be in our current situation.*

You'll get the damned money from the sale of the beds. May you all sleep well.

That stopped the e-mails.

* * *

Friday, August 13th, 2010, 10:00 a.m. MST came and went without a whisper. It was the day after my fifty-fourth birthday, and a normal day at the office for me in Jackson, Mississippi. I didn't mark the minute or even recognize it until an hour later when it dawned on me that the foreclosure had occurred — no tremor in the force such as Obi-Wan Kenobi felt when Alderaan blew up. It just came and went. I didn't feel sad, happy, relieved, depressed, jubilant or defeated, broker or richer. I think the fact that I'd been physically removed from The Riverside and Grand County for so long helped to ease the suffering. But it then shook me to imagine the suffering I would have had to endure had I had no place else to go and had to stand my ground in Colorado and bear witness to the process to which I'd just been subjected. It was also important for our general health and well-being that we had so resolutely decided back in March to walk away from the venture, to quickly shed the pain of the struggle, the failure, and the loss and begin life anew in another locale. As Anheuser-Busch so ironically put it — they also being the promoters of the print hanging in The Riverside's bar illustrating General G.A. Custer's infamous failure to cry "Uncle" in the face of insurmountable odds — "Know when to say when." I strongly suggest to one and all, when the opportunity and the need arise, take heed of those words.

CHAPTER THIRTY
One Last Final Final

Our two-year story of Living Life Riverside is a classic tragicomedy, an all-but-religious experience and undertaking, with the part of God being played by Murphy's law.

I'm often asked if I have regrets.

Knowing what I know now?

Hell yes, I have regrets! There are very few things about this experience that I don't still regret on a daily basis.

"Well," people say, "you can check that off your bucket list."

Dear God, if only I could do it over and have it eternally on my bucket list. The pain of wishing you could do something and not having done it has to be miniscule when compared to the pain of actually having done it and having that experience nearly bludgeon you to death.

I beg of you, please consult with me if owning a bar, restaurant, or B&B is on your bucket list.

Many have lauded us for simply trying. While I truly appreciate the lauding, the folks at Walmart don't yet accept lauds in lieu of cash when purchasing Little Debbie Nutty Bars. The truth be known, I wish I was being lauded for showing restraint and sticking with the dull but sure thing corporate gig. While I wouldn't have the memories of charming Hot Sulphur Springs, $750 per month water bills, and all of the wonderful people we met the past two years ("Yuk! Clean it up!" and "Dog attack at the Riverside!" — titles of two online reviews of our hotel), I would instead have memories of fabulous meals in Paris, quaffing fine wines in

Verona, and, most importantly, memories of quarterly meetings with my financial advisor.

But alas, I opted for that bucket-list thing. And I blame nothing, or no one, but myself for originally selecting that option. However, I did have some help along the way in making it a very bad option to select.

I do know that we bought an old hotel — an icon in the area and an important slice of history in Grand County — and for two years we made it a warm and shining place in a cold, desolate outpost. We welcomed strangers who left as friends. We entertained guests from all over the world who hugged us as family when they departed. I truly believe that we brought new life to a dying town and county, if only for a short while. I've been told by more than a few that when we pulled out of Colorado for the final time on that March Sunday in 2010, we left a hole in the heart of Grand County that has yet to be sutured.

Several years after the fact, and seven hundred safe, warm miles from our ground zero in Hot Sulphur Springs, when discussing The Riverside with friends and family, Julie will say that she has many wonderful memories, perhaps enough good memories to actually drown out the sobering reality of what we lost. I will profess the opposite. From the beginning I knew that we had made a horrific mistake, and as I was the one who bore the daily, nay, hourly burden of mentally dealing with our inevitable date with doom, I could never with a clear conscience enjoy what good there was in the experience. There were the wintertime walks with Julie and the dogs alongside the frozen river, through crystalline snow under the massive façade of Mt. Bross, itself made all the less imposing by the serenity of the blue sky and the whispering cottonwoods. Whenever I'd lose myself in a moment that many would risk all to be able to experience on a daily basis, I couldn't help but zap myself back to the reality of the fact that I had risked all, and the painful foreboding knowledge that all would eventually be lost. It was as if I were renting those good feelings, experiences, and pleasant memories of our time in Hot Sulphur and The Riverside; I knew that eventually I'd have to turn them back in and there would be an ugly bill due at the end of the deal — one that I couldn't afford to pay.

In addition to carrying this psychological burden, there was the physical burden that came with running The Riverside. And truthfully, I have no fond memories of doing ten loads of laundry per day; twenty-plus loads of washing and drying dishes, glasses, pots and pans; setting and unsetting and resetting fourteen tables; making and unmaking then remaking sixteen beds; scouring and disinfecting three showers and six toilets; and chain sawing and hand splitting fifteen cords of wood every fall. I do have very pleasant feelings knowing that I no longer have to work like a dog and net nothing.

But in honest retrospect, I can say that the times I was happiest at The Riverside — when I was able to put the worries aside and get lost in the joy of the moment — occurred in The River Room. With but a very few previously noted exceptions, I enjoyed waiting on customers, interacting with them and watching as they savored the food and the ambience. I derived a great amount of joy and satisfaction from knowing that we were able to greatly exceed the expectations of most who found their way into that rickety old building in the middle of the Colorado wilderness. And although our dream turned into something of a nightmare, for a while, in a small fourteen-table restaurant overlooking the Colorado River, the dream was sweet.

While there were many wonderful guests and moments, there was a particular guest and moment that still makes me think that our adventure wasn't a total failure.

A delightful German couple stopped in one summer afternoon looking for a room for the evening; they ended up staying with us for three nights. The husband played first chair French horn with the Frankfurt Symphony Orchestra — a gentle man of class, culture, and great elegance. He'd traveled throughout the world as a professional musician and was in the midst of a month-long ramble throughout the United States as a prelude to a two-year resident teaching position in China.

During their last evening with us, while dining in the restaurant, I stopped by the table to ask about their dinner. The man's eyes were closed and his hands were clasped, as if he were praying, yet his meal was over. He looked up at me and said, "Everything is perfect. The wine and the food were wonderful; this room is wonderful; and you are playing Schumann's Third Symphony. I can't believe I am here in this place listening to Schumann. This is *Alles klar bei dir.*"

"Come again?" I asked.

"I know you're not familiar with that saying, but it is a German phrase that is even hard for me to explain the meaning of because I don't know of an English phrase that exists to describe the meaning. But I will try. I think a literal translation in English is something like, "Everything is clear with me." But I would never use this phrase in the German language to say I understand something, as it goes far beyond simply understanding.

"And this is not a phrase that I use lightly, as very seldom do I experience the feeling of *Alles klar bei dir.* It describes a sensation of total comfort and wellness, an emotion I have when I am wholly in love and at peace with my life and all of my surroundings. It is a warm feeling, a feeling of quiet joy. I have that very special feeling … now … in this beautiful place of yours."

At that moment, my suffering was temporarily vanquished, my anxieties no longer existent, and all was also clear with me.

* * *

After I assume room temperature, and should my life ever be examined by someone other than creditors, I'm hoping that it will be discussed by close friends at a nice bar, one that pours a good drink, as we did at The Riverside. I'm certain that after the cussing and discussing, all will agree that if I did nothing else, my greatest accomplishment in this life was that my follies were occasionally capable of inducing a feeling of Alles klar bei dir, and, at the worst, my failures did well to serve as a warning to others.

May God continue to bless us all …

Epilogue

After our March 2010 departure from Hot Sulphur Springs and The Riverside, we took up residence in Brandon, Mississippi, both Julie and I gainfully employed and heading back down a path of normalcy (albeit many would argue that "Mississippi" and "normalcy" shouldn't be used in the same sentence, or the same paragraph for that matter). I went back to doing that "Big Company" thing that drove me to the mountains in the first place. Fortunately, after three grueling years of Mississippi meetings and corporate-headquarter displays of male machismo, I landed an opportunity to come back home, back to Kansas City, and back to a small employer. Life has truly come full circle.

Our glorious Riverside Hotel sat empty from March of 2010 until September of 2011. During the eighteen-month period that the hotel was unoccupied, there were rumors that the bank intended to tear the structure to the ground and sweep away the 108 years' worth of history and memories ensconced within the plaster and lath walls, walls that had stood defiant against the brutal Middle Park environment for the past century. I had always imagined that the more than one acre lot the structure occupied — a lot that snuggled up against the banks of the mighty, trout-laden Colorado River — would be worth more without the encumbrance of a 13,000-square-foot money pit. But then I had also imagined that building a beautiful new mountain estate on that beautiful riverside lot, in the setting of Hot Sulphur Springs with the post office across the street and Joe's Auto Repair in your backyard, would be something like placing a glistening diamond in a goat's ass. Perhaps the bank put out their greedy tendrils to test the possibility of this scenario of destruction and saw it like this as well, as the wrecking ball never swung at 509 Grand Street.

In September of 2011, according to the Grand County public record, the hotel was purchased for the sum of $250,000, some $440,000 less than we had paid for the property. The buyers were a husband and wife with children who intended to use The Riverside as a place of residence only and not pursue the cornucopia of financial opportunities that lay fallow in the historic building. The new owners even went as far as removing the large black wooden letters that read HOTEL and RESTAURANT from the façade of the structure, leaving only the RIVERSIDE moniker. My guess is that they were intruded upon daily by potential guests and customers beating down the doors to throw their discretionary incomes at these unintended and unwilling barons of hospitality.

On the night of April 1st, 2013, an unfortunate event put The Riverside and its new owners back not only on the local map but on the national map as well. If you were sitting around watching CNN on Saturday morning, April 6th, you would have seen the unmistakable white clapboard façade of the hotel on the news story.

Late that April Fools' eve, a young man newly relocated to Grand County and Hot Sulphur Springs from Michigan, and under the heavy influence of a smorgasbord of narcotic substances both legal and illegal, began beating on the door of the hotel, rousting the peacefully slumbering and now panic-stricken residents of The Riverside. Both husband and wife were peacekeepers by profession, he a lieutenant for the sheriff's department and she a deputy district attorney for the county of Grand.

Tragically, the situation quickly escalated to violence, and within a matter of minutes the young man from Michigan lay dead in the street in front of the hotel, three bullets of large caliber from the gun belonging to the new male owner of The Riverside fatally embedded in his torso. The victim's death was deemed justifiable as an act of self-defense.

So this small mountain burg that was borne from the violence of the 1860s wild and woolly pioneer west; this desolate, frozen outpost that saw Texas Charlie stumble and fall dead in the street from the blazing guns of vigilantes unknown; this county seat; this placid valley of respite and relaxation; creeps quietly into the new, civilized century still bearing the curse of its bloody past. Add one more spirit to the roster of ghosts who haunt the halls of The Riverside, except this newest member of that macabre fraternity may have a bit of an attitude toward the current earthly residents, the prospects of which I do not envy them.

There is another important loose end that needs to be tied down, and this one adds to the continued sur-reality that was our Colorado adventure. The real-life character that kind of, sort of resembles the totally fictional Damien Farmer character, recently passed away at the untimely and early age of 40 years. This individual was suspected of embezzling from the Grand Lake, CO restaurant that he managed, the reality of which would have landed him in jail due to being on probation for previous nefarious actions involving mismanagement of other people's monies. There would be no hell on earth worse than prison for some, this opinion most probably shared by the gentlemen in question, who took his life as a means of escaping the meats of justice. A tragic ending to a sad, tortured and fragile individual, and perhaps the final weird twist to our Living Life Riverside.

Acknowledgements

Most acknowledgements that I've read at the end of a book thank the family last, as it is them — last but not least — who inspired, encouraged, assisted, coached, and persevered along with the author throughout the most certainly painful process of authorship. My family gets thanked first and foremost, as not only did they do all of the aforementioned regarding the assemblage of these words, they also lived the story: they reveled in the highs and suffered through the lows; they cleaned the toilets, made the beds, vacuumed the floors, and washed the dishes; they loaded and unloaded the U-Haul, five, six times, before and after the numbing trek across I-70 and over Berthoud Pass. Because of their sacrifice — which continues to this day in the form of my daughter, Rachel, inevitably holding her wedding reception in a rent-free gazebo in a county park instead of at a tony country club, due to our formerly owned pile of money now sitting riverside in Hot Sulphur Springs — I owe them thanks and acknowledgements of the highest order, right out of the gate. While my son, Scott, escaped most of the onsite ugliness, as he was finishing up his education at the University of Kansas, our midlife crisis deprived him of a fully-paid-for education, and he had to tap into the student loan program to finish up his final year of matriculation. And then there is Julie, my precious wife of thirty-seven years, who followed me in this folly and worked with me, endured the heartbreak with me, and didn't leave me or strangle me, as would not have been unexpected, considering. To my family, thank you for the continued love and support. But be honest — the ordeal at The Riverside does make for some good stories.

To the citizens of Colorado, Grand County, Middle Park, Boulder, and Hot Sulphur Springs, I thank you for providing the fodder for this story, and I especially thank you for your thick skin, your robust sense of humor, your ability to laugh at yourselves and not take my fictional attempts at personal debasement too seriously, and your intuitive ability to recognize that I am one big kidder, always the joker!

No acknowledgement would be complete without either thanking or cursing the editor. Dawn Petersen got hooked up with me through divine intervention, from my perspective, and most probably wretched bad luck from hers. Her diligence in sculpting this verbal lump of clay that I sent to her into a cohesive beginning, middle, and end was unfaltering. She called out my unnecessary and often incorrect use of the word "literally," literally more times than I can count. She helped me fill in blanks, smooth transitions, check facts, and support assertions.

She also cleared up a major mystery, one that I'm a little sad to report on. But the truth is paramount, even in this fictionalized account based upon real events and fictional characters. Here's the deal: John Lennon did not stay at The Riverside Hotel in the summer of 1974. In spite of almost forty years of local lore, lore that we chose to take at face value, the sedulous Ms. Petersen took the time and effort to chase down the truth and contacted, via e-mail, May Pang, the eighteen-month paramour of John Lennon during one possible period of his purported visit to the hotel. Ms. Pang responded that during their three-day visit to Nederland, Colorado, and the Caribou Ranch recording sessions with Elton John, they did not venture beyond the Continental Divide and visit The Riverside. They did go into Boulder and buy some cowboy boots, but beyond that, all nights were spent at the Caribou Ranch with Elton John, in his cabin. The "John Lennon" room at The Riverside might be, like those made-up bankers, builders, and drunk townspeople; and that made-up Abner Renta character, pure fiction.

I would also like to humbly express my heartfelt gratitude to extended family and friends that helped us in our venture, through either financial support, physical support, or moral support. You all gave more to the venture than you will ever imagine, and even though the venture failed, every success that we enjoyed was on behalf of your efforts.

And finally, I would like to profess my sincere appreciation to all who crossed our threshold during our tenure as owners and proprietors of The Historic Riverside Hotel, Restaurant & Bar, be it as a diner, a hotel guest, a friend, or a neighbor. While I've chronicled, ad nauseam, that there weren't enough of you for us to make a long-term go of it, each and every one of you (with but a very few noted exceptions) enriched our lives and made our journey complete.

May all be clear with you!

THE END

CPSIA information can be obtained
at www.ICGtesting.com
Printed in the USA
BVHW080734260122
627125BV00011B/614/J

9 780692 869475